BEYOND
TOMORROW

BOOK V

BEYOND THOSE HILLS SERIES

BEYOND
TOMORROW

Vernal Lind

REDEMPTION
PRESS

Published by Redemption Press, PO Box 427, Enumclaw, WA 98022.

Unless otherwise noted, all Scriptures are taken from the *King James Version* of the Bible and are quoted by characters in the story.

ISBN 13: 978-1-63232-218-0 (Print)
        978-1-63232-219-7 (ePub)
        978-1-63232-221-0 (Mobi)

Library of Congress Catalog Card Number: 2015934727

CONTENTS

An Introduction
From the Author

Dear Readers,

I want to thank you, my loyal readers, for continuing to read the saga of the Anderson family. I have met many of you, and you have become my friends.

You have taken Matthew and Ellen Anderson and their family to be your friends. You have followed the family, with its joys and sorrows, starting with the last of the Depression in 1937 as told in BEYOND THOSE HILLS. In BEYOND THE STORM, you journeyed through storms they weathered, especially the Armistice Day Blizzard of 1940.

The third book, BEYOND THE DARKNESS, probably brought you through some of the darkest hours during the final years of World War II and the time following. James and Johnie, as well as Joe, returned home. The prayers of many were answered.

Families grow and change and come apart. Even so, BEYOND THIS HOME showed how the Andersons came together. The sixties brought sudden and dramatic and troubling changes, but the strong influence of family and faith and home brought them together. The family weathered those turbulent times.

One of the big changes in life has to do with growing older and facing the last part of life. I felt I wanted to continue the story and also show how members of the family dealt with this part of life. This novel picks up the story in 1985. The story will show Matthew at 85, facing the end of his life. James and the other children are confronted with retirement age and related changes.

It may be helpful to refresh your memories about the characters and where they are as you continue the story of this family.

MATTHEW, now 85, and ELLEN, a year older, face health issues and concerns about the future. They are vigorous and active but realize they are nearing the end of life. They remain involved with and concerned about family. Matthew and Ellen have left the farm and now live in town.

JAMES, the oldest son now 61 and a university professor, experiences a sudden shock. Should he retire from teaching and pursue his lifelong dream of becoming a writer? His wife RUTH still wants to continue teaching. James is estranged from his son RICHARD. The two daughters, COLEEN AND MELISSA, are married and have their own family concerns and family problems. They live close enough so that there are frequent visits and grandchildren around.

JOHNIE or PASTOR JOHN is an active and vigorous pastor who has a dream of doing missionary work. After the death of his first wife, he married CAROLYN. Johnie's three children, JANELLE, JACK, and LEAH, are all married with families. There are frequent visits between parents and children. Should Johnie leave the safety of his present home and pursue missionary work? After all, he is almost 60.

MARGARET, married to JOE NELSON, is on the original home farm. They are both as active as ever, but Joe is getting help from his son-in-law. They suffered the loss of their son, MATT or MATTHEW during the Vietnam War. That loss left deep scars. The other children and their families are nearby: DAVID, DEBORAH, JOEL, JUDITH, and MARLENE.

CAROL is married to HANK STEVENS, and they live in the Chicago area. HANK is a successful businessman. He and Carol are involved with Christian organizations and work. Earlier in her life, Carol was the rebel daughter but now has changed. Her oldest son, JEFFREY GRANT, is in business and the source of family concern and trouble. The other children, NICHOLAS and NICOLE have families and live in Illinois.

MICHAEL, the youngest and only 45, is married to ELISE and lives on the family farm. Elise is a teacher. Michael is trying to branch out and run a greenhouse/nursery and is taking some financial risks. They have four children. The youngest, an afterthought is MATTHEW or called LITTLE MATTHEW.

As often happens, the siblings fade from the scene. The exception is Matthew's older sister, VICTORIA, who is now 95. She is active and

An Introduction

still drives too fast and is involved and interested in her brother's family. The other siblings have all died. That is the sad reality of growing older. At times, Matthew misses his siblings very much.

The parents of Matthew are often mentioned. JOHN and ELIZABETH ANDERSON were a focal part of Matthew's life as well as the lives of the children. PA or JOHN died in 1940 in the first book. MA (ELIZABETH) died in the sixties when she was well into her nineties.

MARTHA, the oldest sister and a favorite, died in the sixties. Her three daughters are in California along with their families. Daughter CORRINE maintains ties with the family.

P.J. or PAUL JOHN left a mark on Matthew for he essentially stole the original farm home from him. When P.J. died, Matthew wasn't sure if he regretted the terrible things he had done. His wife RITA has also died. For a while LARRY played an important role in Matthew's life. Though a nephew he was in some ways more like a younger brother. Larry's children were also involved in the family's life.

LUCILLE, another older sister, is mentioned. She died quite young. Matthew found her death hard to accept.

MARY, Matthew's younger sister, lived on a farm nearby in the earlier novels. She suffered from TB. Her husband ED was a close friend to Matthew. The two families interacted and were close in the earlier novels. Mary and Ed spent time in California. The three children, BETH, JAKE, and IRENE, maintain contact with the family. JAKE and IRENE have their own families.

Matthew's cousin PETER ANDERSON played a small role in the family at an earlier time. GLENN ROBERTSON was Matthew's best friend who died several years ago.

And so life goes on. We see the last of one generation. We see the next generation giving way to a new generation. I am reminded of the Scripture, "The Lord's love endures *From Generation to Generation.*"

Now, my friends, I hope you will enjoy the adventures of the Anderson family as they move forward in life's journey through the late 1900s and into the twenty-first century. May you grow in faith as you see the power of God's love reflected.

May we move forward in faith.

God's richest blessings to you,
—Vernal Lind

PROLOGUE

April 1985

He didn't know what hit him. Suddenly everything went black. The next morning, James Anderson, professor of English at Riverton State University, began to awaken. He moved his head and experienced a throbbing headache.

"James, are you awake?" questioned his wife, Ruth.

He opened his eyes wider. "Where am I? I have a splitting headache."

"You're in the hospital. They found you outside the River View building. Do you remember what happened?"

James looked around at the unfamiliar room, trying to remember. "I was walking outside River View. It was very dark; I think a light was out. I'd been at a meeting and worked later than I had realized. I dropped some books and papers and stooped down to pick them up. Suddenly, something or someone hit me. Everything went blank or black."

"You have a lump on your head.

"My head aches terribly. Someone must have been out to get me."

"Dr. Foster will want to examine you again."

James sat up, straightening himself. "I feel better now, except for my aching head. What about my classes? I have classes to teach."

"Your students will have the day off."

"But, I feel okay—except for the headache. I'll manage just fine."

Dr. Eric Foster, friend of the family, entered, obviously having heard James's words. "Oh no, you don't—we'll x-ray you and run a few more tests."

The next hours James was questioned, x-rayed and given a battery of tests. He returned to his room, exhausted. When it became obvious James wanted to take a nap, Ruth went back to her fifth grade classroom.

In mid-afternoon Eric Foster entered his hospital room. James wakened. "I guess I'm more tired out than I thought."

"James, I come to you both as doctor and as friend. You had a close call. If that crazy kid had hit you in a slightly different place, you would have been in the morgue rather than the hospital. You are very fortunate."

"Who was the kid?"

"I think the name was Mac or Mackenzie—something like that."

"Oh, it sounds like a student who simply quit coming to class. He seemed to have aspirations to be a great writer and teacher. He was obviously not ready for advanced English work."

"Apparently, he snapped—had some sort of breakdown. He's in custody. The person who called the police saw him running after he attacked you."

"I feel bad about the kid."

"Don't. I'm glad they caught him."

"Can I go home? Or I should say may I go home?"

"Just to be on the safe side, we're keeping you one more night for observation. I don't see any problems. But as I said, I'm coming to you as both doctor and friend. We don't want to take any chances."

James wondered what was coming.

"This little incident may have saved your life. Your blood pressure is on the high side. The blood tests reveal you may have some other problems. However, I would say you are exhausted and run down—perhaps you are actually sleep deprived. You were unconscious longer because you simply needed more sleep."

"I have been working hard."

"Being hit on the head may have been a sign—even a warning. You have not been taking care of yourself. You have to slow down. You're stressed out."

"Thank you, I'm afraid you're right."

When his friend and doctor left, James reflected; life has been downright hectic. Full load of classes. Chairman duties. Busy with friends. Involved with church. Not enough time for family . . .

Prologue

"But," he said aloud, "I've often neglected my family. My own son has nothing to do with me. Mom and Dad are old, and I need to take time for them."

He continued to muse. What about my dreams? Before I die, I have to see whether I can really write. Could I write that novel I've always wanted to write?

A disturbing thought entered his mind and he spoke the thought. "The end of my life could come sooner than I think. I'm almost sixty-one, but I've been to funerals of a number of younger people."

The next morning, on the way home, he announced to Ruth, "Being hit on the head made me do some thinking. I may need to make some big changes."

Ruth smiled, knowingly. "I think it's about time."

———◦◦◦———

Matthew Anderson turned off the garden tiller. He surveyed the freshly tilled rich soil that would become his daughter's garden. He felt the same satisfaction as he experienced each year when he had plowed the fields of his farm. The black rich soil held so much promise.

For a moment a shadow darkened Matthew's thoughts. His son James appeared in his mind. Was something wrong?

As suddenly as the darkness appeared, it disappeared.

He walked over to the familiar oak tree, where he loved to stop and think. The green buds had not yet turned into leaves. Nature all around was coming to life. The green-gold leaves of the ash trees reminded him of beginnings everywhere. Soon, plants and small grain would usher in another season. The whole earth seemed alive with music that honored its Creator.

All of a sudden, Matthew felt a strange sensation—as if he were swept back in time. People who had died long ago were around him.

Pa appeared as he had during his prime years. "Son, you've worked hard. You've done a good job plowing."

Ma stood beside him. "You've always been a good son, the one child we could always depend on."

Matthew mentally shed his eighty-five years and felt young again. Martha, his oldest sister, walked into the scene along with three little girls. Victoria, tall and dark and business-like, followed, carrying a brief case. Lucille, a younger gentler version of Martha, greeted him, and then, of course, Mary, his younger sister.

It was strange but P.J., the brother who almost destroyed him, was not present. P.J. had cast that dark shadow over so much of his life. Then, P.J. appeared in the distance but soon disappeared. An indescribable warmth filled his whole being. The physical aches and pains dissolved. Matthew became a young man once more. All the world was filled with beauty and hope and dreams of a better life.

The pastor's words filled his mind. "Since we are surrounded by so great a cloud of witnesses..." "I wonder if I'm not surrounded by these witnesses, encouraging me to go on. To be strong. To keep on believing and moving on."

A gentle breeze and some stiff muscles brought him back to the present. Matthew had the habit of talking aloud when he prayed or thought about life. "Pa, you've been gone so many years, yet I think of you every time I face a crisis. And, Ma, you enriched our family life for so many years. It still seems you should walk out of this little house.

"Martha, I miss you more than I can say. You were like a second mother. In a sense, you were my favorite though each sister played a different role. Oh, Victoria, I'm so glad you're still around. Even at ninety-five, you are active. Not even your driving has slowed down. I think maybe you shouldn't be driving.

"P.J., you were good to me at times, but you stole the home farm. I've forgiven you, and I've tried to understand. But how could you do this to your family? Lucille, you've been gone so many years. I have questions to ask God. 'Why did you create such a wonderful girl and let her have that heart condition? Why did you take her from us when she was so young?' It wasn't fair.

"And, Mary, we were so close together we could have been twins. Why did you have to suffer with TB and then cancer? Why am I still here, and you have been taken?"

Next, Ellen walked into his life. The two had shared more than sixty-two years of married life. What would he have done without this woman? She was more precious than life itself.

Time seemed to stand still. Then, his five children walked before him. He wished he could bring back the time when they were all together. How simple life was. He saw each of the five as they were in their youth.

A voice broke into his awareness. "Dad, thanks for tilling the garden. It looks great." Matthew heard the words but hesitated to leave his reverie.

"Dad," his daughter Margaret said, "you're miles away. What's so interesting?"

Prologue

"I was just thinking back to earlier times. Your grandparents. Your Aunt Martha. And I thought back to when you kids were young."

"Those were good times. We've had a good life."

"God is good."

"And, Dad, we're going to celebrate that life. Your birthday may be in a few days, but we'll celebrate in June when the whole family can come home."

"I don't want you to fuss. I really don't want any big birthday bash."

"You're outvoted."

"I like people, but I don't like big crowds."

"It'll be family. James is planning to be around this summer, and Johnie's taking a whole month off. And Carol and Hank are coming from Chicago for several weeks. And, of course, you have Michael and me around all the time."

"Just keep it to family."

"You do have cousins and nieces and nephews and all the grandchildren. And don't forget all our church friends and community friends."

Matthew grunted. "At least you didn't try to surprise me."

"Dad, what were you really thinking about?"

Matthew hesitated as he looked down tenderly at his daughter. Next to his wife Ellen, she was the ideal woman.

"I've been thinking of that 'cloud of witnesses' the pastor mentioned on Sunday. For a moment as I stood by the oak tree, I couldn't help thinking that I was surrounded by Pa and Ma and many others. They were standing there in front of me."

"It must have been wonderful to have them close to you."

"I think the Lord gave me a foretaste of Heaven."

"Just as the song says, 'a foretaste of glory divine.'"

Matthew stooped down and kissed his daughter.

Margaret looked up and smiled. "Dad, we've lost loved ones, but think of all the family members we have right here on earth. We must be thankful for our past blessings, but we can enjoy one another while we are together. We must appreciate one another right now."

"That's something your mother could have said."

"Or you, Dad. Let's plan and look forward to a great homecoming."

"Yes, my dear."

Matthew thought of the June homecoming, but at the same time he couldn't help thinking of an entirely different kind of homecoming.

CHAPTER 1

May 1985

Matthew set down his cup of coffee and gazed out the window of their recently-built home in town. It was James who occupied his thoughts—especially after last month's episode. He had a sense that something might be wrong—or perhaps his son was facing some big challenge.

"More coffee?" asked Ellen, his wife of more than sixty years. "You're looking out the window, but you're miles away."

"You know, Dear, I miss living on the farm. There was room to walk in the woods or do something. But I'm thinking about James."

"I think Michael might be a bigger concern. He's spending too much on machinery and getting that garden and nursery going."

Matthew sighed. "I'm afraid he's gone into debt a little too deep, but what happens will happen. But I have this feeling that James is facing a difficult decision."

"I was thinking that, too. Last time he was home, he talked about being fed up with some of the university politics. He talked about quitting. That's not like him."

"At least in farming, you don't have to deal with difficult people—not usually."

"I think they'll be home this weekend. James and Ruth have certainly built an extravagant lake home."

"That's the new generation. They want plenty of room for their kids and grandkids. And Johnie and Carolyn will be with James for a while this summer."

Ellen interrupted the conversation. "Matthew, let's have our morning devotions. I'll read Scripture, and you pray."

Ellen read the words, "Let not your hearts be troubled. Believe in God, believe also in Me . . . ."

Matthew prayed for each of the children—especially James.

Dr. James Anderson awakened abruptly. What had happened could best be described as a nightmare. However, the images did not fade as nightmares usually do. He kept remembering and replaying those dreadful scenes.

First, he re-experienced that blow on the head outside the River View building. He felt the blackness come over him as if he were surrounded by evil forces.

The darkness around him dissipated and Mark Goodman, his friend from the history department, kept calling. "James, help me. I'm slipping—I'm going down. I can't breathe. I'm sinking fast."

Hundreds of people moved through the nightmare. People from his distant past, his childhood, and other times in his life kept walking into his presence. There was Grandma, who died twenty years ago, and then Grandpa, who must have died over forty years ago. The people had all seemed so very real. Everyone was so very troubled. In the background Ruth's voice called.

James sat up, rubbing the sleep out of his eyes.

Ruth appeared, fully dressed for a day of teaching fifth graders. "James, it's later than you think."

James slowly got out of bed. "I had one of those dreams—a nightmare."

"It's probably the result of that hit on the head." She paused and added, "Coffee's all set. And I have French toast almost ready."

"I'm hurrying."

James couldn't help wondering about the nightmare. Could it be a sign or warning of things to come?

"I laid out your shirt on the dresser. Don't be too long, I have to get to school."

Chapter 1

James quickly shaved and washed up. Rarely did he sleep beyond the alarm. In minutes he was in the kitchen ready to eat his breakfast.

Ruth placed the French toast before him. "I have to get going. When will you be home tonight?"

"I plan to leave the university early and visit Mark. I'll give you a call."

Ruth kissed him on the cheek and hurried out.

James finished his French toast and took his cup of coffee, and walked out on the deck. The sweet smells of the apple blossoms and the sounds of birds singing seemed to welcome him to the newness of spring. The world beckoned him to leave the ordinary and go somewhere. But at the same time he loved his teaching—and he had his obligations.

"The mind and spirit are fragile things," he said aloud. "They must be nourished or they wither away and die."

―――――⦿―――――

Last fall James Anderson's job at the university changed . . . After many years as chairman of the English department, he decided to delegate more of the responsibilities to the assistant department head. At the same time he heard rumors of eliminating or downgrading department heads and having division chairpersons. He continued to teach his favorite advanced writing classes along with the survey series of American literature courses. Freshman English became part of his teaching load, and that gave him a taste of the more average university student. This experience was his touch with reality.

The Friday afternoon English 132 class did indeed bring James back to reality. The assigned compositions he returned to his students showed little improvement from the woefully inadequate writing that had come in a month ago.

For the first time in more than thirty-five years of teaching, he thought seriously about ending his career as teacher and professor. These years had been good years. He loved his advanced writing classes and his survey of American literature. However, the freshman English class made him wonder about his purpose in teaching.

His mind traveled back to days on the farm. How simple that life was! Good, honest, hard-working people who lived by the Golden Rule and brought up their children "in the fear and admonition of the Lord." The world and the university had somehow gone astray.

"I'm sounding like an old grouch," he said to himself as he got out of the hospital elevator. He walked down the hall to Mark's room.

He knocked on the half-open door and entered. Marcia Goodman, who had been sitting beside Mark's bed, stood up. "Come in, James. I'm going to step out and let you two men visit. I'm sure you have much to talk about."

"I guess you're used to the way we talk on and on."

Marcia Goodman gave James a warm hug. "Try to keep him calm," she said as she left.

James greeted his friend. "I see, Mark, you're looking much better today."

"I'm not ready to check out yet. I have some more classes to teach." Mark clenched his fist, showing some grim determination.

"Perhaps I do, too. Though on a Friday afternoon after freshman English, I sometimes wonder."

Mark sat up in his hospital bed. "You haven't heard what they did to me."

James sensed anger behind those words. Mark, a year older than James, had long held strong political opinions and had some definite biases about history. This colleague could often become quite agitated about a rather ordinary situation. It may have been this liveliness that attracted James to this man—and what helped cement their friendship. James, by nature more quiet and reserved, had a way of calming down his friend.

James hated the indefinite *they*. "Who are they?"

"The administration. The new head of the history and social studies department."

James wasn't sure he wanted to hear what was coming next. "Stay calm. Getting excited can't be good for you."

Mark clenched his fist even more tightly. "Yesterday was an eye-opener. The history department schedule for next year came out."

"I haven't seen the one for the English department. The administration and I usually work things out. I guess I assume I'll be having the same load. However, I could decide to retire."

"Don't be too sure about your same classes." Mark's voice rose in pitch and intensity. "Those jerks took away all my upper level classes. All I'm left with is freshman-sophomore level courses."

"How could they do that? You've been department head for years—until you stepped down last year. You deserve some special consideration."

"Don't fool yourself. Those administration guys are out to get rid of us old guys. The young ones come a lot cheaper."

Chapter 1

"You're older than I. You can resign. You can retire."

"I'll decide when I'm ready to retire. I don't want someone telling me what to do. When I'm ready, I'll quit. I'm staying at the university, and I'll show both the students and the administration a thing or two."

James couldn't help smiling. "I can see you still have that fight in you. They have a formidable opponent. You should keep life interesting."

During the next hour, the two men talked about the university politics and administration politics. They both shared that passion for teaching, a passion that had cemented their friendship years ago.

James began to notice tiredness in Mark.

A nurse entered with his medication. As he finished taking the medication, the nurse added, "Mr. Goodman, I think you need to rest."

Mark grunted. "I'll decide that. I'm not used to being ordered around by nurses or my wife or anybody else."

The nurse smiled and left.

"Mark, I think she's right."

Mark seemed to relax as he lay back. "You know there are some things I'd like to do. You've traveled a bit, but I haven't."

"I'm going to Sweden this summer, and my father's coming with me. I've made some connections with some distant cousins. I'm excited about the trip."

"I've been so busy teaching. And I've been picking up those extra summer classes. That should be good for the retirement check."

"I've avoided those summer duties the last five years. I've been trying to move along with my writing. I've always come away not quite accomplishing what I hoped."

Mark had that far-away look in his eyes. "You know, James, you have writing and gardening and music as hobbies. Teaching has been my whole life."

"Most retirees say there's life after teaching."

"I'm scared of what's ahead. I don't know what I'll do."

"What have you always wanted to do?"

Mark thought a moment. "As a boy and young man, I loved to fish. And I'd go hiking in the woods. I used to sit on a tree stump or lie in a hammock and dream for hours."

"Now's your chance."

Mark's facial features seemed to tighten. "But I'm not going to let them do what they're doing to me. Not without a fight!"

"Are you sure you want to get into a fight with the administration?"

"I will if I have to." Mark's statement put a closing punctuation mark on that part of the discussion.

"Let's talk about something more pleasant. You still like to golf, don't you?"

"I haven't done much, but I'd like that."

"I'll get out my old clubs, and we'll go out on the course together."

Mark smiled. "We used to golf quite frequently in our younger days. And we'd have such good discussions."

The talk of the two men moved on to those earlier pleasant times. They reminisced about the days when the university had fewer students enrolled. Somehow with bigness, the place had become more impersonal—people became numbers. Both professor and other staff and students seemed less important—except as a number or fulfilling a role.

Their talk continued, except for a few interruptions. James realized how late it was when the evening meal was brought in.

"I didn't realize how long we had talked," said James. "I need to get home for dinner."

"Thanks, my old friend. I don't know when I've enjoyed a visit as much."

"We'll have to make time for more of this."

"I'm surprised Marcia isn't back. She's been hovering over me like a mother hen. I'm not giving up like some weak chicken. No one's going to call me some weak old man."

James laughed. "I hardly think that applies to Mark Goodman."

With those words he left, basking in the warmth of a friendship that had spanned most of his professional life. It was hard to think of his university life without Mark Goodman.

———◦⦙⦙⦙⦙◦———

Ruth breathed a sigh of relief as the last of the lively fifth graders cleared the hallway. Friday was always welcome, but this Friday seemed more than welcome. The school year was winding down, and she was ready for summer vacation.

Ruth began to straighten her desk. Her lesson plans were all set for next week. This weekend she would not take home any papers. Hopefully, she and James would drive to the new lake home that they had built a few miles from Lake View. She looked forward to the times she could get away from the city.

Chapter 1

"Ruth, do you have time for a cup of coffee?" The voice belonged to Marcia Goodman.

"Let's make time." Ruth couldn't disguise her surprise, for Marcia was not one of the university wives who had sought her friendship. Marcia Goodman might be described as one of the stay-at-home university wives who was intent on climbing the social ladder. She was busy in volunteer work and entertained the elite of the university and of the city of Riverton.

"You're surprised to see me."

"Yes, I guess so. How's Mark doing?"

Marcia sat down in a front desk. "He's better today. But the doctor said there may have been serious heart damage. I'm afraid what that might mean."

Ruth walked over to the desk and placed her hand on Marcia's shoulder. "Both James and I are praying for him."

Marcia looked away. "I knew you would. I haven't been much of a praying woman—and my husband hasn't been either. I've been surprised our husbands are such good friends. Your husband is serious about his Christian faith. Mark makes it to church on Christmas and Easter and only a few other times."

"The men are both dedicated professors and scholars. They love growing in knowledge."

Ruth could tell that Marcia was on the verge of tears.

Marcia wiped her eyes. "I'm so afraid. I don't know what I'd do if something happens to Mark. My whole life is bound to him and to the university."

"You know, Marcia, there is life beyond this place. Both our husbands will retire soon—at least in a few years."

"Mark has all this energy. He puts that energy into his teaching. And he becomes angry at people and situations that aren't right or fair. Now he's been saddled with lower level history courses, and he is very angry."

"I'm sorry. I didn't know about that."

"Mark just found out. That realization might have been what brought on his heart attack. He's determined to go back to the university as soon as possible. He thinks he can finish out the year, and he's determined to fight."

Ruth could see the problems ahead. "Let's go over to my place. We can have coffee, and I made some chocolate chip cookies yesterday."

The two women drove the few blocks to the James Anderson home. During the next hour Ruth learned more about Marcia than she had known in all the years their husbands had been friends and colleagues.

After a break in coffee and conversation, Ruth commented. "It's strange I haven't heard from James. He's usually home at this time, or otherwise he calls."

"The two men are probably still talking away. I should be getting back to the hospital."

"Why don't you have supper with us?"

"Thank you, I shouldn't have been away this long, but I knew James was with him. I guess I needed to talk. It's been very kind of you to listen."

"Glad to. We have so much in common at this stage of our lives. Stop by or call me whenever you want to talk."

"Thank you. That means more than I can say."

With those words Marcia hurried away. Ruth realized she had received a private glimpse into another woman's fears. She couldn't help wondering about James and about their plans for the future.

As James and Ruth finished supper a few hours later, James appeared to be in a more reflective state of mind. Though James was often reflective, this time he seemed more serious.

"Is something wrong?" asked Ruth. "You haven't seemed to be yourself."

"I can't help thinking about Mark. And I can't help thinking about me and retirement."

"Are you ready?" Ruth paused and went on. "Marcia talked at length with me. I think she and Mark are both afraid of his retirement. Or she's afraid if something should happen to Mark."

"I'm concerned about Mark. He's angry about his teaching assignment. He can handle hard work and decision making, but I don't think he's up to a fight with his department head and the administration of the university. I'm afraid it could kill him."

"I understand."

"In a way, I've always looked up to Mark as someone strong and dynamic. I haven't realized that underneath that bravado, he's like a frightened kid. People often hide their fears very effectively—even from their best friends."

Ruth looked into her husband's eyes. "James, are you afraid of change? Of retiring? I wonder if you aren't ready to retire."

James avoided her gaze. "Yes, I believe you're right. I am somewhat fearful of leaving my job—of facing the unknown. On the other hand, I want to quit while I'm ahead. Today after that freshman English class, I thought more seriously than ever about throwing in the towel, as they say. I think I may be ready."

Chapter 1

"I'd like to teach one more year since I don't have quite as many years as you do. But you could quit, and I could keep going another year."

"If I'm ever going to take this writing business seriously—my dream, I'm going to have to act soon."

"I know you, darling, you can't give up your dream."

"I've been thinking about a line from Tennyson. `To strive, to seek, to find, and not to yield.' I need to move ahead in new ways."

"It's almost time, isn't it?"

As James gathered the dishes and she began to wash them, Ruth knew that changes lay ahead. Life would lead her and James down some new paths. Where those paths would lead, she did not know.

CHAPTER 2

J ames paused as he stood by the garage. He and Ruth were ready to leave for Lake View and their lake home. He began to dream, something he hadn't done in a long time.

What if they moved to this home they had built and finished during these past years? He could walk in the woods, spend time with his mom and dad, work in his beloved garden—and most of all, he could devote his time to full-time writing. Could he write stories that would be good enough to sell? His mind took off and returned to his youthful dreams. In those dreams he had written the best seller. People were buying the books, and he was basking in success.

"I can't wait," he said aloud. "I'm sixty-one years old. If I'm ever going to pursue my dream, I must do it now."

The phone rang inside the house. He could hear Ruth talking. She hung up.

"I have some bad news," Ruth announced. "Mark Goodman died early this morning."

For a moment everything seemed unreal. Mark had been such a part of university life, he couldn't picture the university without him. James found himself speechless.

"James, did you hear me? You were so deep in thought."

"I can't believe Mark is gone. He had that heart attack, but yesterday he seemed so alive and so determined to live and to fight."

"Marcia wants us to help with the funeral plans. She needs us now. I think we better go over and be with her."

"Yes, we need to be there."

"We had better call your mom and tell them we're not coming home this weekend."

"I guess we'll have to. I was looking forward to time at the lake. But we'll go next week and there'll be time this summer."

The hours that followed merged into a type of lengthy nightmare. Marcia was distraught. Both Ruth and James tried to comfort her. James sensed that this woman had few inner resources or spiritual strength. She had been concerned about getting ahead socially and about outward appearances. She was intent on keeping up with the best of people at the university and in the city of Riverton.

"You take charge of the funeral and service arrangements, James," said Marcia. "You know what to do. I'm too upset to do anything."

James hesitated. "I'll do what I can to help, but there are some decisions you have to make."

"Mark always trusted you. I trust you, too."

"Thank you, I'm honored."

James accepted the assignment. This was the least he could do for his friend. In a sense he saw the emptiness of their lives. Marcia had made the decision that they should not be encumbered with children. She filled her time with volunteer and charitable activities. Most of all she had enjoyed being advisor to a sorority of young women who pursued her values.

Ruth smiled up at her husband and then said to Marcia. "When you're ready, there are some matters we need to discuss."

Marcia dried her tears. "It all seems so unreal. But we have to go on."

"You belong to the Episcopal church, don't you? Do you want the funeral in the church or in the funeral home? Did you want James to talk with the priest?"

"We've been members there for years. I wouldn't think of having the funeral any other place. But we haven't been near the church for a year now. Mark wasn't much of a church-going man."

"I've met Father Frank at some of the theater productions. I could call and talk with him. But I think, as pastor, he would want to talk with you."

"You see him first. I knew the previous priest, but we've attended church less and less, so I don't know Father Frank."

"When should we schedule the funeral?"

Marcia sighed. "I think the sooner, the better. Let's go for Monday."

"Okay, I'll work on that, but that might be a little soon. It's already Saturday."

"The sooner, the better," she repeated.

"If we work for a late afternoon funeral, more students will be able to come."

"Yes, his students loved him, and he loved them. Teaching was his whole life."

"We need to go to the funeral home and choose a casket. Now, we might have to delay the funeral until Tuesday."

"I want Monday. And we'll have a catered luncheon at the country club."

The remainder of the day, James completed arrangements for the funeral to be held on Monday afternoon at 3 o'clock. Death had a way of interrupting the lives of all concerned, and for the moment life seemed to stand still.

———

James observed the Gothic architecture of the Riverton's St. John's Episcopal Church. The high arches and the stained glass windows with the familiar Biblical scenes caused him to remember childhood memories from the familiar old country church back home.

He looked around him at a number of the university professors and their spouses. How different this funeral atmosphere was from the academic atmosphere of the university. The rows ahead of him contained Marcia's sister and husband plus some nieces and nephews. Next to them sat Mark's brother and sister. Mark's whole life had been connected to the university and not to his family. Life at the university would be quite different without Mark.

James turned around and saw the sanctuary was full and overflowing. Chairs had been brought in. Hundreds of students filled those chairs and many of the pews in the sanctuary. Their presence bore quiet testimony to the kind of teacher he was.

James' thoughts went off in another direction. "There's nothing I wish for more now than to go back home," he whispered to himself. He thought of his parents, Matthew and Ellen Anderson. They now lived in a small house in Lake View. Younger brother Michael lived on the home place, and at times hired help lived in the smaller house that his parents once lived in for several years. Michael had found himself after those years of wandering as a prodigal son.

He thought of the new home he and Ruth had built on the lake. The property, once considered wasted space, now increased in value. This home had been their weekend or summer escape place, but it could easily become their permanent home. Then he would be close to all the familiar places and many family members.

The farm they called the "home place" became a clear picture in his mind. That's where he had spent the first fourteen years of his life, and now Margaret and Joe lived there. But soon their son-in-law would take over. Some things remained the same, but there was change everywhere.

But the town of Lake View and the rural township of Oak Ridge were home and would always be home. Time was passing so quickly. If he wanted that time with his elderly parents, he could not put it off much longer.

The organ music ended and Father Frank began the spoken words of the service. "In the Name of the Father, the Son, and the Holy Ghost . . ."

Somber words and Scripture reminded James of the transitory nature of life. We are here for a fleeting moment in eternity. We are like a blade of grass.

Much about the service was unfamiliar to James, but he relaxed in comfort to the familiar words of the hymn

> O God, our help in ages past,
> Our hope for years to come.
> Our shelter from the stormy blast
> And our eternal home.

The priest proceeded to read Scripture. A soloist got up to sing. She sang a song that sounded almost like opera, and James could not pick out any familiar words.

"What is the essence of a man's life?" Pastor Frank began his funeral service. "We read the words of an obituary, and those words really say very little about the man himself. Perhaps if we look a bit more closely at those words, we would understand more about the true essence of Mark Goodman's life."

James couldn't help wondering how Father Frank, a virtual stranger to Mark Goodman, could have any kind of understanding of this man's life. In fact, he, James Anderson, knew the man well but was often puzzled about what the man really believed.

"Dr. Mark Goodman was born in 1923. The dreadful Depression of the 1930s made a deep mark on his life. His father, a farmer in northern

Minnesota, lost his farm and then worked hard to buy back that same farm. Mark Goodman knew what it was like to lack many of the so-called good things of life. He also knew what it was like to fight in a war—to see men dying around him.

"I won't go into detail about these events in his life. But these events shaped him into the kind of person he was. He was passionate about life and about history. His students could attest to that."

James smiled as he thought of Mark's reputation for really making history come alive. The students often talked about the way he fought World War II all over again as well as the Civil War and the Revolutionary War. For years, Mark was the most sought after teacher in the history department.

"Mark Goodman remained a fighter throughout his teaching career. I talked to several of his students. They all admired his passion and determination. Although he hated war, he believed in the fight for freedom. If Nazism or communism reared its ugly head, fighting was at least part of the answer. Talk, threats, negotiation might be part of the approach. But if necessary, a war had to be fought."

The pastor continued with other details that seemed less relevant. James' mind took flight to earlier days at the college and the university. "When we were smaller," he thought, "we were more like a large family— or extended family. Big doesn't necessarily mean *it's* better. Perhaps we have lost something when we became a successful and large university. Even so, we have something special."

At the same time, his mind moved to Lake View and family. For the first time in years, he felt homesick, the kind of experience he had had when he went away to college for the first time. Deep within his spirit he felt a need to go home—to stay home.

"Lord, are you telling me something?" he whispered silently. "Are you saying it's time to step back from this teaching job and move home?"

Father Frank's words once more invaded his awareness. "I keep repeating the word, passion. Mark Goodson was ready to lay down his life for his country. He championed the war against communism until it became evident that our country was not really fighting to win. Then, he became a leader in protest. 'We must not move into another dreadful war. We must use every other means possible.'

"Hunger was another passion. He promoted programs that would help eliminate world hunger. He was not a man who attended church, but he supported any program that brought food to starving people. I know that the Lord looks down with favor on a man who would show such mercy."

James' thoughts wandered back to when Mark Goodman was a young man. James remembered him as that brash and boisterous young professor who came to Riverton State College. The young man quickly made his mark as a dynamic teacher and soon became head of the department. Though James had an entirely different personality, they had followed similar paths.

How could such different men become the best of friends? James often wondered how these friendships happened. For one thing, it was timing. He didn't particularly like Mark at first. But as they worked together, respect came first and then friendship followed.

James realized his quieter ways led him to one kind of leadership. His reflective tendencies encouraged the creative and imaginative side of his teachers and students. That had to be an important part of teaching communication and writing and great works of literature.

James had admired Mark's aggressive qualities, his strong and forceful leadership. In turn, Mark respected and admired the quiet and intense scholarship of James. The two seldom argued. They simply acknowledged their differences.

These two men who were opposites in many ways championed many causes for academic excellence in the university. "What will I do without Mark Goodman? Or do I even want to stay on? Isn't it time for me to retire?"

The service ended. James and Ruth followed the crowd to the country club. The burial would take place a few days later because Mark would be buried in a country cemetery near where he was born.

James went through the motions of talking with fellow professors and a number of students. It seemed he was programmed to do and say the right things.

James experienced an emptiness he had not felt in years. Mark's life impacted the lives of many others. But Mark lacked something. He had never come to have faith in the living God. Somehow James felt he should have been able to introduce him to the Savior.

Finally reaching home, James escaped to his study.

Ruth knew her husband wanted to be alone. He would talk when he was ready. She worried about what Mark's death would do to him.

When Ruth needed to talk, she always called Coleen, her oldest daughter. In many ways Coleen was like her. She had been an elementary teacher and married an English teacher. They lived in one of the smaller towns about forty miles from Riverton.

The phone rang. Coleen seemed to know when her mother needed to talk.

"Mother, I heard about Mark Goodman's death. How's Dad taking it?"

"You know your dad. He's in his study. I think it's tougher on him than he cares to admit."

"Those two men were so different. I can't believe they were friends. Dad has such strong beliefs and convictions, yet he became a good friend to a man whose life style was the opposite—whose beliefs were about as far from Dad's as you could get."

"I know. I think Mark actually realized your father was on the right track." She paused a moment. "Your dad and I helped his widow plan the funeral. Your dad did most of the arranging."

"Dad's good at organizing and arranging. He always amazes me."

Ruth smiled. "Even to this day, he surprises and amazes me."

"You have a good, solid marriage. Do you realize how rare that is today?" She stopped and abruptly changed the subject. "Have you heard anything at all from Richard?"

"No, we haven't. Richard's disappearing really hurts your father."

Coleen hesitated. "I guess two free spirits just won't work out in a marriage. The one free spirit won't let the other one be free except in a restricted way."

"As usual, my dear, you seem to be right on. Your father and I think Richard probably headed for California, but you never know."

"I agree. But back to Dad. Is he feeling okay, or is he going to be like Grandpa with those stomach problems or maybe even heart problems?"

"Your dad's puzzling at times. He's so much like your grandmother in looks and disposition. The music and learning and teaching are from her. But similarities to your grandfather sometimes come through loud and clear."

"Dad and you need to take time off. Get out of town. Go on a trip. Or simply go back to the lake and relax."

"I don't know if I'm ready for that. And I wonder if your father would want to leave his teaching. He loves that part of his life."

"But, Mother, he's always had that dream that he would write that great novel."

"I think you're right. We do need a change."

Sounds of young children became evident.

"Mother, I think I need to go. The children need my attention. Let me know if there's anything I can do."

Coleen abruptly said goodbye.

Ruth sighed. "I guess I need to think about another school day. The end of the school year is never easy."

The study door opened. "Who were you talking to?" asked James.

"Oh, Coleen, she called to ask about Mark and the funeral."

"I've been thinking," began James, "I need to—or we need to—make some decisions. But, for now, let's go back to Lake View and our lake home."

"We have school to think about."

"Yes, either fortunately or unfortunately. But I thought I'd cancel my Friday classes, and you could take a personal day. We'll go home to Lake View, and we can talk and think things through."

'That's easier for you than for me.

"This is important. Otherwise I wouldn't have asked you."

"I guess so. But what's so urgent?"

Ruth saw in the eyes of her husband a passion and determination she had not seen for years.

"I can't really explain it now. I feel there are some things we must do now, or we will never have another opportunity. Yet, I'm afraid I've always been too cautious."

"I don't understand."

"Neither do I. It's almost as if God is speaking to me loud and clear."

Ruth knew that life was about to change. She couldn't help wondering what lay beyond the bend in the road. What would happen the day after tomorrow?

CHAPTER 3

"Matthew, dear, is something wrong?"

Ellen put down her knitting. Almost sixty-two years of marriage had taught her to read her husband's moods.

"I'm thinking about James."

"His friend's death must be hard on him. We know what that's like. We've lost enough of our friends and family."

"At least all of our children are okay."

Matthew sighed. "I never thought I'd make it to eighty-five. It's only Victoria and me left out of the six children. Mary had to suffer with cancer and those breathing problems. It's two years since Mary died, and ten since Ed died, but I miss them. I'm glad they came back from California--at least for a little while."

"Mary at least lived a full and long life. It seems different when the young are taken."

"You're thinking of young Matt."

"When Matt was killed in Vietnam, that really affected Margaret and Joe. He was such a sensitive young man with so much promise. He was like James in many ways."

Matthew set down the newspaper. "I think Joe believed in the war he fought in, but he had a hard time believing in the Vietnam War. It's a war that destroyed many families. It shouldn't have happened."

"But Margaret and Joe picked up and kept on moving ahead. It's wonderful the way they have built up their dairy business. It's great that Joel is involved with the farm even though he has his job as county agent. Joe's farm or the old home farm is the biggest dairy farm in the county."

Matthew, however, had a different concern. "I still think about Richard, with all his artistic and creative abilities. I wish he would return to his family. Why can't he come back where he belongs?"

"James and Ruth worry a lot about him"

"There's nothing we can do, but pray." Matthew got up from his chair. "Ellen, those tulips we planted last fall are starting to bloom. Let me show them to you."

Ellen put aside her knitting. "There's nothing like God's Nature to get us away from our problems."

"I still miss the farm. There's nothing like living in the country."

"But" interrupted Ellen, "we're so much better off here in town. We have good neighbors, and Victoria is down the street."

"I hated the idea of becoming dependent on Michael and Elise. They were good to us, but they needed our little house for their hired help. Their dairy business expanded and so did their garden and greenhouse business."

"And," added Ellen, "all their work in the greenhouse business was becoming too much for you. You could have been a full-time employee."

The two stood beside the tulips. Words were not necessary. The two were one in spirit.

———◦◦◦———

"Eight miles to Lake View," the sign read. James and Ruth continued to drive down Highway 210. They were indeed going home.

"Let's drive on and see your parents," suggested Ruth. "You can tell them what you're thinking about, and see what they have to say."

"I hate to disappoint them if we don't decide to move here. I've always been cautious—afraid to do something too radical—like quitting my job."

James kept on driving toward Lake View.

"That's true, but it's a matter of time. If you don't retire this year, you'll retire in another few years."

"I didn't tell you, but I did some checking on next year's schedule. It looks as if I won't be teaching many of my favorite classes. I'll have some of those lower level classes that most of the professors try to avoid."

"That's another reason to retire, isn't it?"

Chapter 3

They drove on to Lake View and the home of Matthew and Ellen.

When they drove up to his parents' home, Matthew and Ellen were standing outside admiring the spring tulips. A gentle breeze blew through the apple blossoms that had just burst forth.

"Mom. Dad!" called out James. "We thought we'd stop on our way to the lake."

"We weren't expecting you," said Ellen. "We thought you'd be busy with all those end of the year papers and teaching, and it's Thursday night."

"How can you be away from school?" asked Matthew.

"We just had to get away," said Ruth.

"We thought we'd play hooky," added James.

"Why don't you come in for some coffee or lemonade?" invited Ellen.

They hesitated. Then James agreed. "Yes, for a few minutes. We should get settled for the weekend."

When they were seated at the kitchen table, James made the announcement. "I've been doing some serious thinking."

His parents waited for him to go on.

"Well, we came this weekend to do some thinking."

"James, if your lake home isn't ready for you, you can stay in our spare bedroom."

"Thank you, Mom, but things are pretty well set at our lake home. And I believe I think better when I walk in the fields."

"He's a farm boy at heart," said Ruth.

"I'm seriously thinking of throwing in the towel with teaching. It may be my time to quit. I'm sixty-one years old, and I think I've been teaching long enough."

"I can't say I'm surprised," said his mother. "Now you can pursue your dream of writing that great American novel."

"I guess it must be now or never."

James and Ruth spent the next hour catching up on family news and talking of possibilities that the future held.

As they left, Matthew made his approval known. "It would be nice to have three of our five children nearby."

"But," added Ellen, "As always, you must make your own decisions. We don't want to push you into anything."

"Thanks, Mom."

When James and Ruth entered their lake home, James posed a question. "Do you think this could become our permanent home? Life in the country would be quite different from life in Riverton."

Ruth took only a moment to answer. "Any place my family is becomes home."

"In all honesty, I love this as a summer place. But in one sense, I'm afraid to leave the safety of our life in Riverton and the university."

"We're both rather cautious, aren't we? I think we need to sleep on our decision."

———⚬◖◗⚬———

The next morning, neither James nor Ruth had a clear picture of the future. A call from Coleen clouded their thinking.

"Was she upset?" questioned James.

"I think she was in shock. They thought their family was complete with a boy and a girl. And now she's expecting. She thought she could continue teaching now that the kids were both in school."

"Every child is a blessing. That's what Dad always said."

"I think Coleen wanted us around for moral support, so to speak. I think she figured that we might be built-in baby sitters if we were retired."

"I love each and every one of these grandchildren, and I want to be part of their lives."

Ruth smiled. "But do we want to be around them all the time? Do we want to be ready-made baby sitters?"

"There are all these 'buts'. Most of our friends are in Riverton. We'll be leaving them. We'll cut ourselves off from the life we've known so many years."

"James, you can retire now, but I need to teach another year or two. I'm not ready to quit at this time."

"I need to mow the lawn, and we should do some cleaning up both inside and outside. Maybe we can think more clearly when we work."

"I'll get the stew going in the crock pot and do a little work inside. When that's under control, I'm coming out."

"I'll get started. When I've finished the lawn mowing, I'm taking a good long walk in the pasture. That's where I do my best thinking—and praying, too."

———⚬◖◗⚬———

Early Sunday evening after supper, Matthew commented to Ellen. "It's really strange we haven't seen or heard from James and Ruth. And they weren't in church this morning."

Chapter 3

"If I know James, he wanted to be alone to think through his problems. He may be creative, but he's also thorough and methodical."

"I would think they'd call or stop here at least."

"But," reminded Ellen, "I'm not sure their phone is connected yet."

"I think we should go for a ride. It's a beautiful spring evening, and we can see the trees budding out and some of the flowering trees."

"Remember they might stop, and we'd miss them."

At that moment, a knock at the door interrupted their plans.

"Mom. Dad," announced James. "I know we should have called, but we've been working around the place and trying to make some decisions."

Ruth added, "You know your son when he gets going on something."

"I must admit we were wondering about you," said Ellen. "We are a bit curious about what you've decided—or if you've decided."

"I think we better ask them to come in and sit down."

"I'm sorry," apologized Ellen. "I guess I forgot my manners."

James looked at the plate containing his mother's homemade cookies. "Mom, those date-filled cookies look awfully good."

"Sit down. I'll warm up the coffee. But tell us your news. You obviously have something to tell us."

Ellen went over to the stove and turned on the burner.

It was Ruth, who spoke first. "We've talked over a number of things. We figure it's time to do some of what we've always wanted to do."

Matthew sat quietly, but curiosity kept gnawing within.

James and Ruth sat down.

"You've probably guessed it. I've decided to retire when school's out in June. Ruth needs to and wants to teach another two years."

"Then you'll stay in Riverton," said Matthew.

"No," said James. "Except for the winter months, I'll live in our new house by the lake. Ruth will come weekends. We're going to sell our house in Riverton, and Ruth will rent an apartment."

"What will the kids say?" asked Ellen.

"I made this part of the decision," said Ruth. "I want to have time with my grandchildren and the new grandchild that will be born, but I want to be a grandmother and not a babysitter or a second mother."

"You're wise," said Ellen. "Parents need to be responsible for their own children. It is their Christian duty."

"There's more," began James. "Yes, beginning this fall, I'm going to live here and concentrate on some serious writing. However, this summer we're considering some other plans."

"James has always wanted to visit Sweden. We've made some contacts, and there's room on a tour the beginning of July. We're serious about going."

Matthew thought of his own dreams. "I used to think that I would go to the Old Country and see where Pa was born. But I'm too old for that."

"Dad, I think you should go."

"No, I'll see your pictures, and you can tell me all about the country. I'm afraid that something could happen if I travelled that far."

"Are you sure, Dad?"

Ruth interjected. "You would have to get your passport. James and I have ours because we went on the European tour. It takes a few weeks for the passport to come through."

Ellen poured the coffee. "We should have taken that trip a few years back. Your father isn't as steady as he used to be. We wouldn't want an accident to happen. I have no desire to go to Sweden."

James took a second cookie. "Mom, you haven't lost your touch. They're better than ever."

Ellen obviously enjoyed the compliment. "Don't forget. There's more."

"We had a note from Richard so we know where he is. I have to see him. We have to resolve the differences—whatever they are."

"I've been praying that this would happen."

"We're going to try."

"It looks like a busy summer," said Ellen.

"Too busy," said Matthew. "Why don't you forget about a birthday celebration?"

"No!" exclaimed James and Ruth at the same time.

"Dad, that's the event that will bring the whole family together. Children. Grandchildren. Great grandchildren. Plus nieces and nephews and the next generations and many others."

"You shouldn't do all this."

"Dad, I think you should consider a trip to Sweden. I'm going to call Johnie when we get back home. We may get you there soon. In fact, I told a friend you were going with me to Sweden."

"Yes," chimed in Ruth. "Now that James is retiring and we're making other plans, I'm not sure I want to go. This could be a father-son trip."

"We love you, Dad. You're special to many people."

Those words stuck in Matthew's mind that night and during the days to come. His family would be coming home. Perhaps he would travel to the land of his ancestors.

"God is good," he said to himself many times.

CHAPTER 4

S ome days mark turning points in people's lives. That following
Tuesday was such a day.

Matthew knelt in their small garden, weeding the strawberries and
loosening the soil. In a few weeks, ripe red strawberries would be the
product of his hard work. He loved getting his hands dirty. He felt closer
to the Creator during those times.

He sat back and thought of the past days. The kids were intent on
having a big birthday party. I'll enjoy all my family, he thought, but I never
feel comfortable having all that attention. I'm not a public speaker like
Ellen or my children. I'm just a shy farmer.

"Dad." The familiar voice of Johnie interrupted his thoughts. "It's
almost lunch time--no it's noon dinner. And I have some surprises."

"Johnie, we weren't expecting you. How about Carolyn?"

"It's a school day for her. I decided to drive over."

"But that's quite a drive. It must be special."

"Let's go in, Dad, and both you and Mom can hear the news."

Matthew wondered what this surprise could be. They had hinted
something about his going to Sweden, but this was a bit sudden.

As Matthew got up from the damp ground, his joints seemed to creak.
Now and then he felt every one of his eighty-five years.

Johnie seemed to stall, refusing to tell what the surprises were.

Matthew washed himself, ridding himself of the garden dirt.

"Dinner's not quite ready," announced Ellen. "I'll keep working and we can talk. Johnie, you can let us know these surprises."

Johnie took out a folder and then produced tickets and laid them out on the table. "Dad, these are airline tickets to Sweden. You and James have tickets for early July."

Ellen smiled. "Matthew, it's time for you to go. I'll be just fine here at home. I have no desire to fly to Sweden."

"But...." Was all Matthew could say.

"It's all taken care of. Michael will pick up you and James and take you to the Minneapolis airport. You'll fly to New York and then change planes and fly to Copenhagen. In Copenhagen, you'll take a tour and then relatives will meet you and take you to the family home."

"I can't believe this."

"You better believe it."

"You know, Pa never talked much about Sweden and the life there. What little he said, I remember well. I used to dream that someday I would see the place."

"And now you will."

"I don't know what to say."

Ellen began to mash the potatoes. She always made the basic farm dinner which had to include meat and potatoes and gravy and vegetable. "Johnie, you said you had surprises. That's plural. What are they?"

Johnie looked at his father. "Dad, you always looked to those hills and you quoted Scripture when you said, 'I will lift my eyes unto the hills from whence cometh my help. My help comes from the Lord, who made Heaven and earth.' You said that you would probably not go far beyond those hills, but your children would. Well, you're going to Sweden, but I'm also making a move."

Ellen looked up in surprise. "We always thought you'd stay where you are until you retired."

"I think the Lord has other plans. I've always had an interest in missions, and the churches I've pastored have supported missionary work. I don't think I've mentioned it, but Carolyn and I have had this dream about doing mission work--perhaps in an area where the church is weak."

"You're not leaving us for Africa or some faraway place, are you?" asked Matthew.

"No, not exactly. I've been called to a larger church. The church has a strong interest in mission work. Eastern Europe and parts of Russia are becoming more open to the Gospel. This church has dreams of sending people over for short periods of time. Short-term missions."

"But that might be dangerous," said Matthew.

"I'm safe wherever the Lord wants me to be."

"Where is this church?" asked his mother. "I hope it's not in some far corner of the United States or Canada."

"That is the good news. This church is in Riverton. Actually, I'll be closer to you when I move than I am now."

Ellen looked over at Matthew and then at her son. "You'll always be a kid to your father and me, but I know you're almost sixty. Churches usually don't try to get a pastor who is that close to retirement."

"I'm not sure it's God's plan for me to retire. I want to go on preaching as long as I can—maybe until I die."

Ellen finished cutting the beef roast and set the meal on the table. "It's time to eat. Johnie, you ask the blessing."

The three bowed their heads. Johnie began his prayer. "Dear Heavenly Father, we come to you with hearts full of gratitude…"

Life would be moving in new directions.

———

"Am I ready for this retirement?" James asked himself as he sat alone in his office. Riverton State University had been his life for more than thirty years. His whole life was bound to this place and to his family. What would life be afterwards? Could he succeed as a writer or in other ways?

He felt butterflies in his stomach. He thought back more than fifty years, when he walked as a frightened little boy across the fields and pastures to the one-room school. In some ways he felt no different from that frightened little boy.

His secretary interrupted. "Dr. Anderson, is there anything more you want me to get ready for your two o'clock department meeting?"

"No, I think I'm ready—as ready as I'll ever be."

His secretary gave him that puzzled look.

"Norma, perhaps there's something I should tell you. It will be general knowledge in a little while, but say nothing until then. I have written my letter of resignation. I'm retiring at the end of this spring quarter."

"Isn't that rather sudden?"

"I've been thinking it about it for a long time. I'll be announcing it to my staff at the department meeting. I see no reason to prolong the departure. It's best I leave quickly."

"We'll all miss you. It won't be the same."

"I guess you already know that the new administration is pushing some of the older professors to step down or leave. I think it's my time."

"Are you sure? I think many of us feel you've made this department what it is--one of the best in this university."

"Thank you. I appreciate your support and confidence. I think I'd like to quit while I'm ahead."

His secretary added, "It may be my time to step down as well."

"The university may need you during the transition. Please don't retire from your job on my account."

"No, not exactly, I'd been thinking about taking more time with family and visiting children and grandchildren."

"And I want to find time to do the writing I've always dreamed of doing."

"Thanks for telling me in advance. I've loved my job—partly because of you." With those words she left his office to return to her desk.

James bowed his head. "This is harder than I thought," he said aloud. He prayed, "Lord, please give me the assurance I'm doing the right thing. I have to admit it's scary to give up the security of a job that I have loved."

He began to think back to the earlier teaching days, his first classes at the university. Those were the freshman English classes that he taught while he worked on a Master's degree. Then he thought of the two years of going elsewhere to work on his doctorate. Although challenging— they were good years, where strong friendships were cemented.

"To strive, to seek, to find, and not to yield." Tennyson's words crossed his mind. There had been something invigorating about the new and uncertain. After receiving his doctorate, he had returned to Riverton and had quickly been promoted to chairman of the English department. But now there had been talk of other changes.

A knock on the door interrupted his thoughts.

"Dr. Anderson, the president just sent a message that he wants you to read at the department meeting. Apparently, all departments are meeting this afternoon."

"Thank you." He trembled as he accepted the letter. But, he thought, I'll be out of here. The changes aren't going to affect me.

He read the letter quickly. Essentially, it said what people had suspected. There would be complete re-alignment of departments. Departments would become a part of a division. The coming year would be a time of shifting.

Chapter 4

At a few minutes before two, James entered the faculty lounge for the English department. His secretary served the rolls he had ordered as an afternoon treat. The professors and teachers entered and took their rolls and coffee. James sensed a tension and uneasiness that was not usually a part of such a meeting.

"Good afternoon," he greeted his staff. "First, I have an announcement from the president of the university. I think you've been expecting this one, though it might give you a slightly better idea of what's going to be happening."

He heard several comments from his professors and teachers, generally negative comments about university politics.

James nervously held the paper. "This is a time of change and a time of challenge as well. As president of Riverton State University, I am aware of the uneasiness of the faculty. I understand, and I empathize with you. Let me assure you as individual professors and teachers that you are under contract, and your jobs are secure for the coming year."

Someone interrupted, "But it's not too sure about the year following."

James read on. "However, because of all the re-alignment, there may be some shifting of responsibilities and classes. We have a tentative schedule of the fall classes, but those are always subject to change, depending on student enrollment. You are being asked to bear with me as we face these uncertainties.

"During the coming year, you will be asked to continue work on various committees. We hope to expand our curriculum, becoming larger but also a university with the highest standards and widely recognized for academic excellence. The new divisions will be in keeping with the trends of the twentieth century as we move toward the twenty-first century.

"Please re-assure your students, who are pursuing specific majors, they will be able to continue their particular plan. However, there will be opportunity to pursue other expanded plans for majors and general education work.

"My door is always open to those of you with questions and concerns. We will work out all these details in the best way possible.

"In the meantime, I wish you the best as you finish the spring quarter and move into the summer season."

One of the more vocal professors called out, "Too many 'however.' And I'm not sure that door is always open. He avoids me."

Someone else chimed in. "I wonder why."

"This is a time of change and uncertainty," continued James. "I also have an announcement. Before I received this notice from the president,

I had made a decision. I think some of you know that I've always had that dream of writing a great American novel. After much soul-searching, I have made a decision. I have here my letter of resignation. I will be leaving at the end of this spring quarter. Lee Morgan, my assistant who is to act as chairman this summer, will be asked to continue those responsibilities this fall."

"You can't leave us now," said one of the younger teachers. "We need you to fight for us. You've always been fair."

"We trust your judgment. We're not so sure of some people."

James felt touched by the kind sentiment. "Thank you. I appreciate your words of affirmation and encouragement. Perhaps I need to say a little bit more."

He waited until he had the full attention of his staff.

"In a sense, this English department has become like a family. Individually, we haven't always agreed. We've had differences. But that's the way it is with family. But there is a time for family members to move out and to move on. It is such a time for me. It could be tempting for me to stay awhile longer. However, I also feel it is good to quit while one is ahead.

"I'd be wrong if I didn't admit that my friend, Mark Goodman, over in the history department, had something to do with my decision. As his life ended so suddenly, I realize something about the brevity of life. Each of us has only so much time. And my family is also important. I have my children and my wife. I also have a father and mother, who are very much alive. I want to spend time with them. In fact, it looks as if my father and I will visit our homeland, Sweden.

"This isn't exactly goodbye. We have several more weeks of classes. I want to keep contact with all of you. I've never felt I was your boss."

Someone chimed in. "You never acted like one. You were more like a father—a mentor."

"That was one of the kindest things you could say. I consider you friends. And friends do stay in touch."

Lee Morgan stood up. "I regret that you are leaving, James. You have been friend and mentor. I will do the best I can to carry on your fine work during the year ahead. I may seek your advice from time to time."

James smiled. "That I can give. But I think it's time to end this meeting. The committees are all in place. The end of the spring quarter plans are all in place. Is there anything we need to talk over?"

To his surprise, there was no discussion.

Chapter 4

"Now for a closing thought. As I was thinking about change and the future, I thought of Tennyson's famous line at the end of *Ulysses*. 'To strive, to seek, to find, and not to yield.' That is good advice for us all as we look to the future."

The room erupted into spontaneous applause.

CHAPTER 5

June 1985

The sounds of cars driving on the state highway broke into Matthew's thoughts. Why were people always in such a hurry? Where were they going anyway? The pace of this twentieth century world disturbed him.

He knelt down and looked over his small garden, which was without weeds. He missed the wide open spaces of the country even after five years of living in Lake View. However, he had to let go of the past and move ahead with his new life.

Matthew stood up. It was a good day and he felt quite limber for being eighty-five years old. I need to get back to the farm, he thought. He moved quickly toward their small but comfortable rambler home.

"Ellen," he called as he entered the kitchen. "Let's drive to Margaret's and then to Michael's. I need a break. I want to get out in the country."

"You go," she answered. "I have work here. And I'm going with the Gray Ladies to the nursing home this afternoon."

"I'm not hungry so don't worry about noon dinner."

"If you stop at Margaret's, I dare say she will feed you."

Fifteen minutes later, Margaret greeted him.

"I just wanted to get out of town and be in the country. I feel much more at home in the country. I'm a farmer at heart."

"I'm glad you stopped, Dad. James called me and wondered if I'd go over and air out their lake home. Why don't we take some sandwiches and have a picnic. Joe's away—helping out at the neighbors."

Matthew was only too happy to agree. He and Margaret had that special father-daughter relationship. But then he thought a moment. "You know there's something else I've really wanted to do."

"Yes, Dad. What?"

"It's June, the most beautiful time of the year. Before we go to James's, could we walk across the hills toward the lake? I used to wander those hills as a young boy."

Margaret smiled up at her father. "Why don't we take our picnic lunch out on the hills near the lake? This afternoon we'll go to James'."

Matthew sat quietly as Margaret went about making sandwiches. Efficient as always, she soon tucked the wrapped sandwiches and cookies in a basket and poured coffee into a thermos. He felt a freedom to talk with Margaret—perhaps even more freely that with Ellen.

As they walked through the pasture across the field and back to the pasture near the lake, they said little. Matthew wanted to drink in the beauty of this June day. How appropriate that as a family they named it Pioneer Lake.

"Dad, something's on your mind. Is something bothering you?"

Mathew mused, "I spend more time thinking—not necessarily doing any work."

"Dad, it's time you took it easy."

"I guess I'm tired. I don't have the energy I used to have."

"Well, Dad, you are older."

"I've been thinking about your mother. She's always busy, but she seems to fall more. She doesn't get hurt. I'm worried about her."

"She'll have to be more careful."

"I try to help more around the house. I do the vacuuming. She doesn't seem to be able to handle something that heavy."

"You're a good husband."

Father and daughter walked on in silence. Matthew wanted to express the thoughts that had come to him during these last weeks. How could he best face the challenges of this last phase of life? Growing old wasn't easy."

"Here's a good spot. There are wild sweet Williams nearby. And we can see the lake."

Margaret took the picnic basket from her father and set it down. "Why don't you share these thoughts you've been having? You and mother are such fine examples and role models to us children."

"You children have helped us grow old."

They sat down. Margaret spread out the sandwiches. "Dad, you ask the blessing."

They bowed their heads and Matthew began to pray. "Dear Lord, thank You for this beautiful place where we can enjoy your world. I thank You Lord for a wonderful life, for health and for family. Thank you for the way you have guided me these eighty-five years. Thank You for Margaret and now for this meal that she has prepared. Bless this food. We pray this in Jesus' Name. Amen."

Margaret handed him a sandwich and leaned over and kissed him on the cheek. "Thank You, Dad. You pray better than most preachers."

A gentle breeze blew. The temperature could not have been more ideal. They ate silently for a few moments as they looked at each other and the lake nearby.

Matthew broke the silence. "This is too perfect a time to spoil with words."

"Dad, I want to hear your thoughts. Something's bothering you."

"Life is scary. Growing old is scary."

Margaret waited for him to go on.

"I think about the trip to Sweden. I've flown a few times in the States, but this is a much longer trip. Being in a foreign country scares me."

"James traveled many places. He'll be with you and take care of everything."

"I think about your mother being alone. We've been apart only a few times, and then it was only because of a health problem. And—we were younger then too."

"Dad, I'll check on her every day. She'll be just fine."

Matthew looked away and then picked up his cup of coffee. "Coffee helps to get us talking."

Margaret smiled. "That is so true. I think of the times when conversations were dragging, and we brought out coffee and cake or cookies. All at once the talk would be lively once more."

Matthew placed his hand over his heart. He had been feeling little twinges, not really pain.

"Do you have pain?" asked Margaret.

"No, it's nothing." In reality, he knew it might well be something. Both Pa and Grandpa had died of heart attacks.

Margaret once more urged him to talk. "There's something you'd like to say, isn't there?"

"I hope I don't get sick on the trip. That would be terrible."

"Dad, you won't. However, there's good medical help in Sweden."

Matthew looked to the lake and the hills beyond. "One thing I can't stand the thought of is being an invalid in a nursing home. That scares me. Or having a stroke the way Glenn did. His last months in the nursing home were terrible. I went to see him, but we couldn't talk the way we had talked for so many years."

"I'll throw back your own words. 'God will be with you there, or wherever you have to go in this life.'"

"One of the hard things about growing old is loss. I've lost so many friends. I've lost my brother and sisters. I'm thankful Victoria is still around and as active as ever. If she dies before I do, that will be really hard."

"You're both hardy people."

"I want to be active and able to look after your mother and be of help to others. I don't want to sit back in the rocking chair."

"Dad, if I get to be the age of you and Mom, I want to do what you're doing. But, Dad, just being around the family is important to us. You shouldn't have to do anything but be here."

"I want to live, really live, until I die."

"I think we all want that."

The sounds of a boat on the lake caught their attention.

"I guess P.J.'s mansion is filled with some of those Chicago people."

Margaret added, "That house has been more of a curse than a blessing. But I do remember that one Christmas when P.J. was so generous. Then, I remember all the problems connected with Uncle P.J. or Aunt Rita or other people."

"I think one of the most terrible moments in my life happened on your grandparents' Golden Wedding. It was then P.J. told me, 'This farm is mine.' It was as if he killed somebody."

"But, as you have said, you were really better off on the other farm you bought."

"Yes, I was able to forgive P.J. and the new farm had richer soil and was better. And now Michael has the place."

"That must have been the worst kind of experience anyone could have. That farm, rather this farm, was your life."

"But I was able to give it up. I had to, I believe God urged me to."

"God works in many ways. Sometimes, it's harder to figure exactly what He is doing."

Chapter 5

Matthew found himself remembering another experience, the time he was close to death.

"Something happened that's terribly hard to explain."

"Dad, you know you can tell me anything."

"Do you remember when I had that ulcer attack when I almost died?"

"I think I was only ten. I remember it was a scary time. That's when Joe came into our lives."

"Joe was only a boy, but he did a man's work as hired help. We couldn't have survived that winter without him."

Margaret reached over and grasped her father's hand. "I think it was way back then that I fell in love with Joe. I think I always knew he was the man for me."

"And he became like a son long before he married you."

"God brings people into our lives at just the right time."

Matthew looked down at the water of Pioneer Lake, glistening in the sun. What a perfect blue, heavenly blue! He looked up to the hills and it seemed, like the song said, "that he could see forever." It was almost as if he had a glimpse of eternity.

Margaret interrupted Matthew's silence. "There was something more you were going to say, Dad. What was it?"

"When I was so sick at that time, I almost died. My heart actually stopped. I had one of those experiences when I was on the edge of eternity. Even after all these years, it's still so vivid in my mind."

Margaret waited for him to go on.

Matthew cleared his throat. He found it hard to put the experience into words. "There was light all around. I had the most wonderful feeling of peace as if I were leaving the world and all its problems. Then, I looked down and I saw the farm. Then, I saw Ma and Pa and your mother and then all of you kids—there were only four of you then. Michael came later."

Matthew cleared his throat once more. "I felt such an overwhelming love—as if I were in the presence of Christ Himself. I believe I was. Then, I felt a new kind of love for your mother and for each of you."

Matthew's face glowed with the remembrance. "There was a door, and someone stood at the door. I seemed to hear an invitation. I saw Christ standing at the door. Then I heard a voice, 'Go back. You are needed. You have a purpose on this earth.'"

"That's a wonderful story."

"That's not all. During that winter as I spent time recovering, I realized God had given me another chance. Christ had become more real than ever. I studied Scripture more than ever before in my life. I sensed that new purpose. And it was then that I forgave P.J. But I'll have to say those scars still remain, and will remain throughout life."

"Thanks for sharing this life experience. I understand some things better."

"And now, I have some new questions. I never thought I would live this long. I thought I'd die at seventy-seven, the age of your grandfather. But I've lived. But now I'm beginning to ask God some questions. What is my purpose at this advanced age? I want purpose in life."

"Dad, you fill a purpose just being here. We need you for moral support."

"Oh, you kids are all pretty well settled in life. You don't really need me. You have your children and grandchildren."

"Dad, I needed to have this talk with you. It's a talk I will remember to my dying day."

Margaret poured another cup of coffee and the two ate their cookies in silence. Some special moments invite times of silence.

It was Matthew, who broke the silence. "I think we need to move on. Maybe we'll see Michael and then go to James's home."

After they picked up the leftovers and placed them in the picnic basket, Matthew looked back, half regretting that this special time had ended. He thought of the road ahead in his life. The familiar lines of a hymn came to him, "The road that short or long will lead me home."

As they walked back to the home place, Margaret mused, "Dad, we should do this more often. I can't remember a time when you and I did this."

"I probably talked too much."

"You could never do that."

Back at the original home place, Margaret suggested she would drive to the other, second home place, now Michael's farm. Matthew quickly agreed. There were times he felt uneasy about driving. No longer did he see quite so well of late.

Fifteen minutes later, they arrived at the other home place, the home of Michael and Elise. Matthew couldn't help remembering all the hard work he had put into this place. It reflected his blood, sweat and tears of half a life. This had been truly his, and now it was Michael's.

Margaret stopped the car, and they stepped out. Loud voices could be heard. Matthew immediately recognized Michael's voice, but it was harsh and angry. For Michael, usually so kind and gentle, this was out of character.

Chapter 5

Margaret looked to her father. "Michael's having an argument. But who with?"

Matthew started to make out some of the words. "Everything will be taken care of," shouted Michael. "You have no business even coming here."

Michael stepped out of the garage, followed by Jeffrey Grant, his daughter Carol's oldest son and his oldest grandson. For a moment Matthew thought he was transported back in time. The likeness of Jeffrey Grant and brother P.J. was unbelievable.

The conversation of the two men continued, though more quietly. Apparently, they did not notice the arrival of Matthew and Margaret.

Jeffrey Grant gestured, though spoke more quietly so that the words were not audible. Well over six feet tall, he was taller than P.J. Dark hair, handsome features, piercing eyes that were almost black, a face that could easily belong to a movie star. He resembled the Biblical character of King Saul, who was taller than any other man in the kingdom.

Matthew had to admire the way his grandson dressed. A casual light blue sport coat with a dark trousers and a matching tie. He looked the way a banker or business man should look. He wasn't careless and informal the way some people were.

A host of memories flooded Matthew's mind. Some of the same feelings he had had toward P.J. began to surface.

The men looked their way and stopped talking. Michael greeted them.

"Hello, Grandfather," greeted Jeffrey. "I'm sorry I haven't been around to see you. You certainly are looking well."

"Hello, son.' Matthew extended his hand.

Jeffrey extended his hand and then embraced his grandfather.

Matthew felt a certain warmth as he felt the closeness of this boy. At the same time, he experienced the discomfort he had felt with his own brother.

Jeffrey continued in the same charming way P.J. would have. "How are you, Grandfather? I'm so glad that I ran into you. I've been meaning to stop."

"I'm fine," said Matthew, "just getting older."

Jeffrey turned to Margaret. "Hello, Aunt Margaret. Lois and I should have all of you over some time, but we're all so busy."

Jeffrey carried forward the conversation about routine matters and then announced, "I have to get back to work. Always business to take care of." He turned to Michael. "We'll talk again soon."

Michael muttered something that was not quite audible.

Jeffrey hurried off.

Margaret turned to Michael. "What was that all about?"

Michael hesitated. "We had business. It will be taken care of."

"Are you sure it's not more serious?"

"How about coming in for coffee?" invited Michael. "I'm afraid Elise went in to town, so it'll just be me."

Margaret hesitated. "We'll take a rain check. I'm going over to James' house to air it out and take care of a few things."

"Well, thanks for stopping by. I guess I have plenty of work myself."

Matthew found himself dredging up past hurts from years ago. Jeffrey reminded him so much of P.J. that he recalled all the terrible things that P.J. had done.

Margaret seemed to understand and respected the silence. When they arrived at James' lake home, Matthew decided to walk around the yard and down to the lake.

The mind does strange things. As Matthew walked beside the sandy beach where the family had gathered many times, his mind seemed like a fast-moving movie or television show. Past, present, possible future all merged together. He felt a sense of pending evil or danger.

He sat down on the stump of a tree. He became a young child. P.J. had told those dreadful stories of Blue Beard and how he locked up his wives and killed them. He experienced again the horror of being locked in the attic by P.J.

Then, his mind moved to the last time he had seen P.J. alive. The man was in torment. "If only I can make things right." The fear in P.J.'s eyes told him that he feared hell. It was almost as if P.J. were in hell already.

"Dear Lord," Matthew said aloud, "I don't want P.J. separated from you. I hope that he somehow repented in those last moments."

"Dad," Margaret spoke gently. "I think it's time for me to get back home. And, if you're much later, Mother will be worried about you."

"Sorry, I was deep in thought."

They walked toward the car. Matthew remained silent.

"Dad, something's bothering you. I think you need to talk. And I think it had to do with Jeffrey."

As Margaret began to drive, Matthew found the words coming quickly and easily. "I'm afraid Jeffrey looks so much like your uncle, Paul John. It's almost as if P.J. were present and a threat to the life of the family."

"You don't have to talk about it, but often talking helps."

Chapter 5

"I think I need to. Jeffrey sounded exactly like P.J. Jeffrey can be so very charming and he can control people. When P.J. manipulated the situation so he owned the farm, he was greedy for money, but he was also wanting to control me and the rest of the family.

"There were many times when P.J. tried to control my life. When I was in the hospital that time, so very sick, he wanted to call in a surgeon to operate. That decision might have just finished me off. We knew the doctors did the right thing at the time."

"I didn't know all that."

"P.J.'s life style of partying and drinking embarrassed the rest of the family. That life style took money. And yet when he had money he could be generous. After I bought the Nelson place, he gave me a very generous Christmas present. I think there was a little bit of guilt, and I think he wanted to control me.

"And I think, too, that the rest of the family was a little bit afraid of him. Victoria could stand up to him at times, but even she was careful."

Margaret looked across to her father. "In a way, he was a very evil man. But that doesn't mean Jeffrey is evil."

"No, I hope not. But I have a hunch that Jeffrey is up to no good. His Grandmother Grant was too much of an influence. She spoiled him rotten and introduced him to a life that wasn't really good for him."

"Dad, we'll have to pray for both Michael and Jeffrey. I know Michael took out a loan for his greenhouse and nursery operation. But he's doing well with the cattle and the farming."

"Yes, but he's bought bigger and newer equipment than he really needs. Joe and I would 'make do' with older equipment rather than go into debt."

"Michael's part of a new generation."

"As his older sister, I think I spoiled him."

As Margaret drove up the driveway of the original home place, Matthew looked to the old oak tree that still stood tall and strong. That tree by itself could tell a story.

"'O what is as rare as a day in June.' I shouldn't borrow trouble before it happens. Most of our worries never come true."

"Dad, how right you are. And look at what you have to look forward to. The big family gathering at your eighty-fifth birthday party. And then your trip to Sweden."

Matthew stood, looking at the lush green of the trees and grain field nearby. "God is good. I have much to be thankful for."

"As I see all this beauty around us, it's hard to believe there's a dark side: evil in this world."

Matthew repeated his words. "God is good, but we live in a fallen world. And there are dangers."

CHAPTER 6

The building seemed eerily empty. As James walked through the halls that Saturday morning, ghosts of teachers and students filled the space around him. This was his final goodbye to the life of teaching.

There was something unreal, almost surrealistic, about this moment in time. All his life he had planned and looked forward to learning or work or teaching. First, the country school, where he anticipated going to the big high school in town. Then, the four years of high school and the dream of attending college or university. Next came those four years at Riverton, then a State Teachers' College. After that, high school teaching, advanced degree classes, and college and university teaching.

He had always looked forward to a step upward. But now retirement. What did retirement really mean? It seemed to be a step down, a conclusion.

Whoever said silence was golden? If this was silence, it wasn't really silence. The voices of former students filled his mind. The students and professors he would meet and greet and talk to were everywhere.

"I will miss these people," he said aloud. "What does life hold for me now? Mom and Dad are older. I have longed to return to the life, a simpler life. I have wanted to return to my people and have time for my family and friends. But so many of my friends are here."

He walked up the steps, marble steps, to the second floor. At the landing stood the whole grandfather clock, now restored and telling correct time. But time was illusive in many ways. The past forty years had passed as if in a moment. This morning, time stood still.

James saw himself first as the young high school teacher, trying hard to project confidence. The confidence did come, day by day and year by year. How quickly he had changed from this youthful teacher to a seasoned PhD and university professor. For a moment he returned to his beginnings in the world of the university.

"Life is transient," he mused aloud. "Like a cloud. Like a mist. Like grass that withers and fades. What about this next phase?"

He walked down the hall toward his office. For years he had walked these halls, noticing little of his surroundings. Today he noticed even the minutest feature. A wall picture depicting the early Mississippi. A bulletin board with the late spring notices. A sign with names of the professors whose offices were located there.

He opened the outer door and saw his faithful secretary's desk, neatly cleaned. She said she planned to retire soon. He walked on and unlocked his office.

He put down the boxes he had carried in. He had already carried out several boxes of books. Now he needed to get out the rest. He placed the photo of Ruth into the box first, then a family picture of him and Ruth and the three children plus the grandchildren. Next, a family picture of Mom and Dad and the five brothers and sisters. These pictures reminded him of what was dearest to him in this world.

Ruth had said she would come and help, but he had declined. He needed this time to reflect. He looked to the wall. Yes, his Terry Redlin painting, "Autumn Afternoon," depicting the mill on the river in late autumn. As he anticipated autumn each year, James looked forward to another school year. Only this year, after fifty-five years of being in school, he would not return.

The enormity of his decision hit him once more. Retirement was final. The university already had replacements. He couldn't change his mind and go back. His retirement pension and benefits would begin in September.

"I have to finish this!" he exclaimed. "I have to get out of here. Enough of this maudlin sentimentality."

With those words he hurried through his tasks. Within the hour, he completed his three trips to the car with boxes and other "stuff."

"I'll turn in my keys on Monday." He double checked the outside door to make sure it was locked. "And now, I look forward to a new life."

—⸺⸺⸺—

Ruth Roberts Anderson's life had always been well-planned and organized. This Saturday was no different. She had vacuumed and cleaned all morning as she always did on Saturdays—unless there were special events . . . Tomorrow would be the day of rest.

She couldn't help wondering about James. She could leave teaching and be as busy as ever, but what about this man whose whole life was teaching? Could he survive without this purpose in his life? Could he re-direct his energies in a new direction or new directions?

Ruth thought of her projects for the summer. She should go through those photographs and put them in albums. The lower floor with the family room and the bedrooms that had become storage or junk rooms needed to be cleaned out. James kept far too much stuff. But that was stuff she didn't dare throw out. He would have to make the decision.

She looked at the clock on the mantle. It was almost one o'clock. They always had their lunch promptly at 12:30.

"I suppose this retirement business is a whole new experience," she mused aloud. "What will he do with the time?" She thought packing up probably took longer than he thought.

The phone rang. Thinking it was James saying he would be late, she answered. The voice was Coleen's.

"I'd like you and Dad to come over for supper tonight. I suppose you won't be around much this summer."

Ruth hesitated. "I'm sure that will be just fine. Your father hasn't come back from his office. He was doing his packing up today. I think it took him longer than he planned."

"That's strange. Dad is rarely late. I thought you'd be finishing your lunch."

The garage door opened, and James drove in. "He came back. I'll say 'yes.' I'll call back in minutes if he says it won't work."

"See you then, Mom. Love you." She hung up.

James entered the kitchen. "Sorry, I'm late."

"Everything's ready." Ruth brought out egg salad sandwiches. "I was going to have soup, but Coleen called and invited us for supper, so we'll stick with sandwiches only."

"So you accepted the invitation."

"I was sure it would be okay."

"I guess I have nothing else that I have to do."

They sat down, said a short grace and ate in silence.

Ruth couldn't help wondering. "Is everything okay?"

James put down the rest of his sandwich. "I should be happy, jumping for joy, so to speak. But it's hit me what I've done. It's a terribly big decision"

"But, darling, you've talked and dreamed of having time to write—to write that great American novel."

"Now that I will have the time, I don't know if I can do it. Do I have what it takes?"

"Oh, James, you've proven yourself as a writer. You can do the novel."

"Those were articles and short stories. I have ideas for a novel, but I've never really written one. And I'm afraid I might get side-tracked."

"You may be busy with many things. But I know when you set your mind to something, you do it. You get it done."

"Thanks for the vote of confidence."

"Why don't we pack up and leave Monday for Lake View and our lake home. Then, you can get outside, wander through the hills, and get started with your novel." Matthew sighed "But I have the last travel arrangements to make for the trip to Sweden. And we have Dad's eighty-fifth birthday party to organize. We can't leave everything to Margaret. And Michael and Elise are so busy with their new greenhouse business that they don't have any time."

"I'll step in and help. Remember, much of the work seems to be women's work. I'll help Margaret with that, but I dare say she has half of those plans already made."

James agreed. "I'll get to work. I'll pack away those books from the office. I'll have to decide later what I want to do with them. And I'll start to pack up what I want to take to the lake."

Ruth got up and brought over the coffee pot for that last cup. "This will be like no other summer ever before."

"It's time to move ahead. We're still relatively young."

Ruth sensed she had a new task, a new purpose in life: she had to make sure her husband got started with the real calling in his life.

Chapter 6

"James, get out of the house. Go for your walk. You think best that way. Take your journal and get started."

It was Tuesday morning after an extended whirlwind weekend. Saturday, James had packed away what needed to be packed away. He then packed for their summer at the Lake View home. In the evening, Coleen gave them a retirement celebration dinner. James would miss being close to Coleen and family.

Sunday, the day of rest, was not exactly a day of rest. There was the usual church service, but someone had a coffee and dessert gathering to honor James on his retirement. Melissa and her husband and the children drove up from southern Minnesota and took them out for dinner. In the evening, a steady stream of people stopped by. Monday morning, he hoped quietly to turn in his keys at the college, but several friends gathered.

It was afternoon before they had finally left for Lake View. Naturally, they had to make quick stops to see Mom and Dad and then they hurried on to the place that would become their home.

"If you don't set out to do what you really want to do, you'll always regret. I had a talk with your mother yesterday. We are in complete agreement about what needs to happen."

"Yes, sergeant," he saluted." I could never win against the two of you."

"Go! Have a good walk, filled with ideas."

James didn't hesitate. "I'm going."

He picked up his journal and walked down the new driveway past the new home place, now Michael and Elise's, and across the highway and on to the east pasture. He climbed the highest hill to look at the surrounding countryside. On that hill, he strained his eyes and could see three different churches, each nearly hidden by trees.

"I will lift my eyes unto the hills from whence cometh my help. My help comes from the Lord, who has made heaven and earth." He spoke the words aloud, words that his father had said many times. He thought of the original home place and the hills that were seen from that point. Like his father, he had always wondered what lay beyond.

He sat down and began to write in his journal. "I sit now on the highest hill. I can view three churches as well as lakes and ponds. The pastures are a rich green, and the wheat fields are a rich, full green. The corn fields are still black with the green sprouts of corn coming up. This is home. I have returned to the hills, to the land of my childhood.

"I see the wonderful life I have had, though it has been a life of change. I want to capture that way of life and show what it means to live the good life. Yet, P.J. was a terrible problem and there were other people and problems. I want to show that as well."

He paused and began to pray. "Lord, show me the way. Show me what to do. I want to do something meaningful in this part of my life. A new chapter in the book of my life."

James continued to walk down the hill and up and down other hills into a neighbor's pasture. He crossed over several fences and then into a school yard. This had not been his school, for he had attended the school a mile or so from the old home place. Even so, this small country school invited him to remember.

He tried the door. It opened. An old water fountain remained. He thought of the times he had pumped water to fill a water fountain like that one. He walked through a hall into the classroom. He saw where the maps had been. He thought of himself sitting in a desk like one of the few remaining. He used to look at those maps and dream of faraway places.

The library shelves were empty. He thought of the books he had read and loved. There had been magic in those books. He had no desire to run off and join the circus, but he couldn't help admiring Toby Tyler, who had done so. He had traveled to Prince Edward Island and Green Gables, and then over to England with Black Beauty and Lassie.

The little country school had nurtured him. He had always dreamed of going far beyond those hills to distant places, and that is exactly what he had done. He had spent time in the service in England. During his teaching career, he and Ruth had traveled to Europe and the Holy Land. In a few weeks he would travel with his father to Sweden. The big world out there was inviting him to come, but at the same time he was being welcomed home.

And now that he was home, he looked beyond all this. Every part of his life seemed to have a different meaning. Many events had been so predictable. What, though, did this next chapter hold for him? How could he find new meaning here?

James walked around the empty school room and then out into the school yard. He stood before a building that was now deteriorating. The school had once been a clean well-painted building that summoned children to enter and learn. The bell once rung by hand for over half a century, was now missing. A culture had changed and a complete way of life had passed away. Was this new culture of the late twentieth century really that much better? Had the world become a better place?

He slowly retraced his steps. "This is the life. This is peace and goodness." He spoke the words aloud, knowing no other human being would hear them.

Somehow he wanted to communicate to the world all he was feeling. Life had been good. Life could be good. "I guess I am a teacher at heart."

Perspective. Life looked to him so different now. Until recently he had always looked forward to teaching another class, working on papers, conducting meetings, interacting with students, and more. But, he had said goodbye to all of that. Part of his life had ended. Realization was both sobering and exciting.

He walked up and down the same hills. He thought of the Negro spiritual. And he sang the words, "Climbin up the mountain children. I ain't got long here for to stay. And if I nevermore see you again, I'm gonna see you on the Judgment day."

"I don't have long to stay here," he mused aloud. How quickly my life has passed. "To use one of those clichés: where have all the years gone?"

His thoughts moved to the play he loved, *Our Town*. The Stage Manager made some profound observations about life. There are some things we don't talk about. "You have to read between the lines." That, he thought, is a direct quote. We usually don't talk about the most important things in life. But that's exactly what I want to write about.

He walked up another hill. This gave him new perspective. He could see for miles around. The farm house looked small from a quarter mile away. The three church steeples looked like small accent marks in the distance.

The scholar part within began to surface. He thought of the books that had changed history, books that lived on in people's lives. John Bunyan's *Pilgrim's Progress* had influenced generations of adults and children. Charles Dickens' books had revealed problem conditions that were later changed. Harriet Beecher Stowe had written a book that started a war.

Could I somehow tell the world that life can be good? That living a life in fellowship with the Lord and in relationship with people makes a good life, that there is a sure way of life that we can emulate? I'm afraid I won't reach millions, but can I make a difference in some way?

A breeze blew gently. "Perhaps I can be that gentle breeze that makes a difference on a hot and sultry day."

His mind zoomed from present to past and back again. The image of himself as a boy, probably fifteen years old, came like a photograph in his mind. A young teacher stood before him and spoke. "You have talent. You should write."

The words echoed in his mind again and again.

Mission statements had been the bywords in business and education. What would be his mission in life?

"My mission is to show that there can be a better life, a life truly worth living."

His steps quickened. He began to sense new purpose and direction.

CHAPTER 7

"Matthew, your pacing back and forth isn't doing any good." Ellen placed the last pan of chocolate chip cookies in the oven. "Why don't we drive out to Margaret's when these cookies are finished?"

"I guess I feel cooped up, living here in town. But I'm glad we're here in town. It's the right place to be."

"Something's bothering you. You're thinking about the birthday party and all the people coming."

"I never feel comfortable in big crowds. I don't like being the center of attention. That's not me."

Ellen smiled. "You'll get to see so many people you don't usually see."

"I suppose I'll enjoy it. But the trip to Sweden. I'm a little scared of that. I've never been overseas before."

"Don't worry a bit. James will be with you all the time. He's been to Europe. Everything will be fine."

"I guess I always worry about these things."

Ellen leaned over to open the oven door. She felt that pain in her back that had come more frequently. Growing old was not easy. The doctor had diagnosed her as having osteoporosis and arthritis. But that was part of being eighty-six years old.

Ellen put aside the pan for the cookies to cool. "Let's go. You'll feel better if we go for a drive and get out a little while."

As they drove out from town into the country, Matthew began to talk. "You know, dear, I've been pretty healthy for a while, but I worry about getting sick in a foreign country."

Ellen had to admit she felt some concerns about her husband. "We'll have to put it in the Lord's hands."

"I guess I've always had a dream that I would see where my father was born. It's interesting that we've made contact with these distant relatives."

"And, you'll be on a tour part of the time. You've always enjoyed the trips we've been on. You have a way of making friends."

While they talked, Ellen couldn't help thinking of how close they had become. They were dependent on each other—more dependent than in their younger years. She enjoyed time alone—time she hadn't had since their move to town. But life would be different when Matthew and James travelled to Sweden.

When they arrived at Margaret's, they had their traditional cup of coffee. Joe, of course was out in the field, baling hay. He had to make hay while the sun was shining. Matthew announced that he'd like to check the garden and fields and go for a little walk.

The minute Matthew left, it was a signal that Ellen would have a mother-daughter talk.

"Mom, how's Dad really doing?"

"I usually can figure him out, but now I can't. In one way, he's been in the best health in years. The doctor seems to think so. He doesn't have to deal with the finances and farming problems any more. The farm is now completely in Michael's hands. But we've kept most of the lakeshore property for all you children. Michael has one part where there is pasture."

"Joe and I have some lake property here."

"We thought of the future and the grandchildren as well."

"Mom, you've always thought of others—we kids. It's time you thought just of yourselves."

"We're well-provided for. The Lord has been good to us. I feel wealthier than I ever thought I could be. There's nothing that I really need."

"We Americans are wealthy. We live like kings, compared to much of the rest of the world."

Ellen sighed. "And we don't really appreciate it."

"But back to Dad, what about him?"

"I'm puzzled. He seems to put his hand over his heart. I ask him what's wrong, but he said, "Oh, nothing.""

"He says he doesn't worry, but I think he does."

"Yes, it's concern anyway. He thinks about the fuss about his birthday party. He thinks about the trip to Sweden and things that can happen."

"Mother, I think it will be good for James and Dad to be together. Dad has always been so close to Johnie. In some ways I think they were more alike—at least in their love of the farm and the land. You were always closer to James. In fact, all of us agreed that James was your favorite and Johnie was Dad's favorite."

Ellen smiled. "We tried to treat all of you alike. We wanted to be fair."

"I think of our six children. I don't think it's possible for a parent to be completely fair. Only God can do what is absolutely right. But I think there was something about you and James. You had a special relationship."

Ellen looked away. "I think it may have had to do with James being so sickly when he was young. And, of course, Johnie came along—big for his age and always bounding with energy. And then there was James, who loved books and learning from his very earliest years."

"I think there may be something about a mother's firstborn. I think of Matt. Even after more than ten years, I still miss him, and think of him every day."

"Margaret, my dear, I think you suffered the worst loss I can imagine. As a wife and mother, I realize that I may lose your father at some point. I've come close to losing him, and that would be devastating. But I always figure that children are supposed to bury their parents."

"That's the usual way. I think of all the potential with young Matt. In many ways he was like James. I don't understand why the Lord permitted him to be killed. But that Vietnam War was not a right war."

"But you were never bitter about Matt's death."

"I think I was in shock at first—and maybe that was bitterness. The Lord dealt with me. And I knew I had to go on with my life."

"I'm proud of you. I'm proud of all my children."

"But back to Dad and James. They will get to know each other in a different way. Perhaps they are more alike than we've thought. They both love family. Both have an interest in genealogy and family history."

"You're right. And do you know I'm interested in family history, but I've never had a desire to go to Sweden. My connection seems more removed."

"And," continued Margaret, "I think this trip might be just the right thing to get James started with his writing. And I'm hoping it will be a highlight of Dad's life."

"We'll need to do a lot of praying." Ellen thought back to the dark days of World War II. "I remember those days when both James and Johnie were in the War. And there were many from this community. There was that time when we thought Tim Robertson had been killed."

"And there was a case of wrong identification," said Margaret. "That wouldn't happen today."

"We women met every week. Your grandmother was a key person in that prayer group. In the end, every one of those soldiers came back alive. I've heard of other situations like that. We are commanded to pray, and the Lord answers prayer."

Margaret looked up at the clock. "Joe should soon be back from baling."

"What about your father?"

Margaret listened. "I dare to bet Joe and he are talking. Joe is like another son to Dad."

Ellen looked out the window and observed the sun shining. "This is an almost perfect June day. As the poet says, 'What is so rare as a day in June?' It's almost like heaven. And another poet said, 'God's in His Heaven. All's right with the world.'"

Margaret smiled and then frowned. "Yes, but…"

She didn't finish the thought.

Matthew walked over the hills to what they had dubbed the "east pasture." This was the area where a cow would go when she was about to give birth to her calf. It was always difficult to get cow and calf safely home.

In some ways, he thought, life was so much simpler then. The children were all safely at home. Life went on in such a predictable manner. He found himself missing his sister Mary and her husband Ed. There had been such a special relationship through those years.

Matthew began to speak aloud his thoughts. "I'm not so sure I like this business of growing old. It's tough to grow old. I never thought I'd live to be eighty-five. But, Lord, You are from everlasting to everlasting."

He knelt down, feeling the intense desire to pray. His eyes settled on some of the summer wild flowers and then looked up to the sky.

"Dear Lord, thank you for this long life. I see and understand some things that I never understood before. I'm changing. My body is changing. I'm no longer so confident about tomorrow. I'm a little bit uneasy about all this fuss about my birthday. And I'm almost a little scared about this trip to Sweden. I need your help."

The noise of the baler stopped. Joe must be finished with baling the hay on that hay field. He thought of the old-fashioned way of haying in his earlier farming days. He knew exactly how to build a load of hay. That took talent. Now, machines did the work, and everything seemed less personal.

He got up and walked over to the field where Joe had been working. Joe stood by the baler, looking around at what he had done. Later, Joe and his son-in-law and the hired man would load the bales.

"Joe," Matthew said to his son-in-law. "It looks as if you've finished one job."

"Dad, I didn't see you. I knew you were walking in the fields. Is there anything that brings you out here?"

"Just thinking."

"Me, too."

The two men stood in silence. Close friends can enjoy each other in silence. Silent moments are never awkward.

Joe broke the silence. "Ordinarily the farm goes to the oldest son. Well, Matt might have taken over, but Vietnam took his life. David's a professor. That leaves him out. Joel's got a full-time job as county agent. He might be interested someday. That leaves my youngest, Marlene. She loves this farm. And Mark likes working with me and his father as well."

"What are you saying?"

"It's this way. I think Mark wants to get out of the hardware business in town. They live in town and would really like to live in the country as they bring up their kids. I'm thinking it might be time for me to step down. In another year I'll be sixty-five."

Matthew looked at his son-in-law who seemed more like a son. In his mind, he rolled back the years to that terrible winter when Joe helped save the family farm—when Matthew almost lost his life . . .

"You're going through pretty much what I went through twenty years ago. I'm so glad Michael took over my farm—or I should say Ellen's and my farm. But you, the son-in-law took over what was really the home farm, this farm. So, this farm is still in the family."

"Yes, if Mark Lundeen takes over, he'll do a good job."

"What about you?"

"That's what I've been thinking about. I'm too young to just sit around. And I think Mark should absolutely take over if he buys the farm."

"Ellen and I moved to the little house. But I did a lot of work."

"Yes, but you stepped back and let Michael decide things."

"Part of that was doctor's orders. I had to step back. And since then, my health is much better."

"I'm not sure I could do that. Maybe I could go work some place. I'm still strong and healthy."

Matthew couldn't help noticing Joe didn't look so young any more. His hair was completely gray and he had a limp. "I think you may need to slow down before the doctor orders you to. Gardens and lawns take a lot of time."

Joe said nothing for a moment. "I don't know that I ever thought much about growing old. And I guess that at sixty-five you're old."

"Think of eighty-five. I'm thankful to be alive and see all my children and grandchildren and even my great grandchildren. Many people don't get to enjoy that much of life."

"We need you, Matthew Anderson. I need you as Dad."

Matthew looked down. "Thank you." He stopped, wondering if he should go on and say what he was really thinking. "I can't help wondering what my purpose in life really is. Both children and grandchildren are on their own. No one except Ellen really needs me. What am I here for?"

Joe stepped back. "Dad, don't say that. Don't even think it. We need you."

"But I do. I can't help it."

"Dad, now I'm going to say something I've heard you saying. You've said it to people. You've said it about people. So long as you're here on earth, God has a purpose for you. Accept that."

"Thanks, son. I guess I needed to hear that."

At that moment, Matthew saw a car park at the edge of the field. A tall well-dressed gentleman got out of the car and walked toward them. In a moment he recognized Jeffrey Grant, his oldest grandson. As he came closer, it seemed that P.J. or Paul John Anderson was walking toward him.

"Well, Dad, it looks as if Jeffrey Grant is coming to see me. Even though he's a member of the family, I don't trust him one bit."

Matthew nodded agreement.

"Hello Grandfather. Hello Uncle Joe," Jeffrey called out.

Matthew and Joe greeted him.

"What brings you out in the hayfield on a beautiful June day?"

Jeffrey extended his hand to Joe and then embraced his grandfather.

Chapter 7

Matthew backed away. There was something insincere, almost manipulative about the embrace. He hated feeling this way toward the grandson he loved.

"I thought it was time I stopped to see my favorite uncle. And I get a chance to see Grandfather as well."

"Oh come on. You have something else on your mind."

Jeffrey looked embarrassed. "Well," he muttered. "As a matter of fact I do. You've got this land close to the lake. I think I have a very good deal for you."

"What do you mean? A good deal? That land isn't really good for anything. Some of it is swamp land?"

"Lake shore land is in demand. It can bring big bucks. And I'll see that we get the very best price for you." He whispered a price that seemed unbelievably high. "I can guarantee that much."

"I always talk everything over with Margaret. But I am not interested in selling. As it is, it's unfortunate that P.J. sold his parcel of land. The Chicago people and those connections have been a problem off and on for years."

"That's the price of progress. And it brings money into the community where we need jobs."

"No thanks, Jeff. I'm not interested."

"Talk it over with Aunt Margaret."

"I will. We'll get back to you."

"Think about it." Jeff stepped closer and showed a slip of paper with a price. "You can get rich from selling."

Joe's eyes widened. He shook his head. "No. I have a good life."

"You'll be turning down a terrific deal. Think about it."

"The answer will probably be 'no.'"

Jeff stepped and extended his hand first to Joe and then to Matthew. "Good to see you both. I'll talk with you later."

He seemed in a hurry to get away.

Matthew looked at his grandson who couldn't seem to get away fast enough. "I didn't know anything like this was going on."

"Jeffrey Grant has been a busy man. I'm hearing things about him—things I don't like to hear about someone in the family."

"I'm afraid people know I'm his grandfather, so they don't say anything."

"His deeds will catch up with him."

"I hope he'll learn the error of his ways. And make changes."

"Come, ride with me," said Joe. "I'm afraid I wouldn't count on a change."

⊷⦚⦚⦚⦚⦚⦚⊶

When Matthew and Joe entered the kitchen, Margaret greeted them.

"I see you had company. What did Jeff want?"

Joe grunted. "He said he had a good deal for some of my land near the lake."

"What did you tell him?"

"I said, 'no.' But he did offer a fantastic price for some of the land that isn't much use."

"I was just telling Mother about what I had heard. He went to Mrs. Jenkins, who has one of those grand homes in town. He convinced her that there were many things wrong with the house. He offered her a low price and then sold it weeks later for several times the price he paid her."

Joe didn't hesitate. "We're not selling any land. We've had enough headaches with the land that P.J. and Rita sold. No amount of money is worth it."

Ellen looked at Matthew and then at Margaret and Joe. "There's not much we can do about our grandson or nephew."

"We can pray."

CHAPTER 8

"James, I'm worried about your father," said Ellen as they sat in the kitchen, having a cup of morning coffee.

"I hadn't noticed."

"He's never been a big eater, but he hasn't been eating—not even his favorite meals. And he's been tossing and turning at night. I think he's had some of those old nightmares."

"Is there anything I can do?"

"Talk to him. Try to get him to talk about what's bothering him. Some things he talks to Johnie about, but Johnie isn't around."

"Maybe he's concerned about the big birthday party and about the trip. He loves people, but he doesn't like big crowds."

"Where is Dad, by the way?" James went over to the counter and poured himself another cup. "I thought he was probably out in the garden, checking things or doing some work."

"He went up town. Probably coffee with the guys. He still misses Glenn Robertson even though he's been gone for several years."

"You know Dad and Johnie have always been close. But lately Johnie's been so busy. I thought he was going to be around this summer, but now he's not so sure."

"I'm concerned about Johnie, too. He's taking on a lot. And he isn't so young any more. It's hard to realize my children are retirement age. That comes as a bit of a shock."

"We live longer lives these days. When Grandma and Grandpa were sixty or seventy, I thought they were really old."

Ellen thought back to her own life. "I didn't have much of a role model in my parents. Mother died when I was not more than eight years old. And Dad was much older when he married, and he didn't live to be very old. You never knew these grandparents. I wish you had."

"I feel I missed something by not knowing them. But you've gotten to know all your grandchildren and even your great-grandchildren. That is a blessing."

Ellen thought of the words of Scripture. "Growing old is clearly a blessing, but it is also a time of new challenges. There are some aches and pains. And there is the loss of friends and family members."

"That happens even to those who are merely sixty-one. I lost one of my best friends, Mark Goodman, only a month ago. I thought we'd be friends for years to come even into our retirement years. But that was not meant to be."

"I miss your Aunt Mary and several of my good friends from church." Ellen stopped a moment and wanted to share thoughts with her son. "I find myself thinking much more about years long since passed. I wouldn't want to go back, but those people and places and happenings keep coming back to me. Maybe that's a part of growing old."

James smiled. "I'd like to hear more of the memories.

"Yes, and I'll share them. However, didn't you say you had groceries to get for Ruth and your family? And didn't you have some other projects to take care of before your kids come."

"Mom, yes, but for now it's more important for us to talk about you and Dad. I need to take time to listen and later to write."

"I used to tell Margaret that the kids wouldn't notice if there wasn't any dust in the house. But they would notice whether or not she had time for them. I felt the same way with you."

"Yes, Mom, you always had time for me. I often talked about what I was going to write."

"And now that you're retired, you must do that writing."

"'The spirit is willing, but the flesh is weak.' I'm afraid it's so easy to put off getting to work. The articles I've written seemed to come easy once I got going. But it's harder to keep going with a full-length novel."

"I'm here for you. I can encourage."

"Yes, Mother, you're a great encourager. You always seem to understand. In many ways we're alike. I seem to take after you and your family. Johnie takes after Dad and the Andersons."

"That's true. But, my dear, you may discover you have more in common with your father than you think. From those earliest years, you were more inclined to come to me while Johnie ran to your father. In all those early pictures I was always holding you and your father held Johnie."

"I hadn't thought of that." James paused and looked out the window, perhaps thinking his father would be coming. "I'm looking forward to that part of the trip."

"You know, your father is a very remarkable man."

"Yes, I agree, but what do you mean?"

Ellen's mind scanned the years and the changes. "I think Matthew Anderson always felt he didn't quite measure up. He didn't finish eighth grade. He must have frozen with that geography exam. And your grandfather found it way too easy to keep him home to do work."

"That wasn't fair. But Dad never wanted to do that to us kids. He didn't want to take advantage of us."

"Your father was—or is—scrupulously honest. There was something about him that attracted me to him from the moment I came to stay at the Anderson place. He was a man who didn't have much formal education, but he was a man I could completely trust."

James added, "That moral integrity is something lacking in many people today."

"You know many people didn't give your father credit for his intelligence. He grew up with horses and the old fashioned farming. Tractors and new machines were not really a part of him. However, he took very good care of his machines—better than the people who were mechanical experts."

James chuckled. "He gave us strict instructions always to change oil on time and grease where we were supposed to grease."

"But your father changed in other ways."

"I remember that time when he almost died. That was the worst time in my childhood. I couldn't imagine how life would be without Dad."

"I didn't think I could face the world with four children."

"Dad has shared much about that experience—how it was as if the Lord appeared and spoke to him."

"He was a different man afterwards. He studied the Bible more than ever before. Before that, I was always the leader in the marriage and family. He became the strong one. The leader."

James interrupted. "I've come to realize that Dad has more common sense than most college professors."

Ellen smiled. "How right you are! He loves each of you children more than you'll ever realize."

"I've known that for a long time. But I still think Johnie is his favorite. They both seem to have a love and respect for the land."

"Yes," responded Ellen, "and it concerns me that Johnie will, for the first time, be in a city church. He just seems to belong in the country."

"It's always a surprise where God calls us. I think He's calling me back home to the country."

An abrupt knock interrupted.

Suddenly, Ellen thought she saw P.J. Anderson appear. Only it was Jeffrey Grant.

Jeffrey greeted them. "Grandma, I thought I'd stop by. And, James, you're just the person I wanted to see. How are you today?"

Ellen said a weak "Hello." She couldn't help wondering about her grandson's purpose.

Jeff stooped down and kissed his grandmother on the cheek. Ellen wanted to respond warmly, but something held her back.

James stood up. "It's good to see you."

"Uncle James, it's been too long since I've seen you. I'm glad you're going to be around here more now that you've retired."

The conversation continued along lines of small talk that seemed to fill in blank spaces. Then, Ellen remembered her manners and offered her grandson coffee.

In his usual smooth manner Jeff accepted. "Yes, Grandma, and I can't refuse one of your chocolate chip cookies."

James changed the direction of the conversation. "Jeff, I have the feeling you have something else on your mind."

"Well, I do have something I'd like to share with you."

"You have piqued my curiosity," said Ellen.

"Actually, I have something that involves both of you. Our family has some land that's going to be more valuable as time goes on."

Ellen quickly interrupted. "If it's business, I want Matthew here. We talk over everything together. And we don't conduct business without the other one present."

"I admire that in you, Grandma. That's why you've had such a wonderful marriage. There's much that you could teach us young people."

"Fire away," said James. "But Ruth and I talk over everything as well. But I doubt that we'll be doing any business right now."

"Give me a chance. Money talks, and there's a lot of money to be had from some of the property around the lakes."

Chapter 8

Ellen gave one of those looks she used to give to the children when she disapproved of something they were doing or saying. "Money doesn't rule our lives."

"Grandma, I beg to differ. I'm in banking and real estate, and you'd be surprised how people respond to money."

"That's what's wrong with this world today."

"You have to hear what I have to say. You might want to talk over with your other half. It's a great opportunity."

"Fire away!" James set down his coffee cup firmly.

Jeff finished his grandmother's cookie. "Grandma, your cookies get better as time goes on."

"You know how to flatter me."

Jeff began his sales pitch. "Uncle James, I believe you had some land in your name on Nelson Lake, and you have built near that area where we used to have picnics."

"Right."

"Some of that land nearby is going to waste. It's not being used."

"Michael has cattle on it part of the time."

"Those would make beautiful lots for people to build homes on. People are wanting to buy lake property and move here—just the way you've moved here. We have to give other people that chance."

James smiled, apparently amused. "I don't think that unselfish reason is the reason you're wanting to make deals."

"Well, yes and no. We all can live better if we have more money. And having more money means we can give other people jobs."

Ellen could see James was holding back laughter at Jeff's obvious sales pitch. "We like the quiet here. We know what happened with P.J.'s property. We've had noise and problems from time to time. That came with those Chicago people moving here."

"Grandma. Don't be so old fashioned. Many good people move in."

"Now, Jeffrey," objected James. "We like a certain amount of privacy. That's why we are moving to the country. If we want a crowd of people, we can stay in the city."

"Let me finish what I started to say. First, Uncle James, on your property there's land that could allow for several homes to be built. And Grandma, on the other side, you and Grandpa have land that could be turned into a number of homes or even a condo that could be in a time-share program. And some of Michael's land could be developed as well."

James didn't hesitate. "I don't think I'd like any of this."

"Wait until you see the amount of money this could bring in. I have all the right contacts. I'd make some money, but you would be the ones to get rich."

Jeff showed them a paper with figures.

"Wow!" exclaimed James.

"That's a lot of money," said Ellen.

"Now, don't you want to do some thinking?"

"I'll talk to your grandfather, but I don't think that will change anything."

"And I'll talk with Ruth, but I'm sure our answer will be the same."

Jeff came back with another argument. "Uncle James, there are expenses with moving from Riverton to Lake View and fixing up your place. The money would come in handy."

"I guess so."

"And, Grandma, Michael's having a tough time with payments. He could use some help."

"I will talk with your grandfather."

Jeff continued with his sales pitch. Ellen and James tried to be polite. Finally, a telephone call interrupted. Ellen answered and gave Jeff the phone.

"Sorry, a call from the bank. I have to leave. But you think it over. And talk with Grandpa and Ruth. I'm sure you'll see all the good from having a little extra money."

When the door closed, Ellen wiped her brow. "I think that boy is headed for trouble."

"Right, and I need to finish my errands."

"James, let's get back to your father. I'm concerned about him. He doesn't need a sales pitch from Jeff or anybody else."

"I'll be back this afternoon. Dad and I will go for a long walk on the old home place."

"That's a beginning."

———⊸≺ℿℿℿ∩ℿℿℿ≻⊶———

James had always felt closer to his mother. He wondered why. Boys should always identify with their father. His mother's love of music and of learning was what endeared her to him. There seemed to be that bond from the earliest time in his life.

He returned to his parents' home early that afternoon.

"Dad," he announced, "it's time we did some talking. About the trip and about some other things."

"I guess I can miss my nap for one day."

Ellen quickly added, "You men go off by yourselves. I'll be ready to help with packing and folding of shirts when the time comes."

James drove over to Margaret and Joe's farm. This place brought back to him his earliest childhood memories. James and his father got out of the car and began to walk through the barnyard and over to the pasture toward the lake.

The men walked in silence. James thought of the times in childhood when he had walked and played and dreamed in these spots.

Matthew broke the silence. "Just last week, Margaret and I walked in these same spots. And years ago, not long before your Aunt Martha died, she and I walked this same path. It was her last time to come out here."

"What are you thinking, Dad?"

"I can't help thinking that one of these times will be my last time. This may be my time to say goodbye to what I have loved."

James wasn't sure how to respond.

Matthew continued. "It's tough getting old. You know I never thought I'd get this old."

"More people are living to be a hundred."

"I'm not sure I want to go there. I'm in pretty good health now, but that might not last."

They walked on in silence and reached one of the hills overlooking the lake.

"Let's sit down," suggested James.

"This is June. I've always thought this is a little bit of heaven. Everything's about as perfect as it gets. Yes, as the poem says: what is so rare as a day in June?"

"You've quoted that poem oftentimes, haven't you? You memorized poetry in those days, and you loved it."

"Yes, son. I often regret I didn't get more education."

"Dad, maybe I'm more like you than I thought. Mother had the formal education. But you have this love of poetry and the land. I think I inherited from both of you."

"Thank you. I'm proud of you."

"Let's talk about what's bothering you, Dad. Are you anxious about the trip? Or is there something else?"

Matthew hesitated. "It's costing you kids a lot of money, for one thing. Others in the family need the money."

"Dad, you're worth it. You've dreamed of seeing the homeland of Grandpa and Grandma and the rest of the family. We want to give you that chance."

"You're so well educated. You can talk with people. I'm just a country farmer. Without even an eighth grade education."

"Dad, you'll be able to get away from all these problems. We'll finally have a chance to talk over everything. Otherwise, we're always in a hurry."

"Yes, I'm looking forward to the trip. I've had questions about what it would be like in Sweden. Many questions will be answered."

"I think there's something else."

"I'm not good with words the way you are. I'm not sure what I really think or what I really mean."

"Just tell me what you're thinking about. Maybe we can figure it out together. You see, Dad, I think we're facing different changes in life. I retired, and I'm not so sure what's going to happen in my life. I have to re-think my purpose. And you're getting used to living in town but love the country. And when you're eighty-five years old, you need to slow down. There are some things you shouldn't be doing at your age."

"I guess you're right."

Once more, the two men sat in silence.

James looked up into the intense blue of the sky. "As I look to the heavens, I can't help thinking about Heaven. I've been so caught up in this life that I haven't thought much about the distant future."

"It's not so distant for me. I can't help thinking about an old Swedish hymn. I haven't heard it for some time. 'We wait for a great and glorious day, all we who love the Lord.' I can't remember some of those other lines. There's something about 'shadows fleeing,' and later about not knowing the day or the hour."

"I've heard it, but I don't remember the words the way you do."

"Then the chorus says something about the wonderful day and a beautiful hope. I've been thinking about that, but I seem to have what they call a split personality. I love what is here. I also love that future hope."

"Dad, to be honest, I haven't thought much about Heaven. There's so much here on earth that I want to do. I look forward to the trip to Sweden. I want to see what I can do as a writer. And I know there is this rift between me and my son, Richard. I wish I could mend that rift."

"Each morning, I look at the family pictures. I pray for each one of you. I know these prayers will be answered. Maybe not in my lifetime."

Silence again prevailed. James' mind travelled many places. "I think it's time to get back."

"Your mother won't worry since I'm with you."

James got up and extended his hand to help his father. Matthew accepted his son's help.

"I guess I am old. Maybe I can't handle this trip."

"Dad, I just thought of something. My friend, Dr. Clark practices at the Atwood Hospital, but he comes one day a week to the River Falls Clinic. I know he'd do me a favor and see you and check your health so you're sure of this trip."

Matthew hesitated. "I don't know about that."

"Dad, you know I'm right."

"I'm always a bit uneasy when I go to the doctor. I keep thinking he'll find something wrong."

"Dad, you're in remarkable shape."

They began to walk back toward the old home place.

James looked at the house and barn and farm yard and thought aloud. "Dad, we're living in a whole different world today. It's a strange new world."

CHAPTER 9

"I can't believe that many people will show up tomorrow," said Matthew. "We never get the whole family together any more. The grandkids are scattered all over, and they have their own children."

"Wait and see," said Ellen.

Victoria set down her coffee cup with force. "Little brother, you will be amazed at how many people turn out. If I were into betting, I'd bet a high number."

"You won't be disappointed, Matthew."

It was Friday evening, the evening before the big family gathering. Matthew felt those butterflies in his stomach, the feeling he always had before a test or a big event.

Matthew looked across the kitchen table at his sister. Her dark hair now was white except for a few dark strands. Her strength and determination remained in her face and demeanor, but there was something of a quiet and kind gentleness. To her students she had always been stern and determined and fair in the classroom and school. At ninety-five, she had not been in the classroom for years.

"I don't think I'm important enough to have all those people come. Not like a banker or a minister or someone like that."

Victoria was never a woman for few words. "I can guarantee you're terribly important to a lot of people—me included. But since you mentioned bankers, I have to say something about my banker/nephew and your banker/grandson. He does insurance, and the rumor is that he collected some premiums and did not make payment to the company. That could land him in jail—if it's true."

Ellen added, "It sounds like P.J. all over again."

Matthew thought of the recent meetings. "When I saw Jeffrey the other day, I thought I was seeing P.J. all over again. It seemed almost as if he were taking the farm from me again."

"He's always wheeling and dealing," said Victoria. "But some day that will catch up with him. It's even worse when you think it's happening to someone in the Anderson family."

Ellen reached for the coffee pot and filled their cups. "Maybe we should change the subject. Victoria, you remembered something about what Martha used to say about the time when Matthew was born, back in 1900."

"Martha remembered so well when you were born, Matthew. She used to tell about the New Year's Eve before the turn of the century. I guess I stayed home, but Martha and P.J. and some other children went down to the country school and rang the bell 1900 times. That must have taken quite a while."

Matthew added, "She used to tell me about the times back then."

"Yes, there was such a mood of optimism. Great advancements in science had been made. A great missionary movement was taking place. Education was advancing and improving. Some believed that the Christian message would take hold. Then, the world would get better and better. At that point the world would be ready, and Christ would return."

"Were you present when Matthew was born?" asked Ellen.

"I was, but I suppose I was preoccupied in my own world. The birth took place at home—in the house that stood before a new house was built. It was a drafty old house. I think I had been sent over to Prairie Center for a day or two. Mom probably wanted to get me out of the house."

Matthew couldn't help smiling.

"How the world has changed," observed Ellen. "There were no cars in this area. Hospitals were few and far between. Babies were born at home with a neighbor woman present or a midwife. In a way, we've moved ahead."

Matthew thought aloud. "We still have as much trouble with sin and wrong-doing as ever before. With wars and rumors of war, we may be closer than ever to Christ's return."

"But," said Ellen, "We can be thankful for long and good healthy lives. A long life is a blessing from the Lord. Matthew, you're eighty-five,

Chapter 9

and I'm well over eighty-six. We have seen our family grow up. We have enjoyed the grandchildren, and now we are even enjoying the great-grandchildren."

"And I've had a full life. I, Victoria Anderson, am ninety-five years old. More than forty years of teaching and work as principal. Then, years of travel and doing volunteer work. And, now, enjoying my nieces and nephews and grand-nieces and nephews even into the next generation. God has been good to me."

"Great is God's faithfulness," added Matthew.

A quick knock on the door, and in walked Johnie.

"Dad, I'm home for your birthday. Happy Birthday!" He opened his arms. Matthew stood and felt himself embraced by his son. "Oh, Dad, I love you. I'm happy that I am here."

The reunion of Pastor John Anderson with his father and mother and aunt was indeed a moment of joy and celebration. He embraced the women immediately after, and there were tears of joy.

Matthew found the next moments were too full for words.

"Where's Carolyn?" asked Ellen. "And are there more?"

"Carolyn's at James's place. And there will be more tomorrow. You just wait and see. You'll be happy and surprised. I wanted to stop by and see how things are going."

Victoria made motions to leave. "We're gearing up for tomorrow. I need to walk back to my apartment."

"By the way, Aunt Victoria," asked Johnie, "how do you like living in an apartment?"

"My dear, I miss my house, but it feels good that I don't have to mow lawn and take care of maintaining a house."

"I can understand. Mom, how about a cup of coffee and one of those favorite cookies."

And so Matthew sat down to enjoy this part of his family. Tomorrow would be his big day. God was being very good.

He thought of the Creation story and how the Lord said, "It is very good."

James awakened early that morning, the day of the big party. Ruth was sleeping soundly. He tiptoed into the bathroom and began to clean up for the day.

"I'm retired," he said aloud. "It's not summer vacation I'm starting. It's a whole new life. My time is my own. Can I make something of this time? Or will I squander that time?"

Then his mind turned to the day that lay before him. His father was "old and full of years" as the Bible said. All five children would be present. He hoped most of the grandchildren would be there, and many of the great-grandchildren. But sadly, his son Richard would be absent. Somehow, more than anything else, he hoped and prayed that rift would be healed.

Grandma's last big birthday party came to mind. He had taken on the task of hearing what she said to each of the families. That was probably the last time so many of the aunts, uncles and cousins gathered at the same time. Some people he never saw again. Life seemed to move on in a faster and faster pace.

He measured out the coffee grounds and started the morning coffee. Sounds from the upstairs guest bedroom told him Johnie was awake. Farm boys of any age seemed to have that habit of rising early in the morning. James sat down, waiting for the coffee to brew. His mind began to calculate the things he should do.

"Good morning, bro." Johnie didn't hesitate but found a cup and poured himself coffee. "The coffee smells good."

"I guess we're up ahead of the rest. It's going to be a big day. I hope Dad will be able to take all the excitement."

"It's our job to help. But right now, I think it's time for some brother talk. James-boy, how are you doing? I never thought you'd throw in the towel."

"Well, bro, so many things happened. Many times the new University presidents want to get rid of the older professors. And I wanted to step back and do more writing."

"Now you can."

"But my good friend, Mark Goodman, died. His death made me do some serious thinking. I realized that there had to be much more to life than my job or profession."

"That's what I preach. That's my calling."

"I'll throw that one back at you. There's more to life than being a minister or a pastor. Have you thought about that?"

Johnie's face showed that determination and that fighting attitude that James had known all his life. Perhaps there was something gentler in that face at this stage in life.

Chapter 9

"James, your calling was to be a teacher/professor. But now you have another calling: to write and influence people in that way. I was called to be a pastor in mostly rural churches. Now, I have a new opportunity to reach out in mission work. God's Plan doesn't include retirement—not for you and me at this age in our lives."

"Wow! That was a real sermon. Right to the point."

"I feel strongly about it. I think the Lord is clearly directing me. I'm excited about being in a larger church and going to Africa."

James thought of his experiences as a teacher and professor. Somehow, he had felt that this business of teaching had no end—that it would go on forever.

"I've thought back to those early years of teaching. I had the feeling there would be no other life—that it would go on and on indefinitely. And for me, suddenly it has come to an end. I hadn't realized how abrupt that was."

Johnie got up and poured another cup of coffee. "That's the way life is. That's the way life ends. And that end will come to all of us—unless the Lord returns."

"I remember something from Grandma and Grandpa's Golden Wedding. And Dad talked about this, too. The minister, Pastor Strand, quoted the verses that 'Jesus Christ is the same, yesterday, today, and forever.' The verses puzzled me at the time. Now I understand a little better. But there's more that I don't quite understand."

"We see only through a glass darkly."

They sat in silence for a moment. Then, James spoke. "We're fortunate to have grown up this kind of family. Mom and Dad—and before them, Grandpa and Grandma—have been powerful forces in the family and the community."

"I'm hungry," said Johnie, "But, brother, you just gave me the ideas for my talk today and my sermon at Oak Ridge Church tomorrow. Thank you."

James stood up and went over to the refrigerator. "And I hear sounds from our wives. It's time to make breakfast. And I'll do my famous French toast."

Johnie walked over to his brother. "We've been fortunate to have each other. Not only have we been brothers, we've been friends."

"We're Andersons. Each very different. You were the lover of the outdoors. I was the lover of books, the bibliophile."

Johnie exclaimed, "We both love the Lord!"

"Matthew, stop that pacing. You'll wear out the rug."

Ellen usually kept quiet about her husband's nervous pacing. Whenever he anticipated a big event, he had that habit. He may have placed his trust in the Lord, but this human element kept coming through.

"All this fuss bothers me," said Matthew.

"Your birthday celebration will bring the family together."

"It's a little much when they all come at once."

Ellen chuckled. "I guess we shouldn't have had five children then."

"Each one is a blessing."

"And," added Matthew, "each grandchild is a blessing. But it's too much to see them all at once. I have a hard time with large numbers of people—even family."

The back door opened and Victoria entered. "I decided to walk down. Even though I'm ninety-five, I can still walk. And, once more, 'Happy Birthday!'"

"Thank you. I wonder if very many people will come. Everyone's so secretive about it. They say lots of people will come, but I can't believe people can get away like that."

"We'll see about that," said Victoria.

"How about a cup of coffee?" invited Ellen. "It's still a few minutes before James will pick us up. He insisted. I think it's possible he doesn't trust Matthew's driving when he gets excited about his big birthday party."

"Well, he complains that I still drive too fast."

Matthew laughed. "There's no question about that. You may be law-abiding in every way—that is except in driving the speed limit."

"I guess I've had a busy life, and I'm usually in a hurry."

Ellen thought to herself and then said, "And now it's time that we all slowed down. We're way up there in years."

The three sat at the kitchen table, reflecting on the gathering that would soon take place. Ellen knew that Matthew would be surprised at what was about to take place. But she couldn't help wondering if his heart was strong enough to take all this excitement.

They began to remember family happenings of the past.

"Do you remember that Christmas when we got our electricity?" asked Victoria. "I think that was one of the most memorable Christmases."

"So many things were new and exciting then," said Matthew.

Chapter 9

The back door opened. "And what was so new and exciting?" asked James as he entered the kitchen. "Everything's ready for the big celebration."

Lord, Ellen said to herself, bless this celebration. Thank You for a wonderful husband and children and family. My heart is filled with gratitude. You have blessed me with a wonderful life.

———

Matthew's thoughts moved away from the conversation of James and Ellen and Victoria. They talked of many things as they drove the few miles to the original home place, the home of Margaret and Joe. His mind was filled with both memories of the past and anticipation and nervousness about what lay ahead.

As James drove up the driveway, Matthew saw that cars were parked by the side and in the ditch. Who could all these people be? Today it was supposed to be family and a few close friends. Tomorrow, church and community would honor him after the church service.

A large tent had been put up so that people could have protection rain or shine. The sun brightened everything this day. The kids must have planned everything so that all the guests arrived first and then he would arrive. Somehow, he wasn't used to all this attention. He preferred being in the background.

"Dad, there are a few people here," said James. "You thought hardly anyone would come. Well, they proved you wrong."

James stopped the car. Johnie came and opened the door for him and then the back door for Ellen. "Happy Birthday! Dad. This is your day."

Matthew was at a loss for words.

James honked the horn and drove on to an empty space. Johnie called out, "Let's all sing together."

The crowd gathered close to Matthew. He could never have imagined there would be this many people. He heard his name called: Matthew or Grandpa and or Dad or neighbor. Then, the group burst into song, "Happy Birthday to you. Happy birthday to you. Happy birthday, dear Matthew. Happy birthday to you!" Then they sang the second verse with "God bless you, dear Matthew."

Matthew liked the idea of the second verse with "God bless you." It served as a reminder of God's presence.

Johnie called out, "We have plenty of chicken and ham and all kinds of other good food. Let's sing the *Table Prayer*."

The singing was better than most of the choirs he had heard.

Johnie once again took charge. "Our guests of honor go first. We'll have some words later on, but important things first: food. The program will be short; we want to hear what's happening with everyone."

One of the nephews shouted, "Don't make it too long!"

"Don't worry," Johnie answered. "Mother and Aunt Victoria, you are special guests as well. You've been in charge for years. Now, it's time for us kids to take over. Line up for food. Let's just enjoy one another."

Once more Matthew thought back to other family gatherings. Pa, he thought to himself, I miss you even after all these years. I think a man always needs a father—or an older mentor. That's why I need my Heavenly Father. Everyone needs a Heavenly Father.

Matthew found eating to be rather difficult. He kept seeing family and some of those close friends.

First he saw people he had expected to see. Then came the surprise visitors.

"Uncle Matthew," said a rugged man with slightly gray hair. "I bet you don't even know who I am."

Matthew looked. "Why, Jake, it's you. I haven't seen you since your mother's funeral."

He stood, and the two shook hands as only uncle and nephew could do.

"It's been too long anyway."

Jake greeted Ellen and Victoria with hugs. Women always responded to a younger handsome man. Jake wore his fifty-plus years well.

"Here's a chair. Why don't you join us? Did you come alone?"

Jake sat down. "My wife and the kids are so busy with everything, but I decided I had to come. I was hoping my sisters would be here, but I haven't seen them."

"I'm surprised how many people are here," said Matthew.

"Uncle Matthew, there's something I wanted to say to you, and it's not easy. You've been a bigger influence on me than you realize."

Matthew listened intently. Ellen and Victoria continued to eat.

"My dad was a good man, but he was tough and hard to please. For years, I rebelled, but we made up before he died. I've changed from the rebel. I have a farm in Iowa. I go to church, and I look to the Lord for my strength."

"I'm glad you've found your way," said Matthew.

"Your grandfather would be proud of you," added Victoria.

Chapter 9

"Uncle Matthew, you were kind and gentle. Your example pointed me in the right direction. You, more than anyone else, showed me the way."

At that point, several other people stopped to visit. The conversation ended. Matthew secretly thanked the Lord for the way Jake had shared the change.

There are too many people all at once, thought Matthew. I don't have time to see everyone. I wish I could talk individually with each one.

People filled themselves with ham and chicken and potato salad and other good dishes. The tables in the tent were filled, and some of the children sat on the ground and then ran about and played. The place was filled with Andersons and a few other people.

Johnie called out and a few people hit silverware against cups. The crowed quieted.

"It's important that we come together as a family. I realize the young children are ready to go out and play and the adults are visiting, but I believe we need this time together. I've been talking with Brother James, and he's more of a philosopher than I am. He had some thoughts, and I'm using them in the few words that I have to say.

"We often don't take time to appreciate one another. We don't take time to say how much we care for and love those people closest to us. Today, we want to wish happy birthday to my father, Matthew Anderson, and to say how much we love you and how much we appreciate you. Though it's Dad's birthday, we also want to thank Mother, Ellen Anderson, and our Aunt Victoria. We love you more than we can say."

The gathering was amazingly silent.

"Each time we get together we have so much 'catching up' to do. We're going to hear from each family—the five of us, sons and daughters of Matthew and Ellen, and then any of the nieces and nephews or cousins or other special friends."

Matthew gazed at the crowd and realized how many people had come out of a simple and small beginning. These have come from me and my beloved Ellen. The Lord has blest me beyond all measure. Thank You, dear Lord.

"Let's be brief," said Johnie, "but let's take time for each family. We'll do this in order with my big brother first."

Matthew looked at his boys. He couldn't help feeling a sense of pride. These were strong and remarkable men.

James began, "I don't feel like the big brother because Johnie became taller and huskier than I. Anyhow, I'm the oldest. Just retired from many years of being a professor and head of the English department at Riverton State University. I—or we—will be spending a lot of time at our lake home nearby. My wife Ruth of 35 years is an elementary teacher. I'm sorry that Richard, my oldest, isn't here. I'm even sorrier that we haven't heard from him. He's probably still in Colorado.

"My daughter, Coleen, also a teacher, her husband Bill, a professor and the two children."

Coleen called out. "I thought we were finished having children, but we're having a surprise addition later this year."

"Congratulations!" several people called out.

James continued. "And my daughter Melissa, a nurse. Her husband, a doctor, couldn't be here. They're from southern Minnesota, and the three children are here."

Johnie stood up once more. "I guess it's my turn. I'm No. 2 son. My wife Carolyn is busy as church secretary. Janelle is a stay-at-home mom with three children. Her husband is a minister and just couldn't get away because he's conducting a wedding. Jack, also named John, and his wife Claudia are both social workers and they have two children. And Leah, a nurse, and her husband were just married. He's in business and didn't get back from his business trip.

"That's my family. You can see how we're growing and spreading out in many directions. And now Sister Margaret, who is close by and keeps track of Mom and Dad."

Matthew couldn't help thinking how much Margaret resembled Ellen. He whispered to his wife, "She looks the way you did a few years ago."

"She looks much better than I do or did," replied Ellen.

Margaret stood up. "I owe so much to Mom and Dad, but I realize this is just the time for introducing family. Joe is still my love after all these years. We've had six children. I still feel that pang of sadness when I think of Matt's death in the Vietnam War. He had so much to give.

"David is a professor in a Christian college in North Carolina. He's here with his wife, a teacher, and the three children, two girls and a boy. Our number three child is Deborah, another teacher in eastern Minnesota, and her husband is a nursing home administrator. They have three boys.

"And now the twins. Joel is a county agent and helps Joe on the farm. His wife is another teacher, and they have two boys and a girl. His twin Judith is a stay-at home mom. Her husband is a principal at River Falls High School. They have two boys and two girls.

"And now our baby, Marlene. She is a teacher, and they are expecting their first child. Her husband Mark Lundeen farms and also does some work in a hardware store. That completes my family. It's one of those rare times when we are all together at the same time."

Jonnie returned as emcee. "That is quite an accomplishment to get everyone together. Now we go on to our baby sister, Carol. We're glad she could come from Illinois."

Matthew couldn't help noticing how Carol now looked like herself and not some movie star. She had gotten away from the high fashion of her younger days. No doubt she colored her hair, but it was that brown hair with a hint of red that was her natural color.

"I'm delighted to be here and sorry I can't be here more often. My husband Hank Stevens has so many business matters to take care of, but he is learning to delegate responsibilities. He and some of the grandkids are coming tonight. We also work in our church as lay leaders and we go on regular mission trips. My son Jeffrey, who works at the bank, is here."

Jeffrey stood and acknowledged his mother. "I'm here and hope to visit with each of you. I'm sorry my kids couldn't be here."

Matthew couldn't help feeling his grandson had an ulterior motive. The image of P.J. kept coming back to him. Here was another P.J., he feared.

Carol continued to talk. "I'm sorry my family is not represented. Nicholas is involved as CEO of a large hotel chain and they are going to move to Ohio. He has responsibilities that really tie him down. He has a wife who works with him and two children. And Nicole married a minister. They're very much tied down to the church and community. They all send their greetings and birthday wishes."

Matthew couldn't help thinking that these were the grandchildren he didn't really know. At least Carol had turned around in her life and the family seemed to be going in the right way.

"And now," continued Johnie, "our baby brother, Michael. We're glad that he's taken over Dad's farm."

Michael, a younger version of Johnie, began his short talk. "I'm definitely the youngest, and I have the youngest children—no grandchildren like my older brothers and sisters."

"You don't have to emphasize the older," said Johnie.

"My wife Elise, who teaches in Lake View, also runs the business side of our farm and nursery. Andrew, now twenty, is at home this summer and will go back to school in the fall. Elizabeth will leave for college in late August. She's eighteen. Then we have Michelle, 9, and Little Matthew, 4. We're proud to be on the farm that was Dad's."

"That completes our family. Now, why don't you sit back a minute. Have another cup of coffee and visit. We have something more."

Matthew sensed a surprise was coming.

CHAPTER 10

Surprises and the unexpected keep a celebration moving along and interesting. James had managed to get several people around the back way. Those last guests had all arrived later either by car or first by plane and then car. They had been served their noon dinners separately and hidden from Matthew's view.

James looked at his cousins and felt the kinship he had experienced through the many years. People had to move on and establish their own families, but there was a time to come home. Something deep within called people home.

"I can't wait to see Uncle Matthew," said Susie, "I remember how much he helped us during those hard years."

"And you're a grandmother."

"Who goes first?" asked Corrine, James' older cousin and Susie's mother. "We should save the biggest surprise until last."

Johnie entered. "It's time. It's one or two at a time."

James nodded to Larry. "You go first. I think Dad was beginning to think you wouldn't come. Then, we'll send in the others."

James ushered Larry outside to the tent. He tried to keep Larry hidden just outside.

Johnie quieted the crowd. "Here's our first surprise."

Larry stepped forward. James held up his camera to attempt to record the surprise on his father's face. Uncle and nephew greeted each other and embraced. The family applauded.

"I thought you might be here," said Matthew. "I knew you were coming back from your mission work in Eastern Europe. This means more than I can say."

"Uncle Matthew, I want to say something to you and the rest of the family. Most of you know my story. I had gone far astray. Money and power and position were becoming my god. I believe money and power brought my father, P.J. Anderson, to his early death. I was following in his footsteps."

James saw tears coming to his father's eyes.

"I had an encounter while I was in prison—an encounter with the Living Lord. That happened through people who cared. And especially when I got out, Uncle Matthew and Aunt Ellen and Grandma helped me to find my way.

"How can I thank you enough?"

The crowd applauded. James could hear from that more reserved Scandinavian crowd words such as "Praise the Lord," or "Thank God."

James couldn't help thinking of his own life. Now that he was retired, the years lay ahead of him. In another twenty-four years, would he be facing what his father now faced? His father had seemed tired and not himself part of the time. Would that be his lot in life?

But these times should be an encouragement to Matthew Anderson. However, would he, James Anderson, have as much impact on people's lives as his father had? Could the rift with son Richard somehow be healed?

Johnie resumed his role as emcee. "Thank you Larry. We're all happy that you could be with us. And now, another surprise. In fact, we have two surprise family visitors."

James ushered in his two cousins, favorite childhood playmates. He hardly recognized Beth, who was stouter but still had some of those athletic features of her childhood. The piercing blue eyes and smile reminded him of the girl he had played with.

Always the exuberant one, Beth threw her arms around her uncle. "Uncle Matthew, I've come home."

"Beth," was all Matthew could say.

"You flew from California," said Ellen.

Chapter 10

"I'm retired from teaching," announced Beth. "I'm going to spend some time with my sister, and I'm going to stay and visit my family here as well. I've neglected you far too long."

Johnie nodded to her, inviting her to honor her uncle.

"My dear Uncle Matthew and Aunt Ellen and Aunt Victoria, you were all such special people when I grew up. You were always there for me. You came to all my plays. You encouraged me in so many ways. Part of my success as a teacher and theater person, I owe to you. Family is important, and you are my family. I thank you from the bottom of my heart."

The family applauded.

Irene, looking like Beth but younger and slimmer, stepped forward. "It's my turn now."

"Go right on," said Johnie.

"I'd say some of the same since I directed plays as well. But I looked to you, Uncle Matthew and Aunt Ellen, as such fine examples of good parents. I looked to Mom and Dad, of course, but I saw in the two of you, such fine examples of godly parents. As I brought up my three children, I thought of the way you brought up my cousins."

Matthew and Ellen embraced Irene and thanked her.

Irene turned to her aunt. "And Aunt Victoria, you were more than an aunt. You showed me what it was to be an educator. During the years I taught—not as many as Beth, for I stayed home with the kids for a while. During those years, you were my model. And I thank you."

By this time, Matthew and his wife and sister all had tears in their eyes.

"But," said Irene, "it's Happy Birthday, Uncle Matthew." With those words she hugged him and kissed him on the cheek.

Irene and Beth found chairs and sat down.

James quietly ushered in the two final surprise guests.

Corrine, now well over seventy, walked slowly over to her uncle and then ran into his arms. "Uncle Matthew, I love you so much. And I'm an old lady now."

"Corrine," said Matthew, "it's been years since I've seen you. I think of you and Warren when you lived on the home place."

"My dear uncle, I think of all you and Aunt Ellen and Aunt Victoria did for us when we went through those difficult times. You helped restore our faith in God."

A voice interrupted. "Don't forget me. I'm little Susie. I used to sit on your lap and cuddle up to you."

"I can't believe you're here."

"I came with Mother from California."

Susie threw her arms around her grand uncle.

"I love you, Susie. You always seemed special to me. Thanks for coming."

"Uncle Matthew, I can't believe it, but I am now a grandmother. That makes you a great-great granduncle. Can you believe it?"

"Wow! I guess it's pretty wonderful to be eighty-five."

Susie extended her hugs to Ellen and Victoria as well. But she obviously had the stronger affection for her uncle.

At this point, family members were moving about and visiting. It would seem the formal part of the gathering had ended.

During this time, James couldn't help wondering about his own role in life—particularly his role as a father. He hadn't been the father that Matthew Anderson had been. He seemed to relate better to his girls. But Richard had never lived up to family expectations. Now he didn't even know where Richard was.

Johnie stood once more and his voice boomed out. "I think there are some things that are very important. We don't often tell those closest to us how much we really care. I think we need to do that now. But behind all this is our faith, our relationship with the Lord. I think back almost fifty years and recall the pastor using the verse, 'Jesus Christ, the same yesterday, today, and forever.'

"So many things are not permanent, but He is forever. Jesus Christ is the same. We can depend on Him at any time. We must depend on Him first. Then let us as family members—fathers or mothers or uncles or aunts or cousins or brothers or sisters—be individuals that others can depend on.

"And now, we want to give our thanks to Matthew Anderson on his birthday as well as Ellen, and we'll add Aunt Victoria. Dad and these other two are the people we honor today. We'll begin with the oldest, James."

Someone jokingly called out. "We don't want a professor's lecture."

James smiled. "A lecture you're not going to get. I retired from being a professor."

Johnie gave him a nudge on the shoulder. "I'm in charge of the microphone so I'll make sure he doesn't start to lecture."

James began, mindful of some restless children in the audience, searched for words that would be most meaningful. "Some of the deepest feelings are the most difficult to express. I speak to you Dad, and Mother as well. How can we five children thank you for sixty years of giving.

Chapter 10

You have given us life, you have loved and nurtured us through all those difficult times. You have been there for us whenever we needed you. All this comes down to three simple words: 'I love you,' or 'we love you.' Words cannot express what I feel for you."

He embraced his father and kissed his mother and Aunt Victoria. He should have said something profound, but those were all the words he could say.

"It's my turn," said Johnie.

As Johnie spoke and then Margaret, James travelled many places in his mind. He saw himself and his siblings as young children, playing in this very spot. He saw each family member seated at the kitchen at his or her proper place, with Mother and Dad at each end of the table. What a wonderful life that had been!

Carol stood before the family, now a mature woman approaching her late fifties. Her reddish brown hair had hints of gray, making her look even more distinguished.

"Dad, Mother—and Aunt Victoria as well, I probably caused you more headaches and gray hairs than any of the other children. I was the prodigal who came back. But Dad and Mom never lost faith in me. They never lost faith in God that He would bring me back. Dad was very much like the Father in the Prodigal Son story. He and Mom welcomed me back and accepted me. And another person who did the same was Aunt Victoria.

"I thank you Dad." She paused. "And Mother and Aunt Victoria. You have strengthened this family. You are the patriarchs and matriarchs of a large family. Words can never express all that I feel."

A quiet applause followed.

Michael, the younger version of Johnie, moved forward. "I'm the kid. I'm the afterthought."

Those words caught his mother's attention. "No, Michael, you were that unexpected blessing. No child is an afterthought. God has a plan and purpose for every child."

Michael continued. "I'm probably the other prodigal. The first three did everything right, and then I came along. I'm not sure I have everything together even at forty-plus."

Does a person ever have everything together? James thought to himself. He realized things about his own life. I was an outstanding professor and teacher. I was a father figure to many of my students, but I was a lousy father to Richard, especially. It seemed I always had a good relationship with my daughters.

Michael went on to talk about his earlier years and how he had come back to buy the farm. "Dad was always there to advise me on what to do. He loved driving the tractor and plowing the fields each fall. That was in his blood. Being there and helping was what he did best. And I can't forget how Mother was always beside him."

Several other people gave tributes to Matthew as well as Ellen and Victoria. After all, they were the last members of that generation.

"And now," announced Johnie, "it's time to hear from our guest of honor or maybe I should say our guests of honor."

Victoria didn't hesitate to stand and speak. "I want to thank all of you for your kind words. I am overwhelmed by the honors you have given me. You are the people who have enriched my life and have given it meaning. I thank you from the bottom of my heart."

The audience responded in applause and even some bravos.

James couldn't help thinking of his father's heart. This excitement might be too much for him. Matthew Anderson had his hand over his heart.

Ellen stood and said of few of those well-chosen words.

Matthew stood up, a little unsteadily it seemed. "I'm not a public speaker like the rest of my family."

"Dad," said Johnie, "you don't have to give a speech. We know you are saying 'Thank you.' That's all you need to say."

"I'm not as strong as I used to be. I can't move around the way I used to. I think of Paul, who wrote the words, 'My strength is made perfect in weakness.' The Lord reminds me that I must depend on Him for my strength. I feel His strength here. I feel His love flowing through all of you, and that makes me feel stronger. Thank you for bringing all this love to me. Thank you for His love that flows through you on this day and in this place.

"I think I've said enough," he added.

Johnie placed his arm on his father's shoulder. "Dad, you've lived the best sermon that anyone could give."

Suddenly, one person stood and clapped. Soon the whole family and the friends present were clapping and encouraging the three elders.

In that moment James felt he experienced a glimpse of what Heaven would be. He had a glimpse beyond tomorrow.

Chapter 10

"Matthew, you lie down for a while before we go home." Ellen's worry and concern came through with every word.

"No, dear, I'll just rest my eyes a few minutes. I can think about the day."

Matthew reviewed the events of the day. Overwhelmed by all the people and happenings, he experienced something of a dizzying effect. He couldn't believe so many people had taken time to come and celebrate and honor him.

"I guess when you're eighty-five, you have the right to sit back," he said aloud. "Lord, it can't be too long until you call me Home. But I still have a reason to be here. So much is happening all around me."

Without realizing what was happening, Matthew fell into a deep sleep. He dreamed of the earlier days with his brother and sisters. Then, his dream took him to the big event, the purchase of the Nelson place. He saw once more how God has brought him to a bigger and better farm. The Nelson place was indeed supposed to be Matthew Anderson's place.

A voice called him back to reality.

"Dad," said James, "are you ready to go home?"

Matthew opened his eyes. "I guess I dozed off."

"It's been a big day for you. Johnie and I will take you and Mom and Victoria home."

Matthew hesitated, not answering. There was a place where he really wanted to go.

"Was there something else?"

"Son, there's something I'd really like to do. Maybe it seems stupid. I was dreaming when I woke up. I'd really like to go to my place, the place I called mine before Michael took over."

"At your service, Dad. This is your birthday, or at least the day we celebrate it, so you get to make wishes."

The women were busy working and talking in the kitchen. Victoria and Ellen were in the midst of the conversation with Margaret and Deborah. Some of the great-grandchildren were still playing outside.

In minutes they were on the way to Michael's place, the farm that Matthew had run for so many years.

The boys, as he always referred to them, were rather quiet. They seemed to be waiting for him to talk.

"Dad, what are you thinking?" asked James.

"I can't help thinking about P.J. and that terrible time when he told me the farm was not mine but his. For that moment he destroyed my world."

"Uncle P.J. was a jerk!" exclaimed Johnie. "We shouldn't speak ill of the dead, but that is absolute truth."

"I can't help wondering if he made things right with the Lord before he died. He was in such terrible torment."

James stopped the car in the farm yard. "As Shakespeare said, 'the evil that men do lives long after them.' He did change the life of our family."

"He did some good things along the way. But in the end, I was better off on this bigger and better farm."

"What did you want to do now?" asked Johnie.

Johnie opened the car door and Matthew got out. "I'd just like to get out and look around. See the house there. It's one of those grand old houses, so much bigger and better than the one on the home place. We even had the indoor bathroom."

The boys laughed.

"That was a step up in the world," said James.

Father and sons stood looking at the grand old farmhouse.

Matthew continued to reminisce. "Remember how hard we worked to paint the house. And we fixed up the swing on the front porch. I'll had to admit it's a great show place—especially after Ellen got the shrubs and flowers in place."

"Planting the garden in spring was always a family event," observed James.

"And harvesting, too," added Johnie.

Matthew looked up at the house. "I don't think Michael and Elise even know we're here. People are always so busy. People often don't have time for others."

"I realize I've been far too busy with being a professor. I missed out on some things with my family, especially Richard."

"Ditto," said Johnie. "Being a pastor demands time away from your children."

Matthew turned toward the barn. "Let's go down to the barn. I think I hear voices down there."

"Sounds like Michael and someone else."

Matthew remembered the added conveniences in this barn. "We had the manure loader. That made life so much easier. And then we had all the work done for selling Grade A Milk."

"For an old barn with its addition, it looks great," said Johnie. "When I was growing up, I always thought I'd be right here on the farm. But God had a different plan for me."

Chapter 10

As they approached the barn, the voices became more distinct. Matthew recognized the voice that sounded exactly like P.J.'s. It was the voice of his grandson, Jeffrey Grant.

Loud and clear came the words of Jeff. "The land of the south and west of Nelson Lake is mine. There's nothing you can do to stop me from bringing in a developer. We'll get the new roads, and I predict the condos will sell like hotcakes."

Matthew couldn't quite hear what Michael was saying, but the words were heated.

"How can he do that?" whispered James. "There isn't that much room on the lake. It would spoil the natural beauty of the place."

Jeffrey's voice became louder and more threatening. "And with your debt, I'll lay claim on even more land."

Michael's voice came through clearly. "I'm too polite. But I'd like to tell you exactly where you can go. And that's exactly where you're headed!"

Matthew and his sons stepped back. Jeff and Michael opened the barn door and came out. Both men looked surprised and startled.

"Hello, Grandfather," said Jeff, suddenly changing his tone. "That was quite a birthday party. You deserved every bit of honor."

Michael cut off his last word. "Jeffrey was just leaving."

Michael eyed his nephew with a stare that said he meant business.

"So long. I'll see you later."

"What was that all about?" asked James.

Michael groped for words. "Well, Jeffrey Grant is talking big. We're not going to let him destroy our lake or our home."

Matthew wondered if serious problems lay ahead. This was not the ideal ending of an almost perfect day.

CHAPTER 11

"Matthew, it's time to get up. James will be here, and we'll be late for church."

Ellen wondered if something was wrong. Matthew had been strangely quiet last night after he came back from his outing with James and Johnie. Matthew was one of those people who never overslept. He was always up at the crack of dawn.

Matthew jumped out of bed, quite agile for his age.

He rubbed his eyes. "I can't believe it's this late."

"I laid out your shirt and trousers. I'll have the oatmeal ready in just a few minutes."

Within fifteen minutes, Matthew was seated at the kitchen table, eating his breakfast and taking his medications. He always moved quickly—though he had slowed down.

Ellen hesitated to ask what was wrong, but she decided to question him. "Matthew, dear, I know something's bothering you, but I don't suppose you'll tell me until you're ready."

Matthew ate another spoonful of oatmeal. "Well, I don't know if there's any problem, and I don't know exactly what it is."

"You've got me wondering."

"Yesterday, when we went to our old place, we heard the end of an argument between Michael and Jeffrey. We couldn't find out what it was all about, but Jeffrey seems to feel he has or can get control of Nelson Lake."

"That's an environmental lake," said Ellen. "There are some major restrictions on lakes like that."

"I think that's why he's running for county commisioner. He believes he can change some rules and regulations."

"Jeffrey has been both a concern and an embarrassment from time to time."

"He's P.J. all over again."

Ellen picked up his bowl. "James will be here any minute."

"I could just as well drive myself," protested Matthew. "I'm beginning to think they feel I shouldn't be driving."

"You'll have to admit that you don't see quite as well. And you react more slowly."

"I don't like getting old."

Ellen gave him a kiss on the cheek. "We're not getting old. We are old."

The back door opened and James called out. "Who said something about getting old? It's time for church, and there's going to be a big crowd with all the Andersons."

"And," Ellen added, "Pastor John Anderson will be speaking."

As she spoke, she wondered about Matthew. Would this busy round of activities and excitement be too much for her husband?

———

The lines of the first hymn stuck in Matthew's mind, words that reflected change. He wondered how many times he had sung that hymn, and perhaps he would not sing this hymn again in this life.

"O God, our help in ages past,
Our hopes for years to come,
Our shelter from the stormy blast,
And our eternal home."

The stormy blast—that was this life and all its concerns and problems. Jeff Grant might be his flesh and blood, but this grandson was thinking only of the earthly values. Eternity was far from his mind. A later verse served as a different reminder.

"Time, like an ever-rolling stream,
Bears all his sons away;
They fly forgotten, as a dream
Dies at the opening day."

Chapter 11

Lord, you are my eternal home. That is my comfort, he said to himself. Houses and property, Nelson Lake included, are all temporal and will pass away.

The opening part of the service, with its liturgy, continued. Matthew couldn't help thinking of the people and the many events of the past days. Many members of his family were present. They would never again all be present in this way. He held that hope that they would all be present in that eternal home.

Johnie rose and went to the pulpit. He began with a short prayer. "I'm Pastor John Anderson, and I'm happy to be here this morning. This is my home church, the church that nurtured me in my faith. Many of you know me simply as Johnie. I see many of you who are family, but I also see a generation of people I do not know.

"In a week or more the Fourth of July will arrive. The anniversary of our country should give us cause to think and ask questions. I have one question to ask you and to ask myself. Are you listening? Am I listening?"

He smiled. "Yes, I hope you're listening to me. But the listening I'm thinking about is a more important kind of listening. Are we truly listening to God and what He has to say? Or perhaps, to put it more boldly, are we letting Jesus into our lives and work place and other areas?"

Johnie paused. His son had always been the bold one in the family. He had been the fighter as well.

"Behold is the word I remember, but here we have the modern words teaching an old truth. 'Here I am! I stand at the door and knock. If anyone hears my voice and opens the door, I will come in and eat with him, and he with me.'

"That is a wonderful invitation. But I'm wondering do we really let Him in? Into our home? Into our classroom? Into our work places? Into every area of life? Is our country letting Him in? And, yes, even our churches?"

Johnie began to speak of some of the moral lapses evident. The dishonesty in various places. The crime statistics. The television and movies that present a way of life far from Christian ways. Finally, the way people hurt and mistreat each other day by day.

"Now I'd like to talk about one of the great Old Testament kings, Hezekiah. The Bible says he did what was right in the eyes of the Lord. Let's look at what he did. First of all, he followed his father, who was a very evil and wicked king. Hezekiah sought after the Lord. And he listened."

Matthew's mind wandered for a moment as Johnie spoke of the way Hezekiah destroyed the idols and other relics of heathen worship. He did what the Lord directed him to do. He restored the right kind of worship.

"But," said Johnie, "there is a *but*. Something happened at the end of his life. Hezekiah did great things for God and his people. He built a tunnel so that Jerusalem could have water if the city were attacked. If you visit Jerusalem today, you can see the tunnel—perhaps even walk in that tunnel. In some ways, King Hezekiah was an engineering genius." He went on to do some more explaining.

"But King Hezekiah became proud and did not rely on God. At one point he was about to die, and he prayed fervently to the Lord. God did give him fifteen extra years, but that pride eventually led to the downfall of the nation.

"I believe there is a strong message here for us today. We have become proud and self-sufficient as a nation and as individuals. I believe the Lord is calling us—Jesus is standing at the door calling to us. In the words of John the Baptist, He says, "Repent of your evil ways."

Johnie paused a moment. "Perhaps I came on a bit strong. I speak to you though as a friend or family member. I speak for myself when I say that I become a bit too comfortable with the way things are in my life and church. I realize, too, that I need to repent. I need to realize that I haven't sought after the Lord's direction as I should. I suspect you may have done—or not done—the same.

"I'd like us to close with one of those old hymns. 'Softly and Tenderly Jesus is Calling' is a hymn of invitation to you and to me. Let's sing it and listen to the words, and take them to heart."

The organist played an introduction. Matthew couldn't help thinking of Johnie and how powerful the sermon was. He joined the rest of the congregation and sang...

"Softly and tenderly Jesus is calling,
Calling for you and for me;
See on the portals He's waiting and watching,
Watching for you and for me.
Come home. Come home. Ye who are weary, come home;
Earnestly, tenderly, Jesus is calling, Calling, O sinner, come home!"

As they sang the second verse about Jesus pleading, Matthew thought of Jeffrey and Richard and some of the other family members who seemed to have strayed. Oh, how he wished they would come home.

Chapter 11

The congregation sang slowly and meditatively down to the last 'Come home!' Matthew couldn't help thinking of another kind of home, his eternal home.

He bowed his head as he thought. He could see Pa and Ma and the very places where they had sat as well as other family and friends. He saw his children when they were young. Then, he looked around to see Johnie, leaving the pulpit, and there was Ellen and all the children and many grandchildren and great-grandchildren. O, how I love them. I want to be with them and be part of their lives. But there comes a time to leave and go Home.

Matthew was scarcely aware of what went on next. The offering. Some closing prayers. The benediction. A closing hymn.

The service ended, and Matthew stood, not moving. Ellen nudged him.

"It's time to leave," she said.

All at once, there were family members and friends crowding around him and Ellen. He heard the repeated comments.

"You must be proud of your son."

"We need more preachers like Pastor John Anderson."

"John Anderson has got it right."

"Johnie-boy has come a long way."

Matthew and Ellen were the last to leave the sanctuary and shake hands with their son.

"Son," said Ellen, "we are so very proud of you. You're doing what God called you to do."

With those words, Johnie embraced her, and she kissed him.

"Son," said Matthew. The words he wanted to say didn't come. He repeated the words, "My son, and my son."

"Dad, I love you more than I can say."

With those words, father and son embraced, and their tears flowed freely.

Time seemed to stand still. Matthew wanted this moment to last. Then, James and Michael stepped forward, as well as Margaret and Carol.

"Time for a family photo!" called James's daughter Marlene. Amid all the commotion Matthew and Ellen lined up with the five children and then with the in-laws included.

As the picture taking ended, Matthew said aloud what he had said and thought so many times. "God is good. My cup runs over."

Beyond Tomorrow

"Where's Dad?" asked James the next morning as he entered his mother's kitchen.

"Your father is not moving very fast. I'm worried about him," answered Ellen. "He's not been himself at times. He's overslept, and that's something totally unlike Matthew Anderson."

"That's why he has a doctor appointment."

"Yes, I want you to go with him and talk to Dr. Martin both before and after. Your father will listen to you or Johnie. He sometimes ignores my advice."

James chuckled. "I suppose I sometimes don't listen to Ruth the way I should."

"Your father went for his morning walk. He should be back any minute."

"I don't suppose he could have headed directly to the clinic. I always used to know where he was going, but that hasn't been the case lately."

His mother poured a cup of coffee and handed it to him.

"Coffee always keeps us going."

At that moment Matthew Anderson returned.

"Did you forget you have a doctor's appointment?" asked Ellen.

"Oh, is that today?"

"Yes, Dear. I think you better leave off the coffee for now. Keep your blood pressure down."

"I'd like to forget all this business with doctors. If my time is up, there's nothing the doctor can do."

"Matthew, don't talk that way. There is plenty a doctor can do to keep you healthy during your life. It's up to you to maintain the quality of life."

"Dad," said James, "I'm taking you. And I'm talking to Dr. Martin. We need to be sure you're ready for our trip to Sweden. We need to have all your prescriptions renewed."

His father grunted.

"Matthew, we want you healthy so you can enjoy your trip. We don't want anything to go wrong with your health while you're far from home."

"Maybe I shouldn't go." Matthew turned to James. "Then, Ruth can go."

"No, Dad, you're going. You've always wanted to visit Sweden and see where Grandpa grew up. You can't back out now."

Ellen took his coffee cup. "Time to go, or you'll be late.

As James drove the short distance to the Lake View Medical Clinic, he wondered if he had taken on a bigger challenge than he had realized.

112

Chapter 11

Maybe Dad can't take such a long and strenuous trip. But he still has a farmer's strength.

He stayed near his father through all the routines of a physical examination. Matthew weighed in. The nurse checked blood pressure and other routine matters. James could feel his father's tension as this was done.

James thought of the changes in his life. No longer did he have a teaching job to go back to. He was free. He was retired. This would be a whole new life. This wasn't summer vacation; this was permanent retirement. His teaching position would not be there as a reason for getting up in the morning. Would he find new purpose during this phase of his life?

Doctor Martin entered the examination room. "Hello Mr. Anderson. How are you today? And this must be your son?"

His father gave one of his annoyed looks. "My wife thinks I need to have someone with me. I think I hear everything I need to hear."

"It's a good idea to have someone with you. You could miss something, and your son will hear it."

The doctor began to poke and probe. James watched and listened as the procedure went on.

"Do you have any particular problems or complaints, Mr. Anderson?"

"Oh, the usual aches and pains. My back gives me some problems, and I don't seem to have the strength I once had."

"You must remember you're not so young." Dr. Martin looked at the chart. "I see you're eighty-five years old. I don't see any problems. You're healthy for your age."

At this point, James decided to say something. "We're a bit concerned because Dad hasn't been himself lately. He's been sleeping more, and he doesn't seem to have the same interest in life."

The doctor began to look at the tests and at earlier records.

"I think we told you that we wanted this check-up because your dad's going on a trip to Sweden, and we hope this won't be too much for him."

"Matthew," said the doctor, "I think the trip will be good for you. From what I understand, you'll go back to the home place in Sweden and you'll meet some cousins there."

"I'll be with him all the time," said James.

The doctor wrinkled his forehead.

"Is something wrong?" asked James.

"I'm the same as I've always been." Matthew sat up straighter. "I'm just older. A lot older."

"Yes, you do well for your age. Your blood pressure was somewhat elevated. You are thin enough so you don't have to think about dieting."

The doctor did some further checking through records. "I see that you have had some stomach problems at an earlier time. And you have had some heart concerns."

"Yes, I think we've done all we can do."

"Matthew, you know as well as I do that your heart isn't as strong as it once was. You need to pace yourself. You've been through this before. Don't do the heavy lifting. Pace yourself. Avoid some of that strenuous climbing."

"I'll see that he does," said James.

"As I look over everything, I can see you've seen so many changes. I think you've been depressed. This happens to many older people. I can give you something for the depression."

James wondered if an anti-depressant might be the answer.

"No! No!" exploded Matthew. "I don't want anything to do with those drugs."

"They do help a lot of people."

"I want none of that!"

James smiled. "I think you have your answer about the anti-depressant."

"I figured that might be your answer. I heard your son John speak yesterday. I, too, believe that a relationship with the Lord is a better answer than much medication. I think I know what you'll do."

"There's a cliché saying about being close to God. If you don't feel close to God, guess who moved. I moved."

Matthew and the doctor shook hands.

Then, James spoke. "Thank you, Doctor. I think we'll have a great trip. Dad sometimes experiences a let-down after all the family excitement."

"Have a great trip, both of you."

James placed his hand on his father's shoulder. "Dad and I will be off on the trip of a lifetime. A trip to the land of our forefathers."

CHAPTER 12

July 1985

Ellen finished reading her Scripture for the morning. Matthew had been away a full week. The house seemed empty without him. Was this the way it felt being a widow? Could she ever adjust to living without Matthew?

She looked out at the lawn. It needed mowing, and this was something she had never done. In fact, her physical strength seemed limited so that Matthew or a cleaning lady she had hired always did the vacuuming. Growing old was not easy. You had to give up so many things. You had to depend on others more and more.

Today, the day lay before her. She didn't feel like cooking for herself. She could call and eat at the senior citizen center. Perhaps someone would pick her up, but she hated to ask. She should have learned to drive a few years back.

A knock at the back door interrupted her thoughts. She hurried back and found she had left the door locked. Ever since Matthew left, she had been careful to lock the doors.

She unlocked the door and there stood her daughter-in-law.

"I'm sorry, Ruth," she apologized, "I forgot to unlock the doors."

"I didn't think you used to lock the doors. It's pretty safe here in Lake View."

"I lock doors now that Matthew's away."

"How about coming with me over to Margaret's? She has a bumper crop of peas and green beans, so I thought we could go over and help. We can do some good visiting."

Ellen hesitated. "I think Carol's supposed to be coming over here today."

"Oh, she's still in the little house. Hank was leaving with the grandkids this morning, but I think she's still there."

"Let me get my keys and purse." She went to the bedroom to ready herself. Everything she did seemed to take longer. That was a part of growing older.

"Mother Anderson, are you feeling all right?"

Ellen returned. "I guess I'm just a pokey old lady."

"You do wonderfully well. Remember you're eighty-six years old."

Sometimes she forgot her age. There were times she thought she was still fifty and there were young grandchildren around. But today she felt every one of her years. It was more a feeling in the spirit, but it made her ache all over.

Fifteen minutes later, she and Margaret and Carol were having coffee in the kitchen as they prepared to get to work.

Ruth announced, "I have a surprise."

"Not another grandchild on the way," teased Margaret. "I thought your girls were about done with having children."

"No, it's not that. I had a phone call early this morning. It was James."

"Is everything all right?" questioned Ellen.

"Good news. Dad has been doing exceptionally well on the tour. James has been amazed at how well he gets around. He keeps going strong from morning until night."

"Where have they been?" asked Margaret.

"They started out in Denmark. Then, they went over to Sweden. They'll be doing quite a bit of touring all around. They'll head up to Stockholm. Then, in a few days they'll take the train down to see the relatives."

"I hope Matthew doesn't over-do." Ellen fingered the wedding band that she had worn more than sixty years.

"James is looking after him," said Margaret. "James can be very protective. And Dad is more careful than he used to be."

"I have to believe what I always say. Matthew is in God's Hands. I've said that all my life, and that is the truth."

Chapter 12

The women began their tasks of shelling peas at the same time they began to rehearse the events of the big birthday party and other details of the past week.

Margaret brought out the freezer bags. "We need to catch up on all the news. However, I'll have to say I don't have anything new. The kids are nearby, and we caught up last week at the birthday party."

Ellen placed her pea husks in the basket. "I suppose you'll put these in the compost pile. But about the birthday party, I have to say again how amazed Matthew was at the number of grandchildren and great-grandchildren who actually came."

"I'm only an in-law," said Ruth, "but I don't think you and Matthew realize how important you are to all of us—and that includes our children and grandchildren."

"Perhaps," said Margaret, "I shouldn't ask, but have you heard anything from Richard? I know how hard it is when you don't hear from someone you love."

Ruth looked away, sadly. "I think Richard was the child we didn't seem to understand. The girls always lived up to family expectations. Richard was brilliant. Very creative. Very much disorganized."

Ellen couldn't help observing. "And James was very creative, but he was also highly organized and planned everything carefully."

Ruth smiled. "Mother Anderson, that is an understatement. James used to be so impatient with all the waste. We paid for a year of college, and Richard failed half the classes. That was something my husband found embarrassing, and he wouldn't tolerate."

Margaret finished putting the last peas in a container. "But he's recognized as a talented artist. He's won prizes."

"James is sorry now that he was so hard on Richard. Sometimes the life style of today's artists is questionable."

"We must keep praying," added Ellen.

"Don't forget Michael," said Margaret. "He was the prodigal for a short while. He took off and disappeared for a while. He resented being compared to his big brother or brothers. But he came back. And Richard will, too."

"We'll keep on praying," said Ellen.

Ruth added, "As the poet wrote, 'More things are wrought by prayer than this world dreams of.' It's true, but it sometimes takes time. Lots of time."

Margaret brought out the cups. "It's time for coffee. I wonder what's keeping Carol. I thought she'd be here by now."

"Carol always did have her own idea of time." Ellen stood up and turned to leave. "I'll go down to the little house and get her. There's something I wanted to ask about."

As Ellen approached the little house, her memory took her back to earlier times. Her mother-in-law Elizabeth Anderson had lived alone there for years. Before becoming a widow, John Anderson and she lived there. They were always Grandpa and Grandma to her and the children. They had established the Anderson family and provided a kind of strength and stability.

Matthew did not have the physical stature of his father, for he was several inches shorter. Grandpa Anderson had been a man whose physical presence filled the room. Matthew exuded more kindness and possessed more of a spiritual strength.

Grandma had changed during her last years in this little house. She had discovered a new purpose for her life. She became a woman of prayer, praying for each child and grandchild.

Her reverie was interrupted by loud voices. Carol's voice came through with sharp tones that Carol did not usually use.

"Mother!" the man yelled. "Why should you care about the Andersons? They weren't that good to you. You were always that other daughter."

"No, Jeffrey that was all my fault. I was a first-rate jerk until I turned my life around. Or rather the Lord turned me around."

"But now that I have the political clout, we can change the rules about Nelson Lake. That small lake can turn into an expensive showcase of homes and a hotel."

"No, Jeffrey, that would destroy the beauty of the area. You would devastate your grandparents and hurt your uncles and aunt."

Jeffrey continued to outline his plans. "On the land I own, there can be several lots for lake homes. They'll make me a pretty penny."

"But you need to get the rights to build a road in there. There's a great deal you have to do before you can accomplish that."

"That's in the works."

"But Michael owns the land, or does it still belong to your grandfather?"

Jeff raised his voice. "On paper it belongs to Michael. But Michael isn't the careful manager like Grandpa and Grandma. I have my ways."

"Jeffrey," Carol screamed, "you can't do this. Your greed is destroying everything this family stands for. You can't do it! You must stop!"

Ellen heard a devilish laugh came from her grandson. "Come now, Mother, you married conveniently. Each time you came up in the world. First my dad, the banker's son. Then a doctor. And finally, a rich businessman. You knew which side of the bread was buttered."

Ellen heard a slap.

"That's only part of the story. Yes, I've made mistakes, but Hank and I are using our wealth to help others, to make a better world. I'm sorry for many things that I've done. I've confessed my sins to the Lord and He's forgiven me. You need to do the same."

"I've had enough!" he yelled.

The door opened, and then Jeffrey immediately slammed it shut. Then he noticed his grandmother.

"Grandma, I didn't know you were here. I need to be on my way."

He stooped down and kissed her on the cheek.

"You should not speak to your mother that way."

"I'm sorry, Grandma, I've got to go."

Ellen wanted to say more. She remembered what she had said to P.J., Matthew's brother who had stolen the home farm. She wanted to tell Jeffrey the same: he was on the pathway to destruction that would lead to a terrible end.

Jeffrey made a quick departure. Carol came out. "Mother, how much did you hear?"

"I didn't mean to eavesdrop, but I couldn't help hearing. I heard all of Jeffrey's plans."

"O, Mother, I'm sorry. Hank and I will do everything we can to stop him."

"Do you think you can?"

Ellen felt relief that Matthew did not know what his grandson was planning. The trip to Sweden should be perfect, not marred by concerns about home.

The minute Joe came in from doing chores, Margaret knew something was wrong. She refrained from asking but simply said, "Supper will be ready in just a minute."

Margaret looked at the man whom she had loved since she was a mere child. Her feelings for him as a big brother changed early to puppy love and then to a love that had endured. But she looked at him now and found he looked older. She saw a tiredness she had not seen before.

Joe proceeded to wash off the dust and dirt of the day and then sat down at the kitchen table.

"You look exhausted."

"It's been quite a day."

"Tell me about it."

The two prayed their short table prayer and began to eat. Just then, the back door opened.

Ruth called out. "Hello. I just had to come over. I had some surprising news."

Margaret couldn't help wondering what Joe had to say, but she invited her sister-in-law to come in. "You can join us for late supper."

"Sorry, I didn't mean to intrude, but I just had to tell someone."

"What is this news?"

Ruth sat down. "As soon as I got home, I had a phone call. The realtor has a buyer for our house in Riverton. It looks like a good offer, but we have to be out by September 1."

"Isn't this what you wanted?" asked Margaret.

"Yes, but it all happened so fast. I can't quite believe it. I've been looking for apartments, but they're not always easy to find."

"This is what James wanted, isn't it?" asked Joe. "After all, he was planning to be here part of the time."

"I guess it's an answer to prayer."

Joe finished the last of his casserole and spoke. "I'm afraid the news I have isn't quite so pleasant."

Margaret gave her husband that knowing look. "The minute you came in I knew something wasn't right."

"It's a long story."

Margaret brought out cups and the coffee. "I think we need coffee for this." She poured the coffee, and the two women looked to Joe to continue.

"I found this out from my neighbor, Bob Schmidt. It's about Jeff."

Both Margaret and Ruth groaned.

"What's he up to now?" asked Ruth. "More land dealings or stealing?"

"This may be more serious. He hasn't really been caught yet. But this is the situation: Jeff's been doing insurance business. He has that business on the side."

Margaret added, "He tried to get us to switch our insurances to him, but we didn't quite trust him."

Joe went on. "It seems he's been collecting insurance premiums, but he hasn't sent that money into the company. That means those people who thought they were insured were not insured."

Chapter 12

Margaret looked at her husband and then at Ruth. "He could go to prison for that."

"Oh my," said Ruth, "I feel so sorry for Carol. She's turned her life around, and so has Hank. And their younger children have become wonderful Christians."

"But," said Margaret, "that hasn't happened to Jeffrey."

"There's more," continued Joe. "He's also been involved in land deals. He misrepresented the value of some land to an owner. Then after buying the land, he sold it for many times what he paid for it. There are some angry people around Lake View."

"I'm afraid that's within the law," said Ruth, "but it's terrible. It's immoral."

Margaret thought of how she had taken care of her nephew. He had been such a precocious lively child. She found it hard to think of him as a forty-year-old businessman who cheated people any way he could.

"What's going to happen now?" she mused. "This can't go on."

Joe held out his cup for more coffee. "I've lived long enough to know that wrong doing like this will never go unchecked. Jeffrey will be caught."

Margaret smiled at her husband. "You are wise. Just like my father. I'm glad that Dad doesn't know of these other developments."

Later that evening Ellen started to play a tape of quiet hymn music. "Carol, I rather like some quiet music this time of the evening. I hope you don't mind."

"Mother, I love that music. I don't hear enough of it. We do so much of that praise music we miss out on some of the good old hymns."

The music began to play.

"I miss your father. It doesn't seem quite right without him."

"I know, Mother. I understand. This quiet time really makes me pause and reflect."

The two women sat in silence, listening to the music, for several minutes. Ellen sensed something was going on in the mind of her daughter.

Carol started to say something and stopped.

"I know something's bothering you. You might as well share it. Maybe your old mother can even be of some help."

"Life is unpredictable, isn't it?"

Ellen thought a moment. "It's more predictable than you think. At least much of the time, life is predictable."

121

"I'm thinking of me. I was a rather hopeless case for a long time. I rebelled against you and Dad and Aunt Victoria and the school system and any kind of authority."

"Your father and I knew you'd return. We brought you up in the way a child ought to go. That's a promise."

Carol smiled. "I guess you never thought Hank and I would do mission work in Haiti. I love the children and I love working with them. It's more rewarding than anything I've ever done in my life."

"But there's something else, isn't there?"

Carol hesitated. "Hank and I are so proud of Nicholas and Nicole. They and their spouses are so involved in bringing up their children in the right ways. They're involved in Sunday school and church. I can see they're doing an absolutely wonderful job."

Ellen gave her daughter a knowing look.

"Mother, it's Jeffrey. And you heard some of it earlier today."

"What he does or what he tries to do will have to run its course."

Carol looked away, "I'm afraid it's more than what you heard this morning. I was in a store this morning and overheard something from two people who were talking."

"There's always gossip, and you can't pay attention to rumors."

"But, Mother, I'm afraid the rumors might be true. The two people didn't know who I was, and they took no care to hide what they were saying. They were saying that my son had cheated several people out of hundreds of thousands of dollars. And they said they thought he had connections with the underworld. They said he was just like P.J."

"He does look amazingly like P.J. And he has much of your uncle's charm."

"I'm afraid the local people are on to him. And maybe that was bound to happen. If something doesn't happen to stop him... Hank and I will have to do what we can."

"I remember all too well how we confronted P.J. There's little a person can do. Why don't we turn on the ten o'clock news and then retire for the night."

"Mom, remember how we used to heat up hot milk whenever we might have a problem going to sleep. I could use some hot milk."

Fifteen minutes later, mother and daughter turned off the music and sipped hot milk. An hour later, Ellen continued to think of Jeffrey. Sleep would not come. At least Matthew was far from the problem.

CHAPTER 13

James looked over at his father across from him as the train sped forward from Stockholm to the town of Linneryd, Sweden. His father had dozed off, no doubt exhausted from the busy tours of the last days.

James thought back over the past days. This journey to Sweden had been one of his dreams, and now it was coming true. He and his father had been part of a tour of the Scandinavian countries. They had landed in Copenhagen and toured Denmark, followed by a cruise taking them to Norway. What could have been more spectacular than the fjords! The next part of the tour had covered the lower part of Sweden up to Stockholm.

They had extended their tour by taking the train from Stockholm to Linneryd. Now, they would meet family members he never knew existed. They would see Grandpa's birth place. In fact, they would see the house where he was born.

Deep within, he experienced a feeling that he was coming home. The countryside he was seeing through the train windows reminded him of the area around Lake View. It was easy to understand why those Swedish immigrants settled exactly where they did. A few miles away, the Norwegians settled in the country that had more hills.

He opened his journal and began to write. "These past days have been like a beautiful dream. I've seen the most spectacular fjords. Each one seemed more awesome than the last one. And then to the Swedish lake country. At times, I thought I was back in Minnesota. I begin to realize now how much a part of me is the country.

"I never could see myself as a farmer. I never felt at home with machines. Never did I feel comfortable on the tractor—not the way most farm boys do. However, I love beauty: flowers, gardens, lakes, trees, and hills—everything that is a part of nature.

"I sense God's Presence whenever I look at this beauty around me."

He put aside his journal.

His mind returned to last night's conversation with Ruth. *"Our Riverton house just sold. We have to be out by September."* He couldn't believe it happened so fast. Houses usually took more time to sell. God must be saying that this was the right time to make the move.

Ruth's tone and evasiveness told him there was something else she wasn't telling him. No amount of prying would get her to tell. "But," he thought aloud, "anything can wait until I get home."

The thought that something was wrong wouldn't leave him. Could there have been word from Richard? Or had something happened in Riverton? Or he had that troubling encounter with Jeff. Could there be problems with Jeff?

Within him the feelings of anticipation returned. Perhaps excitement was a better word. He had been writing to Ingrid for over a year. She had sent a picture, but that didn't really tell him anything. How would he feel about these relatives? Would they be strangers who quickly became friends? What about the language barrier? Most people who were a bit younger than he had learned English from the earliest times in school. He knew only a few Swedish words.

The conductor walked through. "Sir, my young American," he said with a crisp British accent, "we will soon arrive in Linneryd. I believe that is your destination."

"Thank you, sir, it is kind of you to let me know."

"We're always happy to meet American relatives. I hope you are enjoying your visit to Sweden. Your father seems to be relaxing."

"The trip is great," said James, "and my father is exhausted after seeing so much of your beautiful country."

The conductor looked at his watch. "You will arrive in approximately five minutes."

James nudged his father. "We're almost there.'

Matthew sat up and rubbed his eyes. "I must have fallen asleep."

James chuckled. "You were sound asleep. You snored, and I think you were dreaming. You even talked in your sleep."

"I was really tired."

"We'll be meeting Ingrid and Karl at the railroad station."

"I'll get to brush up on my Swedish. I've forgotten most of it, I'm afraid."

Matthew Anderson's enthusiasm and liveliness seemed to have faded. James looked at his father and realized the years were catching up with him. Matthew had always been thin, but now he looked even thinner—even a bit frail. He didn't look like the strong father he had known through the years; he looked like an old man.

How thankful he was that he had had this time with his father. He saw the richness of his character he had not realized before. Matthew Anderson, in his own way, was a great man. He never had the physical strength of his father, John Anderson, but he had a spiritual depth and strength that went far beyond. "Lord," he whispered aloud, "thank You for giving this man as a father to me."

He had always thought his mother was the strength and fabric of the family. But Matthew Anderson contributed far more than people gave him credit for.

The train rattled to a stop abruptly.

James and Matthew picked up their bags and moved toward the exit. James felt that excitement that he experienced every time he entered into a new venture or adventure.

As they moved on to the railroad platform, James saw only a few people meeting friends of relatives. Most of the people looked as if they might be family for they had those Scandinavian features. Then, he caught sight of a woman who could have passed for Cousin Irene. She would be fifty-five. Only a little younger than her look-alike. He set down his suitcase and hurried forward.

"Ingrid Linden?"

He extended his hand. After all, they were Swedish and liked formality.

"Welcome Cousin James." She grasped his hand warmly. "And this must be your father, Cousin Matthew Anderson."

The two exchanged some Swedish greetings that James knew, but he didn't feel confident enough to use the words.

She turned to James. "My car is over by the ticket office. Your Swedish relatives are eager to meet you."

James thought to himself. This is a dream come true. What happens next? I suddenly feel like a shy schoolboy. I don't know what to say.

Ingrid seemed to sense the feelings of her cousins. She began to tell of the plans for the evening. James was relieved that she spoke remarkable English.

They placed their suitcases in the small Swedish-made car. James urged his father to sit in the front seat while he sat in back. While his father and Ingrid visited, using Swedish, James looked at the modest houses as they drove to the home of Ingrid and Karl.

James had a sense of unreality—as if he were here but not really here. It was like a dream where he walked in and out of familiar places with people who did not see him.

These were perhaps the very streets that Grandpa had walked on a hundred years ago, and what was a hundred years in the light of eternity. This life would be only an introduction or a prelude to the whole of eternity.

In one sense this was just another Swedish village. Only recently had any family member lived here. The real home is the place they would visit in a few short hours.

During the supper hour, Karl said very little for he did not understand English. James and Ingrid did most of the talking. They talked of the various relatives. James told of the American relatives while Ingrid told of the Swedish relatives who lived in the area and in cities throughout the country.

"James," said Ingrid in her formal British-style English, "we are family. We may have lived in two different continents, but we are alike."

"I can see that. You have a number of teachers in the family. But all of our relatives here and in America started out as farmers. Grandpa came to America with nothing but a few dollars and the clothes he wore. He left his sisters and brothers back here in Sweden."

"You will meet my mother tomorrow. She always said that there were misunderstandings, and that is why your father left. Sweden was crowded, and there was little opportunity. His older brother was not a very nice person. Sven greedily took everything he could get his hands on. The sisters regretted the way he treated John—or Johann as he was called then."

At this point Matthew spoke up. "I think that is why Pa spoke very little of his family and this country. He had been hurt by his brother."

Ingrid smiled. "That is why it was wonderful that you should come to the home of your father."

Chapter 13

"When Pa died, I believe his brother and all his sisters had died. Pa was one of those afterthoughts—about ten years younger than the next sister."

Ingrid added, "Many in the next generations left this country for America. My grandmother used to tell me how many of our people left their homeland."

"I've heard some of those sad Scandinavian songs—about leaving mother and family in the homeland."

Matthew looked away sadly. "I believe Pa and others felt a call to leave a crowded land and to come to a land of opportunity."

"Wasn't there still another brother who went to America?"

"Yes, but we never knew much about him. I believe he visited when I was very young."

James thought aloud. "There are some things we will never know."

As they finished their meal, Ingrid announced, "Now Karl will drive us over to Nels and Brigitta's. You'll get to see where the whole family started."

James couldn't help recalling what he had read and seen of Roots and Alex Haley. When Haley began his search for his roots, he had a strange feeling that he was not only aided by his relatives on earth, but that some supernatural force was urging him on. James felt he was at a crossroads of history but was also touching the history of one hundred years ago.

—◦◦◦—

Matthew had often dreamed that he would somehow visit Sweden and the home of his ancestors. However, as he grew older, it had seemed rather unlikely. But now he was riding toward the home of John Anderson's childhood.

As they drove toward the Linden Grove Farm, Matthew began to recall some things his father had said.

Ingrid and James were observing the scenery of the country. Matthew looked at scenery that in some ways resembled the Minnesota country-side. Was this really real? Was he actually going to see the place he had only thought about?

"There's our church, the one John Anderson was confirmed and baptized in."

"Could we stop?" asked Matthew.

"That's the plan for tomorrow. There's going to be another family gathering then. We'll visit the church and visit other relatives."

The plain white structure, built in almost a box-like style, seemed so different from the country churches that dotted the countryside in the Midwest. The American churches with their high steeples and gothic windows seemed more like the majestic cathedrals. Somehow, he thought Pa's church looked so very plain.

Once more, Matthew looked at the countryside. Pa must have walked these roads many times. All at once, he saw a meadow and a stream. He sat upright.

"Is something wrong?" asked James.

"No," Matthew responded quickly. "Could we stop here just a minute? There's something I'd like to see."

Karl turned around on the country road, drove back to the spot and parked.

"Dad, this is a strange request."

Matthew got out of the car and stood looking at the scene that stretched before him. Could this be the place Pa had talked about? He walked forward several steps and looked at the meadow and the stream or river that flowed through it. Several cattle grazed lazily nearby.

"I remember something Pa told me." He turned to the three people who looked puzzled by his request.

"Pa didn't ever talk much about his life here, but once he told me a little story. He was herding the cattle by a stream or river. Suddenly, upstream a dam broke and the stream flooded. He chased the cows and ran to safety. That's all I remember of what Pa told me. This looks as if it could be the place."

James walked forward and stood beside him. "Dad, I remember Grandpa told me that story. I think that must have been one of the more pleasant memories. Otherwise, I'd ask questions and he'd look sad. He'd just say, 'That's too long ago to remember.'"

For a moment, Matthew felt Pa beside him. He seemed to be standing with him in this very spot. Could it be possible that a person's spirit returned to these special places? There were times in that old barn back home when it seemed Pa would walk out at any moment.

Ingrid turned to him. "Cousin Matthew, I used to believe in ghosts or spirits. I thought my grandma was with me when I faced difficult decisions."

Matthew didn't hesitate. "I don't believe in ghosts, but I've had some of those same feelings."

They returned to the car. Matthew felt he had come home to Pa's country.

Chapter 13

In minutes they drove into a location of four houses. Two were the traditional old Swedish red. The other two looked like any of the ranch style houses so prevalent back home.

Ingrid pointed to each of the houses. "The first one is owned by people we don't know." Then, she pointed to the two deep red houses that were obviously old. "Those two belong to relatives—your third cousins."

Karl stopped the car in front of a newer house. "This house belongs to Brigitta Johannson. They are my mother's cousins and your second cousins. They own the barn and several acres of land."

They got out of the car. Ingrid pointed to a smaller house, obviously very old. "That's where your grandfather, Johann Anderson, was born, and where his family lived."

"Does anyone live here now?" asked Matthew.

"Johann and I keep it as a museum. It reminds us of the past—the way things were years ago. It is good to remember where we came from."

Matthew spoke slowly. "I'd like to go inside. If that's okay?"

"We can go inside. Johann and his son Staffan are coming in from the barn. They will want to clean up because company will come in a short while."

Karl walked over toward the barn. Ingrid led the way into the house. She unlocked the door and Matthew and James followed her inside.

James sneezed. "I feel as if I'm going back a hundred years."

"I don't think this house has been lived in for seventy-five years. A newer house was built around 1900. Then, only ten years ago, Johann had a new modern house, but he said, 'we'll paint it any color you want, but it won't be red.'"

"There's a lot of red around," said James. "Why is that?"

"The color comes from a product that's very plentiful. Red paint then is very cheap. When people were poor, that's the only color they had."

Ingrid pointed to an old table that had several table leaves. "This is where your father and his parents ate their meals. John Anderson's father would have been great-granduncle. I remember hearing about him."

"What did you hear?" asked James.

"He was a fine, hardworking man, but he died suddenly. I can't remember what happened."

"That I can tell you," said Matthew. "He took care of horses for the King of Sweden. He was kicked by a horse. They didn't get him to a doctor. Gangrene set in, and he died as a result."

"I had heard that but forgot.

Matthew pulled out a chair and sat down. "Are you saying that my father, who I call Pa, could have sat in this spot?"

"That's right. Uncle Anders would have sat at that end, and Aunt Anna would have sat at the end, nearest the kitchen. The youngest, your father, would probably have sat close to his mother."

Matthew stood, reverently looking at the spot. I can't believe I'm actually here, he thought to himself.

"Do you think Grandpa wanted to go back to his home?" asked James. "He never talked much about his home country."

"Pa always said he loved our farm. And that was home. He never thought of leaving."

"I think of the distance in those days. By ship he sailed to Philadelphia. Then, he took the train on west. I think some cousins had come to Minnesota."

Matthew fingered the back of the old wooden chair. It had been sat in many times.

"Come into this room. We have only a little furniture that was in the living room. Here's a small table that we brought back. And here's the old family Bible."

James opened the family Bible to the first pages where the birth records were written.

"Look, Dad, here is his name: Johann, born in 1863, now a hundred twenty-two years ago."

Matthew's fingers touched the page. He could say nothing. Tears came to his eyes as he thought of the hardships his father had endured. To leave home and family for a new country.

"Look!" exclaimed James excitedly. "Here's Grandpa's father. He died when he was only forty-five. The children were still young."

Matthew continued to recall what he had been told. "Grandma was left a widow. Her life was not easy."

"That's why people left for a new land."

Matthew found himself in a world of an earlier century. The few stories he had been told flooded his mind. This place was real. Pa had lived and struggled in this distant land. But even as he saw the upstairs rooms, the bedrooms, he thought of home. His real home was back in the hills of Minnesota, and he found himself lonesome for Ellen.

CHAPTER 14

July 1985

James felt like a celebrity that evening.

After the tour of the birthplace of his grandfather, James and Matthew were ushered into the home of Nels and Brigitta Johannson. This house didn't looked Swedish; it looked almost like any American home, hardly what he had expected.

Nels extended his hand. "Valkommen" he said in a distinctly Swedish way.

Brigitta curtsied, "Valkommen, ve are happy to meet you."

A youthful version of Nels stepped forward. "I'm Staffan. I'm afraid my parents don't understand English so I'll be your translator this evening. I've had twelve years of English in school, and I do rather well."

Brigitta looked up at her son, obviously quite proud of him.

"I do alright, too," added his sister, Linnea.

That introduction set the tone for the evening. Other family members arrived. Each one seemed to resemble a relative back home. The older members depended on Staffan to interpret. Many of the younger members spoke hesitantly in English.

James was overwhelmed by the people and the questions. "What do you do for a living?" became the common question. Or others began by saying, "So, you're a college professor. What do you teach them?"

It didn't seem to matter what he said, they listened politely and seemed taken in by their American relatives. Others kept asking about family. He didn't hesitate to tell them about his three children and the grandchildren. They seemed fascinated by the fact that Richard was an artist.

"You look exactly like Paul," translated Staffan from his father's words.

Several others added their agreement in Swedish.

He could hear other words that were words about him. It was a new sensation to be the center of attention and conversation. He had never experienced anything like this.

Around eight o'clock Brigitta brought out coffee and a generous lunch, consisting of various Swedish cookies and other delicacies. As people finished their lunches, the time seemed almost a signal to go home. This departure reminded him of childhood days when families would visit. By nine o'clock people left for home. After all, there would be the cows to milk early in the morning.

James saw his father yawn. "It's been a long day. I think it may be time for bed."

Johann and Staffan had quietly left the room, for they would rise early in the morning to do the milking and other chores.

Brigitta, followed by Linnea, led the way into the large living room.

Linnea brought out sheets and blankets and placed them on the two sofas. "We thought you would find this room comfortable."

Brigitta began to make up one bed while Linnea did the other.

James saw the piano and walked over to it. "I see you have a piano. Linnea, do you play?"

"A little, but not well."

James sat down on the piano bench and began to play one of the Swedish hymns, "Children of the Heavenly Father."

Brigitta exclaimed something in Swedish.

Linnea added, "We know that one. Let's sing it."

Brigitta found a Swedish hymn book and opened the book to the hymn. She set the book on the piano.

James played the introductory notes and the four began to sing in the language of their ancestors.

"Tlruggare kan ingen vara'
An Guds lilia barnaskara,
Stjaran ej pa himlafastet,
Fageln ej i kanda nastet."

Chapter 14

Four people were united in spirit in a language that James did not know. They were children of the Heavenly Father.

After Brigitta and Linnea left the room, James began to write in his journal. His father undressed slowly, lay down on the sofa and was soon sound asleep.

"I have the strangest feeling," wrote James. "I know there aren't spirits of the dead hovering around me, but I somehow feel the presence of family. I can envision my great-grandfather and great-grandmother here. I can almost see the seventeen-year-old boy walking the pathways outside.

"I experience the continuity of family. The same characteristics. Yet the differences. I saw Grandpa in one older gentleman in particular, and someone saw the distant cousin named Paul in me. The Lord works in many ways in creating a family.

"I am more convinced than ever that God has a plan for each of us. But I must pray for understanding of what that plan is. What is his plan for me at this time in my life? Does He want me to be a writer and really pursue this dream? Doesn't he put these dreams in a man's heart for a reason? It's almost as if I'm seeing a puzzle, and I'm not quite sure how it comes together."

James looked over at his father. "Dad, what a wonderful experience this is to get to know you as both a father and as a man. I know my inclinations are more like Mother's, but now I feel closer to you than ever before. Thank you, Lord, for this opportunity.

"And now, Lord, guide me through this puzzling present time into a future I do not know."

Matthew wakened early the next morning. Light streamed through the windows though it was not yet five o'clock. In this country to the north, the days were long and the nights were short. He couldn't help wondering what winter would be like during the long hours of darkness.

He looked across to his son. James was sound asleep. The last Matthew remembered was the light of a small lamp and James busy writing in his journal. James must have written late into the night. Matthew quietly dressed himself and went to the bathroom and readied himself for the day.

He tiptoed through the kitchen. Sounds from the barn told him that Johann and Steffan were feeding the cattle and milking the cows. Modern machines no doubt replaced the hand milking that Pa had done one hundred years ago.

Matthew walked slowly toward the barn. He took out his camera and snapped a picture of the stone foundation, the same foundation that had been there a hundred years ago. He remembered the pictures of Pa as a young man. All at once Pa was beside him; the young mature man who had been his father for so many years. Then Pa became a seventeen-year old trudging to the barn, perhaps thinking or dreaming about coming to a new land.

Perhaps the spirit of a father remains with his son, at least in the son's mind and spirit. Pa seemed to be speaking to him. "Matthew, my son, you are now old and full of years. The Lord is with you. The Lord will guide and protect you through all the days of your life. Be strong and of good courage."

Matthew looked up at the pine trees that towered above him. This forest had been here one hundred years ago. Something about the land lasted forever. Perhaps the land and this path and this very place reminded him that God Almighty was from everlasting to everlasting.

For some reason, Matthew felt he wanted to kneel to pray. He looked above at the light streaming through openings in the pine forest. The light reflected the face of God shining upon him.

"Dear Lord," he spoke aloud. "You've fulfilled a dream that I would somehow go to Sweden and see the land of Pa and my ancestors. I have a feeling I can't quite describe—perhaps James could. Pa, I feel so close to you."

For a moment, a hand seemed to touch his shoulder. He looked around, and there was no one. "Lord, I feel your Hand on my shoulder. I know I am old, but you are strengthening me. I can go on and face whatever I need to face."

He wanted this feeling and these moments to last forever. He looked at his watch. Time had passed without his realizing it. Ten minutes of eight. Breakfast would be ready, promptly at eight.

Life and Swedish farm ways invited him back to his family. His new Swedish family.

"I never knew I had so many Swedish relatives," James said to Staffan on the way to town and the church.

"They all want to meet you."

"Will the church be open? I'd like to go inside. Grandpa would have been baptized and confirmed in that very place."

Chapter 14

Matthew, sitting in the back seat, remained quiet. James looked back to his father and knew some of what he must be feeling.

Staffan stopped the car in front of the church. "The church has a long history. The first church was built somewhere in the 1300s."

James quickly got out of the car. "Was our family here then? That would mean a long history."

"You'll have to ask someone who knows more. This afternoon at Margarite Johansson's, you'll meet Andrew Johansson, her brother. He really knows history."

Matthew walked over to a tombstone marked with the Johannson name. "Is this a relative?" he asked.

"That's my great-grandfather. We still keep up his grave. Otherwise, the family usually buries someone in that spot. That happens after fifty years."

"I'm overwhelmed by all these family members," said James.

"He would probably be my granduncle." Matthew knelt before the tombstone. "I have the strangest feeling."

James wanted to express what his father must be feeling. "We're in the presence of history. Somehow we feel very close to the relatives who have lived before us."

Staffan walked toward the church door. "I guess I don't feel that way, but I live here. I'm here all the time, though I don't go to church the way I used to."

James wanted to say something, but he thought it better not to.

Matthew, however, didn't hesitate. "What's important is that you know the Lord and have that relationship with him."

"I'm pretty much involved in technical school. I'll think about that later."

"Don't forget," said Matthew.

Staffan opened the church door. James and Matthew followed close behind.

In the narthex, James saw the pictures of an earlier church and the way the present building had changed through the years. Below the pictures, he read bits and pieces of history. Here was history that went back hundreds of years.

James and his father stood silently looking at the pictures and the candles that occupied one corner. This did not in any way resemble the country churches in the Lake View area. As he thought of the centuries of history, he realized that this church had come out of a different tradition.

"Everything is so white," observed James. "It seems so clean and good."

He placed his hands on the white pews and looked up at the large picture above the altar. Jesus stood preaching to the crowds of people below. He stood before the pulpit that stood high above the sanctuary. He couldn't help imagining a somber pastor intoning the words of the Gospel in Swedish.

James looked back and saw the pipes of the organ. "I see the organ is up in the balcony. I'd like to take a look at that."

"I think you should play the organ." said Staffan. "I think it's open. Not too many people come in this church even on Sunday."

"That's a shame," said Matthew. "Beautiful church building and people don't come. It is most sad that people forget about God."

James hurried up the steps to the balcony and found the on switch for the organ. He looked at the stops and selected several. Slowly and quietly, he began to play and then sing.

"O Lord my God, when I in awesome wonder
Consider all the worlds Thy Hands have made.
I see the stars, I hear Thy rolling thunder,
Thy power throughout the universe displayed."

He pulled out some more stops and pedaled to the full volume and sang the words.

"Then sings my soul, my Savior God to Thee.
How great Thou art; how great Thou art.
Then sings my soul, my Savior God to Thee,
How great Thou art, how great Thou art."

James continued to play and slowly moved into some other favorite hymns. At the same time, he sensed that perhaps a family member may have sat at this organ, playing hymns of worship. It seemed he could hear and see family members sitting below in the sanctuary, singing these hymns.

He stopped playing. Staffan and his father applauded. "Play more."

An old hymn came to mind, and he began playing "Take the Name of Jesus with you." What a message this contained. A feeling of worshipful reverence came over him. A century ago, his family faced many struggles. They must have been facing the same problems and struggles every man and woman faces.

Once more he stopped playing. Complete silence greeted him.

"I thought I was at a church service," said Staffan.

136

Chapter 14

Matthew placed his hand on James's shoulder. "I felt I was worshipping with Pa and many of our relatives."

James turned off the organ and looked below at the sanctuary. He left the organ and went down to the sanctuary. Once more he marveled at the white around him and the artistry of the pulpit. The three men all seemed to need those moments of quiet for reverent meditation.

They walked through the narthex and entered the outdoors with the bright sun accenting the green of the country around them.

"Margarite Johannson is expecting us at any time. Her brother, a teacher, is eager to meet both of you. He is from Stockholm."

"I continue to be amazed," said James. "So much is happening. And I can't get over the many Swedish relatives that seem like old friends soon after we meet them."

"Blood is thick," said his father. "That is true even thousands of miles away."

James looked around at the countryside once more. For a moment he thought he was back on the farm in Minnesota. How similar the two places were! For a moment he sensed hundreds of family members, past and present, milling around on this very spot. He stood on sacred ground. He wanted this moment to last. But it was time to move on.

As Matthew left the church, he experienced a need to be silent and reflect. He walked among the tombstones and thought of Pa and his father buried somewhere in this very place. One hundred years ago, these ancestors would have been living and loving and going about the routines of the day.

"Pa," he whispered aloud, "I wish you were here. A man always needs a father. And I need my Heavenly Father. But I need this earthly family."

"Dad," called James, "is something wrong?"

"No, I think everything's right."

"Cousin Margarite and her brother are expecting us."

"Andrew Johannsson is eager to meet you," added Staffan.

"I'm reminded of some words of Scripture. 'Lord, teach us to number our days that we may gain a heart of wisdom.' I can't help thinking how one generation passes away, and another takes over. My generation is mostly gone. My days are numbered."

"Dad, we want you around for a long time."

Matthew held his hand over his heart. He sometimes had that hint of pain. "I don't think so. I've already outlived Pa by quite a few years."

James and Staffan remained silent.

"I didn't want to put a damper on these happy occasions, but I am sure that I will never see these people again."

Staffan walked over and opened the car door. "I'm coming to America someday, and then I can meet all of my American family."

James spoke the very words that Matthew was thinking. "I feel as if I've known these Swedish family members for years, not just a few days."

Matthew couldn't quite find the words he wanted to say. "We're family." That was all he could say.

Staffan drove them to a large home at the edge of town. He began to tell them about Margarite. "Margarite married well. She and her husband inherited the family home. He died, but she continued to live there by herself. In some ways, the house is a museum of family history. She's quite a lady, and I know you'll like her brother."

They made their way up to the front door. The house reminded Matthew of some of the large old farm homes. As they entered, Matthew immediately felt at home.

Margarite must have been in her late sixties, tall with slightly graying hair. There was a strength about her that reminded him of his sister, Victoria. In fact, they looked a little bit alike.

"Velcomen. Welcome, my American cousins." She extended her hand.

"Hello," stuttered Matthew. "I'm happy to meet you.'

In the next moment, he stood, stunned and unbelieving. There stood Andrew Johannson. He thought in that instant that he was seeing himself in a mirror.

Matthew walked forward to meet his cousin. "Hello, Andrew. I can't help staring, I think we look alike."

"You look more alike than many twins do," James said.

The conversation was cut short with more relatives arriving. The comment made again and again was "You look so much alike" or "You could be taken for twins."

Matthew found himself drawn to Andrew. There was something about him, perhaps the similar appearance, which made him want to get to know this relative. Andrew seemed drawn to Matthew as well.

Several hours later, after a meal and lunch, the relatives left one by one or family by family. Soon, only Matthew and James and Staffan remained with Margarite and Andrew.

"Could you stay into the evening?" asked Andrew. "I'd like to talk. I'd like to tell some of what I've been finding in family history. And I'd just like to get to know you better."

Staffan stood up to leave, "James and I can go back home. I'll drive over and get you later."

Andrew quickly spoke. "I'll see that Matthew gets home."

Matthew agreed. He could see that James wanted to hear the family history part, but he sensed this man had more serious matters on his mind.

They said their goodbyes.

"I'll leave you two men alone to talk. I need to clean up in the kitchen."

The men began a talk that went in many directions. They moved into the living room where Andrew guided Matthew to the most comfortable chair.

"I'm an old man who needs to talk," began Andrew. "I guess you knew my wife died, and I'm alone—except for my sister. My wife was everything to me. I came home to her each night from teaching. Then, when I retired, we travelled and enjoyed life to its fullest."

"I think I understand a little. My wife Ellen is everything to me. I don't know what I'd do without her. Anyhow, I'll probably die first."

Andrew continued. "Matthew, I guess I felt I knew you before I met you. I read the letters James wrote to Ingrid. I saw your picture, and James wrote so much about you and your wife."

"I'm afraid I didn't hear about you until the other day."

"I can understand." Andrew paused, groping for words. "I'm usually not at a loss for words. After all, I am a teacher of language, and I do much talking. Right now, I don't quite know where to begin."

"You said you uncovered family history."

"Yes, and that's where I should begin. Again, I have to confess that I know a little about your story. Ingrid said that you had been on the family farm and farmed with your father."

Matthew nodded.

"And your older brother managed to get ownership of the farm, so you moved. I can understand that was very painful."

Matthew sighed and looked away. "When P.J., my brother, stole the farm from me, it almost killed me. The anger and hurt and stress brought me to death's door."

"I understand you had one of those experiences when you were at death's door."

Matthew had recalled many times that life-changing experience. "Yes, I knew I was dying. I was leaving my body. For a moment, I saw each member of my family—including a sister who had died. I saw the farm that I loved. For a while I was summoned to go forward, but then something stopped me. I heard a voice saying, 'Go back. You have a purpose back there. Your family needs you. You have more work to do.'"

"Who said those words to you?"

"I know it was the Lord, Jesus, telling me I had a purpose in life. That I had to go back—that I had to go on. My life changed after that. I had a new relationship with Jesus. I had a reason to go on."

Andrew looked away. Matthew thought he saw tears in his cousin's eyes.

"I've never been a religious man. I went to the state church for confirmation and education. It never meant that much to me. I thought it was an interesting part of history, but I didn't sense much more. But recently I've come across some books, and I've come across something about the sins of the fathers being visited upon the children."

"Yes, that's right out of Scripture."

"I've come across a bit of family history that seems to relate. I found this because I came across an old diary. I'm not quite sure how many greats are in this, but my—or our great-great-grandfather and great-great granduncle had such a dispute. In this case, a younger brother took advantage of the older brother. In some ways it was like the Esau and Jacob story in the Bible. All I know is that he managed this by some clever legal maneuvering."

"That's what P.J. did. The farm was signed over to him temporarily for a good reason. It was supposed to be signed back to my father, but it never was."

"Anyhow, then our great-grandfather came and bought the Linden farm. But, there's another part to the story. These are distant cousins to us. Anyhow, two brothers established a successful family business north of here. Once more one brother got the best of the other. It's like the Esau and Jacob story repeating itself again and again."

Matthew thought a minute. "I guess that only proves again and again that man is sinful. And we are all in need of the Savior."

"This got me thinking. Somehow I felt that you might be a person I could talk with."

"But," said Matthew, "I'm not educated. I didn't even finish eighth grade. And you're educated as a professor. What could I tell you?"

"I think there's much you could tell me. You have something that I don't have, despite my university education."

"James or others could talk better than I. You should talk with them."

"Let me explain. My wife found what you have. About two years ago, she got involved in a women's Bible study. She became a different person—much happier and an even more caring wife. Then, she discovered cancer, and within a month she was gone. But during that month, she showed such strength—far beyond anything in her life before. When I was with her, it was as if a Presence was there also."

"She knew the Lord."

"I know the Bible quite well, but I don't have that faith. I may know too much because I'm just plainly skeptical."

Matthew wanted to say the right words. "You know you need Him. That's the first step."

"But I don't have the feelings my wife had these last years."

Matthew felt uneasy. He didn't want to offend this learned man. They continued to talk during the next hours, but none of Matthew's words brought the feeling or sense that Andrew wanted.

"Why don't you get out your Bible and read the Gospel of John. The first three chapters, but possibly more. Do that tonight."

"I'll do that. I'm sorry I kept you up so late. You know, Matthew, I'd really like to come to America. I think I need a trip like that."

"By all means, come. That would be great."

Matthew realized that he had not only met a cousin but had found a new friend.

CHAPTER 15

J ames helped Ingrid as she made up the sofa beds in the living room. He had come to look on her as a cousin and friend. Even though there were language difficulties, a kinship existed.

"Dad and I could have made up the beds ourselves."

She nodded. In her limited English, she said, "I know how."

James smiled. "Thank you. Good night."

She spoke a Swedish goodnight. Then she added, "Good night."

James took out his journal and began to write. He reviewed first the events of the day and then began to reflect on his father and on life in general.

"I'm amazed at Dad. This trip has made him come alive. He seems to relate to his cousins as if they're old friends. Even those who cannot speak English appreciate and communicate in his somewhat forgotten old Swedish.

"If for no other reason, this trip to Sweden has enabled me to know Dad better. I think I understand him in a different way. We've become not just father and son, but two friends on a journey of life, discovering new truths about life."

The door opened. "James, I thought you'd be in bed."

"You must have had a long visit with Andrew."

"You know, Son, at first I wondered if there was any good reason for me to go to Sweden. Now, I realize God had a purpose for me to come here."

"What do you mean?"

"Andrew."

"You look almost like twins."

"Andrew's alone, and he's searching. I know what that means. He's searching for God. And I can point the way."

"He seems like a remarkable man. I'd like to get to know him. After all, we've both been college professors. I'd like to learn of his experiences."

His father began undressing. "It's strange he wanted to talk with me. He would have more in common with you."

"But, Dad, you seemed to understand what he was facing. I couldn't have gotten him to open up as you did. You were supposed to be here."

His father got into the sofa-bed. "I'm tired, but my mind keeps mulling over the happenings of these last days. I feel as if I have had a lifetime of experiences in just a few days."

"Dad!' exclaimed James. "You're giving me ideas for writing. I'd like to tell a story of a visit like this and how a lifetime comes together in such a visit."

"Son, you know that's the way my conversation went. I heard of Andrew's life from beginning up to now. And I told my story from beginning up to now. He seemed to understand my situation with P.J. He realized what I had gone through. He told me of family situations with brothers just like that. In fact, the same things happened in one generation after another."

"People make the same mistakes." He stopped and thought and added, "They sin in much the same way."

His father lay back. "I'm tired. Very tired."

In a matter of a minute or two, James heard the regular breathing of his father, a sign this tired man who was old and full of years was fast asleep.

He added the final words in his journal. "Thank you, Lord, for Dad. Thank you for letting me get to know him better. Thank you for giving me a godly father. I think I'm a good father to my daughters, but can I become a good father to my own son, Richard?"

He turned off the light, but sleep eluded him.

—◦◦◦◦◦—

Matthew slept soundly that night, but he had strange dreams throughout the sleeping hours. P.J., who had often been a part of nightmares, appeared in a new way. This time cousin Andrew was there, defending him. P.J. first appeared as his childhood tormentor who locked him in the attic. Andrew appeared and saved him.

Other dreams filled the night. Many others peopled those dreams, but Andrew always seemed to appear.

He awakened with light streaming in. James must have gotten up, dressed, and left. He took out his watch. It was after ten o'clock. They were supposed to board a train for Stockholm, stay in a hotel that night, and then fly out early in the morning.

Matthew rubbed his eyes and slowly began to dress. He hurried into the bathroom and took care of the morning cleaning up tasks. Still, no one was around. He had missed breakfast.

He returned to pack his suitcase. James's suitcase was all set. But why had they let him sleep this late? They must have something up their sleeves.

James entered in whirlwind fashion. "We have a surprise!"

Andrew followed close behind. "We've made some changes for you. I'm driving you to Copenhagen. You won't have to take that long train ride. I'll stay with you. We have a hotel in Copenhagen. Then, in the morning at a more reasonable hour you'll fly to the United States."

"How did you manage this?" asked Matthew.

"Good morning, cousin," Andrew extended his hand. "I guess I forgot my manners. I entered rather abruptly."

Matthew felt a special warmth as he grasped Andrew's hand. "Good morning."

"I should explain," began James. "Andrew called early this morning and then did a bit of checking. We found new connections and were able to change the location of the flight. This will be much easier. Before you know it, we'll be in the Minneapolis-St. Paul airport."

"And," said Andrew, "I've made some plans of my own. That's the other surprise. I'm making a trip to Minnesota in September. That is your prettiest time of the year."

"I was hoping this wasn't the last time I would see you."

"I'm planning on much travelling. We have more visiting to do in our lifetimes."

'Remember, I'm eighty-five years old. I have only so much time left."

"We'll make the most of it then."

Matthew remembered a favorite Scripture and spoke the words. "Lord, teach us to number our days that we may have a heart of wisdom."

"Matthew, my cousin, you do indeed have a heart of wisdom."

"Dad," spoke up James. "You must be starved. You were sleeping so soundly I couldn't wake you for breakfast."

"I suppose I needed the sleep."

A chorus of voices in the next room startled Matthew.

"We're having lunch in a few minutes," said James. "Our Swedish relatives are going to say goodbye in the Swedish style."

The Swedish style meant strong coffee and all kinds of pastries and other good things. The next hours brought many of the same people back. Staffan could not be there for he had to return to his job. However, the other people he had met were there.

In the hours that followed, Matthew visited with those many Swedish relatives. As he looked in their faces, he felt he was seeing a different version of the American relatives. He saw in their faces the looks of people who had long since passed from the earth. He thought of Aunt Clara, his mother's older sister. One of the older women looked exactly like her.

What was there about this strange family connection? People he had never before seen appeared, and they were exactly like people who had lived years ago, thousands of miles away. In a sense the whole human race was a family. He felt a strange kind of connection he could not explain.

For the next moments, he experienced being in this world thousands of miles from Lake View and Oak Ridge. He was present there as if in a dream. But this was very real. Or would he wake up in a few minutes?

Swedish family members said goodbye in their restrained Scandinavian ways. However, Ingrid and Brigitta and Margarite all had tears in their eyes.

Margarite moved toward Matthew and warmly embraced him. "Matthew Anderson, you don't know how glad I am that you came. You have become a special friend to my brother."

"We look alike and are alike in many ways."

"Andrew needed someone like you. And maybe someday I will come to America."

"I look forward to that. I hope I'm still around."

Andrew loaded the suitcases into his car. The relatives crowded around, all seemed to want to say goodbye. Matthew was never good at saying goodbye. This goodbye was harder because in reality, he would never see these people again.

In that moment he realized how Pa must have felt. Pa left family here in Sweden, knowing that he would never again see them in this life. He couldn't help wondering how many of them he would see in his eternal home.

Matthew felt a kind of relief as they drove away, soon entering the city of Malmo, then getting on the hydrofoil and sailing on to Copenhagen. He kept looking back toward Sweden as they sailed toward Denmark.

"Dad, what are you thinking?" asked James.

"I have the strangest feeling. I've seen Pa's home. I felt as if I were walking on sacred ground. And I feel sad because as the poem says, 'I shall not pass this way again.'"

"Dad, it's very likely that I shall not pass this way, either."

As Andrew drove into the city, he observed. "I would hope you will come this way again. But anyhow, I shall see you in your country. I believe I have much to learn from my American relatives."

"That will be great for us to have you," said James.

Matthew wanted to speak what he really felt, but words would not come. He couldn't help feeling that this homeland of his father and the rest of his family was a kind of holy land. Many people traveled to Israel, the Holy Land. But he had found his special place of his ancestors. In a sense he felt the presence of the hundreds, perhaps thousands of relatives. Was this a foretaste of heaven where he would meet Pa and Ma and many others?

Life is like a vapor, he thought. Grass withers and fades. But God is forever. The Word of the Lord is forever.

Those were his thoughts as he and James and Andrew entered the hotel. This was a foreign land. For a short while, he had felt at home in Sweden, but now he would travel toward Lake View and Oak Ridge. But he couldn't help thinking how brief life was. It seemed only a short while ago that he was a young man with Ellen by his side and children playing in the yard.

"Time, like an ever rolling stream, bears all her sons away." That is life.

He wanted to express these thoughts, but words would not come.

"Matthew, you're so quiet. Is something wrong?" asked Andrew.

"Life has been good. Life is good. God is good."

———◦∞◦———

James wondered what his father was thinking. He guessed at some thoughts because he must have had the same feelings. Such a strong connection existed with people they had met and known for only a few days. There was a connection with a country.

That evening, Andrew gave him and his father a tour of Copenhagen. What a strange feeling he had as he looked at places that were hundreds of years old. He had a sense of going back in history—as if he were actually living a hundred or more years ago.

He thought of some of the poets he had taught. A.E. Housemen lamented the brevity of life. He thought of Housemen's fascination with the cherry blooms, and at twenty he lamented the fact that he had only fifty more years to enjoy the beauty.

"Life is short," James wrote in his journal later that night. "I am sixty-one years old. I could have quite a few years left to fulfill some of my dreams. Or my life could be cut short. What do I do with this time on earth? I am now retired from a profession I loved. I could sit back and just have a good time. But I want something more. I want to tell stories. I want to write of things that are most important in life."

He heard the steady breathing of his father as he slept. Andrew sat quietly reading. Andrew and he should have much in common, but it was his father that Andrew wanted to talk with. It was perhaps a friend his father needed.

James continued to write. "I am missing my good friend, Mark Goodman. Why did Mark have to die? We could have spent time together in retirement. We've had a lifetime of experiences. Why am I missing him right now? But, I come up with another cliché, so bad in writing. Life must go on. In one sense, I can't dwell on the past."

He put his pen down and sat for several minutes. His mind wandered several places. He thought of getting home to Ruth. Moving would take up much of their time during the next weeks. He would be putting behind him a way of life. Then, his mind moved to Richard. Why couldn't he have a close and loving relationship with his son?

Once more, he began to write. "I miss Mark. I miss my contact with students. I mentored many who are now fine English teachers—or working in another area. However, if I'm honest, I was not a good father to Richard. I was a father to many students, but I never understood Richard. I was always too busy."

His nephew walked into his mind. Jeffrey Grant, what are you up to now? What have you been up to while I've been away? I fear that you have some claim to land that should not be yours. What will I face when I return home?

Andrew interrupted thoughts and writing. "We need to be up early tomorrow in order to get to the airport."

"It's time to turn off these lights and try to sleep. I guess I never sleep well the night before a big trip like this."

"You can sleep on the plane."

Chapter 15

The two men turned out their lights. James got into bed, but his mind travelled in many directions. He must have dreamed one of his father's dreams. When he wakened abruptly early in the morning, he remembered only snatches of the dream. But he had a premonition of danger.

Andrew drove them to the airport. Andrew took care of so many matters with the suitcases and showing them exactly where to go. What a kind and wonderful man Andrew was! It would be a pleasure to have him visit in a few months.

Matthew embraced his distant cousin as they were ready to board the plane. James saw tears in the eyes of both men. In only a few days, a bond had grown between them.

As the plane gained altitude, James felt his ears close up in pain. As he looked aside to his father, he noticed Matthew's hand over his heart.

He turned to him. "Dad, is something wrong? Do you have pain?"

"No, not really."

James looked again into his father's face. "Dad, you look pale. Are you sure you're all right?"

"You're getting to be a worry-wart about me. Just like your mother."

James had heard part of that comment before. He was very much like his mother in so many ways.

"I think you need to make an appointment with the doctor when we get back home."

"We'll see."

The flight was uneventful, like many other flights he had been on. James tried to read, but there were various interruptions—people getting up, a breakfast and later a lunch.

As the plane approached New York City, the captain announced. "If you look to your left, you'll see the skyline and the Statue of Liberty. We are entering the United States."

James felt an unexpected sense of excitement. This was his country. He was home.

Someone a few rows from him began to sing, "God Bless America." He and many others joined in until there seemed to be a full choir.

Yes, this was home. He hadn't realized how much he had missed Ruth and the whole family. He had visited the country of his ancestors, but America was home.

There was safety at home, but the peaceful life of family could be threatened.

CHAPTER 16

Airports both fascinated and frightened Ellen. She felt claustrophobic in crowds. People shouldn't be packed together this way. But she was eager to see Matthew for she had never dreamed how much she would miss him.

Johnie guided her toward a seat. "Mother, you look troubled. What's wrong?"

"I can't help thinking about Michael. I wasn't supposed to hear it, but I did. He and Elise were talking that the bank—or rather Jeffrey—had claim on the farm and could foreclose."

"Mother, you don't know for sure. You heard only snatches of conversation."

"I may not see so well, but my hearing is very good."

"You are not a worrier by nature. How come you seem to be so worried or concerned about something that may not even be true?"

"Son, even though we're not living on the place, your father loves it almost as his own. We struggled to make that farm our home. We struggled to make ends meet. We struggled on that farm to give you children a start in life. That farm is family to him."

"I suppose I understand. I always think of both the home place that belonged to Grandpa and Grandma and the place where we all lived later as home. Somehow I hoped there would always be family there."

"Matthew has done so well these last years. I'm amazed at the way his health has turned around. When I think back to that terrible ulcer attack when he almost died, I have to believe the Lord was part of that healing."

"I was only twelve years old. I was angry at God when I thought Dad was going to die. I couldn't understand how God, who is good, could permit that to happen."

"Those were difficult times, but good came out of it. Your dad learned he had to change and forgive P.J. for taking the ownership of the home farm. I had to learn to forgive him, too. Perhaps your father had an easier time."

"I don't remember that part. I was excited about moving to a bigger house and a much nicer barn. We were better off."

"Yes, and that farm was really our farm. During those early years when we lived on the home place, it always seemed other people had claim on it."

Ellen saw a change come over Johnie. "Excuse me. I'll check if the plane is late and look around a bit. Will you be all right here?"

"I'll be fine. I'll be like your father and take up people watching."

Ellen began to do her people watching. She observed a young mother with two small children, no doubt waiting for her husband. Then, she became aware of a woman who seemed to be staring at her. The woman looked to be about Johnie's age, trim and attractive, wearing a dress that made her look very much a refined lady.

Ellen's eyes scanned the area, looking for Johnie to return. All at once the woman walked toward her.

"I'm sorry to intrude," she said, "but was the gentleman who was here a few minutes ago your son?"

Ellen sensed a sad urgency in the woman's manner. "Yes, he's my second son."

"He's a pastor in Riverton, isn't he? And he has a brother who is a college professor."

"That's right. I'm Ellen Anderson. We're meeting my husband and my other son, the college professor."

"I hope you won't consider me too forward, but you looked like a woman who would understand my concern."

Ellen pointed to the empty seat. "Why don't you sit down and tell me."

The woman proceeded to talk. "I've heard wonderful things about Pastor John Anderson. He has a real heart for missions."

"He's worked with missions in Africa, but he also has an interest in Eastern Europe if that area of the world opens. His church is working with him."

Chapter 16

"I know he must be extremely busy, but I was wondering if you might approach him about visiting my son. He's been sent to what they used to call the reformatory, but now it's the state correctional institution. He's really not such a bad boy, but he fell in with the bad crowd."

Ellen couldn't help thinking of how Matthew had helped his nephew Larry and how Larry had in turn done prison work and prison ministry. "He'll be back in a few minutes. I'm sure he would be willing to help—to visit him."

"I'll just be leaving now. Oh, his name is Jake. Jake Morgan."

"No, why don't you stay and meet Johnie. You can tell him more."

"No, Mrs. Anderson, I don't want to bother you or him anymore. Besides, I've never felt comfortable around ministers. You see, I've made a few mistakes. I wasn't the best mother. But, please, I'm hoping someone will help my poor boy."

Ellen could see the woman was trembling. "Yes, I'll talk to Johnie. He and some of the church members do Bible studies in the prison."

The woman started to leave. "Thank you. My boy needs help."

Right behind her stood Johnie. "Who needs help?"

Her eyes filled with tears, she spoke. "I'm sorry I shouldn't have bothered you."

Johnie placed his arm on her shoulder and guided her back to the chair. "If someone needs help, you aren't bothering my mother or anyone else. What seems to be the problem?"

The woman reluctantly sat down.

Ellen grasped the woman's hand. "You're trembling, my dear. And you don't look well."

"I've been having treatments for cancer, and sometimes I don't do well. I'm picking up my sister. She's coming to stay with me for a while."

"Where are you living?" asked Johnie.

"I live in one of those small, small towns northwest of Riverton."

Ellen continued to hold the woman's hand in order to calm her. "Tell Johnie about the problem. He might be able to help."

The woman began to talk. "I'm sorry, I haven't even introduced myself. I'm Laura Morgan."

Johnie shook her hand. "I'm glad to meet you. You have a beautiful name. My first wife was named Laura. Though I'm happily re-married, I still love Laura and think of her."

"I'm sorry. You seem to be a man who really cares about people"

"I'm Johnie Anderson. Or many people think of me as Pastor John Anderson."

"I haven't led the best life, but I won't bother you with that. I'm trying to make changes. We've been poor. It's my son. That's the problem. He's been a good boy, determined to get away from being poor. He went away to the university. He started out doing well. Then, he got involved with the bad crowd because he was trying to make money to pay for school."

She wiped her eyes and cleared her throat.

"Take your time," said Johnie.

"I don't know all the details. There were drugs involved. There was a holdup and a man was shot. Jake's fingerprints were on the gun. He got the bulk of the blame. And now he's in that reformatory."

"Our church does have a Bible study in the correctional facility, and I sometimes teach. I could visit the young man."

"Oh, Pastor that would make a difference. His father was never around. He needs a man in his life, a man who might take some personal interest."

"Well, Mrs. Morgan, I'll see what I can do when I get back to town."

"Thank you. I don't know how to thank you."

"Is your plane coming in soon?"

Mrs. Morgan got up. "Yes, it's here. I see my sister."

She turned to Johnie and then to Ellen. "Ellen, thanks for helping me." With those words she hurried away.

Johnie took the empty seat beside his mother. "The plane's late—at least a half hour. You never know who you meet at an airport. Sometimes, I think God orchestrates certain meetings to take place. That may have been the case with Laura Morgan."

"She made us forget about our other concerns."

They sat, reading and visiting, for another forty-five minutes. Then people began to mill about. The plane had arrived.

Ellen stood. "Look! People are coming, but I don't see Matthew."

"He'll be coming any minute."

She waited. Straining to find Matthew in the departing passengers, she saw him. "There he is!" she exclaimed. "But he's limping."

"He's just tired from the plane rides. He's been sitting too long."

Ellen waved, and both James and Matthew saw her. "They are home! Finally home."

Matthew limped toward her. Ellen rushed through the crowd in a manner uncharacteristic of her reserved nature.

"Darling," said Matthew. "I've missed you. I'm glad I'm home."

"Did you have a good trip? But I see you're limping."

154

"I took a little fall, and I sat cramped on the plane."

Matthew embraced her, and she kissed him.

"I'm so relieved you're home."

"Hi, Mom," said James, as he threw his arms around her.

The moments that followed involved confusion and picking up luggage. All Ellen wanted to do was get back home.

Matthew expressed her very thoughts. "I can't wait to be home get out in the garden and get my hands dirty."

—◦◦◦◦◦—

The minute James was alone with Johnie, he knew something was wrong.

"Something's wrong, isn't it?" asked James.

"Why bother yourself about it tonight. There's plenty of time when you get back to Lake View."

"Brother, I want to know tonight. Does Ruth know? I'll find out from her."

"She doesn't. And I'm afraid Mom and I don't know the full story."

"Fire away. Otherwise I'll imagine the worst scenario."

Johnie stopped the car in front of the house. "It's this way. Michael's apparently mortgaged the farm. He hasn't been making payments on time. Jeffrey apparently has claim and could foreclose."

"I was afraid of something like that. Michael has always been a free spender. He had those good jobs as a mechanic and lots of money to spend."

"We don't know if this is going to happen quickly or if there's time."

James got out of the car. "I'm afraid this will devastate Dad. He felt so happy that Michael was buying and taking over his farm."

"I hope it doesn't trigger some of those old problems. Jeffrey Grant has become another Uncle P.J. And P.J. could be kind and generous, but he could also destroy."

"History has a way of repeating itself."

Johnie carried his suitcase to the door. "Put it in the back of your mind. There's time to deal with it tomorrow. 'Sufficient for the day is the evil or trouble thereof.'" With those words he waved good night over his shoulder and drove away.

Ruth greeted James at the door. "Welcome home—to a home in a mess."

James set down the suitcase and opened his arms. "That was certainly a sudden sale."

He looked down at Ruth as he held her in his arms.

"I've missed you, but I've never been so busy."

"I can see that—boxes all over. And even our favorite pictures off the wall. Everything seems to be moving so fast."

"I've worked hard to get it ready. I had some help so that most of the work is done."

"We're already used to our lake home. And we'll get used to an apartment here. But the apartment will be temporary. Anyway, you used to say that wherever family is, that is home. You're here, and I know that I'm home."

"Come, take a look around. I think you'll see everything's organized."

They walked through the rooms and downstairs. "Ruth, you've done a great job."

Ruth smiled. "How would you like a cup of hot milk or cocoa milk in the family tradition?"

"Hot milk," he said. "That has such a soothing effect."

He looked around and yawned. The long journey had brought him home. But there would be new problems and an adjustment to a whole new way of life. He didn't really want retirement. He was looking forward to a new challenge.

"It feels good to be home," Matthew mused. "It was a great trip and wonderful to meet Swedish relatives. But there's no place like home."

Johnie began to hum a tune and then said the words. "'Mid pleasures and palaces, though we may roam. Be it ever so humble, there's no place like home.' And there's no place like home at the home farm."

They sat down at that table. Ellen poured the coffee and turned to Johnie. "You ask the blessing. We mustn't forget to be thankful."

Matthew bowed his head. How thankful he was to be sitting right here at home.

"Almighty God," began Johnie. "We come before you in thanksgiving for Dad and James's safe return home. We thank you for the blessings of the trip and for the chance to get to know relatives who live far away in another country.

"And, now, Lord, we thank you for bringing us all to this home. We thank you for family, and I thank you now especially for Mom and Dad.

156

Bless our fellowship. Thank you for this food, and bless it to our bodies. In Jesus' Name. Amen."

Johnie and Ellen tried to keep the conversation moving. Matthew sensed they were trying to divert his attention from a problem.

"Dad, I'm going to stick around until tomorrow. I'd be happy to help you in the garden and even mow the lawn."

"I can do that myself. I haven't done good hard work for almost three weeks. I want to get outside and do something. And I usually help Michael with some of their garden. And James hasn't really taken care of his garden at their lake home."

Ellen's concern became evident. "Matthew, dear, I don't want you over-doing. You have to take care of yourself."

"Ellen, my dear wife, good hard work never hurt anyone. My health is better when I'm outside doing something."

Johnie smiled. "Mom, you'll never change him. But you have so much to do. I can help."

Matthew took up his coffee cup thoughtfully and then spoke. "Yes, Johnie, we'll work together. But now I think something's been going on, and you're trying to keep me from finding out."

Johnie and Ellen looked at one another.

"Have you been over to Michael's?" Matthew asked.

Ellen hesitantly answered. "He's been keeping to himself."

Matthew grunted. "And you think I don't know. I've been keeping this from you. Michael's been making stupid decisions for years. And everything's catching up with him. I knew that would come sooner or later. You can't stop it."

"Dad, we didn't think you knew."

"I know much more than you think."

"Has anything happened while I've been gone?"

Johnie seemed to be measuring his words. "We've been concerned about Michael. I'm afraid there have been rumors about Jeff and the bank."

Matthew sighed. "I'm having a hard time, but it's that time in my life. I have to let go of the precious farm."

"You surprise us, Dad."

"This part of life means letting go."

CHAPTER 17

August 1985

R uth's words still echoed in James's ears. "I'm off once again to get ready to teach a whole batch of new fifth graders. This is your special day: your first real day of retirement from teaching. And your first day of serious writing. I want to say, 'God bless you.'"

Ruth had returned to their new apartment in Riverton. James had remained in their new lake home in the country. Oak Ridge had been the home of his childhood. It was now the home of his retirement. He wasn't sure it felt like home—without Ruth.

He began to write in his journal. "I have a strange feeling in my stomach—a feeling of excitement that I experience every time I begin something new. The past months have merely been summer vacation. Now, with Ruth returning to teaching, and the time I would ordinarily be returning to the University to prepare for fall classes, I feel an emptiness. It seems something is wrong, as if I should be on the Riverton University Campus.

"I admit I'm fearful. I've had this story in my mind for years. I've gathered notes, but now can I really get these ideas down on paper? I've been teaching writing, and I've written articles for many magazines. But do I actually have what it takes to write a novel?"

He put aside his pen and walked across the room to the patio. He opened the screen and walked outside. Nelson Lake had been a source of dreams and inspiration for years. Now he needed that inspiration more than ever.

"Lord," he began praying, "my mind is swarming with ideas for a great novel." He thought of the picnics the family had had in this same area. He looked down the road which passed by the grand old farm home that had been considered home for so many years. He had always thought he would write about the settlers coming to Oak Ridge. After all, he had collected much information about those times.

"Lord, are you telling me something?" he prayed aloud. "Are you telling me to write a story about the Andersons or a family like ours? We need reminders of the life and ways of that time. We're losing something of the personal values of the past. Is this the story I should tell?"

He walked on to the shoreline. He picked up a flat stone and threw it so it skipped over the water. Not bad, he thought. Four skips. But Johnie or Michael would always surpass that number.

The small waves reminded him of the way people influence others. One small stone displaced water for a large distance. Could he write something that had that kind of influence?

"I need to move along," he said aloud.

A ringing phone startled him to action. He welcomed the interruption. He recognized his mother's voice.

"James, I don't want to interrupt your writing, but I thought I'd invite you for dinner tonight. There's a special dinner at the senior center, and I know you're there alone and probably won't make a good meal for yourself."

"Sounds good, Mother. I'll be there."

"Come around five. There's something else I'd like to have you think about. Wednesday afternoon, we have hymn sing at the nursing home or care center. I'm wondering if you wouldn't come over and lead. They would love that."

He hesitated only a minute. "I guess I could do that. I can't write all the time."

After he hung up, he realized retirement could be a busier time than he thought. There were people around who retired and felt they were busier than they had ever been before. "Lord, you may have some new purposes for me after all."

Once more, he left the house and decided to walk--this time a walk in the woods. The walk took him a short distance north and east into the pasture that now belonged to Michael. He remembered that frantic time when his little sister and cousin were lost. The whole community had been involved in the search.

"I wonder," he thought aloud, "if that isn't the kind of family story I should write. But it's tough at this stage in life to start something new. I've been successful in all my work—school and college and degrees. Honestly, I'm afraid of failing."

Mark Goodman appeared in his thoughts. Mark's life had been completely bound to his insatiable interest in history and his teaching. When that chapter of life was coming to an end, he saw himself being attacked and destroyed. What a sad story!

"I wonder," he thought aloud, "if I could tell that story. But now I have two stories, perhaps two novels to write."

James turned his thoughts back to 1937. That was the year P.J. had told his father that he (P.J.) had ownership of the original family farm. The memory of his father's encounter with death had faded from his memory. That would make a powerful story: a conflict between the two brothers. P.J. was such an enigma. He could do such terrible things, but then he could be kind and thoughtful and extremely generous.

I guess the creative process is at work, he thought. Writing a story demands time to think and ponder the possibilities.

He looked ahead to the swamp area, now filled with more water than he had ever seen before. The landscape did indeed change. The trees had grown many feet higher. He came to a small hill that rose above the trees. He sat down, and scenes for new novels seemed to swim through his mind. Writers should always have a journal or notebook nearby.

"I better get back home and get that notebook out," he said aloud.

James hurried, almost running, back to the lake home. His and Ruth's new home was the only one though there were lots for his sisters and brothers nearby. He loved the quiet of that one home on Nelson Lake.

When he came into the yard, he saw a pickup pull into the driveway. It had to be Michael.

"Hello, bro," called out Michael. "I thought you'd be in your office, working away on your great American novel."

"I was having a hard time getting started. But what brings you by? I thought you'd be busy with your fall farm work."

For the first time, James noticed the amount of gray that had taken over the otherwise blond hair of his kid brother. Even at forty-five, Michael retained a youthful vigor. For years, he had seemed like a younger version of Johnie. But now he suddenly seemed older.

Michael looked away. "I guess I wanted to talk."

"I always find time for that. I suppose Elise is at teacher workshops. It's that time of year for teachers—except not for me."

"This must seem different for you."

"It takes getting used to. Sometimes, I wonder if I made a mistake by retiring. I could have gone on for several more years."

Michael again looked away, seeming to avoid his brother's gaze. His usually smiling expression gave way to a somber look.

"I should get back to the farm work. I didn't mean to bother you."

James placed his hand on Michael. "Come now, a brother like you is never a bother. Come inside, and I'll try to hustle up something to eat. I think there's some soup I can warm up."

"I can't turn that down."

"You said you wanted to talk. Start talking."

They walked toward the house.

Michael spoke slowly, so uncharacteristic of his usual manner. "I don't know where to begin."

They walked inside and to the kitchen. James began to heat up the soup and set the table. "I'm listening whenever you're ready."

"I haven't been a good brother or son. I've let other things get in the way."

"Michael, you've been busy. The farm. The greenhouse and nursery business. Responsibility for three growing children. I understand what you're facing."

"I don't think you can understand the mess I've gotten into."

James poured the soup into the bowls. "Let's pray first."

The brothers bowed their heads and James began to pray. "Dear heavenly Father, thank you for being our heavenly Father. We need you as father even more than we need our earthly father. Father God, both Michael and I are at a crossroads. We face problems that are challenging. Be with us and guide us through these problems. Help us to seek your wisdom. And now we thank you for this food and this fellowship. May we honor and glorify you in our lives. In Jesus' Name. Amen."

The two men began to eat their soup.

"Thanks for that prayer," said Michael. "I really need God's help. I also need help from people."

"Fire away, bro. But if I'm honest, I may know or suspect something about the problem."

James thought he saw his brother's hand tremble as he set down the coffee cup. Dad had experienced those tremors in recent years.

Chapter 17

"I suppose my problem is that I didn't really listen to Dad and some of his warnings. Dad never went into debt. His motto was 'neither borrower nor lender be.' Though he did lend money, and he gave generously to the church and to people."

James waited for his brother to go on.

"To get right to the point. I mortgaged the farm. That came when I bought the big machinery and also with the greenhouse business. I wanted the biggest and the best. I should have made do with the older machines I had, but I didn't. I liked the newest and best."

"Michael, if it's money you need, Ruth and I just sold our house in Riverton. We'll help to get you through."

"I'm afraid it's more complicated than that. Legally, the bank or Jeffrey could foreclose right now, but Jeffrey is holding off. You see we have a lot of property on Nelson Lake. Part of that belongs to you and the rest of the family. But I have a chunk that may be quite valuable. Jeffrey wants to do some kind of trade-off. He wants to bring in a promoter who works on getting conference centers in or build large numbers of lake condos."

"We don't want that on our lake."

"I don't know that I've ever been so scared. I always thought this land would be a safety net. It would be ours for generations to come. I'm afraid if I lose the farm, it would be terribly hard on Dad. I can't see doing that to him."

"Foreclosing on your farm wouldn't be very good public relations for either the bank or Jeffrey. There's a lot of talk about Jeffrey anyway."

"That talk makes me feel even more uncomfortable. An outside agency could come in and take over those loans. That might be the worst possibility."

The two brothers talked over the problem during the next hour. Finally, Michael turned to leave.

"I'm glad we talked. I feel better. I've tried to do so much on my own—in my own strength. I need to get back to my dependence on the Lord. That's the only way I can make it through."

"I'll pray for you. We'll get through this no matter what."

After Michael left, James wrote in his journal. "I believe my life is going down a new path. Who knows where this road will lead?

Ellen poured the water off the potatoes. They were ready except to be mashed. Where was Matthew? She wondered as James entered the kitchen.

163

"Hi Mom! Sorry I'm late. I finally got going on my writing." He kissed her on the cheek. "What's this? I thought we were going to the senior center for dinner." James gave his mother a quick hug and began lifting lids on the steaming pots and pans.

"I changed my mind," she said simply. "I think your dad is more tired than he lets on. I can't imagine where he could be. He stayed inside most of the afternoon, and that's not like him. Then, he disappeared."

"Do you want me to drive around and look for him?"

"He always lets me know where he goes. This isn't like him. He's been acting strange all day."

"Maybe it's a letdown after the big trip."

Ellen turned the burners down to low. "I'm not a worrier, but I can't help it when it comes to your father. Earlier in life he had all those health problems. Somehow we never thought he'd last as long as he has. In fact, I never thought I'd be living to be eighty-six. I don't feel that old."

"Dad did exceptionally well on the trip."

"He holds his hand over his heart. I sometimes think he hides things from me. He doesn't want me to worry."

"I watched him closely on the trip. He got tired at times, but I think he was feeling well."

The front door opened.

"Matthew, you're back. Where have you been? I was beginning to worry."

"I just went for a walk." He entered the room and greeted James.

Ellen quickly got everything on the table. James was always amazed at the speed his mother worked.

They went through the usual family routine of praying and eating the first part of the meal quietly.

James decided it was time he said something. "Mother tells me you haven't been your usual self. I'm thinking it might be time for you to go to the doctor."

"Your mother worries too much. She never used to worry, but maybe it's a part of getting old."

"When I find a weed in your garden, I know something must be wrong."

"It's the end of the season. Things are dying."

He paused after the last word, dying. James felt he had something else on his mind.

As they finished the last of the meal Ellen brought out a pumpkin dessert. Matthew brought up the question. "Has anyone talked to Michael? He's been keeping to himself."

Ellen gave James one of those knowing looks.

James stumbled over his words. "Yes, he stopped over late this morning."

"Did he have anything to say for himself?"

Ellen interrupted. "How about some more coffee? And I have some more pumpkin dessert. I baked it fresh this morning."

His mother was obviously trying to stall and give him time to think through his answer.

"I don't know exactly what to say. There's nothing definite."

His father cleared his throat. "You don't need to spare me from the truth. I know Jeffrey is up to something. He's greedy for land that a developer can use. Lake property is what he wants."

"Dad, I know how much the farm means to you."

Matthew didn't hesitate. "Yes, it was my farm for a while. I suppose the real family farm, the place where I grew up and farmed in my earlier years, is the farm where Margaret and Joe live. But I'm learning that we live in a place and farm the land for a while. It was mine for that time, but that has changed."

"But," said Ellen, "it's been in the family. It's been Michael's."

His father had that faraway look that James had noticed during the past months.

"I'm learning —but it's hard to let go."

James wanted to ask him what he meant, but underneath he knew.

They sat in silence the next minutes, sipping coffee and eating the last of the dessert.

After some time of silence, Matthew again spoke. "People are more important than land or things. It's the people I care about."

"Could Michael lose the farm?" asked Ellen.

"That is possible. I'm afraid Jeffrey has him over a barrel, so to speak. He's in a tough position. Jeff Grant has the upper hand."

"I'm afraid," said Matthew, "Jeff Grant will destroy others and himself."

James saw the downcast look in his father's eyes. He saw in his father a depth of character that amazed him. This simple farmer with less than an eighth grade education had more wisdom and compassion than the ministers and professors he knew.

He looked first at his father. "Dad, I love you." Then he turned to his mother. "Mother, I love you. I am the most fortunate of men."

CHAPTER 18

September 1985

Ellen put aside her knitting as she saw her sister-in-law Victoria coming up the front steps. She hadn't seen much of her during the last months. Despite her ninety-five years, Victoria moved quickly.

Ellen opened the front door. "Good morning, Victoria, it's about time we had morning coffee together. It's been far too long."

"I've thought the same. I've been busy driving one of my friends to clinic appointments in River Falls. And since I had that fall awhile back, I haven't gotten around so well."

"You seem to be moving quite well. If I live another ten years, I hope I can do half as well."

"Ellen, I hope you can come my way and see my new apartment. I'm not quite used to this business of senior living."

Ellen motioned for her to sit down on the living room sofa. "I'll do that one of the next days. Things have been different ever since Matthew came back from Sweden. In fact, this whole year around his eighty-fifth birthday has been different. Right now, I'm not sure what to think."

"What do you mean?"

"He's been listless. Sleeps later. Takes more naps. That's not like him."

"I don't take much stock in it, but could it be depression? I know people get medication that seems to help. But I wouldn't have any of it."

"The doctor mentioned that earlier this summer. But I'm sure Matthew wouldn't willingly take any of those drugs."

"I think I need to have a talk with my brother. Is he around?"

"Michael called this morning and asked if he could come out to the farm and help with some things. I think he might be out in the field driving tractor. Matthew used to love nothing more than plowing in the fall."

"It's good to be busy and useful."

Ellen held up the afghan she had been knitting. "Yes, I think you're right. This is my project. This one is for Michael. He's Number Five."

"I like the pattern. I've never been good at sewing and knitting. I'm better at teaching and talking. That's what I've done all my life."

"You have been a great teacher. And you've kept right on teaching in a different way."

"I'm afraid I'm getting too old for mission trips and some of the travelling I did for a while. I just don't get around the way I used to."

Ellen put aside her afghan. "Let me put the coffee on. The kitchen is always a good place to talk."

Victoria followed Ellen into the kitchen. "I probably should do some serious writing the way James does. But this stage in life is a bit late."

Ellen poured water into the coffee maker and then put in the grounds. "Victoria, I think you have something on your mind. There's something you want to ask or tell."

Victoria smiled. "I guess you see right through me."

"I've been in the family quite a few years."

"Yes, and Matthew and I are the last of our siblings and larger family. Most of the cousins have left this earth. I find this part of living hard to take."

Ellen brought out her oatmeal raisin cookies. "Have a cookie. These are healthier than some of my other cookies."

"I can't resist."

"Now, what's on your mind?"

"Many things are on my mind. I don't know where to begin. I suppose I really needed a sisterly talk. We haven't had such a talk for a long time."

"We've been too busy with things that aren't so important. Matthew and I came across an article about the tyranny of the urgent; we have these duties that seem urgent but aren't."

Victoria put down her half-eaten cookie. "Moving has been my urgency. I feel a sense of freedom now that I've gotten rid of so much stuff. I realize how important it is to let go of things."

Chapter 18

"I think that's what Matthew is thinking about."

"Yes, Ellen, I was concerned about Matthew even before you said anything. I've been noticing that he's gotten thinner. He's never been heavy, but he's ever so much thinner now."

"Who else or what else are you concerned about?"

"Johnie stopped by when he was here last time. And he let something slip, or rather I managed to get some information out of him. It's about Michael and the mortgage on the farm."

"I'm afraid that's true."

"I keep thinking there must be something we can do. Now, for example, I sold my house and received a good price. If there's a chance of his losing the farm, I'd like to put my money to good use. I've also made some good investments, so I can afford to help."

Ellen sighed. "I wish it were that simple. It seems because of the wording of the mortgage contract, Jeffrey can foreclose no matter what. Jeffrey wants that lake property and is trying to force Michael to give some of those rights. You see Michael and the kids own several prime lake lots."

"I think I need to have a good talk with Jeffrey Andrew Grant the Third. He will get his come-uppance one of these days."

Ellen sighed. "I wonder if that will do any good."

"What about Matthew? Won't the thought of losing his farm be hard on him?"

"We tried to keep it from him, but Matthew was smart enough to figure it out. And I think Michael has opened up to him in the meantime."

"There's more." Victoria paused a moment and went on. "This I heard from a former student who is in business. This student told me that Jeff has not been honest regarding insurance. He told me that Jeff might well be involved in insurance fraud."

"That sounds serious—very serious."

"This student also told me that if the bank examiners find illegal activity that could be hard on both Jeff and the bank. Even prison time for Jeff."

Ellen closed her eyes for a moment. "I'm afraid that would be very hard on Matthew. Matthew cares so much for each of his grandchildren. He prays for them every day."

"We have to try to do something."

"Matthew is ready to let go. He says that we come into this earth with nothing. We will leave this earth with nothing. He has a wonderful attitude. But I do think the loss of the farm would be hard on him."

"Even so, we must do something. Ellen, how about walking over to the senior center. They serve some good meals though I haven't been there for a while. I have a reservation, and we can call in one for you. How about that?"

"Sounds good."

Ellen and Victoria continued their talk of family. Two sisters-in-law, with a relationship of more than sixty years, had become like sisters.

———

James wasn't quite sure he liked being alone at their new lake home. Yes, there was time for writing after the other chores. However, the quietness was a new experience. Ruth had always been around. A few years before, three lively children and their friends had been in and out of their house, and the university was thriving with activity.

He should be moving along in writing this novel. He knew what to do for he had studied all types of writing. Several hundred of his articles had appeared in magazines and journals. But this writing was the writing he had always wanted to do. In so many ways he had succeeded. Could he succeed in this bold new venture?

"This is just too quiet," he said aloud. "I'm homesick for Ruth and the kids, and I miss the hubbub of university life. Maybe I'm more of a teacher than a writer."

He gathered his journal and notebook and a few papers, went to the car and drove down the driveway. At the mailbox, the mail carrier was placing his bundle of mail.

"You're a popular man," the mail carrier called to him.

"Thanks, I'm helping to keep you in business."

The mail carrier drove away, and James opened the box. Secretly, he hoped he would hear from son Richard. Perhaps the biggest regret in his life was the strained relationship between him and his son. He had been a good father to the girls, but he never understood Richard and had failed him miserably.

He separated the letters from the magazines and *Daily Journal*. No letter from Richard. However, a letter from Sweden immediately caught his attention.

He tore open the letter. Andrew Johansson must have made the necessary arrangements. He quickly scanned the letter. Sure enough, Andrew would be coming, not in September, but the first days of October. That would be a welcome diversion for both him and his father.

Chapter 18

An hour later at the historical society library, James found himself deep in the study of a handwritten family book that retold many remembrances of those pioneer days. Somehow he wished someone in his family had done this work a generation before. Now, these old-timers were all gone from the scene. These times were the times of his great-grandparents.

Another volunteer made a comment he would keep remembering. "Someone ought to retell some of those stories of the Depression. Those people are still with us and remember. In another few years those people will not be around."

The words surprised James. "Are you telling me to research the Depression rather than the 1870s and 1880s? I was just a child, but I do remember a little bit. I remember more of how Mom and Dad kept talking about those hard times."

"You need to write that story. In another twenty years you and I may not be around."

"I hadn't thought of that. In twenty years I'll be almost as old as my father. My grandma lived until she was ninety-four."

"People can live that long, but look at the quality of life."

James began to ponder a new direction. What if I tell the story of the rough times of the thirties? I could tell my family's story, but I'd change it. I could include Uncle P.J. and how he stole the farm from Dad. I could write a gripping story of those hard times.

"Could I get the old newspapers of the 1930s?" he asked the museum director.

"We have all the bound copies."

Within minutes James was paging through the *Daily Journal* of the 1930s. He found himself transported back to his earliest remembrances. The funnies, as they called them then, were the comics he had read as a child. He remembered the crazy antics of "Modest Maidens, and Mr. Doolittle of "Neighborly Neighbors" always had some crazy ideas. "Homer Hoopee" was even crazier.

The news headlines told the story of the hard times for farmers in the area. The serials, or those long continued stories, told him that the newspaper of that time was both information and entertainment. The local news reports told him the lifestyle of city people was distinctly different from the rural ways. The visiting of the country people reminded him of a way of life that was fast fading away. People didn't just stop and visit and do business the way they used to. Maybe some of that happened in the country and the small towns.

James had longed for that simpler way of life. Now that he was living alone at their new lake home, the simpler life was far too quiet. He whispered to himself, "Have I become addicted to busy activity? Have I lost the ability to be alone and to think and meditate? Was there a spiritual dimension that was a part of life back then? Did we have more time for one another? Did we take time to step back and simply enjoy and appreciate our family and friends?"

After several hours of reading the newspapers and jotting down notes, James found his brain seemed to be swimming with ideas and pictures and stories. He took out his journal and wrote, "I've made a decision. I finally know the direction I shall go. My novel will be a novel about a family like the Andersons. I must capture the flavor of those times."

Ellen placed the meatloaf into the oven and then put in a dish of scalloped potatoes. Her mouth watered. This would be a special meal. She checked again the temperature and then left the kitchen for her easy chair and a few quiet moments.

The phone rang, interrupting her quiet moment.

"Mother," said her daughter-in-law Elise. "Michael and Dad are working late in the fields, so I'll feed them supper."

"Oh," said Ellen. "I just put supper in the oven. Your Aunt Victoria is coming by, and I think James is stopping. I had invited him to stay for supper."

"I'm sorry, but Michael wanted to get the work done while he can."

"I understand. We'll enjoy our supper without Matthew. I'm wondering though, is Matthew acting his normal self? He's been acting different lately."

"Michael's been concerned. He thought it would be good for Dad to be busy with something he loves to do."

"You're right. We'll enjoy our supper without Matthew."

Ellen sat back and began to doze off. She thought of Michael and wondered what problems he was facing. He was fortunate to have Elise. What a wonderful woman! Ellen rather liked the way she called her Mother. After Elise lost her own parents, she and Matthew filled a void.

"Lord," Ellen prayed, aloud "give me the wisdom to do what is right for Matthew. Do I sit back and relax hoping things will work out by themselves? Or do I insist that he see the doctor? Oh, Lord, grant me wisdom."

She continued to pray and think so that when James and Victoria entered the room, she jumped up. "I guess I was deep in thought."

"You certainly were," said Victoria.

James came over and gave her a kiss on the cheek. "Mom, something smells awfully good. I've worked hard today. I forgot about lunch."

"Everything should be ready in about half an hour." She took one look at Victoria and she knew she had news. "Victoria, you might as well tell us right away."

"I was going to wait until after supper, but I might as well tell you now. I went to the bank and demanded to talk with Jeffrey."

James smiled. "This sounds interesting."

Ellen couldn't help wondering what this would mean. Jeffrey Grant might be her grandson, but she knew he could not be trusted.

"I've been doing some other investigating as well. First of all, I've been in contact with some of my former students who own an interest in the bank. I think we can stop Jeffrey from doing some of what he plans to do. He's been working with a Chicago firm that specializes in building conference centers in areas around the country."

Ellen couldn't keep from interrupting. "A conference center on the lake would destroy that small lake. The lake isn't large enough for that kind of expansion."

"That's what we know all too well. Now, Michael owns some of the prime property, but I've discovered that part of that belongs to your children, Ellen."

"Yes," said James, "that's how Jeffrey is making it so difficult for Michael."

"I may be almost ninety-six, but my mind is still good. I've been in contact with Carol. She also has a small bit of interest in the bank. That should put an end to Jeffrey's control. And I don't know how we'll do it, but we'll stop Jeffrey from greedily taking the farm from Michael."

Ellen looked away sadly. "I hate family problems. Families aren't supposed to be this way. I love my oldest grandson. I pray for him and all the rest every day. And so does Matthew."

James reached out and touched his mother's hand. "I'm sorry, Mother, I hope something better can work out. This family conflict will hurt Dad."

"I'm sorry about this," continued Victoria. "I am hoping we have enough leverage to get Jeffrey to step back. I'll do whatever I can to keep Michael from losing his farm."

"Thank you, Victoria." Ellen reached over to her sister-in-law. "I don't know what our family would have done without you."

"That's what families are for. And, dear Ellen, I'll do everything I can to achieve the right ends in a peaceful manner."

Ellen smiled. "My dear Victoria, I admire your guts and determination. Jeffrey may even deserve you as an adversary."

James agreed.

"Now, my nephew," said Victoria, "I get the feeling you have some news as well. Let's hear it."

James hesitated. "It's not news yet."

Ellen knew her son had been struggling with questions. "I think you've made some kind of decision. I can't help wondering."

"I hope you're going ahead with your writing," added Victoria. "It's important to fulfill that dream. I know you'll succeed."

"That's part of it. I've been struggling about the direction to go. I haven't been moving ahead. Today at the historical society library, I started researching history of the 1870s and 1880s, but someone suggested that I should write about the Depression, the thirties."

"We lived the thirties, the Depression," echoed both Ellen and Victoria.

"I've made a decision. I'm writing a family story. The family will be fictional, but it will be like our family struggling to live through those tough years."

"That sounds like a great idea." Victoria looked squarely into James's face. "But be sure people know it is fiction. I'll want you to be careful what you do with a Victoria character."

James laughed. "I'll only present a good picture."

"Be honest."

"I have other news, too," said James. "I had a letter from Andrew from Sweden. He is keeping his promise to come. He'll be coming in early October."

"That should be good for Matthew," said Ellen. "After you came back Matthew kept talking about Andrew. He hoped he would keep his promise and come."

"Do you remember those old continued stories in the newspapers?" asked Victoria. "Our lives are like those long continued stories."

"Or like the old radio soaps," said Ellen. "Tune in tomorrow."

James repeated the line. "Tune in tomorrow."

CHAPTER 19

James would long remember the family fellowship of that evening. His mother and Aunt Victoria and he talked of all the family members. He proudly spoke of his girls and their husbands and children. But when mention was made of Richard, he felt only loss and sadness.

"Somehow," he said, "I pray for a miracle and Richard would come home. I'm afraid I never understood the boy. But now he's a full-grown man, and it seems he wants nothing to do with me or his family."

"It's hard being a parent," said his mother.

"But, Mom, I feel that you always did it right."

Ellen smiled. "Well, you have all turned out well. But I always felt I didn't quite do it right with Carol. I thought my family was complete with you boys and Margaret. Then, quite suddenly and unexpectedly, I was pregnant with Carol. Margaret was an easy baby, but Carol was more difficult from the beginning."

Victoria set down her cup of coffee. "I think that Carol and I were alike. Both very determined and headstrong. I finally admitted that to her years later."

"And as a mother, I admitted to Carol my flaws. She had rough going for so many years, but now she does mission work and has turned out right."

The conversation continued for several hours. James and the others lost track of time until the chimes announced the nine o'clock hour.

James looked at his mother and began to feel uneasy. "Isn't this awfully late for Dad coming home? He never liked to work this late when he farmed."

Ellen looked up at the clock. "He hasn't helped Michael for some time. Perhaps they got to talking. But this is unusual."

"Why don't you give them a call?" suggested Victoria.

Ellen went over to the phone and dialed. James heard the phone ringing.

"No answer," said Ellen. "That's strange. Some of the kids should be around at this hour."

James couldn't help thinking something might be wrong, but he hesitated to speak.

The ringing of the telephone interrupted their thoughts. Ellen answered.

"It's Elise," said Ellen. "I think something's wrong. She wants to talk with you, James."

James clasped the phone, fearing what his sister-in-law would say. "Hello, Elise we've been trying to call you."

Elise began to explain. "We're at the River Falls hospital. We don't know how it happened, but Dad fell and hit his head really hard. We don't know how serious it is, but I wanted to explain to you."

"I think we better get there right away."

"Michael's quite upset. He blames himself."

"Is Dad conscious?"

"He's in and out of consciousness. He's confused. He says his vision is blurry."

"Okay. We'll be there as soon as we can."

James turned and explained to the women what he had been told. "Aunt Victoria, I'll drive you home."

"No, you won't," was Victoria's spirited reply. "If my brother's been hurt, I want to see him. I want to make sure they're doing everything they can for him."

His mother was strangely quiet.

Victoria and he did most of the talking—mostly about Matthew and his depression and his early close calls.

As they approached the hospital, Ellen spoke. "I'm afraid Matthew won't make it this time. I shouldn't be, but I'm afraid."

"Mom," reassured James, "he's come through many times before. Where's your faith?"

"Right now, I am a woman of little faith."

"Ellen, this isn't like you."

"I'm sorry." She burst into tears.

When James stopped the car, Ellen quickly dried her tears, and the three hurried in to the hospital. A nurse directed them to a small waiting room.

Michael rushed to his mother and scooped her into his arms. "Mother, I'm sorry. It's all my fault. I shouldn't have had him do all that work."

"What's happening?" asked James. For a moment, he thought his father had died.

Elise stepped forward. This petite woman exhibited such strength whenever a crisis occurred. "Michael, calm down. The doctor is busy examining him. He'll be out in a few minutes."

"What really happened?" demanded Victoria.

Michael started to talk, but he didn't seem to make much sense.

Elise interrupted. "Let me explain. We had late supper. Then the men went out to do some cleaning up. Dad went into the machine shed while Michael did other work. When Michael didn't hear from Dad, he went into the shed. Dad had fallen. He was lying on the floor. We know that he hit his head hard."

Michael could not hold back his guilty feelings. "It's my fault. Dad worked hard and he was tired. I shouldn't have let him work so hard."

"Stop it, Michael," said his mother. "Your father wanted to be there. When he helps you on the farm, he feels useful. You did him a favor by asking him to help."

"I still feel it's my fault."

James wasn't sure if he should say anything. He knew he would feel the same way if he had been Michael.

Michael paced back and forth in the small room.

Elise went over to him and placed her hand on his shoulder. "Michael, dear, your pacing isn't doing anyone any good. And blaming yourself only makes things more difficult."

"I can't help it."

James felt both relief and apprehension when Doctor Blake entered. He feared bad news, but at least there would be news. He missed the familiarity of Dr. Baker and the other doctors who had been around for years. This doctor was perhaps thirty-five, average height and looks. The type of person who didn't stand out in a crowd.

"Are all of you Mr. Anderson's family?" Blake asked.

"I'm his other son, James Anderson, and this is Matthew Anderson's wife."

"I'm Victoria, his sister."

He looked at Ellen. "I'm sorry about your husband's accident."

James wondered for a moment if there was some dreadful news.

"He seems to be resting now. For a while, his vision was blurred, but now his vision seems better. He had some slurred speech when we spoke a short while ago. The good news is that it appears he will survive the fall. However, there could be brain damage."

"Oh, no!" gasped Ellen.

"When will we know?" asked James.

"We may have some idea tomorrow. We'll do some tests, and those tests may determine if there is brain damage and the extent."

James remembered the attack early in late spring. "I didn't realize how devastating a bump on the head could be. I think there's a message about being more careful."

Dr. Blake continued. "There's really nothing more right now. I do believe someone should stay with him for the night just in case of some change."

"I'll stay," said Ellen. "The rest of you can go home."

James looked down at his mother, who suddenly seemed old and frail. "I'll be here. Michael and Elise, you need to get home for the kids, and chores and school in the morning."

Dr. Blake turned to leave. "I'll stop back later in the morning to check. I'll talk with you then."

"And," added James, "Victoria, I think you should go home."

"I'd like to stay. But I suppose I could be a problem. Maybe I better go home."

James followed his mother into his father's hospital room. He stepped back, shocked at his father's pale face and an almost lifeless quality. No, he thought, I'm not ready to lose my father. It can't be his time.

Ellen sat beside the bed and placed her hand in her husband's hand. The others stood back, looking at the pale face of Matthew.

James looked over at his brother. "I'll walk you to the car," he said.

The two brothers walked ahead while Victoria and Elise stayed behind. They must have sensed that need brothers have to be together.

"I feel so terrible about this," said Michael. "If I hadn't asked Dad to come out and help, this wouldn't have happened."

"Michael," James objected. "Dad was not steady. If he hadn't been here, he would have fallen somewhere else. It couldn't be helped. Accidents have a way of happening."

"I feel so responsible. I know I've disappointed Dad. I've taken too many chances financially with the farm. Losing the farm would hurt Dad almost more than anything else."

"You're wrong, brother. Dad is learning to let go of these things. He's been telling me that. You get older, and you have to let go."

"I have to get out from under this financial mess, but Jeffrey has such a legal stranglehold. It was my fault, but the laws and contracts aren't fair."

"There'll be a way." James said the words and tried to sound confident, but underneath he couldn't help wondering.

"I don't know what I'd do without my family."

"I'm your brother, Michael. I'm here for you, no matter what."

"Thank you, bro."

The brothers embraced. Michael, Elise and Aunt Victoria drove off into the night. James returned to the hospital room. As he entered, he saw his mother's head, bowed in prayer.

He felt an overwhelming love for his parents and a strong desire to help and protect.

Matthew loved plowing the fields more than almost any other farm task. That afternoon, he had felt as if he were young again doing a task that he enjoyed. Life was full and productive. He was useful to his youngest son. Life had purpose. He began to relive those moments.

He drove the John Deere into the shed. It's interesting, he thought, the way Michael has remained loyal to this make of tractor. He couldn't help but appreciate the old John Deere, a tractor with lugs, the first tractor he had bought back in 1932. Before that he had plowed with horses.

"I don't think I fit into this new world. I can drive this older tractor, but I wouldn't even try those new machines. I'm an antique."

Inside the tractor shed he stopped the tractor and simply sat. He felt a dizziness come over him. Everything around him seemed strange and unreal. What was happening to him?

"Lord," he whispered aloud. "Are you calling me home?"

Suddenly, he knew he had to get outside—to get some air. He stood and then in a moment found himself falling. His head hit the cement floor. A sharp pain and stars seemed to explode everywhere and then there was complete black.

As he began to regain consciousness, he tried to lift himself up, but he began to see everything double. Double vision and dizziness caused him to call out. He didn't know what he said, but it was a call for help.

"Dad, what happened?" Michael called.

Matthew tried to speak. He mumbled something.

"Don't move. You might have broken something. We need to get help."

"I'm just so dizzy. I'm seeing crazy things. You look like two or three."

He heard more voices. A woman's voice spoke, Elise's. He felt himself being gently guided to the car. They must be taking him to the hospital or the doctor. A lethargy swept over him. He mumbled, not really knowing what he was saying.

Someone was holding his hand. No, it was Elise. She was taking his pulse.

Everything during the next hour was blurred. The dizziness disappeared and a kind of sleep or unconsciousness welcomed him.

His next awareness came when he found himself on a bed. Someone was poking him and asking questions. It had to be a doctor. He answered though only half aware. Michael and Elise's voices told him they were concerned.

A sharp light shined in his eyes. The doctor kept talking and asking questions. All he wanted to do was lie back and escape all this. His head throbbed. This was the most terrible headache he had ever experienced.

"I'm giving you something that will help your headache," the doctor said.

All he wanted to do was escape the pain and get away from the noise of a doctor and nurse talking. He drank the water and swallowed the pills. The doctor left. Complete silence followed. A deep sleep enveloped him.

Dreams invaded his sleep, and they were not pleasant dreams. In some ways the dreams reminded him of his experience years ago. But in that dream he had experienced such peace. Then he found himself returning to life.

P.J., his brother who had been dead for years, invaded his sleep. Matthew became a child again, and P.J. had locked him in the attic. He pounded desperately and couldn't get out. Then, he became an adult, and P.J. again stood before him. "The farm is mine. I have ownership of this place."

He felt his world crumbling again. He had loved that land. He had thought that land would be his legacy, a land he could leave to children and grandchildren.

Chapter 19

He became half aware of voices. James. Ellen. Michael. Elise. But he refused to leave the world of sleep. Those voices faded.

His return to the world of dreams was even less pleasant. This dream took him back to the war, World War II. His sons, particularly Johnie, had experienced all the horrors of war. Matthew thought he was in the midst of the fighting. But he had no gun. He was being chased. He ran, breathless, and the enemy was close behind. He kept running and running and running.

Then, he began to fall and fall and fall. Just before he landed, he wakened.

He looked around him to a darkened room.

"Matthew." It was Ellen. "You're awake. How do you feel?"

Matthew tried to arrange his thoughts. "I don't know. I'm not dizzy anyway."

"Dad, I'm here, too," said James.

"Can we get you anything?"

Something drew him back to the world of sleep.

This time of sleep became more peaceful. He saw around him the most beautiful garden he had ever seen. Was this garden at home on the farm? Or was he in heaven?

In the next scene he found himself driving the tractor in the west field, one of the richest fields on his new farm, the one Michael now owned. He experienced the pride he always felt when he looked at the newly plowed field.

Then, he saw Ellen hurrying toward him. Something important must have happened. Suddenly, Ellen was talking. He knew he was talking aloud, half awake.

"Matthew, you're back."

Matthew looked around him. "Where am I?"

"You had a terrible fall and hit your head. You've given us a real scare."

"I feel strange."

The hours that followed seemed a bit hazy. People spoke to him and he answered part of the time. He did remember the doctor saying, "You won't be jumping on and off that tractor for quite a while. You're not as young as you used to be."

He knew the truth of that last statement all too well.

Matthew remained lethargic throughout the day and into another day. Ellen stayed beside him, taking breaks from time to time. James went home and then came back.

The following day, he suddenly felt different. He announced to the doctor and Ellen. "I need to get out of here. I'm ready to go home."

The doctor smiled. "Yes, but you're going to have to take it easy. You don't need any of those sudden jolts. The tests show a concussion but no serious damage."

An hour later, James came. "I'm here to take you home. And I have some news. Cousin Andrew is coming from Sweden in early October."

At that moment Matthew stood. "I think God may have a purpose for keeping me here."

"Dad," said James, "you're important to us."

Matthew thought of Larry and family members and others who had been a part of his life. "I hate the thought of leaving those I love."

The nurse arrived with a wheelchair. "Are you ready to leave?"

"Yes!" Matthew spoke emphatically. "I can walk."

"Mr. Anderson, it's hospital policy. We have our rules."

Matthew got into the wheelchair. "Some rules are needed. I don't see the sense in some of these other rules."

He heard Victoria's voice. "He's got his old spunk back. He's doing okay."

At home Ellen felt a sense of relief when James and Victoria finally left. She needed time alone. It was time to get the house in order, and she needed time to process all that had happened during the past days.

James had insisted that they have their noon dinner at the Viking Café. Matthew wasn't one who enjoyed going out to eat, but he enjoyed the home cooking of this Scandinavian restaurant. Matthew had ordered the Swedish meatballs and had relished every morsel. When they got home, he seemed exhausted and ready for an afternoon nap.

Ellen had missed her morning devotions ever since the hospital episode began two days ago. She turned to Psalm 27. "The Lord is my light and my salvation. Whom then shall I fear?" She sang the words based on a well-known musical composition.

She had recently started to enjoy a hot cup of tea with her devotions and quiet time. She was having tea with Jesus and she would often speak aloud. "Jesus," she began, "thank you for bringing Matthew safely home. I need him far more than I can say. Lord, let me depend on you more. Matthew needs me to be strong now that he may be weak. Help me to convince him that he can't do everything he used to do. He can't take any chances.

"Lord, this aching back bothers me more and more. And the hip too. I'm afraid of falling. I don't want to end up in a nursing home. I think I could handle it if I absolutely have to. But my dear Matthew could not. I think his limitations and the limitations within the home would drive him absolutely up a wall, so to speak. I'm not sure I can slow him down the way he needs."

She sat for several minutes, reflecting on the ways God had brought her through all those years. Then, she heard a light tap on the back door. She rose from her chair as quickly as she could.

As she entered the kitchen she called out. "Come in."

"Hello, Mother."

"Michael swept her into his arms. She felt certain thrill as she found herself embraced warmly by her strong son. His rigorous work on the farm strengthened the body of a man who was already tall and muscular.

"What a surprise!"

"I had to come and see you. And also check how Dad is doing."

"He's resting. He's supposed to rest if we can keep him down."

"I feel so terrible about his fall. I told him I'd put the tractor in the shed, but he wanted to take care of everything."

"We've said it before. You can't blame yourself. He was doing what he wanted to do. He loved the work, and he needed to be needed."

Ellen motioned for her son to sit down. He sat at the kitchen table, one of the favorite places for a talk.

"Mom, I need to talk."

"I was having some tea, rather than the usual coffee. I was having my quiet time because I didn't have a chance these last days. I've started a little tradition of having tea with Jesus."

"That's a great idea. I'll take some tea—and some of your cookies if you have any."

Ellen smiled. "I think I have a few chocolate chip cookies."

"Mom, I see you have the teakettle on the stove. You know, back on the farm in the old days, you used to have the teakettle on the old wood stove. But we never drank tea."

Ellen put out the tea bags and set down a cup. "I hadn't thought of that. We wanted some moisture in the air. And the hot water was often needed for baking."

'Mom, you let me pour the hot water. But where's your cup?"

"In the living room, by my chair."

Michael hurried into the living room and returned. "I'm young. You've taken many steps for me. I need to do the same for you."

Ellen found it hard to believe how thoughtful her youngest son was becoming. "Thank you."

Michael looked at his tea cup, obviously thinking of something far different. Ellen waited for him to speak.

"Mother, there's more I wanted to say. When I said I was responsible, there's more to it. I was hoping to talk with you before I talk more with Dad. Earlier that afternoon, Dad and I talked seriously about my mistakes. You see there is a real possibility of my losing the farm. I am afraid that would hurt Dad as much as it would hurt me. This contract with Jeffrey and the bank is very strange. Jeffrey has a real hold over me."

Ellen couldn't help thinking back more than forty years. "Your father may deal with this better than you think. Before you were born we lived on the Anderson home place. Your father had worked with the understanding that the farm was to be his. Well, your Uncle P.J. had done some skillful maneuvering so that he had the ownership of the farm."

"Dad has talked about P.J. and what happened."

"At first, that loss practically destroyed your father. He learned that he had to forgive his brother. But something much better came along. Your farm, which was the Nelson farm, had a bigger and better house and better barn as well. The Lord helped us so that everything turned out remarkably well."

"But now I could lose all that. I feel like such a failure."

"But there's hope, isn't there?"

"Yes. But I've made such foolish decisions. I took chances when I shouldn't have."

"Son, bring all these problems before the Lord. He'll show you a way."

Michael looked away. "I haven't done well in that department. I've trusted myself, and I shouldn't have."

"I've made my mistakes."

Michael reached over and took her hand. "Mother, you're about as perfect a mother as a fellow could ever have."

Ellen found her mind traveling back in time. "I remember when you were born back during that February snowstorm. You came as a sign of God's blessing. We were on our own farm. We had overcome some terrible obstacles."

"You never told me that."

Chapter 19

"Your coming into the world came as a result of new life and new energy in the lives of both Matthew and me. A special blessing."

"But look at the problem I've been. Now, my farm situation. And then before Elise, I was definitely the prodigal son. You and Dad didn't know where I was. I rebelled. I went my own way. I wanted nothing to do with you. I was terrible."

"But you came back."

"And I had that terrible accident that could have killed me."

"Your father and I prayed awfully hard."

"I don't deserve you and Dad."

Ellen found herself choking up. "God has been good to us. He's shown more of His love than we could ever deserve."

"I need to be thanking God. And praying for help and guidance."

Ellen smiled. "And the Lord will take care of you. And He'll take care of your father. We are safe within the shadow of his wing."

CHAPTER 20

October 1985

"*Whom the Lord loveth, He chasteneth.*" Ellen thought of those words from her favorite King James Bible. Was he chastening her? For some time Matthew had been the strong dependable force in her life. But now, that all seemed to have changed.

Matthew always insisted on a yard cleared of leaves and perennial flower bed covered well with straw. As usual, he was outside working. At least, she thought, Matthew is in one of his energetic moods. During the other times, he seemed listless and just sat, doing nothing.

He seemed to have made a remarkable recovery from the fall and hospital stay. His usual determination to go on living came through.

Something prompted her to go to the kitchen for another cup of tea. As she looked out the window, she saw Matthew fall. Fear filled her whole being, and she almost ran to the door and then outside.

"Matthew, what happened?"

He looked up at her. "Oh, it's nothing much. I stumbled, that's all."

"I'm not so sure about that. Let me help you get up."

"No, I can manage. I don't have good balance any more. That's why I fell last month."

Matthew remained on his knees.

"Are you sure you aren't a little dizzy. I get that way if I try to stand up fast."

Matthew hesitated. "I think maybe I was a little bit dizzy."

"We need to get you to the doctor."

"No thank you. I've had enough of doctors."

"Dad. Mother," called James. "Did you forget? I'm going to Minneapolis to the airport to pick up Cousin Andrew. I thought you were coming along."

"Matthew," said Ellen sharply, "did you forget to tell me?"

Matthew slowly got up. "I guess I forgot."

"Hurry up and get ready. I can use the company."

Ellen whispered to her son. "Your dad's getting forgetful." She turned to Matthew. "You go with James. I'll stay home and get everything ready. I need to clean the guest room and do some baking. We'll be having people in while he's here."

"Come on, Dad, let's get you ready."

Ellen hurried inside and found clean trousers and shirt. Matthew followed and quickly changed into clean clothes. A farmer could change quickly from soiled garden clothes into clothes that would look good in church or town.

Ellen brought out a cup of coffee for James. "Your father hasn't been himself. Right after the fall, he seemed pretty good. I think he's been depressed and that's not like him."

"I've noticed that, too."

"Maybe you can get him to open up and tell you what's bothering him. He might be worried about his health. He doesn't have the strength he used to have. That happens when you're old."

"I'll try. Johnie would do a better job at that. He's Dad's favorite."

"I think he'll say things to you that he wouldn't say to me." Then she changed the subject. "Have you talked with Michael? Is Jeffrey actually going to foreclose on the farm?"

"Michael clams up about that situation. I do hear from people who are suspicious of Jeffrey and question his business dealings."

"I'm afraid Jeffrey bothers your father more than he'll admit. Jeffrey reminds us of P.J. And I know your uncle had a good side, but he was a crook and could be a first-rate jerk."

"I don't know there's anything we can do."

"Watch closely," Ellen whispered. "There's something else I've noticed. He really shakes a lot in his hands. I'm thinking there might be something more serious."

Chapter 20

"But he's been shaky for years."

"It's more serious now. I don't know what to think."

Matthew entered with a clean pair of trousers and a blue dress shirt, a shirt that seemed to accent the blue of his eyes.

"Talking about me, are you?" questioned Matthew.

Ellen didn't hesitate to respond. "Matthew, dear, you've been dizzy and you had a concussion. We have to look out for you."

James gave his mother a kiss on the cheek and he turned to his father. "Let's go."

Ellen gave her husband a kiss and he hugged her.

"Stop worrying. I'll be all right."

Ellen hoped he was right.

James always felt a spurt of energy when he drove to the Minneapolis-St. Paul International Airport. He loved to travel, and thoughts of the frantic activity of the airport encouraged his creative thoughts. Thousands of people drove to the airport—each facing small or big changes in life. Right now, he thought of his father and the changes that seemed to be taking place.

During the first fifty miles, they rode in silence. James wasn't sure how he could get his father to tell what was really bothering him.

"How's your writing going?" asked Matthew. "You haven't talked much about it."

James chuckled. "I wasn't sure people would be interested in a writer's struggles."

"I guess I might not understand. I don't even have much of an education."

"Dad, you're one of the most understanding men I've met. You're wiser and more sensitive than most college professors."

"That I can't believe. What about your writing?"

James began to share. "I've decided to go a different direction than I had planned. I was going to write about pioneers coming to Minnesota in and around 1870. Instead, I've decided to write a family story—a family coming through the crash of 1929 and then struggling through the Depression."

"Sounds like a story about our family."

"It's going to be fiction. Yes, I'll get ideas from what's happened in our family. In fact, I'll have a character like Uncle P.J., who causes much trouble."

"He's dead, so he can't be hurt by it."

"I'll change a lot of details so the character won't really be P.J."

His father was silent a moment. "I hope the book comes out when I'm still around. I'd like to read it. And I know I'll be proud of you."

"Dad, what about you? I think something's bothering you. I'm your son. You can tell me. If I can help you, I want to."

"I don't think anyone can help. It's just a matter of getting old."

James wanted to ask a question but wondered if he should. "Dad, maybe I shouldn't ask a question like this. But, what's it like to be old—to be eighty-five years old? Understand, I don't think of you as old."

"I'm not sure I know what to tell you. I think I have more of those little aches and pains. I don't really feel that bad. I don't think I feel as old as I am."

James noticed the sign, "Wayside Rest. One Mile." "Dad, I see there's Wayside Rest ahead. Let's stop and have the coffee and cookies Mother sent. We have plenty of time to get to the airport."

"Sounds good. Stopping for coffee this way reminds me of the old days when we would go on family picnics. I miss those times when you kids were all young."

"That's a long time ago now."

James drove off the exit into the parking lot and stopped the car. "I see a picnic table and what looks like a good view."

"I remember back to the days on the home farm. When the cattle freshened in the fall and a cow would go to a far corner of the pasture to have her calf. I enjoyed that because I got to see the beauty of autumn."

"Johnie usually went with you, didn't he?"

"He loved farming and the outdoors."

"I had my nose in a book whenever I could. Or I was writing something."

The two men seated themselves at the picnic table. James opened the thermos and poured the coffee. The aroma of coffee made his mouth water.

Matthew began to sip his coffee. He looked at the trail and the bright yellow leaves nearby. "Nothing is more beautiful than a day in June, but this day and scene almost has a June day beat."

"You always quoted Lowell's words about how rare a day in June is. I think of Frost's poems about walking in the woods. 'And I took the road less traveled by. And that has made the difference.'"

"I've heard you quote those words."

The two men sipped their coffee and sat in silence, enjoying the beauty of the autumn day. A gentle breeze fluttered the leaves, and a napkin blew off the picnic table.

"A perfect day."

"Do you have times when you wish time would stand still? I wish right now that time wouldn't move on."

James searched for the words that would get his dad to tell what was bothering him. "I wish you'd tell me what you're thinking. So many times, I know you're thinking some great thoughts. Or feeling some real concerns. I think—no, I know, Dad—that I could learn from you."

Matthew looked away from his son. "Sometimes I feel I know so little as I think of my eighty-five years. I should know how to face the end of life, but I don't know how. This part of life isn't what I expected."

"Dad, are you afraid?"

Matthew hesitated. "Yes and no. I know in my head that the Lord will be with me always. But I don't feel ready. I'm not ready. Yet I want to go *home,* but I don't want to leave this place."

James took out his journal, which he had brought with him. "I think I understand. At least a little bit."

"Work has always been a part of my life. I guess you call it the work ethic I was brought up with. I was brought up with the belief I should provide for my family and help others who might need help. I can't stop wanting to do this. But I'm not as strong as I was. And I'm afraid of having a heart attack or something so that I land in a nursing home. I'm afraid of that."

"If you're like Grandpa, you'll be sick a few days, and that will be all."

Matthew went on with his thoughts. "When I was seventy-seven, I thought for sure that my life would end. I had the strangest feeling when I celebrated seventy-eight and then seventy-nine. Then, I figured God wanted me to be around longer."

James smiled. "Remember that Moses began his leadership when he was eighty."

"That was a special case. And so were the other old fellows who started late in life."

"Dad, you mentioned being afraid. I think it would help me if you talked about those fears. I could understand better, and I might learn about what I might have to face."

"James, you're college educated. You will know far better what to do. And how to live."

"No, I'm afraid you have more of the answers than I do—despite my education."

"That last fall taught me a great deal. I was careless and in a hurry. Some things happen because a person is careless. And the dizziness makes me feel out of control. As if some evil or other force is controlling me. It's frightening."

"I'd be afraid of that, too."

"I realize that some of what I thought important when I was younger is not so important. Taking time for family is more important than having all the work done right. Yet, I guess on the family farm, we worked together. We had time for one another."

"Dad, you were always there. Mother was always there."

"Life was different back then. Now, people are always in such a hurry. They don't have time for one another."

"That's my generation. And the next two generations. Even more so."

"I've lost so many friends. It was hard to lose Glenn Robertson. We were friends and classmates in the country school. We got together regularly through the years. A few days before Glenn died, we had coffee uptown. I've lost him and so many others. There's your cousin, Larry, who was special to me. Now, he isn't able to get around so I don't see him."

James thought of his own friend. "I thought I'd always have Mark Goodman around, but he died suddenly. But I'm afraid he didn't know the Lord. He taught me how I shouldn't face death."

"I've always planned ahead." Matthew stopped and looked at the bright yellow leaves nearby. "But life doesn't have guarantees. Live one day at a time. Tomorrow may not come."

James wrote down what his father said. "I need to get this wisdom into my writing."

Matthew went on. "Enjoy the people around you. Make the most of this day."

James tried to project his life ahead twenty-five years. What would he be like physically, mentally—and spiritually? Would he be as sharp as his father?

Once more, Matthew looked away. "You know, I have the hardest time remembering names. The other day, someone asked me the names of Johnie's grandkids, and I couldn't remember all the names. I thought I was getting Alzheimer's."

James laughed. "I'm more likely to have Alzheimer's than you. I've forgotten thousands of student names. I can assure that is not happening."

Chapter 20

"I think of Ma, your grandmother. There were times when she was very confused. I'm afraid that could happen to me if I live long enough."

James realized that could happen, but had his grandmother realized she was confused? She may have been troubled at times, but usually she was at peace.

"And," Matthew continued, "I hate the idea of being helpless—out of control. The thought of being cared for in a nursing home is something I couldn't stand."

James listened to his father. He began to understand something about becoming old. Was anyone ready for this chapter of life? How could one live in such a way so as to be ready for the end of life? He couldn't help thinking of *"Thanatopsis,"* by William Cullen Bryant. "So live that when thy summons comes." And then the final line, "Lie down to pleasant dreams."

They talked, but most of the time James listened to his father. "Growing old is tough work," he said as he gathered the thermos and cups. "I hope I do as well as you."

His father got up slowly. "I'm not finished, yet."

"And," James added, "We have a plane to meet and a cousin to bring back home."

<hr />

Matthew thought of what someone had said about troubles. He couldn't remember the exact words, but a trouble shared meant the person had half the trouble. That's the way he felt. It was almost as if James took the part of the father and he became the son. He used to say, "A man always needs a father."

For a while, the two men sat in silence as James drove toward the airport. Both men were deep in thought.

James broke the silence. "You know, Dad, when I was in college, we talked much about 'finding God's will for your life.' That was all about job and purpose and direction. Well, for close to forty years, I was a teacher and professor. Now, I'm realizing I have to look again for God's purpose in my life. I'm wondering if I can succeed as a writer. Or can I succeed in some way at this stage in my life?"

Matthew needed to think about what his son had said. He remained silent, trying to come up with the right words.

James continued. "I think of John Milton, the great English theologian and poet. He lamented his blindness and wondered what God expected of him. He ended that famous sonnet with the words, 'They serve who only stand and wait.'"

"What does that mean?" Matthew asked.

"That's what I'm thinking about. For me, I think I need to do something. But writers need to stand and wait. Perhaps the Lord will reveal something to me. Or perhaps the Lord will give me insight and ideas for my novel."

Matthew considered himself slow to speak. He wanted to think things through before speaking, but he felt an insight had come to him. "I'm thinking that we older folk may need to be here in the background. Maybe we just need to be around for our kids and grandkids."

"Dad, you and Mom are more important to us than you realize. We need you. You help to keep this family together."

"But, son, I don't need another birthday party to bring family together. It's hard when so many people come all at once. But I am glad that people come back home. I think there's something that calls people back home."

"We keep going back to the comfortable and the familiar."

"Some animals return to the place where they were born when they are getting ready to die. I wonder if humans don't do the same."

"You know, Dad, I believe we've been having a life-changing talk. We're both stepping back and looking at what God wants us to do with our lives."

Matthew responded in silence for a minute. "I've learned much from Scripture, but I'm amazed at how much I've learned from my children."

"Dad, really?"

"Your mother and I have learned much about human nature and about living just from bringing five children into the world and seeing what they've become."

"And look how the family has spread out."

"Unbelievable."

Matthew enjoyed riding into the airport and then walking through the terminal to Gate 34, where they would meet the plane. There was something exhilarating about all these people in an international airport. He saw men and women who were obviously Mid-Eastern. What an amazing mass of people. They were all strangers, but every once in a while he would see someone who looked exactly like someone back home.

James checked the screens for information. Andrew would be arriving at Gate 34 on the Northwest Airlines Flight from New York. "The flight should be on time," he noted.

James and Matthew found seats in the waiting area. Matthew looked around, observing passengers hurrying to meet their flight or other people waiting to meet friends or family. He couldn't help wondering about the lives of all these people. James left him to visit a newsstand in order to buy a newspaper.

"Uncle Matthew, is that you?" a voice called out.

In the next moment, a sixty year old woman with a certain dignity, stood before him. It was his niece Beth. She remained a little bit stout and now had slightly graying hair but the same smiling round face he had known years ago.

"Beth, I didn't expect to see you."

"It's so good to see you. I'm afraid I don't see you often enough."

Matthew opened his arms and embraced his niece.

"What are you doing here? Matthew asked.

Beth began to explain. "I'm going on a European tour. I'll fly to New York and meet the tour group there. We'll be traveling all over Europe and England, too. My plane leaves in an hour."

Matthew invited her to sit down and then he explained that James and he were here to meet a relative who was flying from Sweden.

"Uncle Matthew, I just visited Jake and some of his family. I have some news. Jake is selling his farm because it seems none of the kids are interested in staying. He's buying an implement dealership in River Falls."

"That sounds good. Some of the family will be back in the area."

"And I have more news. I've decided to leave California. I may move to River Falls or Lake View. I guess I'm coming home."

"That's wonderful. We'll see more of you then."

Matthew felt the warmth of family as he and Beth talked. The visiting continued when James returned.

Finally, Beth looked at her watch. "I have to move on. My plane leaves in just fifteen minutes. I'm so happy that I got to see you. I think your being here made me decide it's time for me to move back home."

"Thank you, Beth. You don't know how much visiting you means to me. Sometimes, I feel a little bit down."

"Dear Uncle Matthew, you have no idea how much you mean to me. I want you around for a long time. I'm afraid I have to move along to the right gate."

Matthew kissed his niece goodbye. He spoke his thoughts aloud to James.

"I'm meeting my cousin from Sweden. And I think I might just have a purpose here on earth. God isn't done with me yet."

CHAPTER 21

James couldn't help wondering about his father. Would Matthew Anderson be able to take more of this excitement and company? Still tired from his trip to Sweden... then there was that fall and concussion, and the doctor had warned about depression. Many people and situations can become overwhelming.

As James continued to drive away from the airport and then on up north toward home, he listened to his father and Andrew talk about those ancient family connections. It seemed his father had heard more from Grandpa than James ever realized.

Finally, James cut in to their conversation. "How exactly are we related to you, Andrew? I'd like to know. Sometimes that family tree looks way too complicated."

"You explain," said Matthew.

"It's not that complicated. First, your grandfather was known as John Anderson. He had a half-brother Peter, who was much older than he. I'm not sure this half-brother was even acknowledged as family. There were a number of children in Peter's family. Those are some of the people you met. His first wife died, then, he married my mother. I know my father was not a very nice man, but he managed to marry two wonderful women. Most of his children turned out well, though there were some exceptions.

"I am by far the youngest of this generation in Sweden, James. That makes me your father's first cousin."

"Now, I understand why so many people I met were second or third cousins to me—or even further out."

Andrew continued. "Now while I'm here I'd like to meet as many cousins as possible. And maybe if we have time, visit some of your universities."

"I think we can arrange some of that."

"What did you discover?" James asked. He frequently thought of what they had talked about before. He wondered if Andrew had unearthed any more of the family information.

"I was fascinated by the P.J. story. It resembles some of what must have happened in Sweden years ago."

"I don't know that I discovered anything—or I should say—that the whole situation is shrouded in antiquity."

"That's a literary mouthful."

"Let me go back another generation. I never knew my grandfather. Did you know much about your grandfather, Matthew?"

"My grandfather never came to America, and Pa said little about him. That's why I never knew him."

James wondered why his grandfather never talked about his own father. Had Grandfather John Anderson known something of this mystery shrouded in antiquity?

"Those old stories become myths," continued Andrew. "I used to hear the stories as a child, or maybe I embellished the story I heard. There was a treasure. I believe, once again, there were three or four brothers. I investigated genealogy records. I'm the only one of my generation still alive. The next generation, for the most part, knows little or nothing."

"Didn't you find anyone?" blurted out James.

"I did find one cousin. There's story of a valuable treasure—whether there's any truth to it, I do not know. But the story is that the second brother disappeared with the treasure. Years later, he returned destitute."

"What happened then?"

"His family was ostracized. But that's not the end of the story. He had a beautiful and talented granddaughter. Somehow, one of the distant cousins fell in love with her. They eloped. The families still don't get along. What I heard is that the young people went off to America."

"When did they go to America?"

"I think it may have been in the twenties."

Matthew had been silent for a while. "Pa never talked about these family problems in the old country. He was a man of peace. I don't know of another man who had his way with doing the right thing for his neighbors."

"Well," said Andrew, "most of us here in Sweden do get along. We are better off economically. Families aren't pushed together in a small piece of land."

James couldn't help thinking this might be another interesting story to tell—a story of a broken family leaving for America. But he wanted to tell a story of forgiveness and reconciliation.

"It's just one more example of how we live in a fallen world. We are sinners, and we keep on sinning. We are very much in need of the Savior."

His words were greeted with silence.

As James continued to drive, he wondered if he should say something. Was Andrew offended by the words of his father?

Andrew made comments on the beauty of the colors and the scenery that they passed. James moved into the mode of being an American tour guide.

An hour later, Andrew made a sudden comment. "The glorious beauty of this autumn weather almost makes me believe in a Creator. And I wish I could believe and understand how Jesus could die on a cross. I wish I understood."

His remarks were greeted with silence.

After some moments of silence, Matthew spoke. "I'm a simple, unedu-cated farmer so I probably shouldn't say anything. 'But God so loved the world that He gave His only begotten Son that whoever believes in Him should not perish but have eternal life.' These words may be understood by the simplest mind or the most highly educated theologian."

"Cousin Matthew, I wish I had your faith."

"Some day you will," said Matthew.

James sensed there were tears in Andrew's eyes.

"I wish I did," said Andrew.

"And now," said James, "we're almost home."

Matthew experienced a sense of relief as they entered his home in Lake View. This small house was home even after years of living in the country. They had escaped the noise and frantic activity of the airport. James had safely driven them home. He could now relax.

True to Scandinavian hospitality, Ellen had prepared the late supper. Matthew ushered Andrew through the front door. James followed with the suitcases.

Ellen extended her hand to Andrew. "Welcome home. Welcome to America and to Minnesota. I've looked forward to meeting you."

Andrew bowed slightly and grasped her hand. "My dear Ellen. I am delighted to meet you. Your pictures don't do you justice."

Ellen blushed. "I hope you're hungry. Supper is almost ready. We're having some of my chicken soup and sandwiches."

"The aroma is most inviting," responded Andrew. He looked around at the living room and his eyes focused on a picture of the Swedish countryside. "I feel right at home. I feel as if I've come home. That picture reminds me of Sweden."

"James gave Matthew and me the picture as a gift many years ago. It reminded me of what I thought Sweden was like."

"Everything about your home makes me feel right at home."

Matthew yawned. "We've had a long day." He motioned to Andrew. "Why don't you sit down and relax. We'll have supper in a few minutes."

Andrew stood by one of the chairs. "I think I've been sitting long enough. It's good to stand."

Matthew had left all the arranging and planning to James, but he wondered about tomorrow's plans. "Andrew, I expect you might like to take it easy tomorrow."

Andrew did not hesitate. "I know I'll be ready to go in the morning. I am most eager to see the farms—especially that first home place as you call it. Isn't that the farm your father, John Anderson, settled on around a hundred years ago?"

"That will work out," said James. "Dad can show you around. I have an article that an editor wants immediately, so I have work to do."

"And," added Ellen, "I'm sure Margaret will have a noon meal for you. Sometimes we call it lunch and sometimes dinner."

"It's strange," said Andrew, "but I've always wondered about you American relatives. I've had pictures in my mind of the countryside and the farm homes. This is like a dream come true."

For a moment, Matthew experienced a sense of the unreal. Before him stood his Swedish cousin, who very much resembled him. This family connection was stronger than he had ever thought. It seemed almost that a supernatural connection existed. Perhaps Andrew felt the same way.

Ellen dished up the soup and placed a platter of sandwiches on the kitchen table. The three men sat down.

Chapter 21

Ellen turned to Matthew. "We have our Swedish guest. I think it's only appropriate that we use our Swedish table prayer. Matthew, you lead in the prayer."

Matthew began tentatively but then moved forward in confidence. "I Jesu namn till bords vi ga. Valsigna Gud den mal vi fa. Amen."

Silence followed. Matthew experienced a sense that Pa was present. The prayer and fellowship of the small group had bridged both time and generations and space. Matthew felt the continuity of family that crossed time and place. God must have a plan for all these meetings and gatherings.

It was James, who broke the silence. "I had the strangest feeling when you prayed, Dad. I felt as if Grandpa and Grandma were present, and our family was all together again."

Andrew responded to the remark. "I have not been a religious man at all. At least not until recently when I've done some soul searching. But I think I had what I would call a deeply moving spiritual experience. I can't explain it. I've never had such an experience before."

Matthew knew it was best not to try to explain what happened. Deep within, he knew that God was somehow at work. God works in mysterious ways, he thought to himself. I wonder what wonders he will perform.

The telephone rang, interrupting the experience. Ellen answered. Matthew could hear that Margaret had called, wondering about them.

Ellen announced to them. "Whenever you get out to Margaret and Joe's is fine. But Margaret is expecting you for the noon meal."

"I look forward to seeing the home place. A sense of place is important to a family. That's part of a family identity. Perhaps that's why there are family fights and disagreements having to do with the land."

Matthew's mind moved far from the supper table. The trip to Sweden had connected him to family and the past. He couldn't help wondering where this journey with Andrew would take him. Was it somehow necessary for this family journey to go full circle? If so, why was all this happening in the last chapter of his life?

An hour later Matthew fell into bed exhausted. Fear of the unknown toyed with his thoughts as he drifted into a deep sleep. He didn't want to re-live those terrible feelings he had for P.J. He could never forget the torment P.J. experienced just before he died. Even now he loved his brother, but hated what he stood for.

When he awakened, he knew he had overslept. He could hear Ellen in the kitchen, making breakfast. Andrew was in the bathroom, cleaning up. "Lord," he whispered aloud, "guide me through this day. Help me to be strong."

━◆━

Several hours later, Matthew parked the car. "Andrew, this is the home place." He pointed to the stately farm house that Margaret and Joe had maintained so well. "When I grew up, we lived in a drafty old farm house. We lived there until I was about fifteen."

Matthew and Andrew got out of the car. Andrew looked around at the house, then down the hill to the little house. "Who lives in that little house?"

"That little house is where Ma and Pa lived. I guess there's a bit of history. First, when I married Ellen we lived in the big house. Pa and Ma then built the little house."

"When did P.J. take control? I don't quite understand all of that."

"It's this way. I had worked the farm with Pa. We had this understanding that I would take over completely and get the ownership. I didn't realize any of this, but the farm had been signed over to P.J. during World War I or the Great War. That was supposed to be temporary, but P.J. never did what he was supposed to do. So, out of the blue, P.J. told me he owned the farm."

"That must have been devastating."

Matthew avoided his cousin's gaze. The pain of years before overwhelmed him for that brief moment. "I knew immediately I had to get out—to live on a farm that was mine. Everything came together well. The Nelson farm became available, and I bought the place. Actually, it was a much better farm than the old home place. But I felt that seething resentment and anger toward my brother. I had a serious ulcer attack that nearly killed me. The Lord taught me a serious lesson when I almost lost my life. I had to forgive my brother. I did forgive, and I started a new life."

"You're a strong man, Cousin Matthew."

"No, I'm not a strong man. I didn't even finish the eighth grade. The Lord has been my strength. He has guided me through all these years."

"I wish I had your faith."

The two men stood silently for a while.

Matthew continued. "I guess I was telling you a bit of history. P.J. had control for a while, but before he died he must have seen the error of his ways and wanted the farm to go back to the family. Rita, his wife, finally agreed. But something else happened along the way. The original

202

big house burned. We had the house rebuilt almost exactly like the first one. But many of the family keepsakes were destroyed in the fire."

"What caused the fire?"

"Probably lightning."

Andrew looked around and his eyes focused on the large old oak tree. "There have been many changes here. That oak tree has seen much history."

Matthew walked over to the tree and touched it, almost reverently. "When I was a boy, I used to come to this tree when I wanted to think. I think I came here throughout the years we lived here when I wanted to think—when I needed to make decisions."

"This spot seems almost like a chapel or a church."

'Yes, you're right. I love working in a garden or plowing the fields. That's when I become aware of my Creator. I sense the Lord's presence."

Andrew repeated himself. "I wish I had your faith."

"Let's take a walk over to the barns." Matthew pointed to the old barn, where he had milked cows for many years. "The old barn is used for storage. Look at the newer barn. That's where Joe and the hired man milk the cows. They have the new and bigger machines."

Andrew hesitated. "I'm more interested in the way things were when you grew up and started farming. This all seems so modern."

"When I farmed here, we had only ten or twelve cows. I raised wheat and oats and corn, and we always had a big garden."

"I see there's a garden over near the driveway."

"I often come out and help Margaret with the garden. She raises enough for her kids as well. That's the way it's always been."

"I get the impression that many people are dropping these old traditions."

Matthew thought of the many changes he had experienced. "We seem to be forgetting the past. We go for what is modern and glitzy. I'm afraid we're losing something along the way."

"It's that way in Sweden as well."

"Would you like to walk in the pasture down toward the lake? That hasn't changed very much in the last years."

"Where is everyone?" asked Andrew.

"Joe and the hired man are at the neighbors. And Margaret's inside, probably making something special for dinner. She knows I want to show you around."

The two men walked through the barnyard and into the lane that led to the east pasture. Andrew appeared to be deep in thought.

"I walked down these paths when I was a boy. I would get the cows and get them into the barn for milking."

"You must have had a good life when you grew up."

"Yes, I'd say it was a good life. I've worked hard all my life. I can't see myself not working. I have the yard and several gardens to take care of. It's my way of life."

The men walked on down the lane and into the east pasture. As they walked down a hill to the lake, Matthew pointed to a bright blue flower, the gentian.

Matthew pointed to a large house by the lake. "That's the large house that P.J. built. We're not sure who owns the place now."

"So that was part of the farm?" questioned Andrew.

"That's the land that P.J.'s widow kept. It's been bought and sold several times. Mostly, it's been some of those Chicago people."

"Outsiders don't have the same respect for the land, do they? It's a means of making money—not a place to love and enjoy."

"You have that right."

"In Sweden, we have a love and respect for the land. We have the right to walk in the country, but we must respect the owner's rights. We never litter the paths where we walk. We have respect and love for the land."

The men talked of many things during the next hour.

The men walked down to the lake. Matthew picked up a flat stone, carefully aimed. The stone skipped three times. He used to do better when he was young.

Matthew looked above, and noticed how the sun had risen higher in the sky. They had lost track of time. They hurried back to the house where Margaret would be waiting for them.

"Margaret," he called as he entered the back porch. "I'm sorry we're late."

"Everything's fine. I saw you leave for your walk, so I knew you might want to take your time." Margaret extended her hand to Andrew. "Welcome to the home place. I hope you feel at home."

Andrew grasped her hand and bowed. "I feel as if I have come home."

Margaret smiled. "I'm glad. I'm sorry but Joe and our hired man are working at the neighbors. You'll have to meet Joe later."

They sat down to eat. Margaret placed before them the chicken pot pie. "I prepared this hot dish because it would be ready any time."

"One of my favorites," said Matthew.

Margaret and Matthew bowed their heads, and Andrew followed their examples.

Chapter 21

Margaret prayed. "Lord God, thank You for the blessing of family—for the way you bring families together. Thank You for bringing Andrew to us. Thank You for the fellowship that we now experience. Thank You for the food. Bless it to our bodies. In Jesus' Name. Amen."

The meal proceeded with Andrew asking questions and learning about Margaret's children and their families.

As they were about to leave, Andrew turned to Matthew. "You are most fortunate to have this daughter. I wish she were mine."

Margaret smiled. "I feel as if I've just gained an uncle."

Andrew opened his arms, and the two embraced.

Matthew felt the presence of family and love. Such love would sustain him as he looked forward to his tomorrow.

CHAPTER 22

E llen sat down in her comfortable chair, exhausted after doing the breakfast dishes. Andrew had been with them only a few days, but the daily activities for Matthew had doubled and tripled. Matthew usually did the garden and yard work, but he wasn't used to all this running about. She couldn't help worrying that this increased pace of living was too much for him.

A tap on the back door told her that Victoria had decided to stop.

They greeted each other in the usual sister-in-law way. Ellen returned to the kitchen and immediately poured two cups of coffee, one for herself, one for Victoria.

"No need to ask about Matthew and Andrew. They're obviously out some place."

"Today, I think they're over at the cemetery, looking at the tombstones of family members. I think they might be stopping at the church as well."

"Matthew enjoys this Swedish cousin. Andrew seems like a nice sort of fellow. I would have thought he would have more in common with James."

"They do have a lot in common, but Andrew and Matthew seem to enjoy each other's company. Sometimes, they talk endlessly. Sometimes, they seem satisfied to sit near each other and say nothing."

"Just like old friends," added Victoria. "I think Matthew misses Glenn Robertson. They talked over just about everything. It's been a number of years since Glenn died."

"Matthew was devastated by Glenn's death. It took him some time to come back to being his normal self."

Victoria sighed. "That's the sad thing about growing old. I've lost most of my old friends—as well as many of my younger friends. And Matthew and I are the only two left in the Anderson family. And you're the last of your family."

"The Lord must want us here for a reason."

"What about James? Hasn't he been showing Andrew around?"

"I'm not sure exactly what's happening there. He's been working on this novel about a Depression family. I think it's actually a disguised story of the Andersons."

"We did indeed struggle through those years. But those years strengthened us as a family. It brought us together. We had to hang together in order to survive."

"James is headed for a writers' conference in Riverton. He's doing a presentation, but I think he has contact with an editor or publisher."

"I hope he hurries and finishes this novel. I'll be the first to buy a copy."

Ellen looked into her cup as she thought of her husband. "I keep thinking of Matthew and his many close calls. I can't help thinking he's not likely to have another one."

"It's my turn before Matthew's. And I'm feeling quite perky. I walked these few blocks from my apartment. Someone had the nerve to tell me I shouldn't be walking like this at my age."

Ellen smiled. "The kids worry about me when I walk up town."

"We do need to keep in shape."

During the hour that followed, the two talked over all the family and community news. Their relationship and stories were the glue that held a family together.

———✦———

Matthew hated to admit it, but he was out of breath. Andrew seemed determined to climb up the bell tower of the Oak Ridge Church. Matthew hadn't done that in a quarter century. In fact, no one climbed up the bell tower any more. We've used a rope to ring the bell. It wasn't a true sound, but at least the church maintained the tradition of ringing the bell.

"I'm sorry, Cousin Matthew, I shouldn't have made you climb these stairs way up here. But I wanted to see this beautiful countryside."

Matthew breathed heavily. "I'll make it okay."

Finally, they reached the bell and were able to look out at the countryside.

Andrew stood, not saying a word.

Matthew stood a moment, catching his breath. "I'd forgotten how far you can see. We can see at least five miles away." He pointed to the east. "My old place is over there."

"This is awesome. I imagine it was even more beautiful when the trees had their leaves. I can't see how anyone would want to leave this area."

"Most of the young people leave. There aren't jobs here. And farming isn't what it used to be. You have to go into farming really big in order to make a living."

"I love this area. I feel as if I'm home."

"It's home to me." Matthew thought a moment and added quietly, "But, lately I think more of my Heavenly Home."

"There's a bit a heaven in this place. The lakes. The hills. The fields. Heaven could hardly be more beautiful."

"I love this place. I love my family. It's hard to think of leaving."

Andrew placed his arm on his cousin's shoulder. "I will always think of you as I think of this place." He paused and added, "I can see why James wants to write about this special area."

Matthew sensed again the beauty of God's creation. "The earth is the Lord's and the fullness thereof, and all those who dwell therein."

"I think I see what you mean."

The two men stood in silence. Their silence in itself was an act of worship.

James walked down the familiar halls of the building where he had taught so many years. In a sense there was something unfamiliar about the place. It wasn't the same. It was if he were a stranger coming back.

Mark Goodman occupied his thoughts. He thought of the way he would walk over to the history department or of the way Mark would suddenly appear in his office. Why did Mark have to die so suddenly? In a sense, Mark was like Cousin Andrew, who did not have faith. Despite those differences, Matthew had found in Mark a wonderful friend.

He felt the absence of other professors he had worked with.

The minute he arrived, James found himself in the midst of activity. He had directed the writers' conference for years so he knew all the workings. His successor had worked with him last year, but they were acquaintances but not friends. James knew only a few of the students and former students or others who had come to the conference. He was disappointed for he had hoped to interact with a number of old friends.

James helped with the registration and answering questions. In a sense, he felt useful—as if he had purpose. Retirement from teaching had taken away that clear purpose for getting up in the morning and going to work. He had loved teaching, but he knew this was the time to leave the profession and pursue his dream.

His thoughts moved back to Mark. Why were some people denied the last chapter of life? The last chapter of life seemed like a good time to finish what a person wanted to finish. The last chapter could be the time to right the wrongs, to correct what needed to be corrected.

James had a full classroom as he presented his session, "How to Write Articles That Sell." As usual, he found the students or attendees tended to stimulate him. He felt alive as he was back in the classroom. Perhaps he needed more of this stimulation.

Several of the attendees had questions as he was leaving. He felt encouraged because he was able to help people.

"James Anderson, I'd like to see you for a few minutes when the conference ends. Do you think you could spare the time?"

"I guess I can, but do I know you?"

"I'm sorry. I should have introduced myself. I'm Joe Frazer, a publisher from Chicago. You spoke a few weeks ago with one of my editors and you sent him some chapters and a proposal for a book."

"Yes, I've kept on writing. And I would be happy to talk with you."

"Perhaps we could talk later while we're at this conference—when we've finished with our responsibilities."

Frazer hurried away, leaving James anticipating what this meeting was all about.

Late in the afternoon, the conference ended. James returned to the registration area. Most people had left or were leaving.

Frazer returned. "Do you suppose we could find a place that's more private?"

James turned to the conference director. "Could we use one of the offices?"

The director quickly said, "Why don't you use your old office? You can use the place for old times' sake. The door's unlocked."

Frazer followed James to his old office. James couldn't help observing. "Coming in here brings back memories of my teaching days."

Chapter 22

The two men sat down.

Frazer began tentatively. "I've looked over your chapters and your proposal. I'm wondering how far along you are."

"I've been moving along. I should be finished within a month, but I need to edit and revise."

"I wanted to say that your novel looks promising." He opened the folder which contained the chapters and the proposal. "I'm going to make a few suggestions."

James listened as Frazer made the suggestions. Excitement welled deep within him. This was a dream of a lifetime. Could the dream possibly come true?

As Frazer finished his suggestions, he gave the papers to James. "Do you think you can make the changes and complete the novel?"

James smiled. "I certainly can. I definitely will. This is a dream come true."

"I hate to dampen your spirits, but I'm afraid there's a lot of work to do. You'll be working with one of my best editors, and there will be other changes to make. But it's worth it."

"I guess I have some idea from writing articles for professional journals and some other magazines."

"You're many steps ahead of many of the writers we work with."

"How soon do you want me to make these changes and finish the novel?"

Frazer took out his black calendar book. "I hate to rush you. Would it be possible to get this done before Christmas—say December 10. I feel the novel looks promising. Then we can get it in the works next year. We'll work with you on promoting and publicizing the novel. That's part of this whole process."

"I'm beginning to realize much more about this whole publishing process." He shuffled the pages. "I've done quite a bit more. Yes, I'll have a completed novel by December 10. If I have to, I'll work day and night. I have almost two months."

"I'll be sending you a contract. I can offer you a small advance, $1000. I'm sorry I can't offer you more, but we aren't a large publishing house. And there's a lot of competition."

"I'm happy to accept. I'm thrilled at the idea of my novel getting published."

The two shook hands. Frazer left the office.

James wanted to shout out his good news. Instead, he bowed his head. "Thank You, Lord, for allowing me to realize my dream."

———————

Sunday morning, Matthew and Ellen went through the usual process of getting ready for church. Ordinarily, they went to a Bible study, but they decided that might be a little too much for Andrew. They arrived at the Oak Ridge Church about ten minutes before the worship service would begin. Matthew kept hoping the sermon would really come through to Andrew.

The congregation was unusually talkative. Many people came over to greet Andrew. The music that the organist played could barely be heard.

The organist stopped playing. Right on cue, the janitor rang the bell. Some people did not even quiet down with the ringing of the bell.

Pastor Mark raised his voice. "Good morning! Welcome to our service this morning. Today is mission Sunday. We're going to be hearing from our special guest who has returned from a short term mission trip to Africa."

Pastor Mark went on to make announcements. As he came to the end of his announcements, he looked ahead to the next Sunday. "One week from today, we have another special service. October is the anniversary month of our church. We are now 115 years old. A home town boy will be our special guest pastor. Pastor John Anderson, whom most of you know as Johnie. He will deliver the anniversary sermon."

The service continued with the usual hymns and Scripture readings and responses, followed by the sermon. Matthew didn't feel particularly inspired by this mission sermon. He remembered other sermons which made him want to give or even consider going to a foreign mission field.

Matthew kept hoping Andrew would respond well to the sermon. Would it be possible that such a sermon would help him come to faith?

The friendly country church visiting took place afterward. They had dinner at Margaret and Joe's, where some of their children gathered as well. It was a time for Andrew to meet more of his cousins of the next generation.

That evening when they returned home, Matthew decided to ask. "Andrew, what did you think of the sermon this morning?"

Andrew hesitated. "Well, I guess the fellow did a good job of fund raising. Your religious television does a lot of that."

Matthew looked away, surprised at the frankness of his cousin. "Oh, I guess he did talk a lot about raising support."

"To me, religion should be much more than raising money for good causes. I think something is wrong when we talk too much about money."

"What did you think about the people at Oak Ridge?"

"They are a great group of people—really friendly. Your church is a great social organization. The church in Sweden isn't that way."

Matthew was stumped. "The church is much more."

"I'm eager to hear your son, Cousin Johnie."

"You will like him."

Matthew didn't know what to say. He hoped Johnie would provide answers.

Chapter 23

Ellen began to get out the pork chops she was going to prepare for Wednesday supper. "I don't understand why we haven't heard from James. I thought he was coming back from Riverton on Monday."

"He's been working hard on that novel of his," said Matthew. "When he writes, I think he forgets about everything else."

"I was hoping to see more of him," said Andrew, "but I don't want to take him away from his work."

As the family said, James may be her favorite but sometimes he annoyed her. "My son's been working hard as teacher and professor for almost forty years. He's retired. He should have the free time to spend with you."

"Let's give a call and see if he's home," said Matthew.

This turned out to be one of those times when their thoughts about James coincided with his arrival at the back door.

"Hello. Mom. Dad. Andrew. I thought I stop on my way through."

"Where have you been?" demanded his mother. "I thought you'd be home Monday."

"I'm sorry. I should have called. Some things have happened. I have some good news." James turned to Andrew. "I'm sorry that I haven't been here to show you around, but I've had work I felt I needed to do. In fact it was urgent that I keep writing."

"That's all right. I understand. Your father has shown me many places. We've been to Margaret's several times. Michael and Elise have had me over. And your father and I have talked for hours and hours."

"I'm glad for that."

"Your father has been showing me what the heart of the Minnesota family is like. I think Matthew Anderson represents for me the true essence of the Swedish American farmer. That's what I wanted to learn. But I'm afraid things are changing fast here in America. I fear that you could lose something very precious."

"Yes," agreed James. "That's what I'm writing about."

Ellen abruptly interrupted. "I think I'll kick you men out of the kitchen. I'm going to get supper—breaded pork chops. And a cook works best alone in the kitchen. And, James, you by all means stay for supper."

James didn't hesitate. "Thanks Mom. How could I refuse?"

"But, James," questioned Ellen, "what is your news? Your surprise?"

"Saturday, I talked with Joe Frazer from a publishing company. We talked about publishing my first novel."

"Congratulations, son. That's your dream of a lifetime. I'm proud of you."

Andrew and Matthew added their congratulations.

"Now, as I said. Get out of kitchen. We're having early supper because I'm going to church to Bible study and prayer meeting and choir. And Matthew should at least go to choir."

Andrew announced. "I'll go with you to Bible study tonight. I want to see what goes on."

Ellen looked at Matthew and saw his happiness at Andrew's announcement. Then, she looked at James, who seemed to have more to say.

"James, let me hear more. There's more, isn't there?"

"Yes!" He held up a contract. "Here's the official contract, which I shall mail tomorrow morning. And look at what it says. Upon receipt of this contract, I will receive a $1000 advance."

"Wow!" exclaimed Matthew.

"And then," added James, "I'll get more money from royalties when the book sales come in. But that's not what's important. What's important is that my book will be published, and I hope many people will read the book."

"The family will buy your books," said Ellen.

"You and Dad will have a special signed copy from the author himself."

Ellen couldn't help herself. She went over to her son and hugged him. "I'm proud of you. You're doing what God meant for you to do."

"And," added Andrew, "I'm proud to have an American cousin who happens to be an author. You will be read in Sweden."

The men left the kitchen. Ellen went about preparing supper in the same way she had one for more than sixty years. Life takes many twists and turns, she thought. You never know for sure where life takes you.

She whispered quietly. "Thank You, Lord, that I may see James achieve his dream. Lord, you have blessed me beyond all my expectations."

―――――――

The Bible study ended. A lay person had been leading a series of lessons on the prophet Elijah. The evening's study dealt with a tired and discouraged Elijah, who had recently confronted the pagan god of Baal and brought down the awesome power of God. Then Jezebel had threatened him and he escaped. He felt discouraged and wanted to die.

Matthew wondered how Andrew would take to a lesson such as this. "What did you think?" Matthew asked.

"I'm thinking," replied Andrew. "I'm trying to take it all in. I need to think."

Matthew and Ellen left Andrew when choir practice began immediately after the Bible study. Andrew sat in the back of sanctuary and began to page through the hymn book.

During the ride home and immediately afterwards, Andrew was unusually quiet. Normally he was a man of many questions and words.

As they settled down in the living room at home, Ellen asked, "Would you like a cup of hot chocolate?

Both Matthew and Andrew agreed.

After they had drunk their hot chocolate and visited quietly, Ellen excused herself. "I'll let you two men visit. I'm tired. I'm going to bed early."

As soon as she left, Andrew began, "Matthew, I'd like to talk. Some things have been going through my mind."

"Go ahead."

"This Lord that you pray to. He's very personal isn't He?"

"Yes, that's what being a Christian all is about. As a sinner, I can't make it on my own. I miss the mark. I committed my life to Him."

Andrew seemed to be staring into space. "I found some hymns in your hymn book. I wrote down some of the words."

Matthew wondered which hymn Andrew found meaningful.

Slowly and deliberately Andrew began to read the words. "I heard the voice of Jesus say, 'Come unto me and rest. Lay down, thou weary one, lay down Thy head upon my breast.' I came to Jesus as I was, Weary and worn and sad; I found in Him a resting place, and He hath made me glad."

Matthew waited for him to go on. "Those are words right out of Scripture."

"You know, Matthew, the god that I grew up with was a god of the past. A god who was remote and far away. A god that could perhaps be reached in some high place in a cathedral or church building. The God here is very different."

Matthew searched for the right words. "I believe in Jesus as true God. He is love and wants a relationship with us humans. I committed my life to Him, and He became my personal Savior. Jesus is my friend."

"That sounds too good to be true."

"It is true. And He's been turning my life around ever since."

"I think I could come to believe in your kind of God. I'd like to believe in your Jesus. I think the agnostic beliefs of my whole life are getting in the way. University professors are skeptics, and I've been one of those skeptics."

"Jesus is the one who changes people."

"I wonder if it's not too late to change me."

"Never too late. Just ask Him."

Andrew yawned. "I have some thinking to do. Good night, Cousin Matthew."

Matthew responded with a good night. There was nothing more to say. He prayed that somehow the Holy Spirit would work on this lifetime agnostic. Miracles did happen.

—◦◦◦◦◦—

James felt torn between work on his novel and showing Andrew some of the museums and libraries and universities. During the next two days, he drove Andrew to the Riverton University and to several museums. Andrew seemed to enjoy the people he met and whatever he saw. It's too bad, thought James, that we didn't get to know each other much sooner. During those days he managed to squeeze in some writing time. When he had dreamed of being published, he hadn't thought of how time consuming such a career would be.

Saturday morning, he managed to work for a few hours before Ruth arrived from Riverton. She had stayed in the apartment Friday night so that she could relax after a hard week of fifth graders.

James remained so intent on his writing that he noticed nothing around him until he smelled the delicious aroma of a hot dish—or casserole as city people called it. He hadn't even noticed when Ruth came in the house.

He hurried into the kitchen. "I'm sorry I didn't hear you when you came."

Ruth laughed. "You were so intent on that writing. I think you would have completely missed a tornado if it had come through."

"I need to keep moving along to meet my deadline."

Ruth came over and gave him a good kiss on the mouth. "I've missed you. I don't know that I like being alone in Riverton."

"I'll come to Riverton more later on when I get this writing under control. I think I write better when I'm here."

"I suppose that will have to work. In a year I'll be here." She set two plates on the table. "I hope I won't be a distraction."

"No. I could never get through this if I didn't know you'd be coming or that I'd be going back to you in Riverton."

Ruth put out the silverware and placed the hot dish and salad on the table.

Sitting down, they prayed their traditional, "Come, Lord Jesus, be our guest. Let this food to us be blessed."

They ate in silence. James kept thinking of what he needed to do as he would continue to write.

Ruth looked across the table at him. "James Anderson, I hope you're not exchanging the busy-ness of one profession for another one that is more demanding."

"What do you mean?"

"I think your writing is more demanding than your full professorship at Riverton State University. Now, you retired from the University so that you could write and also have more time with your family. Well, dear husband, is that happening?"

Ruth looked straight into his face. He avoided her gaze.

For a moment, James felt as if Ruth had slapped him and that is something she had never done or would do.

"I'm sorry. I didn't realize that was happening."

"I had to be honest."

In that moment James knew he had to do some serious thinking about the importance of the contract and his whole writing career.

James reached across the table and took her hand. "Ruth, dear, let's go for a walk. Let's just enjoy each other and the beauty around us. Let's forget about writing and work and enjoy life."

"Now, you're talking."

⟞⟝

Matthew stood before the Oak Ridge Church. Andrew and Ellen walked ahead. They had arrived early, for both he and Ellen were in the choir. He looked up at the high tower. That same bell had tolled every Sunday since 1875, when the church had been built. They were now celebrating 115 years. The church had survived many changes since 1870.

The service opened with a traditional hymn, "O God, Our Help in Ages Past." Thankful that he still had a good, sound voice, Matthew sang the words with conviction. He thought of the many years that the Lord had guided; how many different ways God had guided and directed him!

He had sung the words many times, but the next words stood out. "Time like an ever rolling stream bears all her sons away." He looked around and thought of the many friends who were no longer present in this congregation. How many more years would he be present here with his family? How about Ellen? The thought of ever losing her was beyond comprehension.

Matthew glanced over at Andrew, who seemed intent on singing the hymn. When the service continued with Scripture and other responses, Andrew kept looking at the words of the hymn.

Anniversaries and birthdays had a way of reminding a person of mortality. Time was passing quickly, and eternity loomed before him and every other human being.

Matthew listened as Johnie made the introductory remarks leading to his sermon. Somehow he hoped what Johnie said would come through to Andrew in his search for truth and meaning.

"We're human, and we hate to admit we have a problem. I kept holding the newspaper farther and farther away from me. I realized I didn't see quite so well. I hated to admit it. Finally, my wife convinced me to see the eye doctor. The remedy was simple. I needed glasses. The right prescription quickly remedied the situation. I could see and read normally.

"Along the way, I've had some other problems. I hesitated to go to the doctor. 'I'm healthy,' I said. 'I don't need a doctor.' Well, that was not the case. A short visit to the doctor took care of a situation. The result was good health."

Johnie paused and looked around at his audience. Matthew looked over at Margaret and Joe. Several of their grandchildren sat nearby. He wondered how those children perceived what their uncle was saying. Several of Margaret's children attended completely different churches. That happened as families grew and spread out. James and Ruth had come in late and sat toward the front of the sanctuary.

Johnie continued. "There's another problem that we don't care to admit. These days, we don't hear much about sin. It all started back in the garden when Adam and Eve hid from God. Eve blamed the serpent, and Adam blamed Eve. We hate to admit we're part of this fallen race. 'We all have sinned and fallen short of the glory of God.'

"There's a time when we first come to believe in Jesus as Savior. We acknowledge our past sins and failures and come to Him, asking forgiveness. That's a step in the right direction. But there's more.

"Sometimes it's hard to accept the fact that we are born in sin—prone to sin. 'Prone to wander, Lord I feel it. Prone to leave the God I love.' Those were words from the old hymn. But there's more that we have to accept. I had to accept the fact that I needed to go to an eye doctor. The problem was taken care of. The same is true about accepting our fallen state. We must seek the Lord. We must come to Jesus; the only way to the Father."

Once more Johnie paused. From that point on he told personal stories of himself and others, including Scripture references as well as words from hymns.

As Johnie ended his sermon, he spoke words of celebration. "Let us think of our past within this church family and what God has done for us. And, as individuals, think of how the Lord is working in your life. Let us celebrate what God has done through His only son, Jesus Christ. In a few minutes, we celebrate Holy Communion. You will be invited to confess your sins and also confess your faith. Then, all who believe in Jesus as Savior are invited to come forward."

A few minutes later, Andrew poked him and whispered, "Do you think it's all right if I go?"

Matthew nodded yes. He hoped that Andrew had truly come into the family of God.

Following the service there was the traditional anniversary dinner. Turkey, chicken, ham as well as hot dishes, salads and desserts made the meal truly a feast. The noon meal at church was followed by a family gathering at Margaret and Joe's. Everyone wanted to meet and visit with Andrew. Andrew appeared to enjoy all the family members he met.

That evening when they returned home, Andrew seemed reticent. Matthew figured that he would want to talk.

Finally, right before going to bed, he asked Andrew, "What do you think of Johnie's sermon and our Anniversary celebration?"

Andrew did not hesitate. "Johnie has it all right. Now I wonder if I can get it right."

Those were his parting words for the evening. Tomorrow, Andrew would fly back to Sweden.

CHAPTER 24

"Dad, you're going with us to the airport. You and Andrew have become good friends. It wouldn't be right if you didn't see him off."

Johnie's emphatic words showed Matthew a son's love.

"But you have to do all that extra driving."

"On the way back, James will pick you up in Riverton. He has business to take care of."

Matthew wasn't sure of James's business. He knew James really needed to concentrate on his writing. He had a deadline.

"Okay. I always enjoy the hustle and bustle of the airport."

"Here's a thermos of coffee," said Ellen. "And I packed some sandwiches and cookies so you can have a picnic along the way."

"Mother," asked Johnie, "are you sure you wouldn't like to come along?"

"No, I think not. Mondays, I always go with the Gray Ladies to volunteer at the nursing home. I think they'd miss me."

Andrew entered with suitcase and carry-on in hand. "Sorry it took me so long. I'm not good at packing. My wife used to take care of such things."

"We're ready to be on our way. Matthew is coming along to see you off."

"I'm so thankful for that," said Andrew. "My goodbye would have been incomplete without Matthew being there."

Matthew smiled.

"I'll be thinking about you," said Ellen.

Andrew went over to Ellen and opened his arms to embrace her. "Ellen, my dear, you are a wonderful cousin. You've made me feel so welcome. I thank you from the bottom of my heart."

"You've been a wonderful guest. I hope you will come back again."

"I promise."

With those words Johnie, Andrew and Matthew left for Minneapolis and the airport.

On the way, Matthew hoped they could continue the discussion of yesterday's sermon, but that was not the case. Instead, Andrew seemed very interested in Johnie's wife Carolyn and the family, as well as the mission trips to Russia and Eastern Europe.

Matthew felt some of the old sadness returning. Once more he questioned his own usefulness in life. What was his purpose here anyway? These thoughts and feelings seemed to come to him when he least expected.

Johnie parked the car and he and Matthew walked with Andrew into the airport. They would see him to the departure gate.

Andrew's parting words stayed with Matthew long after he boarded the plane.

"Farewell, my dear Cousin Matthew. I love you like a brother. I admire your faith. You have taught me much. When I'm back in Sweden, I'll go to my wife's fellowship group. Like Johnie and you, they've got it right."

"If there's any way I can help," said Johnie, "Let me know. I'm only a phone call or a letter away."

"Thank you."

Matthew often found it hard to find the right words. He wanted to say something special. "Andrew, you have become a brother to me. I love you, Andrew."

The two embraced. Andrew walked away, tears in his eyes.

For a moment, Matthew tried to hide the tears. Then, he let the tears flow and found himself embraced by his son.

———❧———

In the days that followed Matthew's trip to see Andrew off, James remained determined to do his daily writing. The day of the trip, James had returned to Riverton to pick up his father and bring him home . . . He had spoken only a few words to Johnie, and his father returned to Lake

View. Most of the time, he was preoccupied with all he had to do. This Friday morning, he would reach another goal in his writing.

The phone rang. It was Johnie. The brothers did not usually talk on the phone—especially not this time in the morning.

"James," said Johnie, "I'm concerned about Dad. Have you talked with him since you returned?"

"No, I guess I haven't. I've been holed up here, working on this novel. I have a deadline. I need to finish the book and then do the necessary re-writing."

"I think maybe you need to be concerned about Dad. Mother is."

"I'll try to get over there later today or tomorrow morning."

"We've been through this before. I think he may be depressed."

James figured he knew the reason. "Johnie, I think it's just the normal let down after an exciting time with our Swedish cousin. He had such a special time with Andrew."

"The way Dad talked, I think it might be more serious. It sounded to me he might almost be giving up on living."

"I can't believe that of Dad."

Johnie's words caused James to do some thinking. He hated the thought of losing Mom and Dad. That was inevitable in the scheme of life. After all, they were past their mid-eighties.

That evening, he drove in to Lake View. Now that he had moved home, so to speak, he must not neglect his parents.

As he entered the front door, his mother sat knitting an afghan. There was something comforting about his mother just being here.

"Mother, how are you?" He stooped down and kissed her on the cheek.

"I'm fine. But how's your writing going?"

"Okay, but lots of interruptions. But where's Dad? I thought I recognized Margaret and Joe's car on the street?"

"Margaret's out back. She's talking with your father."

"Is Dad doing okay? I think all this activity has been a little too much for him."

"'He isn't saying much. He places his hand over his heart. I ask him if he has pain or if something is wrong. He mumbles, 'No, not really.'"

"Is there anything we can or should do?"

Ellen stopped stitching. "I don't think there's anything we can do. Perhaps the best thing happening is that he seems to be talking with Margaret. If he can open up to anyone, he can open up to Margaret."

"You know, Mother, I think a parent seems to have one child he finds it easy to talk with. On the trip I found I had a new communication with Dad. But I find that I'm more like you, and I find it easy to talk with you."

"I think we have that kind of relationship."

James couldn't help thinking of his own life during the past months. "You know we're all going through such big changes. I never realized that retirement from a profession is a real shock to the system. Even now, I haven't completely realized the impact."

"I think I understand. When your father and I moved to town, that was a shock to him. However, he did more work than ever in our garden here. And he would go and help with Margaret's and Michael and Elise's. And then he liked working at your place at the lake."

James laughed. "In a way he didn't really retire."

"And a house wife's task doesn't really change. There are always meals to prepare and a house to keep looking reasonably decent."

In the time that followed, mother and son talked of family and concerns. Time didn't matter. They enjoyed each other and a special kind of fellowship.

<hr>

Matthew always felt more comfortable outside rather than in the house. His garden was mostly cleared for it was past the middle of October. The chrysanthemums still retained some of their yellow and purple blooms. Several zinnias remained with their bright colors. The weather was unseasonably mild—some would call this an Indian summer day.

Father and daughter had been talking for some time when Margaret changed the subject . . .

"Are you feeling all right? Is something wrong? You've been acting different these last days."

"Oh, your mother worries needlessly."

"Are you sure? You seem to place your hand over your heart. Do you have pain?"

"Not really. I don't think there's anything the doctor can do. I don't say anything because I don't want to worry your mother."

"Dad, we love you and want to keep you around."

"I don't know about staying around for years and years. I know Victoria's strong and gets around well at 95. But I hate the idea of having some kind of problem and landing in a nursing home like your grandmother."

Margaret tried to reassure him.

226

Chapter 24

Matthew pulled up a dead plant. "There's a time to be born, a time to die."

"Dad, is it hard to grow old? I'm almost sixty, and I'm in pretty good health. I find it hard to think of what I might be if I get to be Grandma's age."

Matthew scratched his forehead. "I think what bothers me the most is that I don't have the strength I used to have. And I'm afraid it won't get any better."

Margaret reached out and touched his hand. "I'll be here for you. The rest of your children will be here."

"I'm afraid of being a burden to my family. I don't want that to happen. I'd rather just have the end of life come quickly."

"I think many people feel that way. A sudden death is such a shock to the family."

"You know, Margaret, I think there are limits to our lives. I was reading in the Book of Job. That writer says clearly that a man's days are set by the Lord."

"I know that's right. But I think we need to take care of ourselves, health-wise. I heard Billy Graham say something about this. Through our actions and way of living, we can lessen the quality of life. And we can even hurry death. But, he added, we cannot extend life beyond a certain point."

"My life's in the Lord's Hands."

The two stood up and walked in silence. The last rays of sunlight disappeared and darkness settled in.

Matthew looked wistfully toward the horizon. "I hate to leave my family. I think I've let go of the farm. But I'm troubled about Michael. Jeffrey seems to have some terrible hold on the land. Michael is a good and godly man, but Jeffrey has gone the evil ways of my brother. I fear for him."

"Jeffrey can change."

Matthew placed his hand on his heart. "I'm afraid if there's anything that makes my heart actually ache, it's my concern for Michael and Jeffrey."

"We can pray."

The back door opened. "What are you two doing out there? It's dark."

Margaret replied quickly. "We've been talking. Lost track of time."

"How about some decaf coffee and a piece of banana bread?"

227

In the time that followed, Matthew felt a calm settle over him. The routine of family life and small gatherings comforted him. He knew he could depend on his family. God was guiding him in this season of life.

———

In the days that followed, James put all family concerns out of his mind. Instead, he immersed himself in the problems that had been family problems in the 1920s and 1930s. Memories of his growing up years in the thirties gave him rich material for his novel.

He remembered those old ways of threshing—the way he shocked and then they stacked the bundles. Finally, the threshing excitement. He then thought of that special Christmas when electricity came to Oak Ridge. What excitement came with this modern invention!

The next weekend Ruth stayed in Riverton so that she could visit with friends. Her absence gave James more time to work. He went to church on Sunday and had dinner with the family at Michael and Elise's. They lived so close but they were busy and he saw little of them.

He did observe his father often sitting in a corner or walking outside. At one point he followed him outside.

"Anything wrong, Dad?" he asked.

"No. I like being outside. This place has many memories."

"I remember all the excitement when we moved here. We had this bigger house and a much bigger barn. We kids thought we were moving up in the world."

"Those were our best years," said Matthew.

"These are good years, aren't they?"

Matthew looked away. "I suppose. But everyone's so busy. The grandkids go here and there. They're always in a hurry. They don't really have time for one another."

James thought back to the times he was writing about. "Those were different times. I think we went about our business at a slower pace. You and Mom always had time for us kids and our problems."

"I guess I'm older and move more slowly. I think I'm overwhelmed by so many things happening at once. I can't take it all in."

They talked for a while.

Later when the time came for his parents to go home, his father said, "It's time to say goodbye."

The words stuck in James's mind. It was almost as if his father was saying a final goodbye.

Chapter 24

The next day, an afternoon visitor brought him in direct contact with the problems of the present. As he stepped away from his word processor, he heard a knock at the back door.

"Uncle James." The voice belonged to Jeffrey.

"I'm surprised to see you." He hesitantly invited him in.

"I can see you're busy. I won't take much time. I have a favor to ask of you."

"Fire away."

Jeffrey seemed almost hesitant. "As you know, I'm running for county commissioner. And you get to vote for me."

James cleared his throat, not wanting to say anything.

"I'd like to put a campaign sign up near your mailbox, and could you put in a good word for me. After all, I am your nephew—your favorite nephew."

James smiled at the favorite nephew comment. "I'm sorry. I need to be honest. With your hold on Michael's farm and the lake property, I don't feel I can vote for you. And I'm afraid I can't encourage my friends to do so either."

"But we're family."

James felt anger rising within him. "You're not treating Michael like family."

"Business is business. And Michael made unwise business decisions."

Jeffrey turned to leave. "I'm sorry you feel that way. I thank you for being so honest."

James decided he should at least be cordial. "How about if we have a cup of coffee and talk about family?"

Jeffrey hesitated. "I guess that would be good."

Uncle and nephew visited, but the strained relationship remained.

James thought to himself after Jeffrey left. Can this family relationship ever be restored? It seems to me that some things cannot be made right.

He couldn't help wondering about his own son. Will we hear from Richard? Can I ever make right that relationship?

CHAPTER 25

November-December, 1985

James sighed as he anticipated a Sunday evening alone. At these times he really missed Ruth, but he knew this was the only way. She needed to teach one more year, and he had to discipline himself to complete his novel. Anyhow, next year Ruth would be here and establish her residence in Oak Ridge Township and the Lake View area.

James never worked on Sunday. His father had done only the necessary chores on Sunday. He had followed that example most of his teaching life. At one point when he had made a resolution not to do school work on Sunday, he discovered that he accomplished more during the other six days. Working non-stop did not pay off. It was the dedicated teacher attitude that had tempted him to work all seven.

He reflected on the past day. As usual he attended the church service at the Oak Ridge Church. However, he missed the stimulating conversation with friends at the Riverton church. The Oak Ridge minister didn't measure up to Pastor Knutson in Riverton. The morning worship service had left something to be desired. Then, he had taken his parents out for dinner. It was hard to convince them that this was his treat. After taking them back home, he had come home for a nap.

He turned on the television and looked at the schedules that the newspaper included. Only three channels were available in the country. None of the available programs appealed to him.

He switched off the television and spoke aloud. "I'll drive over to Margaret and Joe's. I'm sure they're home."

The short six or seven mile drive brought him to the original home place. Sure enough, Margaret and Joe were home.

"I was just thinking about you," said Margaret as she invited him to come in. "I thought we should talk over some of our holiday plans."

Margaret led him into the family room. The television had been turned off.

"Where's Joe?"

"He went out to the barn to check on a cow."

They began to discuss Thanksgiving. James remembered that Ruth had said his girls wanted to have Thanksgiving in Riverton. It would be their last Thanksgiving in the University town.

James observed, "Getting the family together is much more complicated. I think it's overwhelming to Mom and Dad. Mother would like to have people over, but I think it's too much for her. And there's not enough room."

"I think it's important that we make sure Mom and Dad aren't home alone during those times. And we want to include Aunt Victoria as well."

"I'll be going back to Riverton on Wednesday evening. The girls and their families are coming for Thanksgiving dinner. Now Johnie's life is more complicated. I think he and Carolyn may be joining us. Janelle's husband is a minister so he's involved in a church on Thanksgiving and Leah works as a nurse, and Jack is going to the in-laws."

"Have you heard from Richard?"

"Not a word."

"I'm sorry about that." Margaret got up and motioned for him to follow her to the kitchen. "Joe and I always enjoy some hot chocolate. How about a cup?"

"Sounds good. It's always good for conversation."

"Some of our kids are coming for Thanksgiving. I'm going to invite Michael and Elise and their four plus Mom and Dad and Aunt Victoria."

"That's a big group."

"Mom still insists on making the pies. And I think Aunt Victoria will help. It's almost like the old days on the farm."

James couldn't help thinking of his nephew. "I wonder about Jeff. That's the only other family member around here. He's usually with his in-laws. I think young Jeff is with him this Thanksgiving. Our young grand-nephew will be with his mother at Christmas."

"Divorce really complicates life, doesn't it?"

"That's why the Bible says, 'God hates divorce.' I believe it's as true today as it was thousands of years ago."

The door opened and Joe entered. "Hi Bro. I heard that last remark. Is someone getting divorced?"

"No, we were talking about young Jeffrey and our nephew's first divorce."

"Rumor has it," added Joe, "that things aren't going so well in the second marriage either."

Margaret brought out cups and set them on the kitchen table. "Let's not speculate or gossip about that. The hot cocoa's just about ready. I'll get out the marshmallows, and we can enjoy our relaxing Sunday night tradition."

The three sat and enjoyed their hot cocoa and quiet conversation. James relaxed and for a moment had a feeling that all was right with the world.

That feeling suddenly changed. The phone rang, and Margaret answered. After Margaret's words, James knew something was wrong. He knew Ruth was calling with some kind of bad news.

"James, I tried you at our place, but I figured you might be at Margaret's."

James could hear the fear and concern in her voice. "What's wrong?"

"It's Richard. I had a call from the Denver hospital. Richard's been admitted for something that looks serious. There's an obstruction of some kind. He's going to have surgery tomorrow."

"Oh no, this must have been sudden."

"I'm afraid our son hasn't been taking care of himself. I've been frantic ever since the call came."

James did not have to ponder the question. "I think I need to go. I'll call the Fargo airport. I hope I can fly out tomorrow."

"I was hoping you would say that. I'll fly out later if necessary. Let's pray that it's not so serious."

He and Ruth discussed some other details as they tried to face the problems. Deep within, James had a dreadful fear that he would not see Richard alive. But that couldn't happen. He was too young to die.

When he hung up, he looked at Margaret and Joe. "It's Richard. It could be serious."

"We figured that out. We'll help anyway we can."

"James, we understand how you feel."

"I need to get home and start to make arrangements."

Margaret was quick to volunteer. "Why don't you call from here? That will give you a head start."

That is what James did. He managed to arrange for a flight from Fargo to Denver, a flight that would leave at 7:30 in the morning.

"I'll drive you to the airport," said Margaret. "You have too much on your mind."

"Thanks sis. I need to get home and pack."

James slept little that night. He thought of Richard as a young boy, so sweet and sensitive, the kind of boy who didn't fit in with the tough guys around. Richard had always preferred his mother to him. He might be described even as brilliant and creative, but he worked on his own time frame. Richard's life was disorganized and confused—unlike the highly organized life of his father.

When he did manage to sleep, he dreamed of searching for something but never finding what he was looking for. Then, he was in the classroom. He couldn't find his notes. The students were all waiting, but he wasn't ready. Panic overtook him and he awakened.

Soon Margaret would be here to pick him up. He whispered a prayer. "Lord, be with Richard. Please make him well. Please give me wisdom about what to say and do. Please, Lord, heal that rift between us."

The fear and panic disappeared. A peace settled over him, a peace he did not quite understand.

—————

When Margaret came up the walk the next afternoon, Matthew knew instantly that something was wrong. He hurried to the door.

Without greeting her he spoke. "What's wrong?"

"I guess I'm that transparent." She looked around. "Where's Mother?"

"She's with some ladies, quilting. What's the bad news?"

"It's Richard. He's in the hospital, and it may be serious. I took James to the Fargo airport this morning."

"What's wrong?"

"We didn't really get all the details, and actually the doctors don't know. There's some kind of obstruction. The surgery takes place this morning."

Matthew usually thought through what he would say, but he spoke without thinking. "I hope and pray that this might bring father and son together."

"I knew you would want to know."

"How about coffee?"

"Yes, Dad. Let me take care of this. I know where everything is."

Father and daughter shared their love and concern for Richard and James and the family.

The concerns of the moment brought their lives to a standstill.

———

The whole day had been like a terrible nightmare. The flight from Fargo to Denver experienced some delays during a stopover in Salt Lake City. Terrible fears dominated his thinking. James thought that he might lose his son.

He had trouble getting a cab. That only intensified his anxiety.

That afternoon as he entered the hospital, he felt like a country boy in the city for the first time. The lady at the information desk was quite helpful. She told him where he could get a room for the night if he wished, and then showed him where to find Richard.

The nurse at the nurses' station was able to give him a report on Richard. In her crisp manner she reported the facts.

"The obstruction turned out to be his gallbladder. The gallbladder was removed late this morning. It appears your son hasn't been taking care of himself. He's run down, so it appears that he has an infection."

"Is he awake?"

"He was awake but groggy. Some friends stopped over but they left. You can see him. He's in the first room down that hall to the right."

"Thank you."

James experienced that panic once more. Would Richard be happy to see him? Or would he still feel that old resentment?

"Lord," he whispered under his breath, "help me to know what to say. Or what not to say. Please bring my son back to me."

James stepped into the room. There lay his son, looking pale and much older. How thin he looked. Richard had always had a slight build as a boy and as a young man. As he lay on the hospital bed, he looked even slighter. His eyes were closed.

James hesitated and then spoke his son's name.

Richard opened his eyes and looked up at him. James could not decipher whether he showed any emotion.

"Richard, it's Dad. I came here as soon as I could."

Richard mumbled, "They shouldn't have called you. You didn't need to come."

"Your mother will come, too."

"I shouldn't be such a bother."

"We're concerned."

The nurse came in and asked how he felt.

Richard groaned. "This pain is awful."

"I'll give these pills. They'll knock you out."

Richard took the pills, which did what they were supposed to do. James sat beside the bed, listening to Richard's breathing. Time seemed to stand still.

James began to realize the implications of what had happened. Perhaps Richard was not yet out of the woods. Infections could be serious. "I'm being selfish," he said to himself, "but this is going to delay my writing. Why did this have to happen now?"

Several hours later, he left the hospital and went to the motel nearby. There was nothing he could do.

As he turned off the light and got into bed, he spoke aloud. "This is what I get for being a lousy father." He lay back, but sleep would not come.

"Lord," he prayed. "Help me to make things right."

—⁂—

Matthew always anticipated the family gathering on Thanksgiving Day. He looked forward to the bustle and excitement of the many grandchildren at Margaret and Joe's home. Margaret carried on traditions better than anyone else—except for Ellen. Those gatherings always gave him a sense of well-being and continuity.

He listened intently as Ellen spoke on the phone. He knew the call was from Ruth, and there would be an update on Richard. He silently prayed and wished that the report would be a good one.

Ellen smiled as she hung up the phone. "Well, Dear, I believe the news is good. Richard came home to his small apartment yesterday afternoon. He is still very weak from the infection after the surgery. James will stay and look after him."

"That may be an answer to prayer," responded Matthew.

"Richard will need some looking after, so James plans to stay another week. I can only realize how this puts him behind in meeting the deadline for his book. I'm hoping this doesn't cause stress for him. And that stress might hurt their relationship."

Matthew thought back over the years to the way he related to his boys. He understood Johnie and his ways, but James was often a puzzle. "I guess I never did understand James. But what about Thanksgiving?"

Ellen continued her report of the phone call. "It seems some friends of Richard's are bringing over Thanksgiving dinner. Richard's still too weak to go anywhere. He needs lots of rest. Oh, there's something else that sounds good. We all know that Richard has wandered far from his family and faith. However, he's apparently been going back to church. These friends are from a church he's been going to."

"Thank God."

During the next minutes, Matthew and Ellen had their morning devotions. This was the time they prayed for each member of the family.

Matthew concluded his prayer with requests. "And, Lord, please bring James safely home. And give special care to Richard, and bring him home to us soon. And bring all our children and grandchildren and great-grandchildren to that heavenly Home."

Matthew couldn't help thinking beyond the present. The lines, "Heaven is my Home" echoed through his mind.

———

The short trip to Denver had turned into more than ten days. James had played nurse and meal maker during that time. One night, Richard made a trip to the emergency room for some complications with the infection. This time had definitely interrupted James's work toward his deadline. In reality he would have had little time for the writing anyway. Too many tasks and arrangements and interruptions filled the time.

Richard thanked his father many times, but there was always a safe distance between father and son. James knew of no way to bridge that chasm between the two. In a roundabout way he had tried to apologize for not being a good father.

James finished placing his clothes in his suitcase and the added duffle bag he had bought for the additional clothes that he had needed. He wanted to say something special.

Richard spoke first. "Dad, I can't thank you enough. I couldn't have come through this without you."

Tears came to James's eyes. "I'm glad I could be here. I'm afraid I was always busy when you were growing up. I wasn't the best father to you. I hope you'll forgive me. I don't know why that was."

Richard seemed to back away. "I thought you always favored the girls. They always did everything right. I never quite measured up."

"Oh, Son, I'm proud of your accomplishments in the art world."

Richard cleared his throat. "I'm only part time at the university. And I have to supplement my income by doing commercial art."

"Richard, you do that very well."

"I didn't think you noticed."

James felt as if a tree branch had hit him in the face. "I'm sorry, but I have noticed."

Richard said nothing.

"I wish you'd come home for Christmas. Your mother and I will pay the way."

"Dad, thank you but no thank you. You don't understand. I have to pay my own way. I don't want to be the child who didn't quite make the grade like the others who are successful. I want to do it myself."

"Don't you understand? Your mother and I love you no matter what. We have from the time you were a baby."

"But the girls always did things right."

James wasn't sure what he should say. Silently, he prayed for wisdom. "I'm glad you've found your way back to the church. And you've made friends there, too."

"The church people always figured I wasn't measuring up either. I got sick and tired of that. That's why I wandered far away from the institution."

"But, Richard, that's not what it's all about. The whole business of being a Christian is that relationship, a relationship with the Lord."

"Don't preach, Dad. I don't need that."

"I'm sorry."

"I could say the same. I'm sorry I'm such a jerk."

"I hope you'll think about a visit home. And your mother and I would really like to pay your fare."

"I'll think about a visit. And I'm searching for God, the real God that I need to know and haven't found."

"Your mother and I pray for you."

"And I know Grandpa is."

A knock on the door told James that his ride to the airport had come. He wanted to say the right words but they wouldn't come.

"Thank you, Dad."

"I love you, Son."

James opened his arms. Richard reluctantly embraced his father at first. Then, James felt his son relax into the warmth of a full embrace.

It was a beginning.

CHAPTER 26

Matthew loved Christmas. Next to the satisfaction of a newly planted field in spring, Matthew appreciated Christmas. This was the season that brought people together and seemed to accentuate all that was good.

At the same time, he longed for the way things used to be when his children were at home. Victoria would come and stay over. Ma and Pa were nearby in the little house. Victoria often stayed over and helped with all the work. On Christmas Eve, his sister Mary and her family and brother P.J. and his family would come over.

How thankful he was that he still had Victoria. Otherwise, the other siblings were no longer on this earth. Both Mary and Martha's families lived far away. For one sad moment he thought to himself, "I'll probably never see those nieces and nephews again in this life."

It was now a week before Christmas. Ellen busied herself with baking cookies. Today, he was helping her by putting together her date-filled cookies. After that, he would frost some of the other cookies.

Ellen sighed. "Let's take a break and have some coffee."

"And taste the cookies."

"We'll eat the broken ones—and the ones that aren't quite right."

"The bloopers."

Matthew thought of the years that had passed. "How many years have you been doing exactly what you're doing now?"

"It's 1985. We were married in 1923. That means that this is now the sixty-third year. Even so, I never tire of doing Christmas baking. I'm happy the kids and grandkids like these gifts of cookies. Otherwise they'd be hard to buy for."

"We really have everything we need, don't we? The Lord has provided abundantly."

Ellen reached for the coffee pot and filled the two cups. "I think everyone except Carol will be here to get their cookies. I need to box hers and get them in the mail tomorrow."

"We haven't seen anything of James for a while—not since he came back from Denver. I wonder if everything's okay. I'll be glad when Ruth is back with him next year."

"James will be fine. He always liked being alone with his writing."

The back door opened and a voice spoke. "Did I hear my name, taken in vain?"

"James," his mother answered, "we haven't seen you since you got back."

"I see I'm just in time for coffee and your Christmas cookies."

Ellen brought out another cup and poured the coffee. "How's your writing? Have you met your deadline?"

James pulled up a chair. "I had to make a decision. I realized I've been neglecting everyone."

"We understand," responded Ellen.

"I think the Lord was telling me something when Richard had surgery and was so sick. I learned a tough lesson. I had been so busy with my teaching and being head of the English department that I had not been a good father to my son. I did a little better with the girls."

Ellen reached over and placed her hand in his. "Son, being a parent has never been an easy job."

"I'm afraid I never understood Richard. He was not like most boys. He was artistic and imaginative. He loved beauty and art but had little time for the literature that I loved. He never seemed to fit in."

"But he's teaching now, isn't he?" asked Matthew.

"He has a part-time teaching job at the University, but he does freelance commercial art work. And he's very good at what he does."

"What's the decision you made?" asked Ellen.

"After much struggling, I realized I could not make the deadline and do a decent job. I called my editor last night and explained what had happened. He was very understanding. My deadline now is the middle of

Chapter 26

January. I've decided that my family must come first before my new writing career. I am now retired, and I don't have to be a slave to this new job."

Ellen smiled. "You're making a wise decision."

Matthew thought of the passing of years. "I hope I'm around to see your book. I'm proud of you."

"You'll be around, Dad. We want you here for years to come."

They finished their coffee and Ellen collected their cups. "Now, why don't you men walk up town to the post office and pick up the mail. Then, we can look at the latest Christmas cards. And, James, why don't you stay for our noon meal?"

"Mom, I should take you out. The City Café."

"Another time," Ellen replied. "I have a chicken stuffing hot dish ready to go. So, you get out of the kitchen, and I'll start to clean up after the cookies and get our meal ready."

Over an hour later, Matthew and James returned to the house. Matthew enjoyed the delicious aroma of the chicken hot dish that was ready to be served.

"I see," said Ellen, "we have quite a stack of Christmas cards. Any special ones? Any news from uptown? Matthew, you usually come back with all kinds of news."

Matthew looked to his son. James hesitated. "We heard something that might be considered gossip so I don't know if I should say anything."

"Unfortunately," said Ellen, "gossip or the grapevine is often true. You might as well tell me."

James proceeded to tell the news. "Nora Johnson came over to us, brimming with the news. She seems to delight in bad news. According to Nora, Lois is leaving Jeffrey. She can't put up with his drinking and all the rumors about him."

Ellen set the hot dish on the table. "I'm afraid Nora Johnson usually has her information right. I wish this juicy bit of information was incorrect. I'm afraid this is right."

"If this is true," said Matthew, "Jeffrey will be alone at Christmas. I feel sorry for him. Even though he's not been treating people well, he is our grandson. And we love him."

"He was the first one," said James. "I think we spoiled him. That certainly didn't help."

Ellen invited them to sit down. They prayed the table prayer, and soon were eating their chicken stuffing hot dish.

As they finished their meal, Ellen looked over the Christmas cards. "I see we have a card from Sweden. It's from Cousin Andrew."

Instantly, Matthew spoke. "Open it, and read it."

Ellen carefully opened the card. "The card itself is in Swedish, but I think we're most interested in what Andrew has written."

She began to read. "Dear Matthew and Ellen and other Minnesota family members. I think of you often and the pleasant times we had last fall. I wish I had gotten to know you years ago."

Ellen paused, and Matthew could see that hint of sadness in her eyes. "I fear that I have both good news and bad news. I had my annual checkup. The doctor had me go through numerous tests. The diagnosis was cancer—both in the pancreas and colon. The cancer is in the advanced stages. The doctor says I have less than six months to live."

Both Matthew and James gasped. "Oh, no."

Ellen continued. "The good news is this: I have found the faith my wife found several years ago. I have come to know Jesus as Lord and Savior. I have no fear of what lies before me."

"Matthew, I must thank you for being the example and showing me the way."

Both James and Ellen looked at him and smiled.

"That was your purpose for going to Sweden."

Matthew looked away, tears in his eyes.

Ellen read the closing. "It is with both joy and sadness that I wish you a blessed Christmas. I have many regrets about this life. But I look forward to seeing you in Eternity. God is good. Good Jul. My deepest regards and love, Andrew Johannson."

The three sat in silence for several minutes.

James was the first to speak. "Mother let me help you with dishes. I need to get back home."

"No, James, you go on your way. In the meantime, life goes on. It is time to move on. There is a time for joy. There is a time for sorrow."

James left, and after Matthew helped Ellen with the dishes, he went to his favorite chair to simply reflect on all that was happening. He needed time to be still.

James thought of what his mother always said. "Christmas Eve is a time for worship. But it is also the time to be with those who are closest to you." Each of the five Anderson children would have his or her own Christmas celebration. The days before Christmas, their new home by the lake changed from the quiet place to a place with many people and much activity.

In many ways Ruth was like his mother. She quickly organized everything within minutes of her arrival on Saturday morning. That left several days for her to clean, decorate and bake. James limited his writing those days in order that he could be with her and share in the work. He wondered if he could somehow communicate this family closeness and togetherness in his books.

Christmas Eve 1985 was different in one sense: this was the first Christmas in their new retirement home by the lake. The girls had consented to come to Lake View rather than Riverton. Coleen and Melissa and their husbands and the five grandchildren were all present. The extra bedrooms were in use and Matthew's office and the family room were filled with the members of his family. The absentee was Richard.

That morning, he and Ruth had tried calling Richard, but there was no answer. Somehow, he hoped Richard would at least call back. When Matthew had left a few weeks ago, he felt that a relationship had been re-established. But could he have been wrong?

In another sense the Christmas celebration was like so many other Christmases. They had the traditional lutefisk and Swedish meatballs along with the other Scandinavian delicacies. Doctor Bill, Melissa's husband, rejected the lutefisk but enjoyed everything else. Otherwise, there was full participation in all the eating tradition.

After their Christmas Eve dinner, they gathered around the Christmas tree to open the gifts. James always insisted on having the Christmas story read. For years Ruth read the Christmas story just as his mother had. Ruth insisted that the tradition be passed down to the next generation.

As Coleen, now in the advanced months of pregnancy, read the Christmas story, James thought of another time. He must have been fifteen years old. His mother, then expecting Michael, had read the same story. Coleen reminded him of his mother reading the story. There was something wonderful about seeing the faith continue *From Generation to Generation*.

As eleven o'clock drew nearer, James and Ruth and everyone in the family readied themselves for the Christmas Eve candle lighting service at the Oak Ridge Church. James looked around at his family as they sang "Silent Night" with light only from the candles and the lights on the tree. How peaceful this seemed! Thank God my family is here, except for Richard. He said a silent prayer that Richard would come home.

Afterwards in the larger than usual crowd, he looked for Michael and Elise and their children and his parents. He wondered about their absence. He knew that his parents didn't like to go out late at night. And Michael and Elise had been going to the Lake View Community Church in town. The Oak Ridge Church was changing, and people seemed to leave behind some of the traditional ways.

Christmas Day meant a larger gathering of the Anderson clan. Elise had decided she had enough time to entertain all the Andersons who were still around. James and his family were present. Margaret and Joe were there, but several of their children had left to be with the in-laws. That's what happened when families grew and took in new family members through marriage.

The day after Christmas, the house emptied quickly that morning. His girls had their homes to return to and other obligations. Still, there had been no word from Richard.

"I loved seeing them come," said Ruth, "but I'm glad to see them go. Having four extra adults and five grandchildren is a little much."

James smiled. "I have to agree."

The ringing of the doorbell startled him. James opened the door.

The mailman announced, "You have a large package. I thought I better bring it to you."

"Thanks."

James took one look. "It's from Richard." Ruth quickly found a sharp knife to cut open the package. Eagerly she cut the sides so that they could find out what it contained. James helped take out the contents.

"It's a picture!" exclaimed Ruth. "It's a painting that Richard did.""

Ruth laid out the picture on the table. James recognized the familiar scene, the home place where Michael and Elise now lived.

James experienced a reaction that few works of art evoked. In a moment he was a child back on the farm.

"That's your old home," said Ruth. "And in front your mom and dad and several children. The painting is magnificent!"

James found himself moved almost to tears. "Richard has come home."

———❦———

The day after Christmas could be a letdown for Matthew. He and Ellen slept late. They had spent Christmas Eve at Michael and Elise's, and Victoria had joined them. Michael had driven into town to pick

244

Chapter 26

them up so that he wouldn't have to drive late at night. Matthew hadn't felt quite at home when they attended the Christmas Eve service at the Lake View Community Church.

Christmas Day, many of the Andersons had gathered at Michael and Elise's. Though she was busy as a teacher, she had taken on this added responsibility. "Margaret doesn't need to do the big family gatherings all the time."

Matthew felt overwhelmed by the number of people. When you added together just the three siblings and their children and grandchildren, the number became quite large. Matthew thought, all of these children and grandchildren come from Ellen and him. The Lord has blessed us abundantly.

A gentle knock on the front door startled Matthew from his reverie.

Ellen called out from the kitchen. "Will you answer that, Matthew? I can't imagine who would be stopping by just now."

Matthew went to the door. When he opened it, he was surprised to see his oldest grandson, Jeffrey. Once again, it seemed almost as if brother P.J. were standing before him. The dark, handsome features bore an unbelievable resemblance to his grand uncle.

"Grandpa, I had to stop by to wish you Merry Christmas." He held in his hand a small package.

"Come in. And Merry Christmas."

Ellen came in from the kitchen. "You were supposed to stop by and pick up your box of cookies. You should have brought your wife with you."

Matthew thought he smelled a hint of alcohol.

"I'm afraid I have some bad news. Lois left me a few days before Christmas."

"I'm so sorry," said Ellen. "What happened?"

Jeffrey choked up. "It's a long story."

Ellen moved toward him and kissed him on the cheek. "Where are my manners? Take off your coat and sit down. We'll have some coffee and Christmas cookies."

"That would be great, Grandma."

Matthew, at a loss for words, took his grandson's coat.

"I'll get the coffee and cookies. You sit down."

"I have a little something for you. It's not much."

"Matthew, you open the gift. I'll bring in the coffee."

Matthew, though a bit shaky, unwrapped the gift. When Ellen returned with a platter of cookies, he held up the figurine of an older couple.

245

"That's beautiful!" exclaimed Ellen. "Thank you."

Matthew added a thank you.

"When Lois and I were traveling out East, I saw the figurine and thought of you. I said to myself, 'That's Grandpa and Grandma.'"

"That was thoughtful."

Jeffrey tasted one of the cookies, and then set down his cup of coffee. "Lois left me. I don't know if there's much more to say. Things haven't been going well at the bank and insurance business. I've had some bad luck and felt a lot of stress."

"I'm sorry," said Ellen. "What did you do for Christmas?"

"I was alone. It was the worst Christmas of my life."

"You should have come over," said Ellen. "Have you talked with your mother? Does she know?"

"I haven't told her. I'll call her later today."

Ellen got up to go to the kitchen. "You need family right now. We're having left over Swedish meatballs for dinner. You stay."

"Thanks, Grandma."

Matthew saw in his grandson a young man who was deeply troubled. But, he thought, his wrong-doing is catching up with him. I hope he mends his ways.

The next few minutes were awkward moments for Matthew. He asked about the grandchildren. Jeffrey talked about young Jeffrey, who was in the Cities with his ex-wife. It was hard to believe his great-grandson was sixteen years old. The two girls were with Lois, who was staying with her parents.

Matthew wanted to say the right words. He could smell the liquor on his grandson's breath. It was no use to say that liquor never solved any problem.

The doorbell interrupted their awkward conversation.

The postman appeared at the door. "I decided to deliver your package. Too big for your box at the post office."

"Thank you," said Matthew. "This is a pleasant surprise."

Within minutes, Matthew and Ellen opened the package.

"That's our farm home!" exclaimed Ellen.

Matthew looked closer. "And that's us in front with some of the kids."

"Oh, Matthew, our dearest, Richard has come back."

"What do you mean, 'come back'?" asked Jeffrey.

Ellen reached over and touched her grandson. "It's a long story. But we haven't had contact with Richard for years. And now he paints a picture of home."

"There's a note," said Matthew.

Ellen took the note and read the words. "Dear Grandpa and Grandma. I hope this picture says what I cannot say in words. The home and the family are what give life meaning. I love you more than I can say. Richard."

Matthew cleared his throat. Words would not come.

"This makes our Christmas complete." Ellen looked up at Jeffrey. "And you're here."

"I guess I'm the Prodigal grandson."

"You're home."

Matthew silently prayed that his grandson would return home to the faith of the family.

When they ate their dinner of Swedish meatballs, Matthew experienced the illusion that Jeffrey was a frightened little boy back home with his family.

CHAPTER 27

February 1986

James looked out the window toward the lake. He could see only the white swirls of snow. A full winter blizzard was in progress. His manuscript, *From Generation to Generation*, should now be in the hands of his editor and publisher. He breathed a sigh of relief.

The weeks since Christmas had been rather routine. He had kept close contact with his parents and Michael as well. He hadn't written in his journal for some time. He decided to write.

"I have finished and submitted *From Generation to Generation*. If what the editor says is right, I should soon be a published writer. This has been a life-long dream. But I am not satisfied to sit back. The ideas keep coming for other stories."

He began to write those ideas. Other writers had said that a journal could be a rich source of writing ideas and inspiration. He began to think of his promise from a few months ago.

"I vowed a few months ago that I should put family and friends before my writing. I may love my writing, but I love people more. Ruth and I have spent special times together during the weekends. I have maintained a new telephone relationship with Richard. And I am taking more time with Mom and Dad and Michael as well. I'm concerned about Michael and his financial situation. However, there seems to be nothing I can do."

He got up and poured himself another cup of tea. Lately, he had moved away from the Scandinavian coffee and started to enjoy tea. As he looked out, he could see the storm was abating. He went back to his journal.

"Jeff Grant reminds me of Uncle P.J. I'm glad to hear his wife came back to him—at least for now. As the rumors spread and if they are true, he may well be headed for prison. He is no longer employed by the bank. If he follows in P.J.'s way, his actions affect others seriously. Cousin Larry actually spent time in prison because of what P.J. had started."

He continued to jot down writing ideas. The effects of a deed or a sin on future generations would make a powerful novel. But did he have the skill to put that across in a novel?

Late that afternoon, Michael came with his pickup and snowplow and plowed out the driveway right up to the garage. He left before James could invite him in for coffee. James hurried outside and did some shoveling where it was necessary. He always felt better when he knew he could get out if it was necessary—especially for some emergency.

As he returned to his writing, the telephone rang. He knew it wasn't the case, but the ringing seemed to indicate something urgent. He took up the receiver on the second ring.

His sister Carol's voice greeted him. "James, I'm just frantic. I don't know what to do."

"Slow down, sis, tell me what's wrong."

"Jeff's wife called. She's afraid he's going to take his life."

"Where is he? What can I do?"

"I'm sorry I guess I'm not thinking and talking straight." She paused a moment. "Lois called. Jeff is facing serious charges. He thinks the authorities are going to arrest him. He just found out. He took off. Lois thinks he took his revolver. She thinks he took off for the Grant family cabin. I don't know who to ask, but could you go out and find him. Try to stop him if that's what he's going to do."

James tried to collect his thoughts. "We've just had a snowstorm, so it may be slow going. Is there anything else I should know?"

"I better tell you this. Lois called Dad, and he may have gone out. That's what I'm afraid of. He can't handle anything like that. He shouldn't. That would be too much for him."

"I'm on my way."

He hung up and grabbed a pair of coveralls and his heavy jacket and hurried out to the car. "I better be ready for anything."

Chapter 27

"I need to stop him if I can!" shouted Matthew in a manner completely uncharacteristic of his ways.

"No," answered Ellen. "You are not driving out in the country after this storm. You don't see that well in the first place. And there is drifting snow. That would blind you."

"I need to go. I have to."

"Matthew, you're almost eighty-six years old. If you're going out there, I'm going with you."

In that moment, Matthew realized his age and physical condition. He knew he shouldn't be driving in these conditions. But he wanted to do something. Even though Lois had been ready to leave Jeffrey, she must be frantic.

"Call Lois and see if we can't get other help. James should be around."

Ellen tried calling, but the phone was busy.

"I feel so helpless."

"I'll call James."

Once more, there was no answer.

Ellen hung up. "I guess we can't call the police, considering what's happened. The police presence might push him over the edge."

Matthew couldn't help remembering only too well what had happened almost forty years ago. Jeffrey's father had taken off for the lake cabin. He had been drinking heavily. Matthew and Joe and Johnie had gone searching for him. They had found him frozen to death.

"Could history repeat itself?" asked Matthew.

"What do you mean?"

"Remember what happened to Jeffrey's father. He was messed up after the war. He'd been drinking heavily and he took off for that lake cabin."

"I'm afraid I remember altogether too well."

Matthew began to pace back and forth.

"Dear, that pacing won't do any good."

"I was trying to pray, but I keep thinking back to that terrible day when we found Jeffrey's father."

"I understand. But that is long past."

Before Matthew could reply, there was a quick knock on the door, and James entered.

Without a hello, James blurted out. "Jeffrey's in trouble. Have you heard?"

Ellen quickly responded. "Yes, Lois called. And I've had a hard time keeping your father from going out to hunt for him."

"I came from Lois's. She's frantic. So far, they've been looking in the wooded area where they hunt in the fall. They've seen no signs of him."

Matthew said a silent prayer. "I hope the boy comes to his senses."

"Dad, Lois seems to think Jeffrey might listen to you more than anyone else. I'll drive if you come along."

Matthew didn't hesitate. He picked up his jacket. "I'll go."

"Be careful," Ellen warned. "Matthew, dear, you're not as young as you used to be."

"Neither am I," added James.

Matthew got into the car with his son. He pictured Jeffrey when he was a young child. The boy loved staying out at the farm and playing with the kittens. Why had this handsome, talented young man gone so far astray? Why?

As James turned north, a thought came to Matthew's mind. "Stop! I don't think he's where they're looking for him."

"What do you mean?"

"I recall being with Jeffrey at a church picnic. We walked over to the cemetery, and he said he loved the spot because it reminded him of all the family he had."

James pulled over to the side of the road and maneuvered so that he could turn around. "We'll head for the cemetery."

Whenever Matthew approached the Oak Ridge Church, he had that strange feeling about eternity and the continuity of life. Both his grandmothers sat in their favorite pews in this same building. Ma and Pa had brought him here to Sunday school. It was here that he first felt God's presence. Generations of children and adults had looked at the stained glass window with Christ holding the lamb.

But the church also reminded him of the brevity of life. He pictured those many people who had gone from this earth. James parked the car near the gate to the cemetery. Right ahead of him was another car, which obviously belonged to Jeffrey. His hunch had been right.

Matthew couldn't help wondering about hunches. In one sense, he thought the Holy Spirit may have prompted him. There was the time the girls were lost, and he remembered that abandoned house where he found them. There were other times as well. He thought even further to the way Ellen came into his life as a teacher who happened to stay or board at Ma and Pa's. God did indeed guide and direct the lives of people.

James stopped the car. As he got out, Matthew saw in the distant part of the cemetery a shadowy figure. "There he is!"

252

Chapter 27

The two men said nothing as they trudged through the knee deep snow. The tracks took them to the older part of the cemetery. There in front of the Anderson headstone stood Jeffrey Grant, great- grandson of John and Elizabeth Anderson.

James was about to speak, but Matthew nudged him and whispered not to. Jeff was speaking to himself.

For a moment, Matthew saw himself in this very spot many years ago. Jeffrey Grant looked exactly like P.J. Years ago, Matthew had followed P.J. to this very spot, where P.J. stood holding a revolver. It seemed almost that Jeffrey was speaking the same words. Matthew was amazed that Jeff had not heard them approach.

"Great-grandpa, I didn't know you, but you must have been wonderful to have a son like my grandfather. And, Great-grandma, you showed me so much wisdom. I should have taken more time to be with you, but I was always that wayward child."

Jeffrey knelt in the snow.

"Oh, Lord, can you forgive a sinner such as me? I've taken people's money and misused it. I've taken advantage of people who desperately needed money. I'm worse than any of the tax collectors in the Bible."

Once more he was silent. Both Matthew and James watched him intently.

Then, he reached into his coat pocket and brought out a revolver. "Grandpa, Grandma, you were real family to me. Please understand that I can't go on. Please forgive me. I hope God understands how absolutely hopeless my life is. I can't go on."

Jeffrey raised the revolver.

"Stop!" shouted Matthew. He prayed silently that he would say the right words. "You can't do this. It's not right. Your family loves you."

"It's hopeless," answered Jeff.

"And God loves you," added Matthew.

"I've broken the law. I've hurt people—stolen from them. I'll go to prison."

Matthew thought of Chuck Colson and his prison ministry. "Men have gone to prison and changed. You can do that."

"We're your family," said James. "We won't give up on you."

"I can't go on." He raised the gun. "I can't go on. It's hopeless."

Without thinking, Matthew rushed over to him. He grabbed the gun. "You will not disgrace yourself and the family."

Jeffrey fell back down on his knees. Then, half kneeling, he threw himself against his grandfather. "Grandpa, forgive me. I'm sorry for all that I have done."

They remained in silence for several minutes. Matthew silently prayed a prayer thanking God for stopping Jeff.

James spoke up and took charge. "Jeff, we're taking you back to Lake View and your wife."

In his heart, Matthew knew one of the prodigal sons had returned. But he also knew that challenges lay before him. He had purpose for living; he could at least pray for his grandson.

—⁘⁘⁘⁘—

For a moment James had feared what Jeffrey would do, but his father grabbed the gun. Would this stress be too much for his father? After all, Matthew Anderson was almost 86 and he did have a heart condition.

His father awkwardly held the gun. "I hate this gun. It kills and destroys."

"Here," said James, "I'll take it."

Jeffrey moved ahead to his car.

James grabbed his arm. "No, Jeff, we're taking you back to town."

Jeff looked down, almost in tears. "I've disgraced the family. I don't have the right to claim I'm a part of the family."

Matthew took his other arm. "No, you are my grandson. We're family, and we will stay by you."

"I don't deserve you."

At that moment, the sheriff's car drove up.

The sheriff got out. "Jeffrey Grant, I'm here to arrest you."

Jeff freed himself from the grasp of his uncle and grandfather. "I should have finished the job. I wish I were dead."

The sheriff guided him to the patrol car. "That would be another crime. You have to face the music for your dishonesty. You'll get out of jail someday."

James stood transfixed in that moment of time. For a moment Jeff reminded him of Richard, who had gone his own way for so many years. Then the picture of Uncle P.J. came before him. Jeffrey Grant was the very image of Paul John Anderson. Jeffrey had followed in the steps of his charming and handsome but controlling and manipulative granduncle.

The sheriff seated Jeff in the back seat. Looking down on him, he said, "I'm going to give you a break. I'll take you back to your house so you can say goodbye to your wife and children."

"No! I can't! I don't want my children to see me being arrested."

Another car drove up. Jeff's wife got out and hurried over to the sheriff. Lois looked young enough to be a college student. Her hair blowing in the February wind, she showed fear and concern.

"Oh, Jeff, I had to come. I needed to get someone to watch the girls."

"You didn't need to come."

"I'm your wife. I came back to you. I promised to love and honor you 'til death do us part."

The sheriff stepped away. "I'm going to give you a break. Jeff, you may step out of the car. We'll give you a few moments alone with your wife."

Jeff got out of the car. The sheriff motioned for James and Matthew to move back.

James saw how the couple embraced. Obviously they were still in love. Jeff's dark features contrasted with Lois's blonde hair and light features. They were a handsome couple.

"I love you, Jeff," said Lois. "I'll stick by you. I know you're going to change."

"I'm sorry for all I've put you through. I don't deserve a wife like you."

The rest of the conversation was muffled, and James figured this was private between husband and wife. Jeff's deceit and dishonesty were catching up with him.

The sheriff addressed his father. "Mr. Anderson, I'm sorry we had to do this. Your family is one of the most highly respected families in the county."

Matthew replied, "We've known the boy has gone astray. What a person sows, he reaps. And that is what is happening. You're doing your job."

For several minutes, the three stood in silence. It seemed to James that those moments were a sacred time. The separation and jail time must be frightening.

Jeff's shaky voice broke the silence. "We're ready," he said, and then added, "I'm ready."

Lois kissed him. "I'll be seeing you when I can."

"Goodbye," said Matthew.

James added his goodbye.

The sheriff saluted. "Thanks for being here. You've been a great help."

James added, "We're family."

The sheriff drove away. James saw a young woman, alone and devastated after the arrest. He wasn't sure what to do. The poor woman shouldn't be alone.

He looked at his father, whose hand was on his heart. "Dad, are you okay. Is your heart bothering you?"

"No, not really. I'm okay."

He turned to Lois. "Someone will be over. We'll get someone to see that Jeff's car gets back to your place."

"I'll be all right."

Matthew went over to her. "Lois, we're your family."

"Thank you, Grandpa, you're special to me. And you're special to Jeff."

They hugged until Lois backed away. "I have to get home."

James thought to himself. This is perhaps the saddest family happening I've ever witnessed. How can I weave this into a story?

"Dad, I guess we go back home. You saved the day for Jeff. I don't know how you did it."

"It wasn't really me. I couldn't have done it on my own. It was the Lord's strength that came to me. It was the Spirit nudging me to do what I did."

"Dad, I'm fortunate to have you for a father. There's so much I have learned from you."

Matthew smiled.

He couldn't help wondering what lay ahead for Jeff and Lois and their girls and Jeff's older son. There were often unexpected turns in this road of life.

CHAPTER 28

March 1986

P.J. kept coming toward him. The recurring nightmare wouldn't stop for Matthew. P.J., though dead for many years, towered over him. Then, he found himself locked in the attic. He was once more a boy, and that is what P.J. had done.

In the next moment, P.J. lay in the hospital bed. P. J. reached out to him in desperation. "Save me. I've got to make things right. Help me! Help me!" Then, P.J .became Jeffrey. Matthew desperately wanted to save the grandson, but the boy was slipping away. Matthew tried to catch him. A terrible darkness surrounded them. He tried to reach the boy. All at once, Matthew was falling—falling into a deep dark place.

He awakened with a jolt to find Ellen awake. She turned on the lamp.

"Matthew, you've been tossing and turning and talking in your sleep."

"Sorry, I was having that nightmare"

"That nightmare always comes back when you're upset."

Matthew lay back. "I'll try to lie still."

"I know the remedy. I'm going to the kitchen. We'll have hot milk. That helps make us sleepy. We won't think about getting up early in the morning."

Matthew agreed. Soon they were sitting in the kitchen, drinking their hot milk.

"I can't get over Jeffrey. It's bad enough he's in jail. But it's worse that he's on suicide watch. I keep picturing him in the cemetery when he was ready to take his life."

"That was too much for you, Dear."

"No, I think God wanted me there. Now, I feel helpless. There seems to be nothing I can do."

"We can pray."

"Yes, I do pray. But I'd like to be there. And I think of Michael and how troubled he is. I don't know how Jeffrey's claims and the banks claims will work out. Michael loves the place. Losing the farm would be too much for him to take."

Ellen filled Matthew's cup with more steaming milk. "Michael was brought up to fear and love God. He will come through this stronger, no matter what happens."

"I think of what P.J.'s stealing the home farm did to me. I almost died."

"But you became a much different person afterward. You are a much stronger man."

"Right now, I feel pretty weak." He looked up at the clock. "It's 1:30. We're not getting much sleep. I wonder about Carol, too. I'm glad she's staying near the jail."

"She's working with the lawyers also. And, knowing Carol, I suspect she's going to do the best she can."

"There's no question about jail time. I'm afraid Jeff has that coming."

Both Matthew and Ellen finished their hot milk.

Matthew added, "I sometimes think the kids aren't telling us everything. They think all these problems are too much for me."

"Well, dear, we aren't so young. And added stress isn't good for either of us."

Matthew yawned. "There's nothing we can do now. Except pray."

"That is a good idea."

Matthew bowed his head and began to pray. "Dear Heavenly Father, we have more problems than we can handle. We leave these burdens to you." He went on to pray for all concerned—especially Jeffrey and Michael.

They went up to bed. Matthew and Ellen experienced a peace that passes all understanding.

Chapter 28

"I'm concerned about Mom and Dad," James said to Ruth as they talked on the phone. "This whole episode with Jeffrey is more difficult than he will admit."

"Is there anything we can do? Or you can do?"

"I feel I need to be around. For a while I've been so busy with my book that I haven't taken time for the people I care for most."

Ruth cleared her throat, perhaps a sign. "I think we've been neglecting our own family. We need to take time for Coleen and Melissa and the grandkids. We have hardly seen them since Christmas."

"They're busy. They're busier than we are."

"I've had phone calls from Richard. How about you? Have you called him?"

"I've called once or twice. And he did actually call. Remember, you're the parent he always turns to."

Ruth didn't reply. But he knew what she was thinking.

"If you want me to come to Riverton this weekend I can. We've missed being together the last two weekends because the weather hasn't been good."

"No," Ruth replied, "you don't need to. I have some friends I need to get together with. And I also need to think about packing up to move to Oak Ridge. And that's work I have to do."

James sighed. "I miss you."

They finished their family talk, and James hung up. "This has been a long winter. I can't wait for spring to come and for Ruth to move here permanently."

Before James had a chance to work on other writing projects, the phone rang. "It's Margaret. Carol is here. We're coming over. We need to have a family council."

"Come right over. I'll put the coffee on, but I don't have any goodies."

"I'll take care of that. I baked some banana bread, and I have your favorite chocolate chip cookies."

A half hour later, he and his sisters were seated at the kitchen table. James wondered exactly what Carol had been up to.

"I'm curious," he asked, "What is this family council about?"

Margaret answered. "Carol is wondering how much we should tell Mom and Dad. Though he won't admit it, Dad is definitely bothered by the whole situation."

James noticed Carol's appearance for the first time. Her gorgeous red hair actually had some strands of gray. The bags under her eyes told him that she hadn't been sleeping well, and her appearance announced that she hadn't concentrated on looking good.

"Carol," he asked, "what exactly is the situation with Jeffrey? Why don't we look at the whole situation?"

"I've been talking with Jeffrey and the lawyers as well. I think I have one of the best. I think I've convinced Jeffrey that he has to face up to what he's been doing. In the plea bargaining, he pleads guilty to a lesser charge without the trial. I feel he has to go that way."

"Why wouldn't he?" asked James.

"Actually the authorities are blaming him for some deals that some of his shady friends made. He's giving over some of their names, and he may be able to provide some evidence against them. This might be a long drawn out affair."

James set down his coffee cup with force. "You mean that like Uncle P.J. he has those Chicago connections. And that's what got cousin Larry into trouble even when he was innocent."

Margaret, always the peace maker, added. "But remember how kind Uncle P.J. could be. Remember the special gifts he gave. He loved us. He really cared."

"But," interrupted Carol, "we need to see what can be done for Jeffrey. For some time I've been getting after him. I confronted him last fall. In fact, I think I called him a jerk. We have to somehow straighten out the claims on the farm as well as the lake property."

"What can we do about the farm?" asked Margaret.

"I'm trying to deal with the bank. Because of the bank fraud, the bank examiners have been trying to straighten out everything. I'm hoping we can deal with the late mortgage payments from Michael. Because of Michael's part, the bank could take the farm."

"That would hardly be good for the bank, would it?" asked Margaret. James agreed.

Carol nervously set aside her banana bread. "I'm hoping Hank will know what to do. He's the businessman in our family."

James's thoughts returned to his parents. "What about Mom and Dad? I think of Dad especially. This is hard on him. How can we help him?"

"I'm concerned," said Margaret, "about what this could do to Dad. Have you noticed how he looks older and weaker? I think he's depressed."

James thought of his brother. "I'm worried about Michael. He's not himself. And Elise is worried about him. They have four children to think about. Only two at home, but the other two are at college and technical school."

The three sat in silence for several minutes.

Margaret broke the silence. "It's strange, isn't it, how the actions of one person can affect so many?"

A line of poetry came to James's mind. "I think of the echoes of the soul that echo like the ripples of water. I think of throwing a stone into the lake. Or of a boat on the lake. The ripples extend on indefinitely. Look at P.J. and what he did. Look at Jeffrey and the many lives he has affected or disrupted. It's not just the lives of our family."

Without warning, Carol burst into tears.

"I'm sorry, Carol. I didn't mean to hurt you."

"You told the truth. I'm afraid I do blame myself. In my earlier days I wasn't the right kind of mother to Jeffrey. I was caught up in the lifestyle of the rich and famous. Since then, my values and priorities have turned around completely."

"Carol," said Margaret, "we want to help. We don't want to hurt you or Jeffrey. Right now, what about Mom and Dad. I think they need to know."

James remembered his last time with his father. "I'm more concerned about Dad. He has such deep concern for everyone in the family. And I've been noticing how he places his hand over his heart. I think there's a problem."

"I know that," added Margaret, "but keeping something from them will hurt Dad more. He'll know something is wrong, but he won't know exactly what the problem is."

James knew what needed to be done. "We need to tell them the whole truth and nothing but the truth. No sugar coating. They deserve to know the truth."

"And," interjected Margaret, "Carol, you should tell them. I don't think you should waste any time. There are rumors and the story will break on the media."

"Yes, I'll do that. In fact, Margaret, I'll get my things, and after I've stopped to see Mom and Dad, I'm heading over to Lois's. I'm going to stay there a few days and try to help out."

James thought of his brother. "I wish Johnie were here. Then, all five of us would be together. He has always had a way with Dad."

Carol looked at James and almost timidly said, "I think we should pray."

Both his sisters looked to James. They all bowed their heads.

James prayed. "Almighty God, we come to you in times of trouble when we're not exactly sure which direction to take…"

—⊷⊶—

Ellen had been after him not to drive, but Matthew decided he wanted to see Michael. Spring was in the air, but there was more snow to melt. As he approached the stately farm home, he thought of the many years he and Ellen and the children had lived there. This had been his home, and he hoped it would somehow stay in the family.

As he got out of the car, Little Matthew ran up to him, holding up his arms.

"Hi Grampa! Come see my kittens."

Matthew lifted up his almost five-year old grandson who seemed to grow more every time he saw him. "What are you doing home from day care?"

"Gramma Jo's sick. I'm home with Daddy."

"Where's your daddy?"

"I don't know."

Michael came out of the machine shed. "Hello, Dad, I'm surprised to see you."

"I just wanted to get out of the house. I miss being in the country."

Matthew set down his grandson, but Little Matthew tugged at him. "Come see my kittens."

Michael eyed his son with some impatience. "You go play with your kittens. Your grandfather and I will have some coffee. Then, we'll see your kittens."

"Aw, Dad. I s'pose you don't want me around grown up talk."

Matthew smiled at his grandson. "I'll come out later and see the kittens."

Michael led the way to the old farm house kitchen, a place that held many memories for Matthew. He thought of the many meals there as well as those times when urgent matters had been discussed or company had dropped in.

Matthew knew that Michael was deeply troubled. They hadn't talked for some time. He knew James stopped over frequently. Sometimes, he felt they were hiding something.

Within minutes, they were sitting at the table talking of the routine, the weather, some farming matters, and some family matters. Sometimes

Chapter 28

the transition between the mundane and the serious came suddenly. Matthew enjoyed the coffee and one of Elise's famous date bars.

As he finished the date bar, Matthew observed, "I'll have to say you have a wonderful wife. You couldn't have done better."

Those words must have caught Michael by surprise. He coughed. "I must have swallowed wrong."

Matthew knew there was something more. The two men sat in silence for a few moments.

Michael looked away from his father. "I've never felt so uncertain about my future."

"What do you mean?"

Michael hesitated, avoiding his father's gaze. "It's my fault, I suppose. I went too heavily into debt—something you would never have done. Expanding the milking facilities and the barn as well as working with our small greenhouse. And I realize I can't handle the greenhouse along with everything else. Because of this, I may lose everything."

Matthew didn't know what he should say. "Can't you sell off some cattle, and scale back."

"Everything at the bank is a mess. I can't get straight answers. Jeffrey Grant is a first-rate jerk. It's his mess that's destroying me."

"You can't let him destroy you. There are ways out."

"It's like Uncle P.J. all over again. I know the story."

"My hurt and anger almost took me to the grave."

"Dad, I'm not strong like you."

Matthew silently prayed for wisdom to say the right thing. "I didn't do it in my strength. It was God, who strengthened me in my weakness."

Michael brought out more coffee and began sipping another cup. "I always figured Elise and I would grow old here the way you and Mom did. Perhaps one of the kids would want to farm the place. Maybe the farmer will be Little Matthew. But none of that is certain."

"My life was never certain along the way. There were health problems. Then, we didn't know if you would want to come back to the farm. That left your mother and me wondering what we should do. Life is always filled with uncertainties."

"Dad, you're right. I'm sorry if I burdened you with my problems."

"That's what a father is for. I feel better now that I know that you're facing your problems and thinking them through. I can pray for you."

"You don't know how much that means to me."

The ringing of the phone interrupted their conversation.

Michael answered, but Matthew couldn't tell anything from the one side of the conversation. The answers were the *yes* and *no* type.

"Dad, it was Mother. She was worried about you. Anyhow, I think you're going to get the latest news. Carol is stopping by at your place in a little while. I guess that's an invitation to go home."

"Your mother has started telling me what to do. I'm not sure I like that."

"She's concerned."

"I think I better stop and see Matt and the kittens. I promised."

"Dad, one thing about you, you always keep your promises. And you taught us kids always to keep our promises."

The minute they left the house, Matt ran to his grandfather.

"Here, Grampa, this is Freckles." Little Matthew held up a black and brown kitten. "Isn't she pretty?"

Once more, Matthew lifted up his grandson. He loved that warmth of young child hugging him with the kitten close beside.

Matthew stood a moment, enjoying the relationship that only a grandfather and grandson can have.

"God is good," Matthew said. "His creation is wonderful—right down to little kittens."

"I love you, Grampa."

"And I love you."

———

Ellen was in habit of talking to herself when she was alone. Somehow, saying something aloud made the thought so much clearer. She had done much more of this talking during and after Matthew's trip to Sweden.

"I think I've always been independent and self-sufficient—able to work out anything. But I'm realizing how dependent I am on Matthew. I would have a terrible time living without him. I've had these scares throughout the years, but Matthew has always recovered. He has remarkable resilience."

She couldn't help wondering what Carol would have to say. If there was one child she felt she had neglected, it was Carol. The two boys had arrived first and could manage on their own. And then Margaret had been the model child. On the other hand, from the very earliest years, Carol had tested the limits.

"But all the children have turned out well," she mused. "Carol certainly has turned around her life. Now, she is a strong Christian, a strong community leader. When Carol set her mind to do something, she did it well."

At that moment, she heard Matthew drive up the driveway to the garage. Before Matthew could get out of the car, another car drove up.

Ellen greeted her daughter. "Carol, dear, you look tired."

Carol kissed her mother on the cheek. "I've been on the go with Jeffrey. And the lawyers. And the court representatives, and the bank. Sometimes I'm not sure whether I'm coming or going."

"Why don't we sit down," invited Ellen. "Now, you plan to stay for supper. I have supper in the works."

"You know, Mother, that sounds good. I'm actually hungry."

Matthew interrupted. "We're curious about your news."

"Don't keep us in suspense. What's going to happen to Jeffrey?"

"It's not all settled yet. I'm working with the various lawyers. We're doing a plea bargain. Jeffrey will definitely have to spend time in prison. We're not sure about the amount of time."

"How's Jeff doing? What about the suicide watch?" Ellen asked.

"He's better now, but not out of the woods."

"I'm also working with the bank and those complicated deals that he did. That may take more work. I'm hoping we can somehow work things out for Michael. The local Lake View Bank may very well be taken over by another bank."

Matthew looked troubled as he spoke. "I don't like the sounds of that."

"Neither do I," said Carol. "But we'll do the best we can."

They talked for a while about the various possibilities. Finally, Matthew said he needed to get outside and take a walk.

After he had left, Carol confided in her mother. "I hope this situation with Jeff and then Michael and the farm isn't too much for Dad."

"It's better for us to know the truth. There are rumors all over the place. The community is really talking, but people often spare us some of the talk."

"Mom, I'm afraid there are some people who were taken in by Jeff's schemes. Some of those people are very angry."

"Your father and I already know that. It's good to know the truth."

Ellen stood up and then embraced her daughter. "I'm proud of you and the way you're handling things."

"Thank you, Mother. It's time I'm doing the right thing." She paused and added, "The truth shall make us free."

CHAPTER 29

May 1986

Matthew Anderson had always loved the land. Somehow he felt closer to God, though he knew God was present everywhere. On this particular day in May, he felt weary—almost as if he had been outside working all day. He knelt in the dirt, carefully covering the last gladiola bulb. In a few months there would be beautiful blooms. But this was still early May.

He rested. As he looked around the work that he had done, he thought of the biblical account of *Creation.* "And God said it was good . . . Very good." He looked at one spot that he had left for tomato plants and then to another spot where he would plant some greenhouse flowers. He didn't want to hurry the season. After all, May was notorious for frost.

His thoughts left the peacefulness of the garden. He knew Michael was troubled about losing all or part of the farm. Elise had confided that she thought Michael seemed to be out of control. Matthew knew all too well what that could do to a man.

What about grandson Jeffrey, who had harbored thoughts of suicide? A few months earlier, he and James stopped him just in time from taking his life. What could be more terrible for a family than for a loved one to take his own life? How could a man be so desperate?

Matthew had turned eighty-six the week before. Ellen and Margaret had served cake and coffee at the Oak Ridge Church after services on Sunday. There had been a family gathering at Margaret and Joe's. Why did they have to make such a big fuss? Though he loved people, he was shy. But he dreaded the thought that there would be far too many people all at once.

His mind returned to Jeffrey and Michael. He wondered about Johnie, who should soon return from Africa. All at once, the burden of those problems overwhelmed him. This was more than he could take.

The sun beat down on him, and suddenly he was lightheaded and dizzy. The world seemed to swim around him. He fell back, and suddenly everything went white—then black.

Ellen sensed something was wrong. Matthew usually walked up town to get the mail, but he was still out in the garden. She hadn't started noon dinner because they had decided to go down to the community center for the senior meal. She looked out the kitchen window. Where was Matthew?

"Mother," called James. "I'm here. I'll drive you to the community center for lunch."

"I'm wondering about your father."

"Worried again?"

Ellen looked more closely and then she saw her husband lying in the garden. "Oh, James, something's happened to your father. Look!"

James looked and immediately hurried outside. Ellen followed.

James felt of his pulse and spoke urgently to him.

Matthew mumbled something. Then, he spoke some words that were not quite coherent.

"Dad, can you hear what I'm saying?"

Matthew tried to talk, but the words couldn't seem to come out.

Ellen stood, speechless, fearing what may have happened or might be happening at that moment. "We need to get help."

"Can you move?" asked James.

Matthew started to sit up. Then, he mumbled something.

James looked up to Ellen and then spoke to his father. "Dad, we're going to take you to the emergency. I'm driving the car close up."

James left to get the car. Ellen bent down to her husband. "Oh, Matthew, can you hear me?"

Chapter 29

He nodded but couldn't speak.

During the next half hour, Ellen sat in the back seat of James' car, holding her husband's hand and feeling his pulse. She whispered a prayer. "Oh, Lord, please don't take him now. I can't give him up yet. I need him."

She remembered another trip similar to this. That was more than forty years ago. Matthew had almost died. The Lord had spared him, and there had been all these good years. James drove at high speeds, breaking all the speed limits.

Ellen and James waited while the doctor examined Matthew. Under these circumstances, waiting seemed like an eternity. Finally he came to the waiting room.

"He's speaking more coherently now. It appears he may have had a slight stroke. We'll keep him overnight for observation, and we'll do some tests."

"You don't really know anything?" questioned James.

"He seems to be responding normally. You can go in and see him. I think he probably needs to rest."

"He's not been sleeping well. He's been under a lot of stress."

The doctor smiled. "Stress can cause all kinds of problems. If people could only relax more and take life as it comes."

Ellen thanked the doctor. "He usually takes things as they come. He's a man of faith, but lately he's had some situations that have really bothered him."

"Well, we'll do the tests."

Ellen felt a sense of relief as she entered her husband's room. "Oh, Matthew," was all she could say.

"Dad, you gave us quite a scare."

"It's strange," said Matthew, "I don't remember anything except I know I was feeling dizzy. I remember the warmth of the garden soil."

"That's where we found you."

Matthew straightened himself. "I feel okay. I think I can go home. No use taking up this space."

"Oh no, you don't. You're staying here. They're checking you out."

Late the following morning, Ellen and James met with the doctor.

"Mr. Anderson, we can't find anything wrong—other than your heart isn't as strong as it used to be. You should avoid heavy lifting and work that is too strenuous. Otherwise, avoid all kinds of stress. Just enjoy this beautiful May day."

For Ellen, the past day had seemed like a lost day. They returned to Lake View in the afternoon, and Ellen looked at their house in Lake View. "How wonderful it is to be back home!"

—◦⟪⟫◦—

James began to write in his journal a week after the episode with his father. "Life seems to be made up of waiting. We always seem to be waiting for someone or something. Right now, I wait for the galleys of my novel. I wait for and look forward to Ruth coming here for good. It doesn't seem right that we should be apart.

"I think back to Dad's episode, and the way he scared us. I have a hard time trying to realize what it would be like to be 86 years old. I know he thinks about his own death. We are so busy with the details of daily life that we forget that our earthly life is only an introduction to eternity. Eternity is something that is hard to fathom. We humans are so clearly finite, and God is infinite."

Remembering an old hymn, he put aside his journal. He found the words of the hymn and spoke them aloud. "We wait for a great and glorious day, as many as love the Lord, when shadows shall flee, and clouds pass away, and weeping no more be heard. O wonderful day that soon may be here! O beautiful hope, the pilgrim to cheer! Thy coming we hail in tuneful accord, thou glorious day of Christ our Lord."

He recalled hearing the hymn sung in Swedish; the language his parents had learned but had now almost forgotten.

Once more, he began to write. "How do I put all of life into perspective? How can I write in such a way as to prepare a reader for the life to come? I wonder, too, if a reader would really want to read something like this."

Something prompted him to leave the journal and go outside. He looked down the driveway to the road, and he saw the mailman drive off. He could see a package attached to the outside flag. This must be the long-anticipated galleys of *From Generation to Generation*.

He hurried to the mailbox and tore open the package. There it was! The book he had thought about for years and written this past year.

"Dad and Mom need to see this!" he exclaimed aloud.

Fifteen minutes later, he burst in the front door of their house. "I have something special."

It happened that his parents were just finishing their noon dinner and their last cup of coffee. "We're in the kitchen."

"My galleys just came. Here is my book."

He placed the book on the table between his parents.

"James," said his mother, "the book looks great."

"We're proud of you son."

James sat down and opened the book. "Dedicated to Matthew and Ellen Anderson, the parents who provided the inspiration and wisdom to write this novel. They instilled in me the Christian values and desire for education that went into the writing of this book. I pray the Lord's blessing on you, the reader. May you experience some enjoyment from this reading and appreciate the fullness and richness of this family's life. James Anderson."

James saw in his parents' eyes the love and pride that they felt.

They sat in silence.

Finally, his father, the man of few words spoke. "We can't put into words what we feel at this moment. Thank you, son. And thank God for this blessing."

———

During the weeks after his medical episode, Matthew had felt cooped up. He drove up town as he sometimes did and then decided to take a drive. Spring would soon move into summer. Memorial Day would arrive in a few days.

Thoughts of Memorial Day prompted him to drive out to the Oak Ridge Cemetery. He hadn't visited the cemetery alone in a long time. He loved to walk around and remember the people who had been a part of his life.

He walked slowly up the hill to the area where his parents lay. He didn't move as fast as he used to. In fact, he couldn't do the many things that he liked to do.

Something made him want to kneel. He knelt before the Anderson headstone and looked at the tombstones of John and Elizabeth Anderson.

In the next moments he experienced a strange presence—as if he were back in time and Ma and Pa were there in front of him.

"Pa. Ma," he addressed them. "I miss you now even after these many years. Pa, we always talked over the farming matters. We always took care of problems together."

He remembered again the terrible rift when P.J. had essentially stolen the farm, tricked Pa and Ma into signing over the land. He had forgiven his brother, but the evil P.J. he never forgot.

"Pa, I can't help wondering what you would think of this modern world. The whole business of farming has changed completely. Big tractors and new farm equipment. No horses today. Combines and other equipment that is extremely costly. Everything is big and impersonal."

He thought of the recent events. "Pa, your great-grandson would have humiliated you. He has broken the law—essentially stolen money from many people. He has a debt to pay. He deserves to be in prison. Ma, you would be praying for him. I must pray more fervently that he will find the Lord—that thoughts of suicide will disappear.

"Why, Pa, do people in a good family go astray? P.J. did, and others have. They have the same upbringing, but just seem to be bent on doing what is wrong."

Matthew fingered his mother's tombstone. "Ma, I remember how you and those other women prayed for all the service men during World War II. All returned alive, though some had been in situations where most would not have survived. 'The prayer of the righteous availeth much.'

"And, Michael, why did he go so far into debt? I reminded him of the Depression and how many people lost their farms for that reason. Why can't people learn from mistakes out of the past?

"What would you say, Pa? Ma? What would you suggest I do?"

A light breeze reminded him that spring could be as changeable as people and situations.

Then, it was almost as if Pa spoke. "Children of each generation have to work out their own problems in their own way. The older generation doesn't necessarily understand."

Matthew stood up, strengthened by a new realization.

"Lord," he said prayerfully, "You are our dwelling place through all generations."

Matthew felt a new strength as he walked to the car. Spring was moving forward to summer. Life had a way of moving on.

CHAPTER 30

June 1986

Matthew Anderson wakened later than usual that morning in early June. He could smell Ellen's coffee mixed with breeze coming through the window carrying a fragrant hint of lilacs.

For some reason he felt lethargic. He didn't really have anything he needed to do. Some of the friends he used to have coffee with had either died or gone to a nursing home. He thought to himself, growing old isn't that great.

What's my purpose in life? He had been asking that question from time to time. He liked to be useful, but his children and Ellen were always saying, "We don't want you to over-do."

Matthew looked at himself in the mirror after he had finished shaving. "I am old and full of years, as the Bible says. Sometimes I feel old. Other days like today, I feel good, but I feel lethargic. I don't know if I feel like doing anything."

The phone rang, and Ellen answered. He heard her say, "I'm sure he'll come as soon as he's had breakfast."

He entered the kitchen. "What was that all about?"

"Elise called. She wondered if you would come out and look after Little Matthew. I have my ladies' group. Michael and Elise are coming into Lake View to work on their situation with the bank."

"Why don't they just leave Little Matthew here?"

"It seems that Little Matthew has been playing outside in the dirt. He's good and dirty. Elise thought it would be better to let him play, and you could be there. You always like going out to the farm."

Matthew gave her that knowing look. "Maybe their garden needs a little weeding."

"I think Elise may have given a hint."

"I figure I'm no earthly good, but now I can help a little."

As he finished his breakfast and drank his coffee, the lethargy disappeared. He began to look forward to being with his grandson.

He had the strangest feeling that something was not quite right.

James hadn't written in his journal for some time. Ruth had moved to their new home, but she was back in Riverton for a few days to finish cleaning up the apartment. No distractions. It was almost too quiet. He began to think of all that had happened during the past year.

"I've been retired a year," he wrote. "It's over a year ago that I had that incident on campus. That blow on the head helped me to stop and consider that it might be time to retire. And then came Mark Goodman's death. Death of a special person confronts a person with some very basic truths. Or, I should have said, truth about life."

He thought of the galleys he had sent back to the publishing company. *From Generation to Generation* would be in the bookstores before August. He would have achieved a life-long dream. But he also realized there was more to write—more to say.

The editor had encouraged him to go on with a second book. That's exactly what he did. *From Generation to Generation* was moving along in the publicity phase. He knew he needed time to get a new story into shape.

His thoughts returned to his own family. Somehow he would weave these problems into this second novel and perhaps the third one. He wanted to go on writing the rest of his life. He had stories to tell and ideas to put into articles.

He began to write about family. "Michael. I can't help wondering about what is happening with him. Dad and the rest of us certainly lived always within our means. Dad rarely borrowed money—except when he needed to be able to sell Grade A milk. And he paid that debt quickly. Why would Michael do something so foolish?

274

Chapter 30

"I fear that Michael has also strayed from some of our family's Christian values. His social standing in the community seems to have taken on great importance. We never felt we had to keep up with the Joneses. It seems this younger generation has to have everything—all the newest and biggest farm equipment. When Michael expanded his milking operation and then had the idea of a greenhouse-nursery as a sideline, both Dad and I thought that was a hair-brained idea."

Kids tend to go their own way, he thought. I guess I had my own destiny to fulfill: Ruth and my family, my teaching career, my writing. Those were all things I had to do—whether Mom and Dad understood or not. I think they did understand me. I guess many things about me were so visible.

He continued to write in the journal. "I've been propelled into the middle of these family concerns and problems. In some ways, it's really hard to be retired. When I was teaching at the University, my whole life seemed to center around the university and my teaching. Now, there are all these other concerns." He paused and added, "But now I have time."

He glanced at the family picture, taken a number of years back. There was Richard. "The restoration of a relationship is taking place," he wrote. "Richard is coming home. And he has a surprise. I wonder what that can be. He's leaving Colorado this morning, but he said he's taking the long way home. What I really wonder about is that surprise. He said, too, that he was eager to see Grandpa and Grandma. I guess he realizes they aren't going to be around forever."

The last words he wrote caused him to think more deeply. His father had been showing his years more during these last weeks. His mother looked the same, but he could tell she was concerned or worried. She tried not to let people know how concerned she was.

A newspaper lying near by caught his attention. Jeffrey had been sentenced to a five-year prison term. That left his wife Lois alone with two girls at home and his ex-wife with a sixteen-year old son.

"Jeffrey Grant. I think we spoiled him, for he was the first grandchild and the first nephew in the family. His circumstances weren't the best either. Carol was a young mother, widowed and eighteen. She had to struggle to get her feet on the ground. She did a remarkable job. But I don't know what got into Carol. Mac, Mackenzie, was a wonderful father to Jeff and the two girls. But he was a busy medical doctor. I suppose Carol was into the glamorous life style, and Mac didn't pay enough attention to her. She felt he was neglecting the children."

He put down his pen and poured another cup of coffee. "I'm so thankful that she turned her life around. Or should say there was a God intervention. And fortunately there was such an intervention with Hank. He's turned into such a wonderful Christian, who uses his money to promote missions. God does indeed work in mysterious ways."

James thoughts turned to a writer he admired. Thornton Wilder. "I think of *Our Town* and one of Wilder's novels, *The Eighth Day*. I'm not sure of the exact words, but Wilder said, 'We always like to know how these things began. Emily Webb and George Gibbs 'life together began in subtle ways long before the marriage.

"I think I understand why Jeffrey went in the direction he did. He was spoiled by us as a young child. Then, he had the doting grandmother, Mrs. Grant, who spoiled him and kept him from being accountable for his actions. He was exposed to a lavish life style that was quite different from the simple life of the Anderson family."

He thought ahead to next week and the trip to the prison. "What will visiting Jeffrey in prison do to Mom and Dad? As a family, we believe in loving and supporting one another, no matter what. This visit may well be a serious strain on both of them."

His thoughts turned back to his writing of novels and articles. "How can I weave all these strands of life into a believable family novel? How do I keep from giving away family secrets? How can I weave these same concerns into a good story?"

At that moment, his elbow brushed some mail he hadn't checked. A letter fell out. He picked it up and saw the Swedish postmark. He slit the letter open and quickly read the words from Andrew's sister. Andrew had died.

James looked at the date. Andrew had died two weeks ago.

"I'll wait to tell Dad when the time is right."

He set aside his journal and the letter. "There are no simple answers in life."

He couldn't explain the urge within, but he suddenly felt an urge to go over to the farm. He could easily walk the half mile, but he decided to drive.

———◦◦◦———

The minute Matthew got out of the car at the farm, Elise met him. "Dad, it's great that you could come on short notice. Michael and I are hoping to take care of some problems. And we know how Little Matthew enjoys having you all to himself."

"I'm glad I can be of some use."

Michael waved to him. "Thanks Dad. We'll see you later."

Michael and Elise drove away, and Little Matthew ran toward him.

"Hi Grampa. You gotta see my calf."

"Hello, Johnie."

"I'm Matthew. Little Matthew."

Matthew experienced the strangest sensation. He felt dizzy, and everything around seemed unreal. It was as if he were seeing through a light fog. In that moment, he felt Johnie was a child, excited about a young calf.

The fogginess cleared. "My boy, you remind me of your Uncle Johnie. For a moment, I thought Johnie was a little boy."

"That was a long time ago."

The haziness had disappeared, and Matthew felt he was back to normal life. "A long time ago. I'm afraid Grandpa's getting old."

"I love you, Grampa. Very much."

Matthew bent down and picked him up and hugged him. "I love you, too."

"I'm too big for you to carry. Come, see the calf."

Matthew felt the warm feeling of love as well as pride. This blond, blue-eyed boy was the perfect example of a robust and energetic farm boy. He was the future.

When he finished looking at the calf, Matthew led his grandson to the garden. "I think this garden needs some weeding."

"I'll help you."

Matthew, followed by Little Matthew, walked to the edge of the garden and started the tiller. His young grandson followed close behind. He loved the looks of the rich black soil after he had tilled the row. Matthew had always loved plowing and cultivating. Plowing under the weeds gave him such a sense of closeness to the Creator.

Matthew felt tired as he finished the last row. He stopped the tiller.

"I see there are some weeds to pull. Why don't you go and play with your kittens."

"No, I'd rather stay with you. Why don't you tell me about when you were young or when Daddy and Uncle James and Aunt Margaret were youngsters?"

Matthew walked over to the first row of potatoes and knelt down. "What would you like to hear about?"

"That time when Cousin Irene and Aunt Margaret got lost."

He started to tell the story, but then a sudden sharp pain cut through his heart. He fell forward even as he was talking.

First, everything around him seemed to be whirling as if he were on a merry-go-round or one of those faster rides. The world around him became unreal.

"Pa, is that you?" he said. "You look so young. Where have you been? And Ma. I've missed you."

Other people walked before him. Lucille, who had been gone for so many years. Then, Martha, who had been like a second mother. P.J. There were others he had loved long ago. Then, Ellen stood before him. But she was young, the woman he had married over sixty years ago, and the children when they were young: James, Johnie, Margaret, Carol, and baby Michael.

A figure appeared and beckoned him to follow. Suddenly, a familiar person stood before him. "Andrew, it's you!" he shouted. Pa and Ma and Martha stood close by.

In the next moment, he felt he was above his farm, looking down on Little Matthew. A car drove up, and James got out. He saw the beauty of a June day all around. But a hand seemed to beckon him away from all this.

Then, he saw something that was far beyond the beauty of the land he loved. He saw hills and streams and lakes and then a garden. This garden had to be a restored Garden of Eden.

A voice seemed to call. The scene below became dark and ugly compared to the light and beauty before him. Andrew stood there, holding out his hand. Then, Ma and Pa and Martha and a host of other loved ones welcomed him. Suddenly they faded into the background.

A man who resembled the paintings he seen many times, stepped forward and motioned for him to come.

"Oh, my Dear Jesus. Is that You I see?"

Matthew felt the most perfect peace he had ever known.

———

James drove on down the road to the family farm. The moment he got out of the car, he sensed something was wrong. His father appeared to be lying on the ground in the garden. Little Matthew stood near his grandfather.

"Grampa," Little Matthew called, "are you tired or something?"

James's heart seemed to jump up into his throat. A fear gripped him for he knew what he was about to face.

"Dad," he called. "Are you all right? Is something wrong?"

Even as he called, he knew what was in store for him. He ran toward his father.

Matthew Anderson mumbled some words, unintelligible to James except for the words, "Jesus, is that you?"

"Dad, I'm here. We'll get help."

All at once, James noticed his father's chest seemed to heave. He grasped his hand and looked into his father's eyes. One moment, his father's eyes spoke to him. Then, the recognition was gone.

James felt for a pulse. He knew already that his father was dead.

Little Matthew touched his grandfather. With tears in his eyes, Little Matthew looked to James. "Grampa's in heaven, isn't he?"

<hr />

For a moment James thought he was in a different world, a place unreal. He wanted to reach down and help his father get up. But then the reality hit him. He was stunned. He could not move. He knelt there before Matthew Anderson, the man he had known as Dad for more than sixty years.

An unseen power or energy came to James. He knew he had to take action.

"Come with me," he said to Little Matthew. "I need to call for help."

"Will Grampa come back?"

"No, I'm afraid not. Come with me. Show me where the telephone is."

Little Matthew ran ahead, and James followed. He would first call 911 and then Margaret and others in the family. He did that calling and went outside.

Little Matthew continued to ask questions.

"You mean I won't see Grampa til I get to Heaven?"

James reassured him. Little Matthew threw himself into his uncle's arms. Uncle and nephew then let their tears flow freely.

It seemed to take an eternity until the ambulance came. James went through the motions of showing the ambulance driver where to go. He felt a weakness come over him as the ambulance drove out of the yard. Matthew Anderson was leaving this beloved farm forever.

"I miss Grampa," said Little Matthew. He began to cry.

James knew that life kept moving on. He had to drive to town and tell his mother.

—◁◁◁◁◁◁◁▷▷▷▷▷▷—

Ellen said goodbye to the other ladies as she got out of the car. She enjoyed volunteering as one of the Gray Ladies. Many of the nursing home residents were older than these faithful older Gray Ladies. She had helped some of the residents play bingo and then she had read letters to several residents who had sight problems.

"I'm thankful I can get around the way I do," she said aloud. "Someday I may need someone who will read to me."

She thought Matthew would be home, but he wasn't. She opened the refrigerator door, took out the chicken. "I think Matthew's going to need a full meal. He always likes baked chicken."

Ellen went through the motions of preparing the chicken and the baked corn pudding that Matthew liked so well. I'll wait to turn on the oven, she thought. Matthew could be late. It's strange that he hasn't called.

Ellen's mind travelled many places. She couldn't help wondering about Michael and Elise. How would their financial crisis be resolved? Could they lose the farm?

What about Jeffrey—would she have a chance to visit him in prison? How would he survive in prison? She had heard some dreadful stories about what happened in prison.

She decided to sit down in the living room. Perhaps she would just close her eyes and relax a little. She had been busy all day, and her eight-seven plus years seemed to wear her down at times. She must have been dozing off when she heard her son's voice.

"Mother. Hello."

She rubbed her eyes. "I must have dozed off."

She looked up at her son, wondering why he stopped at this time. She saw the look in his eyes—a look that seemed to be hiding something.

"Mother, I have some bad news."

He sat down beside her on the sofa. "It's Dad."

She turned and instantly knew what he would say. "He's gone."

"Yes," James replied. "I decided to stop at Michael's. When I came, I saw him lying in the garden. Little Matthew was nearby. I hurried over. He had passed on."

"He must have died quickly. How terrible for Little Matthew!"

Chapter 30

"I'm amazed. Little Matthew seemed to know. He simply said, 'Grandpa's in Heaven, isn't he?'"

Those words brought tears to her eyes. "That's the way he wanted it."

Ellen felt the warmth of her son's arm on her shoulder. She somehow knew that such a message would someday come to her. "We have to call the other kids."

"Margaret is doing that, and she'll be over."

"I don't know what I'd do without you."

Ellen leaned against her son. For some reason the tears would not come.

"Mother, I'll be here for you. We won't leave you alone."

She knew that God would give her strength, but even so she felt alone and cold and empty. Matthew was gone.

She forced herself to stand up. "But life goes on."

CHAPTER 31

Death had come quickly and quietly for Matthew Anderson. It was the kind of passing that he would have preferred. His passing brought life to a standstill for many people. The regular day to day work stopped, and family and friends came together.

In a sense, James became the head of the family. With his mother and sister Margaret beside him, they made the funeral arrangements. He had never realized how many details had to be worked out. They scheduled the funeral for Saturday. That meant people could come from a distance, and other matters could be taken care of.

Life seemed to move in slow motion during the next days. Ruth came home to their Oak Ridge home. James felt his life was more complete now that his wife was with him. He spent much of his time with his mother. She appeared amazingly strong, always in control. During the next day and the following day, he and Margaret made all the funeral arrangements. Michael and Elise stayed in the background. Johnie and Carol needed time to come home.

In the late afternoon of the second day following Matthew's death, after all the final arrangements had been made, James and Ruth returned to their new home. They entered their home as the telephone was ringing insistently.

James answered.

"Dad, it's me. Richard. Where have you been?"

"We've been busy. I'm afraid we have some bad news."

Richard hesitated. "Dad, I'm almost home. We're approaching River Falls. But what's the bad news?"

The reality of his father's death became even more real as he spoke. "Your grandfather died very suddenly two days ago. We've been busy making the funeral arrangements."

Richard cleared his throat. "Oh, no. I've been away so long. I've been dreaming of seeing Grandpa and Grandma. I'm so sorry."

"We've been looking forward to your coming. You didn't tell us when so we've been wondering."

"As usual, I'm your inconsiderate son. I'm trying to change. I do have a surprise for you."

"Are you going to tell me before you come?"

"I'll wait until I see both you and Mom. In fact, I have two surprises."

"Well, son, hurry home."

James experienced many deep emotions as he thought of his son's return. More than anything, he wanted a relationship with his son.

Ruth stood before him. "Richard is on the way home, isn't he?"

"He should be here within an hour."

Ruth moved toward the kitchen. "I have to get something ready for supper."

"Remember how he loved your chicken dumpling hot dish?"

Ruth opened the refrigerator door. "Guess what. I have leftover chicken. I'll have to work fast, but we'll be ready."

James began pacing the floor in the living room. Father and son had made many inroads during Richard's hospital day during Thanksgiving. But there were still fences to be mended. He had years to make up as a father.

Ruth called to him. "You're pacing the way your father did."

"Maybe I'm more like my father than I thought. I always thought Johnie was like Dad, and I seemed more like mother."

"I wonder what his surprise is."

"I think he said there were two. I'm really curious."

The hour and some minutes seemed to pass slowly as James and Ruth waited for the arrival of their son.

When the car with the Colorado license drove up, James and Ruth hurried outside to welcome their son. In some ways it was like the father in the parable of the prodigal son. Both James and Ruth would welcome their son with open arms.

Chapter 31

Richard got out of the car and stood there. He looked older and thinner. Even though he was only in his mid-thirties, he showed signs of ill health. His Anderson blue eyes had that sharpness that must be part of an artist's look. For a moment Richard reminded him of Cousin Pete, who had been a part of his life years ago.

"Oh, my dear Richard." Ruth threw herself into his arms. "You're home at last. Our family will be complete."

Richard looked down at his mother and then up to James. "Yes, there's more. Don't forget my surprise."

Richard stepped back, shook hands with James. Then the two men embraced.

"Oh, my son, I can't tell you how thankful I am that you're home. Home at last."

Richard walked around the car to the passenger side. He opened the door. A petite young woman, probably in her late twenties, got out of the car. Her brown hair and eyes accented a face with kindness and gentleness.

Both James and Ruth stood in surprised silence.

"Hello. I'm Jennifer. Mr. Anderson, I believe I met you when James was in the hospital."

"Yes, we welcome you."

Ruth added. "We knew Richard had a surprise, but he didn't tell us what it was. We're delighted to meet you."

Richard reached for her hand and held it up to display a simple gold wedding band. "This is the surprise. Jennifer and I were married just before we left Colorado. This is our honeymoon."

Jennifer appeared more composed than the other family members. "I'm sorry that you have lost your father. I was so looking forward to meeting Grandpa Anderson. And I'm so glad to be here."

Ruth embraced her new daughter-in-law. "Welcome to the Anderson family. Congratulations, son. You must come in and see our new home. And I think we have Richard's favorite meal."

"You mean chicken dumpling hot dish?" He hugged his mother once more. "You're the greatest, Mom."

James added his congratulations. In the minutes that followed, he felt left out. From the earliest months of his life, Richard had always preferred his mother. James recalled the many times when he felt deliberately left out. Perhaps the rift in their relationship hadn't been entirely his fault. In a sense, they may have each rejected the other.

"James, why don't you and Richard bring in the luggage? Then, you can show them to their room. We have three large bedrooms upstairs. We built this home with the idea that our children would visit and all three might be here at the same time. Our basement or downstairs has two other bedrooms and a large family room."

"I'm impressed," said Jennifer.

During the next hours, Ruth and Jennifer seemed to take over the conversation. James wasn't sure his son's health was the best. He still looked terribly weak.

As they finished their supper with dessert and the last cup of coffee, Richard stopped them in the middle of other conversation. "We haven't told you about the second surprise."

"Do tell us!" exclaimed Ruth.

Jennifer beamed proudly as only a wife could. "I'm so excited about this announcement."

Richard looked at both his parents as if he wanted to observe their reactions. "This is the deal. We'll probably be moving to Minnesota. There's an opening for an art professor at the university in Riverton, and there are some opportunities in other colleges and in the Twin Cities area."

"Oh, Richard," exclaimed his mother, "that's wonderful. You'll be nearby, and we'll get to see more of you."

"And, son, you'll be at the same university where I taught for more than thirty years. I used to know the head of the art department, but I haven't met the new person."

"I may go elsewhere than Riverton, Dad. I don't want to get a position there because I'm your son. I want to be hired on my own merits."

"You're a fine artist and teacher," said James.

Richard's face reddened with anger. "I'm tired of being considered James Anderson's son. I am *me*, not the son of that talented professor."

James thought it best to think before he said anything.

Ruth interrupted. "Your father never meant that to happen. You are both very talented men, but in different ways."

"Son," began James slowly, trying to forget the words of anger. "I'm very proud of you. You will make your own name wherever you go."

"I'm sorry, Dad. I shouldn't have spouted off the way I did." He stopped a minute. "Do you think it's too late for me to go and see Grandma?"

"Why don't I call and let her know you're here. Morning would be better. Besides, I think Johnie and Carolyn are there. And Carol might be there, too. Carol's husband and many of your cousins are coming tomorrow."

"Besides," said Jennifer, "we're tired from the trip."

"Richard," began James, "I can't begin to tell you how wonderful it is to have you home. We've been hoping and praying for this reunion for a long time. And, son, I am so very proud of you."

"Dad, thank you. I guess I didn't show it, but I was actually proud of you, I guess I felt I could never measure up."

"Let's just enjoy being together. And in the re-wording of a poet's thoughts: forgetting what is behind us, we go on to maturity."

"Dad, you are smart and wise. And I am finally home."

<hr/>

During the days that followed Ellen walked through some of the daily duties as if she were walking through a nightmare. The sense of the unreal would not go away. Matthew couldn't really be gone. He would return from his drive out to the farm.

"It's good of you, to stay here," she said to Victoria as she finished washing the last dish. "I guess I needed someone to be around—especially until Johnie and Carolyn came. I think I'm still in shock."

"I think I'm in shock. Especially during these past years, Matthew and you have been such a focus in my life. And your children are like the children I never had."

"You've helped in so many ways. You were always there for each of the kids. And your gifts and your financial help made such a difference."

"Family is very important."

"Let's get out of the kitchen." Ellen hung up the towel and wrung out the dish cloth. "I guess I feel like talking, and the living room is more comfortable."

The two women seated themselves on the sofa and sat in silence for a few moments. Silence between friends is never awkward.

"So many memories come to mind as we sit here."

Ellen began to reminisce. "I can't believe all these years have gone by. Sometimes, I wake up from a dream and think that I'm back on the farm and the kids are small."

Victoria adjusted her glasses. "And I dream that I'm standing in front of a classroom of students, and I'm not prepared. But in reality I was always prepared."

"That takes me back to my teaching in the schoolhouse that you went to as a child. It was my second teaching job, but I remember how scared I was. The year I came, there were twenty-seven children, and some of the boys were almost as old as I."

"But," said Victoria, "You were a spunky young lady. You were small and petite, but you were every bit as good a disciplinarian as I was. Sometimes, I envied you. I think you had a kinder way of disciplining. I know I could be harsh—especially during those early years when I was proving myself."

"I loved teaching during those years. If it hadn't been for Matthew, I think I would have been a career teacher."

"Dear Ellen, you were meant for Matthew. He always had the feeling that he didn't quite measure up. You were good for him. You helped build his self-esteem."

"He never got over his failure to finish eighth grade. Yet, he has more wisdom and common sense than many college professors."

Victoria smiled. "I noticed that you used the present tense. He has more common sense."

"He's still so very much alive."

Victoria blew her nose. The women sat in silence until Victoria spoke.

"I think of all those times we were together for Thanksgiving and Christmas. I would come out and stay at the original farm place where Margaret and Joe are now. And then to your new—rather older—big house on the new farm. Those times cemented family relationships."

"You helped cement the relationships of Matthew's and my five children."

"You always included me."

"I'm looking back now at those turning points in my life. There have been many."

The ringing of the telephone interrupted what Ellen was going to say. She went into the kitchen to answer.

She returned a few minutes later. "That was another turning point. Richard has come home at last. James called. Richard will be in to see me tomorrow morning."

"That's an answer to prayer, isn't it? There have been many answers to prayer through the years."

Ellen's mind moved back to an earlier time. "I can't help thinking back to other funerals. Mother died when I was only nine. My seventeen-year-old sister, in a sense, became my mother. Then, when I came here, my father died soon after. My sisters and brothers were all older and married. That left me all alone. That meant the Andersons became my family."

"You've become my sister." Victoria reached over and touched her sister-in-law's hand. "You have always included me in your family."

"I'm having this sense that God has guided me and this family all the way. I think I had lapses though. I was going through a difficult period a year after Margaret was born. I wasn't ready for another child when Carol was expected. Margaret was always the perfect child, but Carol was always the spunky and difficult one."

Victoria smiled. "It took me a long time to realize it, but Carol and I were much alike. When she stayed with me, we often clashed."

"I suppose if we had prodigals, it was Carol and Michael. Carol's first marriage was ill-advised and ended in a tragic death. Her second involved a fine husband she divorced. But she and Hank have come around and returned to the faith of the family. And Michael strayed, and then returned to take over the family farm."

"I hope his financial problems can work out."

"Michael's made some unwise decisions. I sense that he's strayed. He hasn't been seeking the Lord in all his decisions. But I know he's coming back. I have faith."

"You're a great example to me."

Ellen's thoughts returned to Matthew's brush with death. "I remember those times when Matthew almost died. I had four children. I didn't know what I could do alone on the farm. But Matthew came back with new purpose and direction. And Joe, also, came into our lives at just the right time. And all the time Margaret loved him. They were brought together."

"I'm thinking of something else," interrupted Victoria. "You and Mother and a number of area women would get together to pray for the soldiers. All the soldier boys were involved in life and death situations. They all returned, miraculously. That had a lot to do with prayer."

"I remember when Margaret and Irene were lost. We had a church prayer meeting. All at once, Matthew had an idea where they were. He left, and sure enough he found them."

"Amen."

"And I think of Johnie coming back from the War. I suppose he might have had what we called shell shock. Then, it was almost like God calling Moses, he felt the Lord calling him into the ministry."

"And what about the future? Our futures?"

"I'm eighty-seven, and you're ninety-seven. The Lord has permitted us to see these many changes. And we've been a part of this."

"I strongly believe the Lord has a purpose for each of us." Victoria's strong teacher voice came through. "We must encourage the next generation in the faith. We must remind the family of how the Lord has guided and directed in the past."

"Yes," added Ellen. "We are writing this history as well as speaking it."

Victoria yawned. "I think it's about time for bed."

"Not quite. I think it's time for hot chocolate. That's how our family closes a time of family fellowship."

During the next hours, two old women sipped hot chocolate and talked of days gone by. There was a strange blending of past and present. For a short while, time seemed to stand still.

—⚭⚭⚭—

James observed the events of the day. Life, which had seemed to stand still, suddenly moved into a "fast forward" mode.

After breakfast, James and Ruth, along with Richard and Jennifer, drove into Lake View to his mother's home. James wished he could put the reunion into words that would show the depth of the love and emotions that were a part of coming home. There was so much he wanted to preserve for people to appreciate and understand. There would be future generations.

When they entered Ellen Anderson's home, she was sitting in her chair, reading her Bible. Norman Rockwell could have painted her as the ideal godly mother and grandmother.

She looked up as her guests entered. "Richard, you're home."

She stood, somewhat unsteadily.

Richard scooped her into his arms. "Grandma."

Perhaps more words would have spoiled the perfect beauty of the reunion. Tears came to the old woman's eyes. James thought to himself, my heart overflows with joy and thanksgiving.

Richard's tears flowed freely. "I'm sorry about Grandpa. I was hoping to have one of our good talks—like the ones we had when I was a kid."

"He's in a far better place. We just need to be ready to meet the Lord and to meet your grandfather."

"I know that. I walked away from the Lord, but I've come back. I've come home to the faith of my childhood."

"Our prayers have been answered."

Chapter 31

Richard turned and placed his arm around his bride. "This is Jennifer. She's partly responsible for getting me where I am."

Ellen extended her hand, but Jennifer embraced her and kissed her on the cheek. "May I call you Grandma?"

"I would love that."

Those words set the stage for the warm welcomes that followed. First there was talk about Matthew Anderson and his last days. Next, Johnie and wife Carolyn arrived. Commotion followed. In a short time Carol arrived. Then, before they settled down, the door opened and Margaret arrived with a box containing a full noon dinner for the family.

Confusion followed with everyone greeting everyone else, with special attention to Richard. This was the way the Andersons were when they gathered.

James greeted Johnie with the strong brotherly hug. They needed to spend more time together while they had time to enjoy each other. Margaret was around all the time. He took her for granted.

He hugged his sister Carol. "I can't tell you how happy I am to see you." Hank and the kids would be arriving the morning of the funeral. Carol would be staying with her daughter-in-law and grandchildren.

Like clockwork, Margaret brought out the paper plates. She spread out the food on the dining room table. They sang the table prayer and continued visiting as they sat down to eat.

James stepped back a moment. He thought of the words to a song, "There is beauty all around when there's love at home."

The Andersons had come home, but the head of the family had gone to his Eternal Home.

CHAPTER 32

E llen laid aside her Bible. "Lord, give me strength for today. I want to honor you and I want to honor the wonderful man who was my husband."

She heard her daughter-in-law stirring in the bedroom. How fortunate it was that Carolyn came into Johnie's life after Laura died. Carolyn had been a good wife to Johnie and a wonderful mother to the children. Now she was right beside him in his mission work.

Ellen knew that Johnie had driven somewhere in the country where he could walk and plan his funeral sermon. She and Matthew had been proud of all the children. However, she knew Matthew was always especially proud of Johnie. She had to admit that Johnie was the most like Matthew, and James was the most like her. Of course, all the children had the blended qualities of their parents.

She had appreciated Victoria being with her the past days, but she was thankful her sister-in-law had returned to her own apartment. She needed this time alone.

She took off her glasses, thinking she would relax a moment before Johnie returned and other people stopped in. She was tired and she found herself dozing off. Her thoughts took her back to the time when she came to the Andersons as a young teacher. She wasn't sure afterwards whether these were her thoughts or a dream had taken over. Matthew had come to her, only he was twenty-two years old. It was the moment she knew she loved him.

She wanted Matthew to stay, but subconsciously she knew this was a dream. "Goodbye, my love. I miss you."

Johnie stood before her. "Mother, it's almost time to get ready for the funeral."

"I'm sorry, I'm not a very good hostess."

"Mother, you don't think about a thing—except getting dressed and ready to go. You took care of us kids. We'll take care of you."

All at once, Ellen felt a peace coming over her. "I'll always be a mother—until the day I die."

"Carolyn will help you get into that new black dress that you decided to wear. I'm leaving early for the Oak Ridge Church. James and Ruth will pick you up."

"This is all so unreal. I knew somehow that I would outlive Matthew. But I can't believe that he's gone, and I'm alone."

"Dad isn't really gone. He's with us in our thoughts and minds—just as you are."

An unseen strength came to Ellen. She must go on.

The Oak Ridge Church and community, as well as the Anderson family, had a definite order for funerals. Johnie wanted everything to be right. On the other hand, he felt a freedom to break away from the usual pattern.

Johnie wanted to spend time alone before the funeral. He arrived at the church soon after 12 even though the funeral wasn't until two. Several women were in the church kitchen, getting food ready for the lunch they served after the funeral and burial. The Oak Ridge ladies always did their lunches in style. This lunch might well be considered a banquet.

Bible and notes in hand, Johnie walked down the hill to the cemetery. The grave had been dug, not far from the tombstones of John and Elizabeth Anderson. He stooped down and spoke as if his grandfather were present. "Grandpa, I am proud to bear your name. Somehow, I feel I don't have your strength, but the Lord keeps leading me to preach the Gospel."

He knelt and began to pray. "Lord, thank You for my heritage. Thank You for Grandpa, a strong godly man. Thank You for Dad. I know he has prayed for me every day. And Mother and Grandma, both women

294

of prayer. Lord, how can I transmit this wonderful faith to the next generations?"

His own children came to mind. Janelle, now over thirty and a stay-at-home mother, had three lively children. She was the ideal helpmate to her minister husband. This son-in-law had a life similar to his own. His namesake, whom they called Jack, loved nature and outdoors and thrived as a science teacher. He and his social worker wife had two children.

Perhaps the baby in the family always received extra attention. Leah, a nurse and about to become a mother, had married a doctor whose beliefs did not fit the Christian framework. He had wondered about the marriage. Would it survive? They were both such busy people. It was hard to see his precious little one having to face the harsh problems of life.

Families spread out, he thought. The five Anderson children had each produced children, and now those grandchildren were growing up. "Dad, I think you were overwhelmed by all those great grandchildren. They were hard to keep track of, but you loved each one."

A gentle breeze blew. The almost perfect weather reminded him of the line of poetry, "And what is so fair as a day in June." Those lines were his father's favorite. He couldn't seem to remember the next line, but there was something about heaven being close to this June day.

Johnie walked back to the cemetery entrance. He looked up this hill at the grand old country church with its new entrance addition as well as the new fellowship hall. In a sense this structure symbolized something of permanence in life. Though the structure was in no way permanent, what it stood for was permanent and eternal. "I need to impart the truth that only Jesus Christ is unchanging and eternal. Everything else changes, but Jesus does not. He is the way, the truth, and the light. He is the only way to the Father. He is the only way to salvation and eternal life."

Johnie walked back up the hill to the church. He saw his siblings and the in-laws outside greeting people. James saw him and hurried over to him.

"Well, brother, I'm sure you'll do a great job with the sermon."

A handshake turned into an embrace. "You're the expert with words. You could probably say it better."

"No, Johnie, you're the one. You and Dad always had a special bond. I think my special bond is with Mother."

"We each have our place."

"I'm thankful Dad and I had our trip to Sweden last summer. I learned more about him, and I realized what a wonderful father he was."

"That's what I'm talking about today."

Pastor Dale motioned for the family to gather in the basement of the church. They met there, and he gave them some direction about what to do and what the service would be like.

The family had chosen the opening hymn, which looked forward to heaven as "a great and glorious day."

"We wait for a great and glorious day, as many as love the Lord.

When shadows shall flee, and clouds pass away, and weeping will no more be heard.

O wonderful day that soon may be here! O beautiful hope the pilgrim to cheer!

Thy coming we hailed in tuneful accord, thou glorious day of Christ, our Lord."

As the congregation sang the stanzas that followed, Johnie couldn't help observing the different expressions on the faces of the family. This Second Coming or time in heaven seemed far away to many of the younger ones. No doubt there were those who did not believe. Others were close to the Kingdom or on the edge of coming to faith.

He couldn't help thinking of the Swedish ancestors and the way they faced such difficulties in the coming to America and in living during pioneer days. They thought more about eternity and Christ's return or the end of their own lives.

Pastor Dale proceeded through the opening part of the service. He read the obituary of Matthew Anderson. In some ways the reading of the obituary seemed cold and impersonal. Matthew Anderson's life was more than a series of dates and a list of ancestors and survivors. He hoped that he could get that truth across to people. Dale read several Scriptural passages and then Johnie read the third chapter of John, the chapter that his father wanted read. This chapter did, after all, contain the heart of the Gospel. More than anything Johnie wanted this truth to come through.

At this point, a soloist got up to sing one of Matthew Anderson's favorite songs, "If I Gained the World but Lost the Savior." Johnie couldn't help thinking the church ought to bring out those old hymns more frequently.

As a pastor, Johnie had mixed feelings about tributes to the loved one. Pastor Dale called for people to come forward if they wanted to share some thoughts.

When Carol came forward, he was surprised. Dressed in black, she appeared strikingly beautiful in these mature years. Her reddish hair with strands of gray accented a face that was filled with compassion.

Chapter 32

"I'm Carol, the youngest daughter and fourth of the five Andersons. I'm the prodigal."

She paused and looked over her audience of family and friends and people she didn't know.

"I won't dwell on the prodigal part. I made many mistakes in my life—especially in my younger years. What I do want to say is this: Dad and Mom never gave up on me. They kept on praying all the time. They were always there to help when I so desperately needed help. Dad welcomed me even when I didn't acknowledge the errors of my ways. But he more than welcomed me when I returned to the faith of my childhood. I thank you, Dad, but I thank You, Lord, for a father who loved me and cared for me and forgave me."

Once more, Carol paused as she brought out a piece of paper.

"I have a letter here from another prodigal. My son. I made many mistakes as a young person. Some of those mistakes impacted my son. I'm afraid he followed in my footsteps."

She wiped away a tear. "I read Jeffrey Grant's words. 'Thank you, Grandpa for being the most wonderful grandfather a boy could ever ask for. You are the example of what a Christian man should be. As I write these words, I am shedding tears. I am not shedding tears for you, Grandpa, because you are in a far better place. I shed tears because I'm missing you. I regret that I was not a better and more considerate grandson. Grandpa, it is your example that showed me the way. Your prayers and kindness and encouragement helped bring me to the point where I realized how sinful I was. I now come to Jesus and ask for forgiveness.'"

Johnie could hear the muffled sobs and see people wiping their tears.

"My son, Jeffrey, also asks forgiveness from all of you who have been wronged by him or his actions. Forgiving and being forgiven mean a new kind of freedom. That was Matthew Anderson's way."

Carol paused once more. "I ask you, on behalf of my son Jeffrey, to forgive him. I will do whatever is in my power to help. May God bless Matthew Anderson's memory."

She stepped down. Johnie couldn't help wondering about Michael and Elise. Would Michael lose the family farm? Or could something be done to keep that special place?

As Carol sat down, a dignified gray-haired gentleman came forward. In a moment he recognized him as his Cousin Larry's son.

"I'm from another branch of the family. I'm Lowell Anderson, son of Larry and grandson of Paul John or P.J. I came to speak for my father, who is not well and very much wanted to be here."

Lowell took out some notes. "My father, Larry, spent time in prison for his wrong-doing. It was Uncle Matthew, who visited him and later encouraged him to lead a good and productive life. He prayed for him during those times and encouraged him along the way. My dad eventually became a prison chaplain so that he could help others who had gone the wrong way. Uncle Matthew also helped me and my wife during a difficult time in my life."

Lowell looked down on the casket and over to Johnie and then down at grand uncles and aunts. "You and I have a wonderful heritage. May we carry forward Matthew Anderson's heritage of faith."

As Lowell returned to his seat, another man came forward. For a moment Johnie thought he was seeing a ghost. The man was the very image of his father's best friend.

The man began somewhat hesitantly. "I'm not used to speaking in public. I'm more at home on the tractor. My name is Tim Robertson. Glenn Robertson was my father, a special friend to Matthew Anderson. Matthew was that friend my dad depended on. They talked over everything. But what I want to say is that Matthew Anderson served as a light to the community. He was a man of faith and integrity. I look to him as a man who knew what was right and always did what was right. I thank him for being my father's friend and my friend as well. You have many stars in your crown."

Two friends and fellow church members added their thoughts. Johnie hoped this wouldn't go on endlessly as tributes did at some funerals.

The pastor announced the next hymn, which everyone sang with deep emotion.

"Children of the heavenly Father safely in His bosom gather;
Nestling bird nor star in heaven such a refuge e'er was given."

Johnie moved to the pulpit as they began to sing the last verse.
"Though He giveth or He taketh, God his children ne'er forsaketh
His the loving purpose solely to preserve them pure and holy."

Johnie had a sudden inspiration to add something. "In this church, we've had a Swedish tradition. I'd like to ask those who know the words to sing the Swedish with me."

"Trygga re kan ingen vara an Guds lilla barna skara;
Stjaarnan ej pa himla fastet, fageln ej I kanda nastet."

Chapter 32

The words reminded Johnie of the passing of time and the changes. The family of Swedish immigrants had come to this very place over a century ago in the 1870s and 80s. Now they were gathered here near the end of the twentieth century. They were facing a whole different world.

"I'm Pastor John Anderson, known as Johnie to many of you. I come to you as a pastor, a son of Matthew Anderson, a brother or cousin or friend to others."

He paused a moment and gave an invocation.

"Years ago, my grandfather John Anderson worshipped in this very church. Grandma Elizabeth Anderson worshipped here for even more years. A few minutes ago we sang about being children of the Heavenly Father. Dad said something I cannot forget. 'A man always needs a father.' The more I think of those words, the more they mean. I have always looked to and depended on my earthly father.

"I believe each of us needs our Heavenly Father." From this point on, he brought forward Biblical illustrations as well as personal ones.

Johnie looked at the clock on the wall. He had preached longer than he should have, yet he seemed to have everyone's attention, "I believe this is the time to come before our Heavenly Father. Let us sing that favorite old hymn, 'Just as I am without one plea.' As we sing those words we come before our Heavenly Father. He is with us to guide and help us through all our doubts and fears and hopes and dreams."

Once more, the congregation sang the words with deep emotion. When they finished the hymn, James got up to sing another favorite. James sang of the future as presented in Revelation and in the song, "The Holy City."

Johnie had heard his brother singing the song so many times, but he never tired of hearing the words. There was something better beyond this life.

"Lord," he prayed silently, "let this funeral service truly honor and glorify you."

"Hosanna forevermore!" James sang the final words of the song. He felt an excitement that he rarely felt—it was as if he were approaching the Holy City at this moment.

He returned to his seat beside his mother. She grasped his hand and whispered, "Your father would be proud of you. He would have loved it."

299

At this point an unexpected interruption took. Five-year-old Little Matthew ran to the front and announced, "I want to sing for Grandpa, too."

In a clear child-like voice, he sang, "Jesus loves me this I know. For the Bible tells me so. Little ones to Him belong. We are weak but He is strong. Yes, Jesus loves me. Yes, Jesus loves me. Yes, Jesus loves me. The Bible tells me so."

A mixture of smiles and tears filled the congregation. All reserve broke down, and the dignified men and women of Scandinavian descent broke into exuberant applause.

The funeral service continued with the closing, "The Lord's Prayer," and the benediction. The family began to exit with the final hymn, "For All the Saints." James thought of his father who indeed rested from his labors, a sometimes hard life, but a fruitful one.

The funeral directors, followed by the pallbearers, proceeded down the aisle. James guided his mother as they moved forward. He saw the faces of family and friends. There was something final about a funeral and saying "goodbye." The unevenness of the steps outside the church reminded him of the ordinary realities of life.

"Do you think you want to walk down the hill to the cemetery, Mother? Or you can ride?" he asked.

His mother looked up at him. "James, I want to take this one last walk with your father. He deserves that, and I am sound of limb."

All at once this woman, his mother Ellen Anderson, looked old and alone. Throughout life there had always been the two, Matthew and Ellen. Life would never be the same.

Joe took charge of Aunt Victoria. She remained strong but not so sure-footed. He convinced her to take the short ride of the cemetery. Several other older people rode with him, and Michael took another group.

The conversation of the mourners was rather subdued. Something happens to people when they are in the presence of one who has died. Even though these were believers who knew of eternal life, there was a sadness and reverence in the presence of death.

James had always loved the gentle rolling hill that was part of the cemetery. Four large evergreens had been planted years ago and were now full grown. Oak trees would have been more appropriate for this area.

The five Anderson children and their spouses sat or stood close to the grave. James looked down into the hole and momentarily felt a hopelessness. Death and the grave remained the enemy of life. He didn't want to think about this aspect of the scheme of life.

Chapter 32

Other family members and friends crowded nearby. The minister proceeded with the last rites. The "ashes to ashes, dust to dust" part pointed to both the beginning and the end of life. The service closed with the pastoral prayer.

The family remained in silence. Someone began the lines of the hymn, "Blessed be the tie that binds our hearts in Christian love." In moments everyone joined in singing the familiar words. As they finished a second verse, James thought of another familiar hymn. He began the song. "God be with you til we meet again."

The farewell seemed complete as they sang through the stanza a second time. "Til we meet at Jesus' feet."

The collective mood of the mourners and congregational members changed almost as if a signal had been given. There was a fellowship that seems to take place only during a time of loss. It seemed people realized the limitations of their time on earth. James heard someone say, "We need to appreciate each other while we are here. Our days may be numbered."

The funeral meal of hot dishes, sandwiches, various salads and luscious desserts seemed to encourage people to visit and laugh and cry at the same time. Catching up on the latest news was an important part of what took place. The visiting and eating took place inside the church building as well as outside. It was one of those times when there was an overflow crowd.

James tried to visit with each of the nieces and nephews as well as the cousins. That proved to be a challenge because the working world and other obligations called people to be on their way. Most people had left, and cousins Jake and Irene stopped him.

He shook hands with Jake or Jacob and embraced Irene. "Where's Beth? I thought she would be here."

Irene's sadness told the story. "I'm sorry but Beth is having a rough time. The doctor says she has just weeks to live. It's cancer."

"Oh, no," responded James. "I always felt that special bond with her. It's hard to think that this would happen so soon."

"We never know," said Jake.

James began to remember childhood days. "I remember all the crazy things we cousins did. I'll never forget the time the girls were lost."

Jake looked aside. "I think I was something of a jerk back in those days. But I've made a few changes."

Irene poked Jake. "You've become a wonderful brother."

The three began to reminisce about all those times. Soon they were joined with other Anderson cousins. Then, one by one or two by two, they left.

Ruth announced to James. "I'm taking your mother home, and Carolyn and Jennifer are coming with me. You can get a ride with your brother."

James gladly agreed.

James stood looking to the hills that Matthew Anderson had looked to for so many years. "I will lift my eyes unto the hills from whence cometh my help. My help comes from the Lord who made heaven and earth."

Johnie and Richard came over.

"I think I know what you're thinking," said Johnie. "We know where our help comes from. And I know you want to write those thoughts. I want to preach those thoughts to people from another world."

"And," Richard added, "I want to paint that beauty and convey the truth in that way."

James began to think aloud. "Dad always dreamed of going beyond those hills. He never did until his later years. But in spirit he went way beyond."

Johnie added, "Look at the way the family has spread out. In a sense we've gone all over the world—at least all over this area of the country. Dad has left quite a legacy."

"I want to paint a picture of Little Matthew. He's the future in these hills."

The three men stood in silence, looking to the hills.

CHAPTER 33

October 1986

Ellen wasn't at all sure she liked this role reversal. It was good to have James and Margaret and Michael nearby to help when needed. However, James and Margaret had gotten more in the habit of telling her what she shouldn't be doing or what she should do. "I suppose this happens when you're almost eighty-eight years old," she said aloud.

This was one of those crisp October mornings. She had been outside with James, who had dug the potatoes that Matthew had planted in the spring. This day brought back so many memories of Matthew. She missed him, especially on the weekends. This was Saturday, and James realized her loneliness and came over to help. He would soon come in with a sack of potatoes and a number of squash.

Ellen did not cook the way she used to when Matthew was alive. During most weekdays she went to the senior citizen center, where she met Victoria and a number of other friends. It was more than a meal for her, it was friendship and fellowship. On Saturdays, she was often alone, and that meant she missed Matthew much more.

The chicken soup, which contained vegetables and an ample amount of potatoes, simmered. The egg salad sandwiches, James's favorite, were ready. She had mixed together eggs and flour so that she could put in the dumplings any time. She felt more like eating when someone was with her.

She put aside the tablet that contained her writing of memories about earlier days. James had been quite emphatic that she must do that writing. She remembered the many questions she had after her older generation of relatives had passed away.

The back door opened and James entered. "I'll take this sack of potatoes down to your dark room. I'll bring a few of them up for your next meals."

"I'll come down and show you where I want them."

"No, Mom, you stay there. We don't want you climbing these steps more than you have to."

"I'm not an invalid."

"We don't want you falling."

"I'm very careful."

Ellen followed her son into the storage room. After all, she needed to know exactly where things were. After the potatoes were put in place, he hurried back to the garden and returned with two pails of squash.

A few minutes later, they were seated at the kitchen table. Ellen could tell that James was really enjoying the chicken soup.

"Mom, there's nothing like your chicken soup. I believe this soup is good for both body and soul."

"You do know the right words to say." Ellen looked over to her son. "James, we've been so intent on this work that I haven't asked about your book sales."

"The book just came out in late June so it's too early to tell. The early sales have been pretty good, my editor says. People seem to like the picture I've given of rural life in the twenties."

"It's a wonderful story. I'm proud of you."

"My publisher does want a second book. I'm working at it. I know I want to keep on writing during this chapter of my life. I didn't want to quit work anyway."

"The Bible doesn't say anything about retirement."

"Johnie is excited about the possibility of mission work in Hungary and some of those countries. There's an interest in teaching Bible and the English language. That's something I could do. And Ruth is interested as well."

"I think you should use your talents that way—even though I hate to think of you so far away."

"The Lord is giving us this time, free from the obligations of a day to day job. I think He intends for us to make good use of the time."

Chapter 33

Mother and son ate for a few moments in silence. Ellen realized how much her role in life had changed. Without Matthew to care for, she faced a different kind of life. If the Lord decided to take her, she was ready any time.

"Mother, is something wrong?"

"I'm having to re-think my purpose here on earth. Until June, I had your father to care for. I've done quilting and other volunteering. But now I'm not sure any more."

"O, Mother, you don't know how important you are to the whole family. We depend on you. You have a way of keeping us all connected."

Ellen thought of her son's role in the family connections. "James, you are the one now that your father's gone. You take an interest in people. It's your turn to keep them connected."

"Maybe that's part of my task at this stage in my life. You realize until a year ago this spring, my whole life was centered on the university and teaching. Ruth and our lives were centered in Riverton. Now, all that has changed."

Ellen thought of Ruth. "You know in some ways a woman's life is centered on her husband. I'm not so sure Ruth is as comfortable being here. She has lost some of her opportunities."

"That's why she's back in Riverton for the day."

Ellen brought out the coffee and poured cups for the two. "I guess now we have coffee and dessert. I quickly made some of your favorite butterscotch pudding. I don't think it's even cooled."

James smacked his lips. "Let's put some ice cream on the pudding."

James took charge of dishing up the pudding and added the ice cream. Ellen enjoyed sitting back and being served by her son.

As they finished their pudding, Ellen voiced what she had been thinking. "I keep thinking about the earlier years of this century. I can't get over how different the world is now. We do indeed live in a different world."

"Mother, I've been doing some thinking. I'd like to tell a story of someone like you growing up and teaching in the earlier part of this century. When did you start teaching?"

"It was 1916. I was just seventeen years old."

"How could you start so young?"

"The rules and laws were different then. I finished eighth grade. Then, I could go directly to Normal School. Actually, I took two years of classes and then I was certified to teach I was seventeen years old."

"You weren't much older than your students."

"Actually, I had two students who were older than I. But they were good boys. In fact, one of the boys wanted to go out with me."

"You must have taught several years before you came to the Oak Ridge School."

"Back in those days, a country school teacher stayed only a year or two and then moved on to another school."

"Where did you teach?"

"I taught in several schools not far from Prairie Center. I boarded with a family. Most of the time I had a mile or two to walk to school. Only once did I live across from the school."

"I want to hear all about what happened. What brought you twenty miles over from Prairie Center? Why didn't you stay over there closer to your family?

Ellen thought a moment. "That's a long time ago. I think I wanted new opportunities away from my family. And the superintendent of schools had encouraged me to apply for this particular school. She thought they needed a good strong teacher at Oak Ridge because the enrollment was up, and there were a number of older students."

'Mom, when I finish this book, another family story, I want to tell your story. But I want you to keep writing down those stories of the earlier days."

"I hope I can live to see these books. Your father didn't quite get to see your book in print. He would have been proud of your novel."

"Both you and Dad were an inspiration for the main characters."

"I could see myself. You had your character of Marie say exactly what I would say."

"I am thankful for the life we had. You and Dad nurtured us in the Christian faith. Many people don't have that privilege today."

"The Lord saw us through all those years. Now, I must have faith that He will see me through this last chapter of life."

James cleared his throat. "I guess I don't want to think about you not being a part of my life and the life of this family."

Ellen yawned. "This time of the day I feel my years."

"It's time for a nap."

At that moment, a voice called out. It was Michael. "Hi Mom. James. I'm glad I caught you both. I have news."

Chapter 33

During the time with his mother, James's mind had been brimming with ideas for a novel about a country school teacher. This would be one way he could honor his mother.

The voice of his brother nudged him back to the reality of the day. He had wondered if Michael and Elise would be able to keep the farm.

Michael appeared happier than he had in months. "I'm glad you're here. There's something I wanted to tell you in person. I'm afraid otherwise you may hear other rumors."

"Come in," invited his mother. "Tell us."

"I suppose it's a long story. I'd like to explain everything."

James turned to his mother. "I believe that requires a cup of coffee and some chocolate chip cookies."

His mother smiled. "Then, to the kitchen table we will go."

Michael stooped down and gave his mother a kiss.

"You're keeping us in suspense," said James. "You must be going for dramatic effect."

"I'm learning from my two big brothers. Johnie preaches and knows how to keep people interested. You write books and try to keep us interested until the very end."

His mother started a pot of coffee. "Michael, you were always a fast learner. If you had decided on college, you could have really gone places."

Michael shrugged his shoulders. "Back then, I was the prodigal. I had to do my own thing in my own way."

James thought to himself but said nothing. Michael had kept on doing things his own way. That's why he got into financial trouble.

As Ellen poured coffee, James observed, "It's amazing how many family problems are hashed out over coffee. It's amazing how much happens while people drink coffee. One person observed about my characters: they're always drinking coffee."

"And now," said Michael, "it's time for full confession. I think I have to go back to the beginning to show how my problems progressed. If I'd followed Dad's advice, I wouldn't have gotten into this mess in the first place."

James waited for him to continue.

"Over twenty years ago, I had a pretty good start. Dad didn't ask a very big price for the farm. In fact, he deducted one-fifth, which was from my inheritance."

"We wanted to treat each of you kids the same."

"I'm afraid I got into trouble when Jeffrey talked me into the financing for my big machines and for improving my dairy operation. His side schemes were way out of line. Some of it was downright dishonest and illegal."

"We suspected that," said James.

His mother had the look of sadness. "Your father felt terrible about Jeffrey and what he was doing. I think the whole community suspected before we did."

"What's your news?" James asked. "This is all history."

"I think I'm having a hard time admitting how wrong I was for quite some time. It's my way of confessing and asking forgiveness."

"You don't have to ask for forgiveness. You got yourself into the mess."

"But," continued Michael, "I did something to hurt the family name. I was greedy for money and land and good machines and other equipment. I wanted to get ahead socially with the right people. All of this hurt my marriage. Elise told me a few months ago that she didn't even know me."

James had no idea the situation was that bad.

"Elise and I started going to a Bible study about two months ago. It was a wonderful group—very committed Christians. It was during this Bible study that I realized what was happening to me. I realized that in all of this I was moving away from the Lord. Jesus was calling me back to Him. To use an old fashioned word, I needed to repent."

"Son, I'm proud of you."

"I'll get to my news. As you know, Carol worked with the bank and the lawyers and did the best she could for Jeffrey. She paid off some of what Jeffrey had taken. She also offered—rather Hank—offered to help me.

"To make a long story short, I have sold off part of my herd of cattle. I have agreements to take care of combining for several older farmers. I'm planning to lead a simpler life. Also, we're going to board horses because we have so much pasture. Anyhow, I have an agreement with the bank to pay off the rest of what I owe. I'll be able to do that and keep the farm as well as the lake property. Also, I'm scaling back on the nursery-greenhouse because it's not making much profit. I may sell a lot or two of the lake property, and that will go toward paying off the debts."

"Your father would be proud of you."

"I wanted the family to know. Once this debt is paid off, I'm making other changes. Right now we're returning to a much simpler style of life."

Ellen looked first at James and then at Michael. "My prayers have been answered."

Chapter 33

Ellen knocked at the door of Victoria's apartment. Victoria was usually the one to walk the two or three blocks to visit Ellen, but she hadn't for over a week. Ellen had decided she would take the walk. She knocked again, but heard no response.

"I think Victoria's getting hard of hearing," she whispered aloud. She tried the door and found it unlocked.

"Victoria," she called out.

Victoria, sitting in her easy chair, rubbed her eyes. "I must have fallen asleep."

"Is something wrong?"

"I fell yesterday. I had so much pain I didn't sleep well last night. I took some pain pills and they must have taken effect."

"Are you sure you didn't break anything?"

Victoria tried to get up but groaned in pain. "I've had little falls before, and I've been okay."

"Let me call Margaret. I think we should get you down to the clinic. You know it could be serious."

Victoria lay back. "I'm not used to being this way. I think I'd make a terrible invalid or nursing home patient."

Within half an hour Margaret arrived. During that time Ellen thought of her own situation. She wondered if she shouldn't leave the house she lived in. If she were in an apartment she would be around other people. Then, if something like Victoria's accident happened, she would be near help.

It took Margaret only a minute to call the ambulance. After following the ambulance to the hospital, Ellen spent the next hours waiting with Margaret.

Once in the hospital, the medical team moved forward. They performed surgery on the broken hip. Ellen and Margaret went to the cafeteria for noon dinner and then returned to wait.

During their talks of many matters, Ellen sensed Margaret wanted to say something. "Margaret, I think you have something on your mind but you're not saying it."

Margaret hesitated. "Mom, I can't help thinking of you alone in that house. It was fine when Dad was there, but now you're all alone. I'm wondering if you should stay there."

Ellen smiled. "I've been thinking about that myself. I know I have good neighbors, but many of them are not around part of the day."

"Victoria's accident made me think of you. They're building some nice new senior apartments that are supposed to open soon."

"Margaret, I think you're right. But it's hard to move."

"We'll take care of everything. You have five children, and it's time for us to take care of you."

"I like some of this role reversal, but there are some parts I don't like. I'm used to taking care of people and helping. I'm not sure I like being looked after."

"You deserve to relax and enjoy being taken care of."

At this point the doctor came to the waiting room. "Mrs. Anderson. Mrs. Nelson." He addressed them. "Miss Anderson came through the surgery. This has been a serious jolt to her system. She may have had a slight heart attack that caused her to fall. We didn't detect that until her surgery was completed."

"Is she going to be all right"?" Asked Margaret.

"She's going to need nursing care for some time. We do have extended care in connection with the hospital. That might be best."

"Can we see her now?"

"She will be somewhat groggy, but you can see her. She probably won't be clear in her mind until tomorrow."

Ellen couldn't help wondering how her sister-in-law would adjust to being an invalid. However, a half hour later, she realized what Victoria was thinking.

Victoria did not remain groggy very long. She looked at Ellen and Margaret and remarked, "You didn't need to waste a whole day waiting for me to come back."

"We were concerned," said Margaret.

"I guess I'm going to have to be here in extended care. I've visited a few people there. I know what it's like."

"They have good therapy," said Ellen.

"Yes, I know that. I may be 97, but as long as I'm living, I don't intend to give up. As long as the good Lord gives me life and breath, I intend to live."

Later, Ellen returned home. As she said goodbye to Margaret, she added, "Victoria is a fighter. She'll keep going to the end."

"And so will you, Mother."

—◦◦◦—

"Life has its strategic moments," wrote James in his journal. "For Mother and Aunt Victoria, their lives are winding down. We brothers and sisters are getting more serious about visiting both these special people. We realize we can't take them for granted."

He looked out the window at the lake and then across to the trees that were almost bare of leaves. "For us five children, except for Michael we are in retirement years. We all choose to be active and to pursue special interests. The Bible says nothing about retirement."

He walked back to his office and computer. There before were the words of a half-finished second novel. On the desk lay a copy of *From Generation to Generation*. He would be doing book signings during the next weeks. Though not a best seller, the novel was selling, and people were reading and enjoying it.

He returned to the living room and continued to write. "The next generation of Andersons is in the fray of living—always busy with jobs and family. So little time. How quickly those years pass by. We can miss so much by not taking time and really appreciating those around us. I must take time for my girls—as much time as they'll allow me. I must do my best to be a father to Richard."

Taking his journal, he walked outside. Like his father before him, he enjoyed the large oak trees, so sturdy and permanent. A wind moved some of the leaves. He picked up a leaf and an acorn and then sat down to write.

"The acorn may sometime become a large oak tree. The tree has lost its leaves, but there are buds of promise for another year. I have hopes for this life. I see hope for today and tomorrow and for eternity. There is hope here and beyond those hills."

CHAPTER 34

December 1999-January 2000

Ellen sat at her desk at the Lake View Care Center. She steadied her hand on the writing tablet as she prepared to share some thoughts. She had felt her mind was slipping, and that frightened her. She had seen what happened with some of the residents. She didn't want her grandchildren and great-grandchildren to remember her that way.

"My dear children," she wrote, "I want to share some thoughts and concerns. As I write these words, we stand on the edge of the twenty-first century. If I live a few more hours—and I expect I will—I shall have lived in three centuries. Few people can claim such an accomplishment. I can speak of this only because the Lord has richly blessed me."

She paused as she remembered that James said all five of the kids were stopping by. More of the family would have come, but they didn't want to tire her out. She did tire far too easily.

"I prefer being remembered for earlier stages of my life. I began my life, dreaming of becoming a dedicated country school teacher. I achieved that dream and taught for seven years. I began at the tender age of seventeen. I'd like to be remembered as a teacher."

Her mind pictured herself back in the one-room schoolhouse in front of fifteen to twenty-five students. Those old rural schools had something that could never be replaced in the most modern schools of today.

The school itself was a community, but there was a wider community connected to that little school house.

"James, I shared much of the wonderful values of a rural school in the book you wrote. I believe you captured well that time in my life."

Her thoughts seemed to fast forward through more than sixty years. Matthew entered her life during those last two years of teaching. She liked to remember him as that young man who captured her heart.

"I believe my most important role in life was my role as wife and mother. When I married Matthew Anderson, I never realized what a truly remarkable man he was. He had a spiritual depth and faith that surpassed mine many times over. I am all too aware of how I could have been a better mother to you five children, but I did the best I knew how.

"I also realize that the Lord was teaching me and guiding me through all these years. During those times, I know I was always the teacher. I felt it was my duty to prepare you for life."

She looked at the many pictures on the wall or placed elsewhere. All the grandchildren were now adults, and she wasn't sure how many great-grandchildren she had. Now the great-great-grandchildren were entering the world. The numbers were overwhelming.

"I loved being a grandmother. Each child was special and unique. Please remember me as the grandmother and great-grandmother who enjoyed each one. Now, I must confess I sometimes get names mixed up. And some of you remind me of someone from the previous generation. I keep wanting to call you by names belonging to your parents or grandparents."

She put down her pen, looked around at the pictures, and continued to write.

"Please remember me as someone who loved you dearly. Forgetfulness may come over me, but in eternity my memory will be fully restored. Above all, remember that I love you and that God loves you. I pray that you realize that 'Jesus Christ is the same yesterday, today, and forever.'"

Ellen took a leaflet out of her well-worn Bible. "I found an old hymn by Fanny Crosby, 'My Savior First of All.' The words are speaking to me—especially the first and third verses. Please have these words read or sung at my funeral."

"Verse 1. When my lifework is ended and I cross the swelling tide,
When the bright and glorious morning I shall see;
I shall know my Redeemer when I reach the other side,

And His smile will be the first to welcome me.
Chorus. I shall know Him, I shall know Him (repeated)
By the print in the nails of His hand.
Verse 3. Oh, the dear ones in glory how they beckon me to come,
And our parting at the river I recall;
To the sweet vales of Eden they will sing my welcome home,
But I long to meet my Savior first of all."

She paused and then signed the letter. "Lovingly yours, Mother. Grandmother. Ellen Anderson."
She added the date: "December 31, in the year of our Lord, 1999."
Ellen put aside the letter. She would give it to James. Then, she whispered a prayer aloud. "Lord, I know you are with me even to the end of my life. Please let me sense Your Presence during these times."

When James arrived at the care center late that afternoon, he found his mother napping. "Mother, I'm here. Your other kids will be coming soon."
Ellen opened her eyes. "Matthew?"
"No, Mom, it's James."
His mother took a moment to look at her son. "I think I was dreaming. Your father was so very real. I felt he should be here. And you have his eyes."
"We are all home this evening, along with our spouses. We decided each of us would come, but you'll see others tomorrow."
"I have a hard time when many people come all at once. I think I get mixed up."
"That's why we're coming in small groups."
She handed him her letter. "I wrote down some thoughts. I seem to have times when I'm not quite 'with it.' I don't want people to remember me that way."
"We won't. And, Mom, you're amazingly sharp for someone who is almost 101. We are amazed at all you remember."
"I forget some things. I want each of you to help me catch up on all the grandkids—no grandchildren. I never really liked the word, kids."
In the next minutes the rest of the Anderson children arrived. Each one hugged and kissed Ellen in an individual way.
"All my children," she exclaimed. "You are such a blessing to me. Now, let's hear from each of you about you. Bring me up to date."

"I guess that means we go by birth order," suggested Margaret.

"That's not fair," said Carol, "but I'll go along with it. That keeps us from arguing and trying to figure a different way."

James proceeded to tell of each of the girls with their children, grown or almost grown. Then, he mentioned Richard and his two younger children.

"Tell me more about Richard and his children."

James knew there were problems. "Richard is doing fine at the university in Riverton. Jennifer is a wonderful mother who does secretarial work. Their younger girl does everything right. Then, we have Robert. I'm afraid Richard is making the same mistakes I did. I never understood Richard and his art. Richard doesn't understand Robert, who is obsessed with football and baseball."

"The Lord makes no carbon copies." Ellen smiled. "There will always be problems so long as there is life."

"Johnie's next," announced Carol.

"I wish I could say everything's okay." He went on to mention each of the three children and the grandchildren. "I'm afraid Leah may be heading for a divorce. She and her husband are separated."

"I'm sorry. These problems happen in the best of families."

Ellen's words were a signal for Margaret to talk. "Even after these many years, I miss my Matthew. But I know this wonderful kid with all his potential is in a far, far better place." She then went through each of the children and grandchildren. "And I have news. I have two great grandchildren on the way. And my other news is that Marlene's husband, Mark Lundeen, is interested in taking over the farm. Joe really needs to retire from all that hard work."

"I'm so glad for you."

Carol began her review. "I might as well begin with my heartache. Jeffrey disappeared after he got out of prison. He wanted to start fresh some other place. I believe he changed his name and seems to want to separate himself from the family. I keep contact with Lois and the grandchildren. My Nicholas and Nicole and their families are doing well. I have six great grandchildren. I can't believe these years have flown by."

"Carol, I'm proud of you the way you turned your life around. I'm proud of all of you—each in a different way."

"And now, it's time for Michael, the baby—the afterthought."

"Not an afterthought," objected Ellen. "You were and are a special blessing. You came after your father's brush with death. Your father's life had new purpose and meaning. You came as a special sign from the Lord."

"I was a first rate screw-up twice in my life. I was the prodigal, who went astray. First, I really caused you some grief when I got into drinking and the wild ways. But Elise came into my life. And the Lord had a way of setting me straight." He spoke of each of the older three children and his grandchildren."

"And there's Little Matthew."

Michael quickly added, "He is definitely not so little. He's the tall one, over six three."

Ellen sighed. "Little Matthew and his grandfather had a special relationship—almost a special spiritual one. Little Matthew will follow in his grandfather's footsteps."

With those words, his mother seemed to fade away.

"I'm sorry, but I'm suddenly very tired."

"Time for us to leave."

Each of the five kissed their mother and wished her a Happy New Year.

James couldn't help wondering how much time his mother had left. Eternity somehow seemed very near.

Johnie and Carolyn entered the Oak Ridge Church that had stood on this spot for almost a hundred twenty years. The sanctuary had been built at that time by Swedish pioneers and had been enlarged several times through the years.

"I hate the thought of this beautiful old church being abandoned," said Johnie. "But I suppose that's what the new generation wants. And it's amazing, but this is one of those rural churches that is growing."

"I'll miss this old church. It won't be the same to come back here," said Carolyn.

"People don't seem to come to the Watch Night services the way they used to. But that's part of the changing times."

Within minutes the rest of the family arrived. James and Ruth came first. Then, Margaret and Joe, followed by Michael and Elise.

"I'm usually last," announced Carol as she and Hank walked down the aisle that creaked under their footsteps. "I'm afraid it's habit that I either hurry too fast or else I don't get around to something and I'm late."

"We're here. All five plus our spouses."

Joe, usually so quiet, spoke up. "I wonder if we'll ever all be together again at the same time. We're not so young anymore."

Johnie immediately quoted Scripture. "Lord, teach us to number our days that we may gain a heart of wisdom."

"I think we should ring the bell at midnight, just the way we used to." said James.

Michael turned to go to the bell tower. "I'll do the honors. I'll climb up faster than the rest of you."

"Don't brag, brother," said Johnie. "It's still only 11:30. Let's gather up front near the altar. I think it would be good to share some thoughts. And we should pray in the New Year."

"And, James," said Margaret, "you know some history, I believe. You seem to keep all the family history straight in your mind."

"I heard this from Aunt Victoria and Aunt Martha. I may have even heard it from Grandma. Grandma always talked about these things."

"Tell us."

James began to re-tell what he had heard. "Aunt Martha said that they had a New Year's Eve Watch Night Service on December 31, 1899. They had a young student minister who was quite bright and extremely well-educated. Some Christians of the time believed that through education and science and all kinds of learning the world would become better and better. Then, the world would be ready to welcome Christ when He returned."

"That sure hasn't happened," said Joe.

"Yes," continued James, "we had World War I, a Depression, and World War II. That proved we weren't getting better. There was indeed evil in the world."

Johnie held up his Bible. "Amen, brother. Amen!!"

James looked up that large picture in the front of the sanctuary. "I love what that picture shows. There are the three disciples looking up in amazement as Christ ascends into heaven. That same picture has been there for a hundred years."

Carol walked forward to the altar as she looked up at the picture. "I feel certain the Lord will return soon. Definitely, He'll be back in the 21st century."

"But," interrupted Johnie, "no man or woman knows the day or the hour."

James spoke his thoughts aloud. "So much change. I'm overwhelmed with change. It is good to reflect on the way life was. We should think of what we want to preserve for our future and the future of our children."

"Do you remember 1950?" asked Margaret.

"Yes, we had a *Watch Night Service* then. Ruth and I were home and we attended. It doesn't seem that long ago. I remember Aunt Martha talking about 1899. Also, there was an older gentleman who told how they went down to the old schoolhouse and rang the bell 1900 times. That would be a real workout."

"When it's twelve," said Johnie, "I'll ring the bell, but I won't do it two thousand times."

Carol came forward with the next idea. "Let's each of us share something of what was most important in our lives during these past years of the twentieth century."

The sharing moved along quickly. Much was said in a few minutes. James wanted to remember, but everything blended together. Ten lifetimes blended together in one family.

"It's almost time," announced Johnie. "I think of the words of Scripture, 'O Lord You are from everlasting to everlasting.' The Lord has guided us through the twentieth century, and now we stand on the brink of the twenty-first. He is with us through all generations."

"Why don't we all go to the altar and kneel," suggested Carol.

They followed her suggestion and Johnie began to pray.

"Lord Jesus, I pray that you may steal softly over the world of sin and strife. We face an uncertain future as we move into the twenty-first century. You guided our family 100 years ago. You were with us here fifty years ago. And you are here now.

"Each one of us faces new problems. We are growing older. We all have our family concerns—children, grandchildren, and even some have great-grandchildren.'

Johnie began to mention each sibling and spouse by name, along with some of the grandchildren.

As the time neared midnight, Michael quietly left the group and climbed the stairs to the bell tower. As the Andersons knelt in silence, he tolled the bell to welcome in the new century. After ringing the bell twenty-one times, Michael returned.

"I rang it twenty-one times—once for each century."

"Let's join hands," invited Johnie, "and pray the Lord's Prayer."

The ten formed a circle and prayed the prayer Jesus had taught his disciples almost 2000 years ago. The circle of faith and love gave the Andersons strength to face whatever the new century would bring.

James thought aloud. "We know the One, Who knows the future."

CHAPTER 35

September 2001

James kept remembering the words of the night nurse at the care center. "I don't think she has much time. Her systems seem to be shutting down."

He held his mother's hand. He had come here several times in the middle of the night. He sang the old songs, "Amazing Grace," "Children of the Heavenly Father," and others. She seemed to rest peacefully as he sang those words.

He sang, "When peace like a river attendeth my way. When sorrows like sea billows roll." He didn't want to let go of his mother. She had been here all his life; it was hard to imagine life without her.

"Lord," he whispered aloud. "If this is her time, Lord, then quickly come."

He let go of her hand and sat back in his chair. His tiredness took over, and sleep and dreams welcomed him. It was hard to tell where his thoughts ended and those dream recollections began. In a moment, he saw Ellen Anderson as a younger woman in the farm kitchen or in the church basement, teaching Sunday school. She had always been so vital and alive.

When he awakened, he reached over and felt his mother's pulse. She was still on this side of heaven.

The morning staff people were coming to work. There was activity in the halls, and he could tell those in neighboring rooms were waking up.

The night nurse stopped to check her vital signs. "I thought I'd stop before I went home."

James thanked her.

"Why don't you step out a minute."

He followed the nurse into the hall.

She spoke softly. "I'm sure it's a matter of time. You may want to call your sisters and brothers if they want to see her before she passes. I didn't want to talk in the room because she may hear more than you think. Hearing is the last sense to go."

"I think I'll go home and make the calls."

Margaret greeted them. "I'll sit with her now. Is there any change?"

"No," said both James and the nurse.

"You need to be prepared," said the nurse as she left.'

James opened his arms and embraced his sister. Tears came to his eyes.

"James, I'll stay with her. I know this is the hardest for you. You're the most like Mother. And I think she relied the most on you these last years."

"It's hard no matter when it comes. I'll call Carol."

"Michael is coming in later this morning. And Johnie will be flying home from New York the day after tomorrow. I think we can reach him at his hotel this evening."

"This will be hard on Carol. Her cancer treatments aren't going well."

An hour later, after cleaning up and breakfast with Ruth, he called his sister. At first she sounded tired. Then she said, "I'll catch a plane in a few hours. There's flight from Chicago to Fargo. I'll rent a car and be there this evening."

James experienced a sense of the unreal. Death was not God's original purpose. Death was an intruder. God's purpose was life. Death was but a doorway to eternity.

———◦◦◦———

Ellen gasped for breath. "O, Lord, why are you keeping me in this world. I want to go Home. Take me." Her breathing returned.

She experienced a cold haze around her, as if one of those fogs had entered her world. She recalled walking across the fields and hills to school on a foggy autumn morning. All at once she found herself in front of a classroom with twenty-five children.

Chapter 35

Her mind returned to this hazy place. Her teaching days went back eighty years. Even so, everything seemed real.

Her mother walked into her awareness. Unlike Ellen, her mother was tall and had that commanding presence. Ellen was petite but had her mother's commanding and forceful presence. Perhaps it was something she learned.

Her mother's death when Ellen was only eight entered her mind. The long funeral procession—two miles from the home place to the church cemetery—played before her. That event left an indelible mark on her life. Though not quite nine years old, she needed to be a big girl. Her seventeen-year-old sister became a substitute mother. But no one could ever replace her mother.

Her father walked through her awareness. Dad had become the single parent who raised seven children, most of them older than she. Only a remarkable man could have survived such a challenge. She had wished both her parents could have been alive to be grandparents to her children. But such was not meant to be.

This fogginess of mind was getting to her. All these people walked through her awareness, but they seemed distant or obscured by these shadows and fog.

For a moment, she felt herself leaving her body. She heard whispering in the hall. Then Margaret and Michael returned to her bedside. Michael took her hand.

"Mother, I should have been a better son. I should have visited you more. I'm afraid I gave you and Dad a hard time."

She wanted to say something but words did not come. Then, she thought she spoke but no one seemed to hear. "Michael, don't regret the past. You have more life to live. You need to think about your son—especially Little Matthew, though he's not so little."

"We all could have done more," said Margaret.

At this point, James entered. They greeted each other.

"Any change?" he asked.

Margaret nodded.

"Carol is coming this evening. And we can reach Johnie in New York when he returns from the mission trip."

Ellen desperately wanted to say something. She formed words but no one heard. "My children, I am proud of you. I am humbled that the Lord has blessed me with you. I hate to leave you. But you are in God's Hands."

All at once, Ellen experienced a fatigue she had never before felt. It was as if the work she had done for a hundred years had taken over. She welcomed the most deep and restful sleep she had ever had.

Evening arrived. At least she thought it was evening. She opened her eyes for a moment.

Carol had arrived. She wanted to greet her but couldn't. Margaret sat nearby.

Carolyn grasped her hand. "Look! Mother just opened her eyes. She's not leaving us yet."

Ellen opened her eyes again, but keeping them open was simply too much effort.

"I think she's back to sleep," said Margaret.

James entered the room. "I called Johnie and got him at his hotel. He and Carolyn are all tired out. They're taking a bus tour tomorrow to see the World Trade Center. They'll fly back home the day after."

Ellen wanted to say something, but her eyes would not open and her voice could not say anything. Everything seemed so muddled and confused. She wanted to escape but seemed bound to the hospital room.

Danger. She sensed danger for Johnie. Until now she had felt a peace that she couldn't quite understand. Something flashed before her. A terrible fire. Was it a terrible accident? After being in Eastern Europe, was Johnie about to lose his life in a plane crash?

Once more, she was lifted out of her body. She saw herself in the hospital bed. Michael entered the room. That meant four of her five children were there. They meant well, she thought, but they should be home with their spouses or family.

Though she still saw herself and the four children, she seemed to rise above that world. Everything below was dark and hazy. She looked above and saw light, the most beautiful light she had ever seen. The world below looked dark and evil. She felt she witnessed the fallen world and the fallen nature of man.

"We see through a glass darkly." The Scripture echoed in her mind. Below and around everything was dark and hazy. Above the light became more brilliant.

For a moment she was in the room. The children sat or stood, talking quietly. "Oh," she said though unheard, "why don't you let me be alone."

She wondered if they heard her.

"Let's go down to the lunchroom," said Michael. "The coffee's on."

All four left the room.

Chapter 35

Ellen breathed a sigh of relief though she had the experience of sinking—not being able to breathe. Suddenly the foggy haziness she had been experiencing disappeared. All at once, she was in the light . . .

"Oh, my Dear Lord, I'm Home at last."

⚬⫘⫘⫘⫘⫘⚬

Margaret poured the cups of coffee for her brothers and sister. "I'm glad you could make it home for Mother. You look tired."

"I am tired. Perhaps I can stay at your place."

"By all means. We can have our sisterly talks."

James added, "Both Michael and Elise and Ruth and I have plenty of room."

"Thanks. I feel more than welcome."

Margaret reached for a plate of cookies. "That's what families are all about. It seems strange for Joe and me to be in the little house where Grandma and Grandpa lived. I feel a sense of relief now that Marlene and Mark have moved to the big house. It was past time for Joe to step away from serious farming."

"Life moves on," said Michael, "whether we're ready or not."

James added, "I don't think any of us is ready for what's happening with Mother."

Margaret looked over to Carol. "Sis, have you heard from Jeffrey?"

Carol looked away. "I'm afraid no one has heard from him or knows where he is."

"I'm sorry."

"I have family nearby. They have been wonderful during these times."

The four Andersons sat contentedly, drinking coffee and talking about family. Margaret knew that her mother's time was short.

"I think we should go back," said James."

"Would it make any difference?"

A nurse interrupted. "I'm afraid your mother died just a few minutes ago. I stopped in to check her vitals. In those moments she gasped her last breath. She spoke in a whisper, 'I'm Home.'"

"What a beautiful end," said James.

The nurse continued. "You might want to go down there. We usually gather together a few of the staff and have a very short prayer service."

Margaret was the first to speak. "This is hard even after all these years. I never liked saying goodbye."

They gathered for a quiet prayer service. Margaret experienced a love and support she had felt from her mother and from her Lord.

"Mother is Home," she said.

CHAPTER 36

September 11, 2001, was to be a day James Anderson would always remember. "I knew this would happen," he said to Ruth, "but there's something unreal about it. Death is a reality we dismiss. We don't want to face our own death or the death of those we love most."

"Your mother has been in the center of many people's lives for years. You've created characters that embody your mother."

"I guess you write about what you know."

"Now, Dear, I'll do these breakfast dishes. I know you want to write in your journal."

'Yes, I like to write while everything's fresh in my mind." He paused and looked at his watch. "I'm surprised Johnie hasn't called. He said they were going to do the city tour because there was no use rushing home."

"He knew your mom's passing was a matter of time."

James began to collect his thoughts. He wrote though his thoughts came faster than he could get them on paper.

The phone rang, and Ruth answered. It wasn't Johnie. He could tell it was Margaret. The conversation must have been one sided until he heard Ruth call to him as she switched on the television set.

Ruth's voice communicated fear. "Come, James, look! Two planes have flown into the World Trade Center. And isn't that where Johnie and Carolyn were going this morning?"

James hurried into the living room. He heard the announcer's voice commenting on what had happened and then saw the images of the two buildings and the fire.

"America has been attacked."

James remained speechless.

They saw people actually jumping from the World Trade Center.

"Could Johnie be there? That's where they were supposed to go this morning. This afternoon they were going on a bus tour of the city."

The two stood like statues, their eyes glued to the television screen. The commentary explained that two planes had flown directly into the Twin Towers. Each one was a regular passenger plane.

Other reports soon followed. Another plane had crashed into the Pentagon. A fourth plane had crashed in a rural area of Pennsylvania.

"I can't believe what's happened."

James got up and began to pace back and forth. "This is too terrible to believe. Our country is being attacked. How many people have been killed?"

"It could be thousands. The World Trade Center is the hub of business activity."

James could not take his eyes off the scenes on the television set. Could his brother have been at the World Trade Center? Not only had he lost his mother, would he lose his brother, perhaps his closest friend in the world?

He wanted to pray, but he couldn't. He experienced only a deep fear in the pit of his stomach.

It was Ruth, who reminded him. "James, we need to pray for all those people and for Johnie and Carolyn."

"I feel such fear and even anger. I can't pray. You pray."

Ruth reached over and clasped his hand. "God is telling us something. We need to listen."

"I've never had such a feeling of dread and fear. I remember though during the Bay of Pigs in the sixties. Some of my students had such fear. They felt we might not be back in our classes the following Monday."

"James, dear, it's time to pray."

James replied with a timid, "Yes."

"Dear Heavenly Father," prayed Ruth. "I thank You that You are our Father. You are ultimately in control even though things seem out of control at the moment. Lord, comfort those who are in peril. Be with those who are experiencing their final moments of life. We pray selfishly at times. But we pray that Johnie and Carolyn may be kept safe. We love them, and we can't imagine life without them."

Ruth paused a moment. "Lord Jesus, you are with us even in the 'valley of the shadow of death.' We will fear no evil."

There was silence. A peace settled over James.

"Let's pray the Lord's Prayer."

James thought wherever two or three are gathered in My Name, there am I.

◦━◦

Johnie looked across the restaurant table at his wife as they finished breakfast. "Carolyn, I can't believe how late we slept. We're always up at the crack of dawn."

"We're both exhausted from teaching and mission work in Hungary. We needed the sleep."

"But if we're going to see the Big Apple, we need to move along. On the other hand, I really don't feel like moving at all."

The waitress came over. "How about another cup of coffee?"

Both Johnie and Carolyn held up their cups.

Jonnie took a sip. "From that last phone call, I suspect that Mother is no longer with us. We'll probably be going home to a funeral."

"She's had a good life. And most of the time, she's been sound of mind. I hope, when I grow old—really old—I'll have all my marbles."

"As the older versions of the Bible say, 'she is old and full of years.' When you're over one hundred, you are indeed old and full of years."

Johnie became aware of sirens—first just one in the distance, then of many more sirens blending into a dreadful cacophony.

Carolyn shivered. "Those sirens scare me. I keep thinking that someone has been killed or been in a terrible accident."

"We're safe right here. I should call home and find out about Mother."

They continued to drink their coffee, and the sirens kept increasing in number and volume. Then, a voice boomed out.

The waitress ran past them and into the lobby. Loud voices spoke excitedly.

The waitress returned. "Two planes have crashed into the World Trade Center. The buildings are on fire. They're collapsing. It's already on television."

Within minutes, Johnie and Carolyn were in the lobby, watching the spectacle on television.

"We need to make that phone call," he said to Carolyn.

Another hotel guest nearby answered him. "You needn't try. The phone calls are not going through. The lines are jammed."

Johnie began to realize what had just happened. Thousands of people had been killed as a result of the planes crashing into the towers. If he and Carolyn had done as planned, they would probably have been victims of the terrible attack.

They returned to their room and immediately turned on the television. They sat, glued to the screen. President Bush's announcement was replayed several times. All air traffic was shut down. No planes would be either coming or going.

"We don't have much choice," said Johnie, "we're going to be stuck here until the planes can fly again."

"We have been spared."

For years, Johnie had left the horrors of his war experiences behind him. As those scenes flashed before him, he once more remembered the bloodshed and the death of his army buddy. This bombing was war at its worst.

Why was I spared? Why were those people taken? Why, God, why did you permit this atrocity?

"I need to get outside," he told Carolyn. "I need to think."

"Remember what the hotel clerk said. The police are saying that onlookers and curiosity seekers are to stay in. And besides, this terrible dust is not good."

"We're ten blocks away."

"We're close enough."

Johnie began pacing back and forth. "I'm going out. I have to."

When he stepped out of the hotel into the street, the many sirens brought him a splitting headache and deadness. The dust was heavy in the air. People shouting and running brought the horror of the situation close to him.

He began to walk. In a moment he was lost in the crowd. Fear gripped him. Never before had he felt claustrophobia. In those moments he did. He had to escape. He looked back where he had come from. He would return to the hotel and minimal safety.

"Lord," he whispered aloud, "I want to help, but there's nothing I can do. My place is with my wife. I'm not in a state of mind to comfort anyone."

In that moment, he longed for the peaceful Minnesota hills. "Lord, take me away from this war. Take me home."

———✦———

Late that night, James wrote in his journal. "I expected Mother to depart from this earth. But somehow, I thought Johnie would always be around. Calls do not go through. He could have been at the Trade Center at the time. That means he and Carolyn could have been casualties of this tragic event.

"But Christians should feel differently. I do feel different about facing death. I am assured that Christ has saved me and my brother. However, I don't want to let go. This life here is precious. At the same time, we have only a glimpse of that tomorrow, only 'through a glass darkly.' I want to see my grandchildren grow up, and it's exciting now that great-grandchildren are now coming on the scene."

He put down his pen, turned off the light, and went into the bedroom. Ruth appeared to be sound asleep. He slipped into bed beside his wife. Ruth had been this reassuring presence for more than fifty years. This is what marriage and life were all about.

His mind would not stop. All the times he and Johnie had been together kept replaying in his thoughts. Could Johnie's life come abruptly to an end?

He drifted into a restless sleep, a sleep with strange dreams or nightmares. For some strange reason, Uncle P.J. played a strange role. Sometimes, P.J. became the very incarnation of evil, the man who stood before his father, saying "This farm is mine." Then it seemed that Jeffrey Grant took over the role of the evil man, trying to control those around.

When the phone rang, James wasn't sure whether it was night or morning. Sunlight told him that morning had arrived. The smell of coffee and the absence of Ruth beside him told him that he must have overslept.

"James," Ruth called from the kitchen, "it's Johnie. He's safe."

"Praise the Lord!" James shouted.

He hurried to the phone. Ruth gave him the receiver.

"James, by a miracle, I'm alive and well."

"Did you go to the Trade Center as you had planned?"

"That's the miracle. Both Carolyn and I overslept. We had breakfast later than we usually do. We didn't feel like doing much of anything, so we missed being there."

James found comfort in hearing his brother's voice. Johnie was alive. "Mother passed away Monday evening." He didn't even try to soften the news for his brother.

"Somehow, I knew that had happened. It was her time."

"She went peacefully."

"This is the last of a generation. The end of an era."

The brothers went on to talk of the routine and the mundane. After all, Johnie and Carolyn had to catch a plane home and a funeral had to be planned.

James hated to end the conversation because it seemed almost as if Johnie were present. He needed this family connection.

"I have to be on my way," said Johnie.

"Have a safe flight home, whenever that happens. Let us know when you know so we can set the time for the funeral. God bless you."

"I love you, bro."

James choked up. "Me, too," was all he could say.

Pastor John Anderson stood once more before the Oak Ridge congregation and his family. The past days were something of a blur or nightmare. The mission trip to Hungary seemed like a faraway dream. The 9/11 Attack seemed unreal—something like that had never before happened in America. It was as if a safety net had been removed.

Johnie made his opening remarks and then went on to his mother's request. "I don't want my funeral to be all about me. I want it to be about Jesus. That request tells us much about my mother, Ellen Johnson Anderson. Though I've known her in everyday settings, I can still say she was indeed a Godly woman."

He paused a moment, not quite sure how he should proceed. "I believe all of us are very much aware of the atrocity that took place last week. Each of us can remember exactly where he or she was or what he or she was doing. Perhaps I remember even more vividly since I was in New York City.

"I'd like to honor Ellen Anderson's request to preach about Jesus for that is also my story as well as her story. We sing the favorite hymn about what a friend we have in Jesus. Just a week ago, I learned again that truth. The Lord is our protector and preserver.

"On September 11, 2001, Carolyn and I slept later than we intended. We were supposed to walk or take a cab to the World Trade Center. We ate a leisurely breakfast and had a second or third cup of coffee. It was that delay that saved our lives. In fact, we had moments of guilt because we were spared and others were not.

"There was a reason for this. It was not our time. God apparently wants us around for a while. However, if it had been our time, the Good Shepherd would have been with us all the way. He would have seen us through the valley of the shadow.

"Now, let me change the scene. Let us look at Jesus and the way He befriended my mother. The friendship began early in life. When Mother was very young, she had a respiratory infection. Her parents did not expect her to live. The minister was called and felt he should pray for her and perform an emergency baptism. He prayed and something happened the minute he said the words, 'in the name of the Father, in the name of the Son, in the name of the Holy Spirit.' Ellen immediately began breathing normally. God wanted her to live. God had a purpose for her life."

Johnie looked over the audience and continued to recount the many times in his mother's life where God was present as a friend. He went through the many years until he arrived at her later years.

"Mother wanted us to remember her for being a loving and caring mother and grandmother and great-grandmother. She was fearful of losing memory and saying or doing what she wouldn't have ordinarily done. She said, 'I know whatever happens that God is with me. I should have nothing to fear.'"

As Johnie prepared to end the funeral service, another thought came to mind. Graduation. Commencement. Several of his mother's great-grandchildren had graduated from high school.

"Ellen Anderson has gone through another version of what's happened with those great-grandchildren. Graduation points to an ending. Yes, like those graduates who ended their high school careers, her life on earth has ended. But graduation is called commencement. Commencement has to do with a beginning. Ellen Anderson has begun her eternity. And we now look forward to our eternity.

"Our life here on earth is but an introduction, a beginning of eternity. We know our task on earth is to love the Lord and to love one another as He as loved us."

He then pronounced the Benediction. The congregation sang with gusto Ellen's favorite hymn, "How Great Thou Art." Johnie experienced a feeling that he was on the edge of eternity as they sang, "When Christ shall come with shout of acclamation."

Though exhausted from his 9/11 experience, he sang with the joy that filled his heart.

A half hour later, James and the Andersons as well as friends stood in the cemetery near the Anderson graves. He looked down at his father's grave and then over to his grandparents' graves. The headstone words seemed to jump out. "Till we meet again."

His mind moved far away as Johnie intoned the familiar words of the burial service. He looked over the heads of the crowd and to the hills that lay beyond.

Those were the hills his father had looked to. This was the place the family had returned to. He couldn't help feeling that in other ways people, like animals, came home to die. People wanted to be near the dearest and most familiar.

In his mind he saw his parents when they were much younger. He could almost hear his father saying the words: "I will lift my eyes unto the hills from whence cometh my help. My help comes from the Lord, who made heaven and earth."

EPILOGUE

November 2001

James began to write.

This last chapter of my life began when I was hit over the head, and everything went black. I realized then that the time had come for me to make some changes. Right now as Ruth and I draw closer to the age of eighty, I need to make some decisions.

First, my brothers and sisters want me to write some personal thoughts about family—about legacy, and the meaning of all that has happened in our lives. I'm not sure I know where to begin or end. After all, every good story has a beginning, a middle and an end. However, a family story goes on and on because there is always the next generation.

Each generation and family has its new set of concerns.

What about the legacy of Matthew and Ellen Anderson? That legacy goes on to the next generation and the next. But I suppose the legacy really comes through each of us five children.

What about my legacy? Maybe I'm not the best judge of that. Perhaps I should leave that judgment to my children and grandchildren. However, I will reflect on this matter.

In a sense, my personality was most like Mother's. I seemed to inherit her love of learning and teaching. She had the wish to see that history was written down. Since my earliest days, I've always wanted to be a writer. I can't remember a time when I didn't have that desire. Mother encouraged that desire, and Dad began to understand and encourage as well.

What about my legacy? Aside from my three children, my legacy lives on in thousands of students. They have gone on in just about every walk of life. They are all over the world. In a small way, the world is different. But it is the Lord who guided me in all these ways.

And my writing. My family stories and mysteries and other novels all had an underlying or even an overt Christian message. I pray that readers were encouraged in their faith. I wonder if some stories might have led people into a personal faith in the Lord.

My children seem to have found their way as Christians in a troubled world. Even Richard and I have a relationship that I would never have dreamed possible a few years back. In a sense, the Lord leads people back home. As Scripture says, "If you bring up a child in the fear and admonition of the Lord, when he is old, he will not depart from it."

I feel so privileged to have been a part of this Anderson family. I could not ask for better brothers and sisters. So many families have had rifts in them. We've had differences along the way, but we always return home and to each other.

Johnie's road has perhaps been more exciting. He was always the fighter. Even as a younger brother, he was a protector. As a youth, those took the form of fist fights. As a pastor, he always fought for causes and for the underdog.

His first wife Laura's cancer and death brought to him a depth of understanding and compassion that caused his ministry to blossom. Now, though he is getting up in years—just a year and a half behind me—he has this love and enthusiasm for missions. He loves the people of Eastern Europe and has a heart for them.

Interestingly, none of his three children followed in his footsteps. His son is a lawyer. His daughters are teachers. Those families have their legacies. They have great pride in their father and grandfather. It seems I heard a rumor that a grandson has an interest in following in Johnie's footsteps.

Our relationship as brothers has deepened through the years. I feel that I have been able to write some of what he has been preaching. I know of so many brothers who are odds with each other. I'm saddened by some of those situations, and I've written stories about brothers who even hated each other. God's plans are so much better than ours. In a humble way, I would say that Johnie and I are a little closer to God's plan than most.

Epilogue

Number three in the family is Margaret. I cannot think of a more perfect wife and mother, though I know she had difficult struggles in managing six children and then losing her special Matthew or Matt. Joe has remained the sensible and stable "salt of the earth" farmer. In many ways he was a brother to me, though not a brother like Johnie.

Margaret taught country school only a few years, but she was in the center of education. In the church, she was Sunday school superintendent and was always very much involved in teaching and in music. She showed children the way. Then she became a community leader—4-H, member of the school board for Lake View Public Schools. There were very few areas of town and country living that Margaret wasn't involved in.

It is interesting that now that youngest daughter and husband are taking over the farm. The two Anderson farms still have family members on them. That is unusual. However, these big farms—almost corporation farms—are not at all like the small family farms of years ago. In the process of supposedly getting better, we are losing some of the family and community togetherness that was a part of life sixty years ago.

All five of Margaret's living children have gone on in the world of education. Now there are the many grandchildren making their way.

Without a doubt, Number Four child was a rebel. Carol would say that herself. For years she was the wayward child. As a teenager she eloped, became a mother, and soon became a widow. She turned her life around when she went to secretarial school and became productive. She was determined to make her own way, and she did.

Sadly, she divorced her second husband, the good doctor. It was later that she realized the error of her ways. Hank came to the realization as well. The result was a couple deeply involved in philanthropy of varying causes as well as mission work. Like the work of so many people, it would be difficult to assess how their influence had far reaching effects.

One sad part of Carol's story is Jeffrey. Jeffrey spent time in prison. When he was released, he tried to get back into business. Things did not work out. Suddenly, he disappeared. He has probably changed his name. Now with Carol's struggle with cancer, I hope and pray that he will return home while there is yet time.

Nicholas and Nicole and their families remain in Illinois and Ohio. Jeffrey's son has turned out well and is in the bank at River Falls. The girls remain in this area.

That leaves the baby in the family. Michael was the one family member who says his weakness was that he took chances—too many chances. For about two years, he was the family prodigal. But when he came back, he took over the family farm just when Dad needed to step away.

Michael always bought the biggest and best machinery and expanded the dairy. Then, decided to go with nursery and garden work. Once more, he found his way out. He scaled back, and now uses those pastures for horses and a riding stable. Who knows what comes next? Michael is a bit younger than the rest of us.

The three older children have all caught Michael's spirit of adventure. His children are on the East coast, the West coast, and the military in Germany.

We Andersons pray a lot. I pray that these young people find their ways in an increasingly complex world. Michael was half a generation younger than the rest of us, and that means his children are still very much finding their way. I like to think they have experienced a relationship with the Lord along the way.

There is an old saying that I've heard many times. "Only one life, how soon 'tis past. Only what's done for Christ will last."

Mother and Dad, Matthew and Ellen Anderson, this is your legacy. May we all remember who we are and what that means.

James sat back and looked at what he had written. "I'll need to go over this again," he said aloud. "The legacy goes on. What will my writing mean to this next generation or future generations? Lord, what does my life mean in the whole scheme of things?"

He stood up and went outside, walked across the yard. He looked to the hills and repeated the question. "What does my life mean in the larger scheme of things?"

Only during a few times in life had he felt God speak to him. A voice seemed to speak the words. "James, that is not for you to know in this life. Your task is to have the vision to write and live. It is not for you to know the future. Your life and writing are in My Hands."

"O, Lord, forgive me."

He knelt and silently prayed. Then, he looked again to the hills. The Lord's strength did come through looking beyond those hills to the real source of strength.

"Uncle James, I wanted to talk with you."

Epilogue

James turned around and stood, looking up to his nephew, who towered above him. In those vivid blue eyes, he saw both his father and grandfather.

"Little Matthew, you caught me deep in thought—and prayer."

"Sorry to interrupt."

"No, my boy. I've been writing about family legacy. And part of family is taking time for one another."

"Uncle James, I miss Grandpa more than I can say. We seemed to have a connection, and it wasn't just our names. It was as if something else connected the two of us. You're a man of words. You could probably explain it."

"Little Matthew—and I think we need to stop calling you Little Matthew—I saw the connection. I think you might call it something of a spiritual connection."

James motioned for his visitor to sit on a bench nearby.

Little Matthew started to say something and then asked, "Uncle James, when did you know what you wanted to do with your life? How did everything come to be?"

Matthew smiled. "You know I've been doing a lot of thinking about this very thing."

"I'm getting started and I have some dreams. But how did you know what to do?"

James' mind travelled back to those early years. "I went to a little country school, not far from your Aunt Margaret and Uncle Joe's. We lived there at that time. I would walk to school and look at those hills and wonder what lay beyond. I saw the maps in the front of the room, and I'd dream about going to faraway places. I saw all that was happening around me—the people, the happenings, the drama of life, and somehow I wanted to write. I read the Sugar Creek Gang books and some Hardy Boys books as well as Anne of Green Gables. I just kept on wanting to write."

"But you became a teacher, a college professor."

"As soon as I got to high school, I fell in love with English and I read voraciously. By the time I was sixteen, I knew I wanted to be a teacher. My English teacher encouraged me to write, and I saw the difference she made. And there was always Aunt Victoria, who was such a part of our lives. She was not only an aunt but a mentor."

"Why didn't you just go ahead and write? Why bother to be a teacher?"

James didn't hesitate. "I needed to move ahead and live and earn a living. Also, when I came to know the Lord, I wanted to do something that would make a difference. I realized then that teachers make a difference in the long road of life."

"I've been thinking about life. I'm twenty-one, and I will soon have a college degree in business. I want to do something that makes a difference—that makes this a better world."

"Where do you want to be? In the city, I suppose. That's where you can make the money—and it may sound cynical, but money talks."

"No, I've been talking with Dad. I love growing things. I've been learning about the nursery business. And the horses on the ranch. People need places like this to come to. We need the quiet of the country. I've been in the city enough to know this is what I want."

"You have wonderful values."

"But, Uncle James, I want to help others find their way to a better life. I want to live and work and make money so that I can help people right here in Oak Ridge and Lake View. I want to help them keep this good way of life and lead an even better life. I know the answer is in finding Jesus as personal Savior. I want to serve Him in that way."

"You're a man after my own heart."

"Do you think this is possible?"

"Yes, by all means. Life is a struggle. Fulfilling a dream is not easy, but it's the only way to find happiness in life. You can do it—with God's help. God puts these dreams in our hearts. These dreams come from God."

"Then, I'm not some foolish kid with so-called pipe dreams. And I've just found a beautiful girl who shares these dreams. Her name is Elizabeth. Elizabeth Robertson."

"Don't tell me it's Glenn Robertson's granddaughter. Glenn was your grandfather's best friend. This will bring the two families together."

"I love her more than I can say. She's a teacher, just like my mother."

"Ruth was part of my dream. We dreamed together. That is important. Don't be afraid to dream and strike out in new ways."

"Thanks Uncle. You understand."

"Come, my boy, look at those hills. My grandfather, John Anderson, came from Sweden to a new and strange land—learned a new language and new ways. My father, Matthew, dreamed of what lay beyond the hills. He helped his family realize the dream. And he did in many ways go far beyond the hills. Your father continued on the farm and loved this land, which he almost lost. I, as your uncle, struggled in different ways."

Epilogue

Little Matthew looked away. "I'm staying here. I've been beyond. And I think I'm seeing beyond to something much better."

"This is home, our earthly home. But the Lord has given us dreams to go far beyond."

The two men stood in silence.

James looked to the heavens. "The Lord has given us hints of what comes beyond tomorrow."

Contact Information

To order additional copies of this book, please visit
www.redemption-press.com.
Also available on Amazon.com and BarnesandNoble.com
Or by calling toll free 1-844-2REDEEM.

CPSIA information can be obtained
at www.ICGtesting.com
Printed in the USA
LVHW031703130220
646864LV00001B/137